Cars

Cars

A Romantic Manifesto

KENT GRAMM

RESOURCE *Publications* · Eugene, Oregon

CARS
A Romantic Manifesto

Resource Publications
An Imprint of Wipf and Stock Publishers
199 W. 8th Ave., Suite 3
Eugene, OR 97401

www.wipfandstock.com

PAPERBACK ISBN: 978-1-6667-0334-4
HARDCOVER ISBN: 978-1-6667-0335-1
EBOOK ISBN: 978-1-6667-0336-8

JULY 7, 2021

for

Eileen Johannsen

Anyone separated from someone he loves understands what I say;

Anyone pulled from a source longs to go back.

—RUMI[1]

1. Quoted in Huston Smith, *The World's Religions* (New York: HarperCollins, 1958), 259.

Contents

Note to the Reader

This Manifesto is about the Meaning of Life and How to Save the World. Those interested in car repair, car buying, and related subjects can consult my *Systematic Theology*. Those interested in a handbook for your everyday, down-to-earth romance can consult my *History of Modern Ergonomics*. Those interested in love, happiness, and personal fulfillment, read on.

Prologue on Earth

Spontaneous, fun-loving German Lutheran seeks lost love.

I AM FIRED

For twenty years I was a sprocket engineer for Clark Bicycle Manufactury, UnLtd, a business founded by God in the 19th century. It is a totalitarian company that doesn't permit anything, so I was fired for wearing a beret. I did so in solidarity with the French, who, I stated in a press conference, "are fellow human beings, who worship the same God as we do." This God happens to be the automobile, but the reporter at the press conference, who was a new hire at the *West Fargo Evening Gazette*, did not report my entire statement, which led to an ironic result because Clark produces an alternative to the automobile that might help to save the planet. I stand by my statement.

Clark's rules on how to talk, think, and act are written in an inerrant book. But since only the Board of Directors knows how to interpret that book, I had turned to other books, primarily those of the great German, Goethe, whose works comprise an excellent guide on How to Live, and are not inerrant.

Still, I was confused by my firing because of a vision I had received twenty-one years earlier one blazing afternoon while walking the streets of Las Vegas looking for work.

I SEE ELVIS

I had just consumed the remnants of a veggie burger smothered in mushrooms behind a restaurant; and though you, Reader, might attribute my vision to the day-old shrooms, I do not. As I wandered dejectedly along the sidewalk in front of the Golden Nugget, I noticed that a car was slowly accompanying me. The street was strangely quiet, a soft glow outlining all the parked and passing automobiles. I knew I was having a vision: this was an avenue in heaven. The vehicle slowly rolling beside me was a pink Cadillac.

There he was: the sequined white shirt-jacket with the high collar, an arm resting on the door's ridge—Elvis himself.

"Hey man," he said. "Been lookin' for you."

"Sir? Me?"

"What d'you want to do with your life, boy?"

"Translate Goethe, Sir. Compose the definitive English version of *Faust,* Goethe's masterpiece."

"I know it, man. Why ain't you doin' that right now?"

"I need to support myself, Sir. Translating doesn't pay money."

"What do you need money for, man?"

"Well, to be honest, Sir, I want to get a car like this one. It will remind me of you."

"Go get it, man. But remember."

"Remember what, Sir?"

"Keep the faith."

"I'll try, Sir."

"Go after that job at Clark's. It's meant to be, baby."

"But am I qualified?"

"Moses gave me the same story, man. Tell 'em you've seen the King." Then I saw the famous Elvis sneer. "That'll fetch 'em every time, boy. But remember that one thing."

At first speechless with gratitude, I finally stammered, "Th-thank you, Sir!"

He was about to pull away when he spotted my shoes. "Hey one more thing, man. Take care of them blue suede shoes." The sneer transformed into the great Elvis smile, a dimple on his cheek. "Never know when you might need 'em."

Therefore the firing confused me, because in addition to the beret, I had been fired for wearing those particular shoes. When Management called me in I had them on, and the High Officials of the Company rent their garments. I had thought that "keeping the faith" meant keeping my job, but it struck me in a flash of insight that I was to keep the faith *in spite of* my job, and then "*step out in faith*" into a new life after Clark. Then I saw it all: my blue suedes were the same style and color as Johann Wolfgang von Goethe's favorites, his so-called "lucky shoes" (*Tvönkelspitzen*). The message was clear: I was to translate Goethe's works on Automotive Theory and walk back civilization's destruction of the environment.

Chevy: Where it All Begins

Everything has a beginning. A French monk bored with God tinkers with some metal and invents the automobile. Good, or bad? An innocent cluster of Satanists in colonial Pennsylvania distills the first drops of gasoline. Bad.

Two centuries later, I was taught to drive by a man named Art, a son of Norwegian immigrants, a farmer and a fisherman all his life. Art is good.

Good and evil: two words, one world.

1.

"It's a nice little car," Art said as we leaned against it, he at the front fender and I at the rear. It was the summer of '63, the year of John F. Kennedy and the Beatles. He was about seventy then, and I was a kid, tall enough to be resting my posterior against the fender of the '62 Chevy Bel Air that Art had just bought one year used.

You might remember that those Chevys had circular tail lights: one for the Biscayne, two for the Bel Air, three for the Impala. Art's dark turquoise Bel Air had the six cylinder engine and a manual transmission. The shift stick was on the steering column: three speeds and reverse in the old H pattern. It was easy to shift into Reverse by mistake: no fancy European requirement of having to push downward to get Reverse, just straight back from Third. The shifter and clutch were pretty rough by today's standards. It was kind of a bolt action arrangement, and I remember it well because I learned to drive in that car.

We stood in my Grandpa Martin's driveway, which was only two tracks in the gravel and grass, looking at his white house about five feet away. Grandpa had owned a '48 Chevy and had sold it when he stopped driving, at about the same time Art's wife Sonja moved in to take care of him. Martin was going blind and deaf. She had taken care of me before that, as I had been an infant and it would have been counter-productive for me to see to my own affairs. But the good old days ended. Sonja moved out of our house and I was forced to grow up and learn literature, "philosophy, law, and regrettably also theology."[1] And cars. Legend has it that at age four I could name any car I saw. So it began early. Neither my mother nor my father drove; we were the only people I knew who didn't own a car. When Sonja was laid off at our house and went back to my grandpa's small town, she bought herself a car. I think she spent her life savings on it.

So my first love was Sonja's 1956 Chevrolet. That was one good car. Buffs know this baby as a classic. Hers was green, two-toned: dark green on the lower half with a very pale green upper half and roof. The upholstery was green and I can still smell it, warm and comforting. She had bought the "Sport Coupe" version with the booming 265 cubic inch V-8 that put out 245 horses and could be jacked up to 270. Manual transmission. Whenever Sonja went out, she dressed up, which is what decent people did back in the 1950's. She emerged from my grandpa's tiny white house in her floral print dress, shiny two-toned shoes, hair set (by herself), purse gripped by the strap. Whoa, Nellie! From the moment she let up the clutch, the car flew—except, of course, when she remembered "her boy" was in the car. Those were the days of no safety engineering and 50,000 fatalities per year in a comparatively low population of cars.

At the conclusion of our family's visits, Sonja would drive us sedately from that western Wisconsin town back to Union Station in the heart of St. Paul, thirty miles away. As the train pulled out, she would be on the platform waving goodbye. We were on the old "400" that did the 400 miles from St. Paul to Chicago in 400 minutes, supposedly, stopping at many towns along the way, including good old Milwaukee, our home. So this bullet train pulled out of Union Station, gathered steam (it was a steam engine until the mid-50's), and then shot toward Wisconsin. It passed through our old home town, but no longer stopped at the station. Sonja would be waiting on the platform in the floral print dress, purse in hand, waving to us—her hot Chevy steaming behind her in the parking lot. She had negotiated city traffic in St. Paul, falling miles behind the train—and then slammed that baby to the floor all the way home. She must have done over 100 mph.

---

1. *Faust,* l. 354–6.

The car had two straight bench seats, which Sonja bought covers for. She was proud of that car—it was all she had. She and Art married in their fifties, didn't live together until their sixties, and never showed affection. Though display of affection is considered to be aberrant among Norwegians, this was an arctic, perhaps polar, marriage. The two were placed together in order to hammer each other into Lutherans.

So Sonja, who was full of sentimentality and hugs and love, had nothing but her car; and Art had fishing and his pipe. I was lucky. I had both of them. Some of my earliest memories are of waking up on summer visits to the sound of Art's Chevy truck. He'd come into town on his morning break when we visited. He'd look into the bedroom where I was, smile a broad, tanned smile, and wiggle his fingers at me. His huge, rough, farmer hands would enclose my little hand. With thumb and forefinger, he would neatly pinch my whole upper arm, telling me to make a muscle. I grimaced suitably, and he would laugh and slap his knee. And Sonja would cook white and wonderful Norwegian things for me and pay attention to what I said and hug me; so love and Chevrolet are associated in my soul, and Chevrolet stands for everything good. It is the car of my heart.

The odds were very good that Sonja, a Norwegian immigrant, would have bought a Chevrolet. It was the most American car. The 1956 model sold a phenomenal 1,600,000 units that year. I use the word "phenomenal" only because in groping for an adequately colossal word I have failed and given up. You have to consider that figure of 1,600,000 in today's context to appreciate it fully. Today the population of the United States is twice what it was in 1956. Not only that. Families have two and three cars today. People commute much farther today. *Still*, the largest-selling sedans today, the Honda Accord and Toyota Camry, sell only about 265,000 and 330,000 units apiece. Even the best-selling vehicle, the Ford F-150 pickup, sells only about 900,000—being bought not only by farmers and businesses, but by consumers who need them to haul their golf balls and groceries and make them feel safe and powerful. So, that sales figure of the 1956 Chevy is astonishing. Of course, Chevrolet did not make as many different models then—and so on and so forth—but you would be quite correct in feeling astonished. Not until the "world cars" came along—the Volkswagen Beetle, for example—did such sales figures receive anything like a challenge.

And then you had Dinah Shore, the most American woman on television—wholesome, blonde, sound of mind and body—singing,

See the USA
in your Chevrolet,
America is asking you to call.
See the USA
in your Chevrolet,
America's the greatest land of all.

Years later, when Chevy made the shameful rubbish of the 70's and 80's, their ad campaigns drew on the old account by talking about America, apple pie, and Chevrolet. And later still, Chevrolet was "the heartbeat of America." No other manufacturer has been able to take away Chevy's identification with America—even though a lot of General Motors vehicles are made in Canada now, and Camrys and Accords are manufactured in the USA.

The 1956 Chevy was the bridge between the tall, rounded cars of the late 40's and the long, low, finned bodies of the late 50's and early 60's. The next year, Chevy lengthened the car a little, lowered it, enlarged what was a small fin—but except for a hotter engine (a 283 ci with Rochester fuel injection, developing "one horsepower per cubic inch!") it was essentially the same car. Back then cars were restyled every year, "planned obsolescence" being one of the drivers of booming postwar American industry. But all those late-50's Chevys were heartwarming gas-guzzlers.

Aerodynamics? Only apparent, not real. The cars plowed through the air by dint of sheer force. The neatest exercise in aerodynamics put on by Sonja's 1956 Chevy occurred one afternoon when she drove my grandfather and me out fishing. Actually, not me. They fished, but I was too young. It was a hot summer day, and of course only the swank cars like Cadillac had air conditioning. So we had rolled the windows down. Grandpa was meditating in front, gently working the *snuss*—snuff— pocketed in his cheek, and I sat behind him with the wind adorning my good-natured face. Aerodynamics played their part when Grandpa decided that his oyster of salivated tobacco was worn out. So he ejected what ordinarily would have been an artistically pure, horizontal, ten-foot long, heavy squirt of brown juice. Our forward motion and the slipstream created by those humped fenders and that enormous grille caused the outbound load of hydrated *snuss* to peel back in a perfectly defined arch, delivering the entire quantity perfectly onto the middle of my cherubic face. The wash lasted several seconds, it seemed, splattering in all directions. We heard a high-pitched reprimand then. Followed by rumblings and aftershocks dating back to the Viking period.

But Grandpa took the reprimand in stride—of course not apologizing, mild and genial though he was, because there are no expressions for "please" or "I'm sorry" in Norwegian, and hence not in his English. He knew he did everything wrong and accepted the fact. He had my nutritionist father to remind him, for example, that he shouldn't smoke strong cigars, chew snuff, drink coffee in bulk, eat butter and cheese in more bulk, use heavy cream in that coffee, and sugar on everything conceivable and inconceivable; he knew all that would kill him and it did, at age ninety-five.

The 1950's was the decade when the unhealthy American love of cars came into full flower also. The cars were massive floats of horsepower and chrome, and for the first time they were really used. That is, previously the American love of cars was adolescent, Platonic: we had the hardware, but our software was not yet in place. But during the Fifties we learned to think like automotive people. We built the superhighway system, and we built suburbs. In the Fifties, teenagers started cruising on weekends and going to drive-ins. Cars were less overtly functional and were made to have more aesthetic and sex appeal. The '57 Chevy, for example, was called "Sweet, Smooth, and Sassy" by its ad men. Now the software was in place, and on a mass scale—no longer only among the Duesenberg and Stutz Bearcat crowd: cars meant sex. Regrettably, during the Fifties of Marilyn Monroe and the Sixties of the "sexual revolution," sex was assumed to mean love. So in the Fifties you had the motives: bleak prosperity, culturally arid exuberance, boredom, and Hollywood romanticism; and you had opportunity: cars. True love was as rare and problematical as ever, but if you had romance and you had cars, you could entertain yourself. Roll over, Beethoven.

But now Art owned not the '56 Chevy but a 1962 Bel Air. Not much chrome. No big grille. Six-cylinder engine. It was long and low, symmetrical and straight instead of looking like a wedding cake. It had four doors, which was handy. It certainly was an up-to-date, plain car. Sonja never drove it. When Art traded for the '62 and the '56 was gone, Sonja never drove again.

But Art liked the new car. He took care good of it. There was no garage, but whenever a rainfall quit, he went out and wiped the car off. He would keep that car 21 years. He never drove much farther than downtown (one mile) or a few miles out fishing. Maybe three two-hundred mile trips back to Minnesota to visit his old family farm. So after 21 years, the car had about 24,000 miles on it. What Art liked about Chevys is that they always started. For twenty-one winters the temperature out where the car stood plunged below minus ten regularly, sometimes for a week or two together. But no matter how cold, the car started. Near the end, the body and interior were pretty far gone. The seat covering was fraying and unraveling, the front right fender was banged up from the time Art and another driver had a small misunderstanding at an intersection a few blocks away, and you could see the street through the floor behind the driver; but the car always ran, faithful as the proverbial old man's clock. After twenty-one years, Art lay in the local hospice dying of cancer. Nearly every day before going up to visit him I would start the car, sometimes drive it, to make sure it stayed healthy. It never failed. The day Art died, I went to start the car and it was dead. There might be some "stretchers" in this book, but that is not one of them. It took more than a new battery to start the car, too. A service station sent a guy out to start it and he failed. The next month somebody bought it for the engine and had to tow it to a garage and work on the engine to start it. There are more things in heaven and earth than are dreamt of in our philosophy, and cars are more than we think.

This was the car Art and I stood leaning against that warm day. So warm, Art had said, "even the rabbit, he walks." There was a drought, too. The St. Croix River was low, and water for lawns had become, to Art's way of thinking, more expensive than beer. I had been standing there, either thinking a boy's long thoughts or remembering the '56 Chevy, for a good twenty minutes. Another ten or so passed. I stopped thinking about cars. I thought about my girlfriend. Well, she wasn't exactly my girlfriend. I was nothing in particular to her, but I liked her the way a young adolescent does—religiously; that is to say, purely, almost nostalgically. No boom-boom ever entered my mind. This is when boys and girls are supposed to marry. At thirteen, you are at your wisest and best. After this, you marry for sex or nannying, and nine times out of ten you get nasty surprises. You marry for sex because you are disappointed beyond repair, ideal love never having materialized. Most men go through their entire lives without learning that you can't pull yourself up by your own whistle. In the strange and basically illogical human mind, sex becomes a stand-in for immortality. The sex drive is connected to the fear of death. Once you find that sex won't do it, or that you can't get sex, whichever, you go for cars. It has been that way since pre-historic times. (Don't kid yourself that cave men didn't have cars. They did, and they still do.)

So I stood there against the '62 Bel Air lost in reveries about Nancy Hueple, or whatever her name was. Probably some song lyrics went through my mind, but I did not understand them:

I got a girl, she's my steady date:
When she's good she's good;
When she's bad she's great.

That was sung by Rick Nelson around 1960, and truer words as to male fantasy would be hard to find. But this knowledge was in the mercifully opaque future; I did not know what further heartbreak and painful knowledge awaited me, as I stood looking at the old white clapboard of Grandpa's house.

Grandpa was my ideal. His wife died back in 1919. He had never wanted anyone else. His was the truest love I could ever imagine, and I admired and respected him for it without limit. That's the way love is supposed to be. When people asked him why he never married again, especially with two daughters to take care of, he said he never would find anyone like her—never find "a lady" like her, as he phrased it. A lady has a knight. This one smokes old cigars, drinks coffee, grows big around the middle, gets tipsy now and then down at the Oslo tavern, sits all day thinking, and once—once on an early summer morning—sings an old Norwegian love song in a deep, rich baritone I had never heard before— and have never heard since.

Art shifted. "A-yuh," he said, "it's a nice little car."

2.

A couple of years went by and I passed my second shot at the written driver's test, and because my parents had no car I began learning in Art's car. Learning to drive is a man's whole education compressed; it is Goethe's *Wilhelm Meister's Years of Wandering* and *Wilhelm Meister's Apprenticeship* rolled into a few months, without the tedium. The '62 Bel Air had no power steering, no power brakes, and it was heavy. I had started lifting weights by then and it was a good thing.

The weights and the years had changed the boy who had leaned against that car back in the summer of '63. Now he had grown to six feet, he had arms and shoulders and a chest, he shaved, and he knew everything. Knowing everything when you are fifteen and sixteen is definitely a good thing because in all other respects you are an ass. Whoever thought up the idea of putting a volatile keg of hormones, ignorant and feeling invulnerable, behind a 250 horsepower engine in a mobile 3,000-pound machine deserves some kind of population control medal. Anyone who doubts that like Faust, we modern people have made a deal with the devil, should ponder the concept of teen-age driving. Not that adults are much better.

The changes one undergoes while getting to be 16 prompt me to expand on my theory about 13 years being the ideal marrying age. If your wife marries you at 13, she is marrying a boy. If she marries you at age 16 or later she marries a man. Men are always worse than boys. Boys are more honest than men, more idealistic. They are nobler and wiser. Take for example my idea, at age 13, of floating down the Mississippi River like Huckleberry Finn. I have never had as good an idea since. Not one that approaches it in sublimity or purity.

My second best idea of that year was probably to marry Charlotte or Gwen or Paige, or whatever her name was. It's true that I was not physically attracted to her and never even smooched her, but she made me feel my best self. The best self is a fiction we should make ourselves into. Whenever I was anywhere near that kid, I felt like a king and I had no other needs. That is what thirteen-year-old love does for you. Adult love usually turns out like this: you marry someone who proves to be shrewder than you, smarter than you, morally superior to you, thinks of affection as just another one of your problems, and shows you continually and audibly your worst self. It is hard to be noble as a married man with a job, health insurance, a retirement plan, and a mortgage. It is hard to be idealistic. It is hard to buy as many cars as you want.

I am not being cynical. I am simply a Romantic without a new car. Some will point out that having children redeems all the dull reality of post-adolescence, and I agree. But if we married at thirteen, we would still have children, plenty of them; and we would never become the Faustian adults we almost inevitably become. Why not? Because the girl has married a boy and the boy has married a girl. This business of adults marrying adults leads only to cars.

Proof? The ancient Hebrews married at puberty, and they had absolutely no cars. When Solomon used the phrase "the wife of thy youth," he meant what he said. She married the youth in you. She sees that youth when she looks at you. She remembers it for you when you forget it, and you can read that youth in her eyes. When you look at her and you see those old days, it keeps you honest. Try lying to someone who has known you since you were 13. Of course, there were unhappy marriages back then too. All I claim is that early nuptials would increase the chances of happy marriage from 3% to 10%. That is a whopping increase.

There are other favorable results. How to end war? Get people taking care of several of their own children by age 16, and who has the hormonal oomph left over to enlist? The Western World, in its bad aspects, not its good, is based on two things: cars and postponement of marriage. Could we have had industry, wars, or theology if everyone married when they were biologically ready? I know what you are thinking: So we would be better off without the Industrial Revolution? Are you a Rousseauian Romantic? Are you a neo-Neanderthal? You wish to undo progress?

Listen, we still would have had progress. Progress is unavoidable. People would always figure out better and better ways to do things. But to do what? Kill? With marriage at 13 and death at about 25, the progress would have been made by boys and girls, not men and women. Consider. Boys and girls think of factories that spume out smoke, that employ people working like machines on assembly lines, and that gradually destroy our air—as a nightmare. Only an adult could think of industrialization as desirable. Only an adult could tell himself that the compensations were worth it: cars, more factories, more people working as drones. In short, children value freedom, and they are afraid of the devil. Angels are sometimes depicted as children, for "of such is the kingdom of God;" but Mephistopheles is an adult. Can you imagine an American adult dreaming up this sublime universe?

Oh, I know that children are not innocent. Anybody who remembers his or her childhood knows that. Children can be cruel. I do not deny human nature. I merely want to ask you when you believe yourself to have been more noble: at 12, or now? Did you own a car at age 12? I rest my case. And one more thing. Where were you just before you went wrong? You were thirteen. When did you still believe? You were thirteen. Believers are better off not because their beliefs are correct. Ninety-nine percent of all beliefs are fiction. Believers are blessed because no innocent believer mistakes himself or his car for God.

However, I really like Chevys. They are an exception to whatever I might have said just now. If you love an old Chevy, you can't go wrong. No one ever followed his love for an old Chevy to where it misled him.

So, I loved that old '56 Chevy. And I felt quite warm toward the faithful '62. Of course in 1965, Chevys lost that straight look and revolutionized automobile design. The '65 Chevy Impala was a great car! It had a 350 engine (396 in the Super Sport version), responsive acceleration, smooth curves, would always start, would cruise through every day without whispering a complaint, shifted gears smoothly, and is still one of the greatest-looking things out there—everything you'd want in a woman. She was comfortable but not too comfortable. Compared to the alternatives, she was very economical. I am convinced that she was religious, but not sectarian. She was poetry in motion. If you think the 1966 Mustang was a better car, built like a tin can and overpriced, then you no doubt spend a lot of time in adult video stores and you drink Miller Lite and you own a big SUV. Chevy love is proof of character and a gauge of idealism.

I just wanted to get that one thing straight; now back to the Industrial Revolution, Mephistopheles, and Western civilization's determination to destroy the planet. As I said, I learned to drive in Art's '62 Chevy Bel Air. It was early August; fish were jumping and the cotton was high. The Little League players on the athletic field had been replaced by early football practice, Lyndon Johnson was picking his dog up by the ears back in Washington, and I was deep in Art's Bel Air by myself, parked next to the garden, working the clutch and the shift lever. I had the window down, and Art called over to me as he straightened up from the tomato plants.

"How's it goin'?"

"I think I'm getting the hang of it."

"Good idea, to get the shift down pat before goin' out on the road."

"Thanks. Second and third are easy."

"First is kinda rough, ain't it. You'll catch on."

"Thanks. Want to try it?"

Art stood with a handful of weeds, looking as though a horrible reality had just struck home.

"Hah?"

"Wonder, do you think I'm ready?"

He recovered himself. "Ain't no trick to it at all. I'll get the keys."

"I got 'em here, Art."

"Oh. I'll get my wallet."

I waited. Art came out with Sonja following after. She bent into the window next to me.

"You aren't heavy on your foot, are you?"

"I don't know. No. Not at all."

"Well, I suppose you got to start sometime. Don't kill Art."

She backed away and Art got in. "A-yuh," he said. "Think you got the shift down?"

"I think so. First goes in rough."

"A-yuh."

I looked at the white double door of the shed my grandfather had made out of old boxcar boards. Years ago he had kept his Chevrolet in there. Now it was full of old furniture, dead appliances, and fishing tackle.

"Ain't you gonna start?" Art asked.

"Oh, yeah. Just thinking. What if I hit the shed instead of going backward?"

"Ain't much of a shed anyhow."

I wiggled the shift lever in neutral. Art's low-key approach to everything was reassuring. On earth, everything has a price; in heaven, everything is free. I was glad to be riding next to an angel.

It came in handy. I pushed the shift lever forward, then pulled it down. Letting out the clutch, I pressed the accelerator. The engine raced, but nothing else happened. "Still in neutral," Art said as if thinking about other things. "Pull 'er down harder."

I crunched the lever down, and because I had already let the clutch out pretty far, the car moved backward with considerable alacrity.

Later that afternoon, Art and I were meditatively fitting some boards onto the corner of the neighbor's garage, replacing the bite that the Bel Air had taken out of it. Those cars were solid, body-on-frame affairs, with steel and chrome bumpers rather than today's collapsible plastic. The Chevy had a little white paint on the corner of the bumper, but no grooves or dents. Art applied a layer of primer to the upright corner board we had nailed into place, and I asked him what he thought of cars, in general.

"Oh, they're all right. Ain't what they're cracked up to be, though."

"You mean they're, I mean, what?"

Art brushed a few leisurely strokes and said, "A-yuh. We used to have horses on the farm. Didn't have no cars, tractors. We were mighty glad to get a tractor. But cars, I don't know. A guy would get to love his horses, you know."

"Some people love their cars."

"A-yuh." Since he said nothing more, I figured that was his answer. I didn't get it.

"I mean, really love their car."

He looked at my face sort of like trying to figure out for the first time the map of a foreign country, which way was supposed to be upward. He bent down to the paint can. "A car ain't nothin' but glass and metal. A horse is a person. Like a cow." He brushed over what he had already done, just a touch. "That's good enough. Let it dry." He wiped his forehead and I picked up the can, the hammers, saw, bag of nails, two pieces of wood.

"I'm awfully sorry about this, Art."

"It don't hurt nothin'. Old man Stinson, he don't care. Stronger now than it was before anyhow. Goin' to have to take out a bigger piece next time."

After we washed the brushes in turpentine, we sat down and Art pulled out his pipe. He got it lit, and we sat quite a long time.

"A-yuh," he said. I noticed that he inhaled the pipe smoke sometimes, which I had heard pipe and cigar smokers did not do. "My dog Mike, he was a huntin' dog, boy. Those gray eyes of his wouldn't miss nothin'. Got to where he knew if I had missed my shot or hit, soon as I fired. Got to where he knew whatever I was thinkin', and me him." He took a deep pull of smoke. "In town ain't no place for a dog." He looked at the Bel Air.

That was the conclusion of that conversation about cars. The next morning we were out on the street, after I eased the car by jerks carefully between the neighbors' spanking fresh garage corner and Grandpa's house. "Made it okay that time," Art observed. The red bandana came out of his pocket and he wiped his neck and face. Yep, everything has a price, including an easygoing personality. I shifted hard into First, and let out the clutch. The engine raced and we inched forward.

"You'll get the hang of it," Art said. "You'll find the sweet spot."

We moved up the street, one sour spot after another, screeching and crawling by turns. After quite a bit of that, I began moving a little faster, feeling the place on the let-out where the gears caught. It felt pretty good to make progress.

"They're talking about making it a law to wear these seatbelts, you know," he said, reaching for his. They were like airline seatbelts, the buckles heavy, chrome, and square. "A fellow ought to get used to wearin' em, I s'pose."

I had been trained to fasten mine before even starting the car: Driver Education. We turned a corner slowly, the heavy steering making the car feel like an institution. I pulled it down into Second, then pushed it back up to Third.

"You're gettin' the hang of it. Nothin' like a manual transmission. I wouldn't want an automatic for nothin'. No good in the winter, you know."

"Do you put snow tires on in the fall?"

"Nah. Ain't worth it, the little I drive. Wait 'till the streets are plowed before I go out. Ain't nothin' I need so quick I couldn't walk to get it." I made a careful left turn, and soon after that a right, feeling more confident every block.

"Some people put studs on their snow tires now," I said casually.

"A-yuh." He rolled down the window another few inches to flip out a match. I could feel him looking at me out of the corner of his eye as he puffed. "Studs ain't what they're cracked up to be neither. We ain't in a hurry."

I slowed down and signaled for another corner. Coming carefully to it, I climbed the wheel like a monkey, then straightened us out. We went up on the curb a little again.

"You know, you don't need to turn a corner so square."

"Sorry," I said.

"Just a little rounder-like."

"Okay," I said.

"It's all right if you don't sort of stalk 'em. Just go up to 'em normal speed kind of, and go round 'em smooth. You'll catch on."

We drove quite a bit that summer, finally going out to the fishing spots along the Willow River with me behind the wheel. Art began to look convincingly relaxed. Once we drove out to the Rattle Bridge, which is what they called the old bridge way upriver. There was a new bridge a hundred yards away, where the traffic went now. But the old bridge was down where it was quiet, except when you walked on it.

There were already three people on the bridge, an old couple and a little grandson. As we walked toward it carrying our rods, bucket, and can of worms, Art slowed from leisurely to doubtful. "Maybe we better not both walk onto the bridge at the same time. Already three people on it. I'll go first, sort of to test it, like."

I suggested we fish from shore, so we started moving away from the bridge. The boy jerked up his rod about then. A tiny fish dangled from the end of his line. "Hey Grandpa!" he shouted. "The sunnies are in!" Art shuffled along through the trees coughing. We went around a small point where we couldn't see the bridge and he turned toward me, his mouth open with silent laughter. "The sunnies are in!" He continued suppressing and suffocating his laughter and finally we reached a good place to stand.

The river widened there to a pond. On the other side someone had parked one of those loaf-shaped Airstream campers. A middle-aged couple sat in lawn chairs on the riverbank, fishing. After about an hour of silence, fishless silence immeasurably good for the soul, the woman reeled in, got up, and went into the trailer. About ten minutes later, the man reeled up and went into the trailer, like an Ole and Lena joke in the making. Art looked at the trailer contemplatively. Aside from the occasional repetition of "The sunnies are in," he had said nothing for the last hour and a quarter. Now he stood his rod against a tree and fished his pipe and tobacco from his pockets. In the midst of lighting, he observed,

"A-yuh. Goin' to take a bump at the old lady."

Those were heroic times, the Sixties—elevated times, Homeric times, eloquent times. As the flaming darts of Apollo struck off the silver Airstream, gleaming into our squinting eyes, Art repeated, "A-yuh," then picked up his pole and pulled in the line to check the worm.

As we drove home a couple of hours later, I asked Art whether he thought having a pretty car was a practical way of trying to get girls. "I don't know; I suppose so. But it ain't cars that get women. It's having a woman that makes you get cars. Just as bad as not havin' 'em." He drew on the pipe, inhaling. "A-yuh."

We were coming to a one lane spot in the road where it went under a railroad bridge, a blind entrance for both directions because it was on a sharp curve. Art would work the non-existent brake and clutch on the passenger side just as if he were driving, out of habit I thought then, but now I realize it was a way of communicating without the odium of having to henpeck. Now he slammed down his air brake and air clutch, and even spoke.

"Slow down, Boy." We were almost at the blind underpass. I braked so hard that I killed the engine. I flushed red and turned the key, "Don't hurt nothin'. Better than steamboatin' through to beat the band. You can't see what's comin', you know. Never know when some screwball's runnin' through the other side."

I inched forward and a dump truck coming at a respectable clip bulled through the underpass, and I swerved off the road, killing the engine again. This time I felt like all little pieces inside. "That was a big truck," I said.

"Pretty lucky," Art observed calmly. He looked out the window. "A guy ain't always so lucky."

I took it easy all the way home, and when we arrived, my grandpa got up from his chair. "No fish?" he said, shuffling toward the pail.

"Oh, we got a few," I answered.

We heard Sonja clomp from the kitchen onto the small porch. She peered through the screen. "No fish?"

Art shuffled up next to me. "Too many to throw back and too few to want to clean."

"Fishing!" she said in disgust, turning back to the kitchen. Since the '56 Chevy had been gone, she not only had not driven again, she had not fished.

We went to the shed to clean the fish. "But the sunnies were in," Art said, laughing. "Don't that beat the band?"

3.

The difference between fiction and nonfiction is a literary distinction and has nothing to do with truth or lies. Anything we read, we read for its truth. So I must confess that my memory of the following event is indistinct; but it's vivid.

There were two fishing places in that small town on the rivers. Where the Willow River flows into the St. Croix you have two dams, both built as work projects during the Great Depression. Art had worked on the Big Dam, which backs up the Willow to form a good-sized lake. Off to the side they made the Little Dam as a bleeder, to take a little pressure off the high, three-section Big Dam from time to time. The Little Dam was a good place to fish. It's hardly wider than a sluice, and it drops only about ten feet. Usually there's a little flow over the top; I have never seen the gate fully open. Trees reach over both sides of the dam and surround the lagoon it spills into. It's a quiet place, shady and peaceful in the summer.

The Big Dam is out in the sun, and you approach it not over a car-wide dirt pathway, but across fifty yards of concrete catwalk. On one side is the big lake, pressing toward your feet. On your left the dam is as wide as a city lot. Water plunges with a constant roar, down it seems a hundred feet with all the force of the Pond behind it, bursting silver-white into the half-mile wide St. Croix. You have to shout to be heard. At the bottom, sometimes the big fish of the St. Croix wait like hulking subs for whatever spills over the top of the dam. Sturgeon, big channel cats, pike the size of logs. If you want to fish them, you step and slide along the steep, rocky dirt rut on the north side of the dam, or carefully walk on the concrete wall of the dam itself as it slants down beside the rushing water.

One summer evening after I had learned to drive, Art and I went down to the dams to fish. We pulled our fish pails out of the big, bare trunk, and each of us went his own way. Art liked the Big Dam. He clambered down along its side, gingerly and holding onto the concrete wall, and set up for big fish at the bottom corner. Maybe he liked to think of the 1930's, when he had helped build the thing. He thought of FDR—still a New Deal Democrat, Art was—and the peaceful town before the dams and the big bridge across the St. Croix to the Cities; or maybe he liked the hypnotic rush of the water. But I liked it quiet, down under the trees, fishing for sunfish with the pail next to me; and I thought about Kennedy and Johnson and Goldwater. Art stood with the setting sun in his face, and I stood in the shadows in the cool evening breeze.

It was warm. The fish exercised an enviable degree of aloofness, regarding the worm I suspended among them with humorless passivity. I soon sat down on a rock, my back against the trunk of a black walnut, and began considering the particulars of the twigs and stones at the water's edge. I had done that for a while, when the sound of gravel scraping underfoot caused me to look up and see Art approaching the top of the Little Dam. Using an imperative gesture I had never seen him use, Art simply gave me a full-arm wave and turned back toward the Big Dam. This seemed uncharacteristically urgent. I picked up my rod and reeled in like I was beating egg whites, and hot-footed the short slope up to the little roadway. Art was ahead, almost running—something I had never before witnessed. He always shuffled, which seemed exactly appropriate to his hunched profile. He had a severe humpback, and his neck jutted forward from his shoulders. You noticed this once, and never again, because his low-key personality took over, but he might have been six and a half feet tall had his spine been straight. As it was, Art seemed almost a head shorter than I was. I began running, and caught up to him just at the walkway over the Big Dam. He slowed down, steadying himself by moving his hand along the cable that was posted waist-high. I followed after as the water roared to our left. No use trying to shout any questions.

But when we got to the far corner, I saw the answer. Way down below at the shoreline, Art's rod stood wedged by the butt between a large rock and a tree stump. It was bent over like a rainbow.

"Holy Matilda!" I exclaimed—possibly employing different words. "What have you got on your line?"

"Big one," he shouted over his shoulder.

When we reached the bottom he stood for a moment to catch his breath. "Catfish the size of a cow."

"The size of a locomotive," I said. "Surprised you didn't cut the line."

"Wanted you to have a look. His back's big and black like a whale."

"You've seen it?"

"Look!" He pointed. Thirty yards out, a dark hulk hovered just under the surface.

I figured Art would go ahead and just break off. "Wait! I know a trick," I said. He handed me the bowing pole and I strummed the line with my thumb. "I read that this irritates a sulking fish."

"We don't particularly want to irritate him," Art observed. "That's only twelve pound line."

I bent back a little and the rod didn't double any farther. The fish was budging toward shore. I kept gently but firmly tipping the rod back, thinking it would bend more before the line snapped.

"Well, ain't that something," Art shook his head. The black shape was rising, breaking the waterline. "It's a car."

"More or less," I said: "I think it's a Ford."

It was buoyant enough to horse in with the fishing line until the back wheels caught on the bottom. Immediately we both walked into the water, and each of us gripped one of those wheels. The bicycle-like balloon tires were still firm, full of air. Maybe that's why the car was buoyant; they were light cars.

"Ain't a Ford," Art said. We pulled and rolled the car back until the running boards cleared and water poured out. "I used to have me one of these. First car I ever owned. Nineteen-thirteen Chevrolet."

We stood back and looked at it. The top was up. From the rear it had looked like a Model T. But the sides were tan, not black, as clean and shiny as the day they were born. The wheel's spokes were a matching golden-tan. The seats were trimmed in nickel plating, and were still smooth and firm. The steel body was perfect, no rust, and there wasn't a single ding or chip that I could see in the baked-enamel finish.

"Swing low, sweet cha-a-ariot," I murmured. "Come for to carry me home. Hoo-ee."

"A-yuh," Art said. "Ain't in too bad a shape at all. Ain't bad at all." He looked at me smiling. "Must have been in a cool spot out there."

I opened the passenger door slowly, expecting to find silt and sludge and beer cans and who knows what—but the floor was clean, and there lay the hand crank. "Art," I said like a madman. "I'm going to try it."

"Well I s'pose it don't hurt nothin' to try."

I took the handle around front, clicked it into place, took a deep breath, and gave it a lunge. It hardly moved.

"Those cranks always were hard to turn," Art observed.

"Holy cow," I said, holding my shoulder with my free hand. I gripped the handle with both hands now, reared up, and lunged for all I was worth. Nothing. The crank moved about one-twentieth of a turn.

"You get in; let me do it." Art waded over and, rather amazed, I went around and got in the driver's side. "Give it a little gas with the choke out, but not too much," Art said. I looked at the dashboard and saw a little silver rod with a round wooden ball on the end. I pulled, and waited. Art put one hand on a headlight like an old friend, stooped over and gave a turn—at which the engine coughed and grunted. I stepped on the gas; and the car jiggled, shook, and then hummed as smooth as butter. Art came around and levered himself into the seat next to me. "If this don't beat it all. I thought there was nothin' under the sun I ain't seen, but this is somethin'."

"How—" I began, but the wooden wheel gave a lurch, a quick turn, and I reached instinctively to straighten it. As soon as I gripped the wheel, I felt a sensation of motion. I slammed for the clutch and the brake, but they had no effect. The front end seemed to tip up, and Art laid his index finger on the end of the big shift stick. "It ain't nothin' to shift these, except they shift hard. Give it a good shove."

As I had learned, I stepped the clutch in and threw the lever forward. It went, and there was a sudden upward movement. Art stamped both feet for the non-existent clutch and brake pedals on his side, I slammed the brake again, but the car lurched up and forward once more—there was still evening sunset in front of us, but when I looked out my open side I saw the River and the dam rapidly receding. Then we were over the new interstate bridge and the cars looked tiny and then like specks.

I gasped and clutched the wheel but Art said, "A-yuh. This ain't usual, all right. Somethin's fishy."

I nodded, no doubt with my mouth open. There was only a mild sensation of lifting, but suddenly we were surrounded by impenetrable white mist and the windshield was uniformly covered with moisture. The car began to drop and kick as if struck by drafts and currents. When it gave a sickening fall, I exclaimed, "Art!"

He put his hand on my tense, knotted forearm. I was still gripping the wheel. "Take 'er easy there, Partner. Nothin' we can do. We sure ain't gonna step out." I sat back but continued to grip the wheel. "I don't think you're doin' nothin' by steering. Got a feelin' the wheels ain't exactly on the road."

My mouth was so dry I couldn't answer. I closed it and several times unsuccessfully tried to swallow. "We're going to die," I croaked.

"You don't say."

I swallowed. I felt better, somehow not afraid of it after I had said it. The car continued to slip up and down.

"Art," I said with a fairly even voice. "If these are our last moments, I want you to know—to know that going fishing with you has meant, meant very very much to me. And back when the Twins won the pennant, when we used to sit and watch."

"A-yuh." Art unconsciously fished for his pipe, but absently gave up. "Them was good times."

"Ha ha," I laughed a little hysterically. "That was a great team. Jim Kaat, Mudcat Grant, Zoilo, Richie—and of course Harmon Killebrew."

"Killebrew," Art said, his right hand in a strangely gripping posture. "Either he hits a home run, or he fans out"—accompanied by a one-armed swinging gesture.

"Right," I said. The atmosphere seemed to be getting lighter. "But it was fun to see him bat." Suddenly we broke out of the clouds.

Below us was a carpet of cottony hills, and ahead, far ahead, a range of snow-capped mountains stretched across the horizon. One peak stood taller than the others.

"Looks like a regular Mount Everest," Art said. "Course, I ain't ever seen Mount Everest."

"Looks like the pictures," I said. There was little sensation of movement, but the mountain range came closer rapidly. "I bet it is Everest."

"Thoughtful of someone to leave a map," Art said, reaching over into the back seat and coming up with an old map. "Wonder if it was left for us." He unfolded the heavy paper and spread it across his knees where I could see it. "India down here," he said with his weathered finger jabbing the bottom left.

I reached across to the word "Himalayas" under a silhouette of a range looking like what was ahead of us. "Looks like we're going over them." Below, the peaks jutted up in all directions, and Everest was massive as it passed beneath us.

"Wish I had my readin' glasses," Art said. "It feels kinda like we're lowering."

The next range of mountains on the map was right in front of us, so we must have lost altitude quickly. I read out the name under the mountains on the map.

"Kuen-Luns, it says."

"Kuen Lunds? That ain't Sweden, I hope. Course, if it's Swedes at least we'll land on something soft."

"No, it's Luns, not Lunds. We're over Tibet."

"You bet. Always had a hankering to see Tibet, you know."

We were descending. "I do wonder why we're here," I said, gripping the wheel again.

"You mean alive, or in Tibet in particular?"

"I'll take either one—look!" We approached a mountain dead-on. Art gripped my arm again.

"Easy partner. We all gotta go sometime."

The mountain resolved into two, one behind and to the left of the other. We passed around and between them. Art took off his hat and wiped his forehead with the back of his sleeve.

"That was sorta close."

Again my mouth was dry. The car shuddered briefly in an air current, then lowered rapidly. Ahead was a high, narrow pass between two mountains. With a bit of a tilt to the right, we shot through and banked directly in front of a sheer wall. As we passed across its face we suddenly banked sharp left toward the rock. Art slammed both feet against the floorboard and my arms went up across my face—but we slipped through a narrow diagonal archway and straightened.

In front of us loomed what seemed to me the loveliest mountain on earth, an almost perfect cone of snow, radiant gold and white in the sunshine. Behind it in all directions, snow peaks, but between us and the mountain stretched a green valley—into which we almost immediately settled, rolling perhaps a hundred yards and coming to a stop.

"Chevys always had good brakes," Art observed. "And they always start again, too." He seized the crank and opened his door, saying, "I'll give her a crank."

But it didn't start. Art tossed the handle back in and tipped up his hat. In the clean air and sunlight he looked years younger; his hair was thick and curly brown. "Nice an' quiet here," he said.

I pointed ahead, and then got out. Coming toward us was a single-file procession of some kind. A row of Tibetans dressed in sheepskins, fur hats, and yakskin boots was approaching, two of them in the middle carrying a hooded chair. We walked toward them cautiously.

"Unfortunately, the only Tibetan I remember from school is *La*," I said.

"What does it mean?"

" 'Mountain pass.' "

"Probably ain't gonna be enough." We stopped and let the procession cover the remaining thirty yards. I recalled that Asians value the ritual of meeting, and it ought not to be rushed. They drew up in a line facing us, letting down the chair. A hand from inside parted the cloth, a slippered foot emerged, and a man stepped out. He looked to be Chinese, and he was dressed in a long golden silk tunic, split up the side. He wore the traditional tight-ankled trousers, orange with ornate gold stitching. The man appeared to be aged, yet his face was not wrinkled, the eyes were very clear, and the expression was youthful. He stepped forward and bowed.

"Good day. My name is Chang. It is a pleasure to meet you." He spoke flawless English.

"My name is Buster," I said as I stepped forward and bowed. "Pleased and delighted, I'm sure."

Chang nodded toward Art. "You would be so good as to present me to your tall friend?"

Art, who sometimes when under stress reverted to the Norwegian he had spoken as a child in Minnesota, awkwardly held out his hand and said, "*Jeg heter Art. God aften. Vi har komme med bilen.*" I was about to translate that he had given his name and a greeting and said we had arrived in the car, when to my disconcerted amazement, all the Tibetans looked wide-eyed at Art and suddenly knelt on one knee. Chang bowed very low. When he came up, he said, "I am deeply honored." He turned and lifted a hand to the mountain behind him, upon the face of which I now noticed the pavilions of a monastery. "Welcome to the lamasery of Shangri-La." Art and I both bowed. Chang continued, "It will be my pleasure to escort you to the lamasery, where you shall find shelter, rest, and refreshment."

"We could not think of putting you to the trouble," I said.

"It is no trouble, I assure you."

"It is exceedingly kind of you, but really—"

"I quite insist."

"Very well," I replied. "We shall be forever in your debt."

"Not to mention it," he said. He re-entered the hooded chair, the men hoisted it, and the procession about-faced toward the lamasery. We followed immediately behind the chair.

As we passed through the valley, I took careful note of the dwellings, most of which were made of wood, no doubt rare in that region. The clapboards were vertical instead of horizontal as in America, and the houses were painted bright white or red, the windows trimmed, and flowers and gardens were everywhere. I recalled that the Tibetan plateau has one of the most prohibitive climates in the world, but this valley must be so sheltered and favored by the sun that fruits of all kinds could be cultivated.

"I wish I knew where we were," I said quietly to Art.

The sun was overhead. I had no sense of direction. "I seem to have lost the horizon as we came in," I continued. "The name sounded familiar somehow. I feel I should know it."

"Why, we're back home," Art said smiling down at me. "I recognize everything—'cept the monastery."

"You do?"

Art pointed past some houses. "I bet there's a baseball field right over there. Remember it well."

"Baseball field!" I exclaimed.

Chang put his head out from the chair. "Did you say 'baseball'?"

"You bet," Art replied. "Spent many an hour watching baseball."

"You played, of course?"

Art flushed, and looked down.

"Ah," Chang said. He turned and said something to the lead bearer, who caused it to be passed all the way to the front. The column abruptly changed course and moved in the direction Art had pointed. We crossed a little arched bridge, passed through an overhang, and emerged from a stand of willows. Before us stood a fenced ball field.

A game was being played. The team in the field wore Yankee uniforms; the team at bat were also dressed in baggy pinstripes. "Art!" I exclaimed. "This must be heaven."

The scoreboard said "Us" and "Also Us." It was the bottom of the ninth. I noticed the bases were loaded. Nobody out. As we walked to the right field foul line, two trainers jogged out to the mound. In a minute, they led the pitcher back toward us. He was holding his right wrist.

The trainers recognized Chang, who had exited the chair and was standing next to Art. He bowed to them and said, "Not to worry, gentlemen. I have brought you a closer." He reached out and took the ball from the pitcher; then he carefully placed it into Art's right hand. We stood breathless for a moment. Art turned to me and there was moisture in his eyes.

I said, "Look who's at the plate." A broad, tall figure stood with the bat resting on his shoulder. He removed his cap to wipe sweat from his face. It was Harmon Killebrew. I saw Art swallow hard. "Remember," I whispered, "he either hits a home run or he fans out. Fan 'im!" The injured pitcher handed Art his cap and glove, and Art walked out to the mound. It had been thoughtful of the pitcher to have given him the cap, because Art looked a little odd, dressed in his everyday fishing clothes: work pants, work shirt with T-shirt. His pipe and tobacco protruded from his back pocket.

I was a little nervous, but Art looked down to the catcher, rotating the ball in his right hand. His face took on the expression of a man who was about to do something he had wanted to do all his life—a mixture of determination, fear, and joy. He brought the ball to his glove, then went into a full wind-up with bases loaded—looked a little awkward on that first pitch—and dropped the neatest screwball I had ever seen. The umpire bellowed "*Steeee*," shooting up his right arm.

"*Hoo-ee!*" I shouted, raising a fist toward Art, which he acknowledged with the most modest of barely-perceptible nods. On the next pitch, Killebrew unloosed a prodigious swing but came up sucking air.

I took a step toward the mound and called loud enough for the whole field to hear, "Throw him some garbage, Big Fella!" Art looked blank for an instant, then a faint knowledgeable smile came over his face. It was like playing whist. Art shook off a few signs, finally nodded, and brought the ball and glove to his chest. As he wound up, I could see Killebrew relax just a fraction. The ball blew past him right down the middle. He was called out with the bat on his shoulder, expecting garbage.

"Hot dog!" I said, punching the air. "Hot-diggity dog-diggity!"

Killebrew looked up at the mound. "Not bad, Buddy. Not bad at all!" He smiled and Art touched the brim of his cap. They were all good sports here—or nearly all, as I would find out.

Without thinking, I had edged down into the dugout. One of the players said to me, "They got the heart of the line-up coming. Think he can do it?"

"He can do anything," I said. But when I looked toward the plate I saw a very big man kneeling in the on deck circle, and a hulking pear-shaped man at the plate. "Oh, man," I exclaimed softly. "Art's pitching to Ruth and Gehrig."

The Bambino pointed right into the dugout and tagged the first pitch so hard that I didn't even have time to flinch before the ball hit the wall behind my head. Art looked shaken, so I walked out to the mound.

"He hit that pretty hard," Art said.

"Yeah, he did. But he hit it foul. Didn't hurt nothin.'" Art nodded, with some reservation. "Remember, he's also the major league strike-out king. Fan him. The bigger they are, the harder they fan. You can do it."

I turned just as Art said, "But he's Babe Ruth."

"Yeah," I said over my shoulder. "And you know who you are."

The next pitch was a hard sinker and Ruth missed it by a full inch. It made him a little angry, however. After Art had received the next sign, Ruth stepped back out of the box. He pointed to the stands behind right center. Then he stepped back in. A chill went through me.

Art stepped off the rubber, and pointed at Ruth.

"Hot *cha*!" I said. "Hot *damn*!"

I felt a tiny tug at my trousers. The player sitting nearest me looked up respectfully. "Nobody speaks like that here, Sir. It just ain't done."

"It's all right if you're a pitching coach," I said.

"Yeah, I suppose. A bit irregular, that's all."

Art missed on the next pitch. Ruth fouled the next, a towering arc behind the stands. The next two pitches broke a bit too early, just barely missing the plate. I figured Art was not losing it; he was trying to set Ruth up. But the next pitch Ruth fouled off, a shot like a bullet just over the umpire. It hit the backstop and seemed to shake the rivets loose. I saw Art breathe deeply. He kicked high, and delivered the sweetest change-up I ever saw. Ruth was five feet ahead of the ball and swung himself into a corkscrew.

Art's cheeks puffed, and he blew out some hot air. Ruth grunted toward the mound, "Not bad." Art touched the tip of his cap.

But now our catcher stepped out and walked toward me, looking like he had just been in a combat zone.

"I can't catch dis guy no more."

"How's that?"

"He's got me divin' all over da place. I can't tell what's comin' next, no matter what pitch we call. Da last ball looked like a butterfly."

"We only got one more batter."

"Says *you*. It ain't over 'till it's over. Dat's Gehrig comin' up."

"Okay. You did great catching a pitcher you don't know."

"Yeah, I know him. But I don't catch Scandinavians too good."

"Munson!" I shouted, but Munson already had his shin guards and chest pad on, and was walking toward the plate adjusting his mask. "What a team," I said quietly.

I knew you couldn't throw any loop-de-loop stuff past Gehrig. He had the eyes of a hawk and the reflexes of a mongoose. I knew Art would have to heat that ball like a gob of mercury on a frying pan to stand a chance.

The first pitch snapped in Munson's glove like a slingshot strap on a bare bottom. The next pitch sounded like a firecracker on a flat tin pan. But I knew that Gehrig would learn from those two pitches. If Art had any heat left, the next pitch would have to burn like a ball of lightning.

Art wound up. There had been no sign, no nod. Everybody knew that the only pitch was the prime fastball. Gehrig knew it. Art knew it. Every player knew it. Every monk watching from the lamasery on the mountainside knew it. The pitch came and it glinted like a yellow-white ball of lightning and the next thing I knew, Gehrig was walking away from the plate nodding respectfully at the mound, and Art was touching his cap brim.

Both benches emptied and all the players went out to shake Art's hand and congratulate him. Amidst the din and the hubbub, I walked to the plate. I knelt down on one knee behind it and traced with my fingers the grooves of the catcher's spikes. On that last pitch, Munson had been moved back a full inch.

As I straightened up, a man came toward me shouting and gesticulating vehemently. It was George Steinbrenner.

"Hey, you bush-league so-and-so," he shouted five inches from my face. "That's my team you just cheated out of the win they deserved! That pitcher of yours isn't even in proper uniform!" He sprayed spittle everywhere except in my face. "Who is that guy and who gave you permission for him to pitch and how did you two good-for-nothing slab-faced nose-picking pieces of pond scum even *get here*!!!"

"Go to hell," I explained. "And back out of my face." As he backed off I poked my finger into his chest. "And take your junior league chumps with you."

Steinbrenner looked down, and quietly said "Oh." Then tears gushed from his eyes, and he held his hands to his face and hurried away.

"This is heaven," I said as Art came over. "Sure enough, this is heaven."

"Naw," Art said. "It's just home."

Well, whatever it was, we continued through it with that procession of Tibetans and the Chinese lama. Chang had allowed us a proper interval of rejoicing as the two teams shook hands and the fans, Tibetans all, came down from the stands and got autographs. Then he discreetly sidled up to me and said that it would be most convenient if we would resume our journey.

"The air grows quite chill here at evening, even in the summer, and we have yet before us the long ascent to the lamasery."

As we resumed our journey, Chang asked that the hood of his chair be rolled up and tied so that he could speak to us.

"I regret that I must resort to this rather privileged-appearing mode of transport," he said. "I would far rather walk beside you than be obliged to be transported as if I were a potentate. It is not our custom in Shangri-La even to appear to lord it over others."

"I should think respect flows toward you naturally," I replied.

"And flows outward as well, I should hope. We all respect each other, peasants and lamas alike. I hope you find that I bow toward others quite as often as they bow toward me."

I nodded, having noticed already that what he said was true. Yet it occurred to me that the people all around were exceptionally well-behaved, courteous, and self-controlled, as though governed by some gentle force.

"I can see what you are thinking," Chang said. "Indeed, we are all governed by a gentle force, but it is a force from within. None here is a governor, and except for the Dagli Lama, none could be considered an authority. And he chooses not to exercise the force of his position. That is why I so deeply regret the debilities of age that necessitate my being carried in this manner."

I observed the sincerity in his eyes. At the same time I could not help doubting what he said, as despite his being gray-haired, his almost youthful face was smooth and firm, and his eyes betrayed no fatigue nor the cynicism and resignation one might expect of an elderly intellectual as he so clearly was. He interrupted my thoughts: "But you think I cannot be very old after all. Regrettably I am not at liberty to enter much into detail, but I am well past my hundredth birthday."

My eyes must have widened, because he exclaimed delightedly, "Your evident astonishment compliments me, young man. But I assure you, what I say is true, for who would choose to exaggerate his age?"

Recalling my high school text, *Grundlagen des Tibetischen Mystik,* I said, "I have read that many monks in this country reach advanced ages, but I have never known whether such reports were written by gullible travelers."

"I assure you, they are not. Oh, bother," he suddenly exclaimed. Motioning me over, he bent toward my ear and said quietly, "I shouldn't tell you his, but—now don't repeat this—I arrived at the lamasery in 1748."

"Great Scott!" I exclaimed. He put his finger to his lips. Quietly, I said, "I never would have imagined."

Again quietly, he said, "And I am far from being the oldest here. The Dagli Lama—but I should allow him to tell you himself."

"We shall see him?" I had heard that monks at Tibetan monasteries were cordial, even scampishly cheerful in the uniquely Buddhist way—as Chang had just demonstrated—but the senior lamas were absolutely unapproachable, and were never seen by foreign visitors.

"I am certain that you will. As you know, it is very far from customary for visitors to be granted such conversations—they would be called audiences elsewhere, I believe—but your friend has introduced a most unusual consideration." I recalled the strange reaction to what Art had said right after our landing. "This consideration, I am certain, places you in a unique position. Furthermore, the Dagli Lama has an avid interest in American automobiles. After you are refreshed and rested, you will be invited, I have no doubt."

"Can you tell me anything about the Dalai Lama?"

"Regrettably, I cannot."

"Is he a severe man?"

"You will find him to be most gracious. I must say there is something peculiar in the way you pronounce his title, but I cannot put my finger upon what it is."

"My unfortunate accent, no doubt," I apologized. Chang assured me there was no need for apology, but added somewhat to my discomfiture that he suspected Art would pronounce it quite satisfactorily—the correctness of which supposition Art immediately confirmed by saying the title entirely to Chang's approval.

"Is it permissible," I enquired, "to tell me something of how this community, or valley, of Shangri-La operates, how it came to be, and so on?"

"It is, and I shall do so with pleasure. But first, only the lamasery is properly called Shangri-La. The valley derives its name from the mountain." He nodded, with what I detected to be elements of both affection and respect, toward the perfect cone of the mountain, at the foot of which we had nearly arrived.

"It is Blue Moon Mountain," he continued. "This is the valley of the Blue Moon. The valley has been here from time immemorial, as has the mountain of course, but the lamasery has existed only a thousand or so years.

"The valley is fortunately situated, and uniquely blessed by Nature. Were it not accessed by several low passes, it should have become an alpine lake long ago. As it is, the valley is wonderfully temperate, fertile, and unaffected by the seasonal extremes one finds nearly everywhere else in this vast, uninhabitable region.

"The people are governed by the lamasery, but it is a gentle governance marked rather by moderation than by anything else. We govern moderately; the people obey moderately. People only rarely misbehave, for everyone has what they need and all are raised to think first of others, then themselves. When they misbehave, it is only moderately; and they are punished only moderately. Seldom—perhaps a half dozen times in a thousand years—is anyone given the extreme and ultimate punishment, which is to be put out of the valley. No-one wishes to leave."

A sort of bell chimed faintly in my mind at that, and I asked, "Not even visitors?"

"No," Chang said very earnestly, looking briefly but not impolitely directly into my eyes. "No visitor wishes to leave.—And we cannot permit them to, of course."

He read my thought, which was one of alarm and resistance. "I do not mean that we compel anyone to remain, by force of any kind. Oftentimes, we even escort one away. We offer hospitality. Before long, one stays because one wishes to. I myself am an example. I was a wandering Buddhist monk, and now I no longer wander."

"But suppose one is not a Buddhist. Would the lamasery still appear to be so congenial?"

Chang smiled a warm, wise smile. "But everyone is a Buddhist. It is merely that most people in this world have not yet awakened to that fact."

"Then, for those who have not so awakened, is this valley congenial?"

"No less than for myself. We believe in moderation. Buddhism is only moderately Buddhist."

"But Buddhism is the right religion?"

"Of course. But that does not mean other religions are wrong."

"That is a unique attitude."

"I am all too aware that it is. But rest assured, we try to persuade no one. And of coercion there is none in Shangri-La."

We had reached a dismaying array of paths at the foot of the mountain. I wondered how a person was to know which was the correct one. No doubt the false ones had been cleared as a measure of defense.

Chang appeared to understand my thoughts. He smiled patiently. "You see before you a demonstration of Buddhist thought. There are many paths to the top of the mountain."

I nodded, observing with satisfaction that the monks had not even presumed to set up at the top, but along the side. As I looked up, the pavilions—for I do not know what else to call them—appeared to cling to the mountainside like petals to a flower. In the setting sun, the graceful buildings glowed violet, gold, vermilion, azure, and the pristine air gave the colors an ethereal purity that made them seem to be abstract perfections, yet also subjects of life rather than objects built by human hands. They appeared to be fruits of the spirit.

Art tapped me on the shoulder. I realized now that he had been in a deep study all the while we had been walking.

"You know, I been trying to figure out what the strangest part of this whole thing is. I got it."

At that point I realized that nothing seemed strange to me. A feeling of strangeness was completely absent. But I had misunderstood Art.

"Strange enough to be born, and go to work, and get sick, and go fishin', and die, and fight wars and all. But you know the darndest thing?"

I was dazed. The speed of his thought transfer almost made my head whirl.

"It was them bumper stickers."

"Bumper stickers?" I asked. "What bumper stickers? Where?"

"On that Chevy."

"The Chevy—oh, the 1913 Chevy? That we took here?"

"Now, we just got it backwards. It took us away from here. But ain't they the darndest screwball stickers?"

I hadn't noticed any bumper stickers on the car. But now that he had brought my attention to it, I could recall seeing something.

"The one on the left side said UFF-DA. He he. Don't that beat all?"

"*Uff-da?*"

"And the other one. 'Honk if you love lefse.' He he."

Chang watched me with kindly amusement.

"*Uff-da?*" I repeated. *Uff-da* is what Norwegians say when it's too hot, or too cold, or when they spill something, or when they suddenly remember something, or realize they have forgotten something, or when the coffee tastes terrible, or when the fish they've caught is twice the size they expected, or when they realize marriage entails a mother-in-law. "I don't get it," I said.

"Everything makes sense," Art said. His face seemed to radiate light reflected by the mountain. "Why was I so darn slow I didn't see it right away?"

"What? *What?*" I cried. I turned to Chang. "I don't get it. I don't get it at all!"

He put a frail hand on my shoulder, as I walked and he sat. "Old Man," he said, rather as if we were sitting in a club in London, "Old Man, you are really quite delightfully obtuse." Seeing my dismay, he added genially: "It is no sin to be obtuse, Old Man. In fact, there are no sins here at all."

*

Sure enough, the next day we were summoned to see the Dagli Lama of the Lamasery. Rather I should say we were invited, for there was no sense of compulsion, only privilege.

The previous evening we had been given an exquisite yet decidedly unshowy dinner. The cuisine was Chinese, characterized by subtlety of flavor, yet the clarity and freshness of the locally-grown vegetables were quite extraordinary. Chang presided over a congenial assemblage of lamas and valley people, only a few of whom spoke English. A young woman who dined with us rose from the table as we finished, and seated herself at a piano. I had wondered during the meal how a grand piano had found its way into this lamasery—indeed, had wondered how many of the furnishings and books had been brought in. The piano was a Narvik, a name I did not recognize, but it produced exquisite tone, of a depth and clarity I had never before heard.

Rather, I should have said that the young woman produced that exquisite music. She was, like Chang, Chinese in appearance, though less so then he, as if she were of equally European lineage. Her hair was dark and skin exceptionally fair; her eyes were profoundly dark yet somehow luminous. She had spoken not a word during the dinner, and when introduced by Chang—her name being Fayaway—she had lowered her eyes. But she played Edvard Grieg with a grace and understanding that seemed quite beyond her years. The music coming from her hands on the keys of that Narvik was almost hypnotic in its beauty.

After what was perhaps a half hour, though it seemed to be but minutes, she turned to us and said quietly, "I shall play more, if desired."

I rose involuntarily and said fervently, "Oh yes! By all means do!" Then I looked around, quite embarrassed at my outburst, and sat down. Art yawned the widest yawn I had seen in some time. Fortunately Chang, with unerring perception and grace, said that as the evening was now late, let those retire to their rooms who wished, and let those who desired more music remain; Fayaway would be pleased to play quite as long as anyone liked.

All, including Art, departed with bows and expressions of thanks— all except the young woman and me.

"It pleases you for me to play?" she asked, turning toward me on the bench. Like Chang, she wore the traditional slit gown of embroidered orange and gold silk but without, however, the narrow-ankled trousers. The collar of the gown was joined by a delicate brooch of gold, decorated with jade and lapis. Her long sleeves were embroidered with simple designs reminiscent of vines about to fructify with delicate grapes. "You may come sit," she said, placing her hand on the cushioned bench.

Awkwardly, I walked to the bench and sat beside her. It was a feeling I cannot readily describe. "I—I should love to hear you play more—of anything you wish. If only I could play also—half, even one-tenth as well!"

"You not play?"

"To my sorrow, no. Not at all."

"Yet you are musical, it seem to me."

"I love music."

"Why you never learn play?"

"As a boy, I only wanted to play baseball and football, and read about cars. Now I fear it is too late."

"You play nothing at all?"

I seemed to sense something indefinable behind that question, but could answer merely, "Only drums. I am no musician."

"I like drum. You play for me sometime?"

I nodded. "I would love to."

"And you play this piano for me now."

I thought that she had understood none of my awkward English, and so I began a halting, awkward repetition of what I had said—but she placed her finger to my lips. With the kindest, momentary shake of her head, she smiled a patient smile such as Chang often exhibited, and said simply, "You play."

Her small hands guided mine onto the keys. At their touch I felt an ability in my hands, and a longing, and when my fingers rested on the keys I felt that the notes were words and I had merely to speak them. The keys felt as smooth as Fayaway's hands. I began to play the adagio from Beethoven's Third Piano Concerto. The music emerged naturally with all the pathos of my young life's longing. The sadness of beauty's fragility passed from my heart into music.

At first Fayaway listened calmly, sweetly, but as I finished, her eyes glowed with tears. "Much beauty," she said. "Very sad; very much beauty in sadness."

I straightened up and inhaled deeply. Her fragrance, so ethereal and clean, filled me with melancholy and elation at the same time. "Can we play together?" I asked impulsively but quietly. Before I could even consider the nature of my request, the first simple, clear notes came from her fingers. I knew the tune immediately, and played the harmony. The words went through my mind.

> *I give to you, and you give to me.*
> *True love,*
> *True love.*
> *So on and on it will always be*
> *True love,*
> *True love.*

And then I realized we were singing it aloud together.

We rose from the piano, but it was as if the music played on. I found myself reaching for her hand and placing my arm around her waist; and she laid her head softly against my chest. At first slowly, then with flowing grace, we waltzed to the clear, unheard music and words,

> *love forever true.*

Play on, soft keys, play on!

*

In the morning, Art remarked, "A-yuh. Didn't hear you come in last night."

I answered, "Oh. Ah."

"Maybe you could use some coffee. You have a kinda starry look in your eyes."

"Eyes?" Cough. "Coffee? Oh." I blinked at the bright, clear panorama out the window. "I don't think they would have coffee here."

Art pointed to a small table near the door. On a mahogany tray stood an insulated glass carafe of coffee, and next to that was Art's half-empty cup. There was another cup and saucer, a tea towel with the embroidered words "Oslo Hilton," and a bowl of sugar cubes.

"Sugar cubes? At a lamasery in Tibet?"

"Yeah. Coffee ain't bad. 'Bout the best I ever had."

Though normally not a coffee drinker, I rushed to the table and poured myself a cup. Instantly its effects radiated through my body. It was the richest and strongest coffee I have ever tasted. With shaky hands, I put the cup back onto the table.

"Holy mackerel," I said.

Art smiled slyly. "It ain't any too weak, though. That fellow Chang was here."

"While I was asleep?"

"Didn't want to wake you. We was quiet. He said we see the head man this afternoon."

"Oh good," I said with relief. "I have an appointment to have lunch with, ah, with Fayaway. If it's okay with you."

"No problem." Art said casually. "Nice-lookin' gal."

*

We explored the monastery that morning. It had been built in many separate parts over the years, which, as Chang explained, permitted many different philosophies. At a questioning look from me, Chang continued, "The architecture varies from pavilion to pavilion. It is well that this is so. At first, one wishes to be surrounded by a familiar atmosphere, as this seems to be congenial to one's thoughts and beliefs—the ones we were brought up with. I myself came here as a Confucian as well as a Buddhist."

Again, I must have registered surprise, for he quickly but patiently explained,

"Those of us who choose to enter the lamasery have come from the greatest variety of religious and philosophical backgrounds. Roman Catholics, Jews, Hindus, Jains—"

"Formerly," I broke in without thinking.

"Formerly and still. Because one religion is true does not mean all the others are false."

"Of course." Hearing it then, I thought it made perfect sense.

"Oh, it must do more than make sense," Chang said, reading my thoughts. "To be persuaded of a truth is only superficial. It is merely to have an opinion. You will find that the clarity of our atmosphere, free from contaminants of civilization—"

"Contaminants?" I interrupted. Then as I was about to apologize for my repeated interrupting, Chang held up his index finger.

"No need to apologize. This is a place of dialogue. You do understand, I believe, that by contaminants, I do not mean only pollution of the air."

"Yes," I said. "I think you mean what I would call civilization."

"I truly doubt that, Buster. What you mean by civilization is Beethoven and Grieg, Goethe and Shakespeare, Keats and Milton. Such civilization we have here, as you know."

"Indeed I do."

We had reached a partition that was quite large. It had the appearance of a domed stadium, in fact. But Chang continued speaking and my attention was drawn back. Art walked ahead.

"What I mean by contamination is what you would call popular culture, the corporate ethic, and industrial production; the idea of profit, the useless luxuries and conveniences of a bored and arid society. We try to import only the best." With a nod, he pointed to the stadium.

"You have been wondering whether Shangri-La is heaven or hell." He was correct. It seemed perfectly heavenly, but I wondered whether it would merely unfit me for the outside world and give rise in me to an indelible yet unsatisfiable longing that would turn everything else to hell.

"How people deal with the contrast is what determines whether they exist in a hell or in a heaven," Chang said. "But strictly speaking, this should not be termed either heaven or hell. The words come from the various religions and carry many different and absurd and unhealthful meanings to most people. Shangri-La is simply home.—But to reassure you." He pointed to a tall scoreboard, visible above the ramparts of the stadium. It read:

Green Bay 14
Dallas   0

"*This is heaven*," I said with considerable warmth.

"You may make further expressions of happiness, if you wish."

But I kept a considerate silence. Chang then said, "There is more. Quite a bit more, unless I miss my guess." He glanced at a nearby sundial. "I believe the first half should be nearly completed. If you would be pleased to enter?" He gestured toward one of the entrances. Already I could hear the roar of the crowd.

We went through an underpass and emerged behind the Packers' bench. The field was the freshest turf I had ever seen. The Green and Gold had never looked so beautiful. I could smell brats.

The clock was running down the last few seconds and both teams were walking off the field. Two Packer linemen were assisting a big man limping between them. It appeared to be Willie Davis. "This is very bad," I said to Chang.

"What is bad, and what is good—usually it is too early to say, when we still think of those words."

A man in the familiar fedora walked out to them, and they stopped to talk near where Chang and I stood. "What's the matter, Davis?"

"It's the ankle again, Coach."

"I don't want you on it. Shower and sit out the second half."

"The replacements are down, Coach. There are no other defensive ends. I have to play. Wood and Adderley are injured. If we don't keep nailing Staubach in the backfield, they'll turn the game around in the second half."

Number 15 had jogged out to the little group and now stood listening.

"We're in trouble," Lombardi said. "We're in one helluva mess."

"Coach," said number 15. With a nod of his head, he directed the Coach's attention toward me.

Lombardi yelled at me, "Suit up! You're playing the second half!" I looked at Chang, who nodded benignly.

As I stood waiting for the defense to go in at the beginning of the second half, I sort of growled. Coach Lombardi, who was standing alongside, said,

"It's only a game, Buster. Remember, winning isn't everything."

Through my teeth I said, "Coach, winning might not be everything, but losing is nothing."

His face lit up in a great, toothy smile. He slapped my back hard. "You got a way with words, Kid!" As I trotted onto the field I looked back and saw Coach writing it down on his clipboard.

The second half was good.

After I showered and was interviewed, I went to the entrance we had used to come in, and found Chang and Art.

"Well done," Chang said. "Smashingly well done."

"Thanks. It was a team effort. You gotta give credit to all the guys." Art put up a fist, and we knocked fists.

"Good game," he said.

"Call it what you will, I call it heaven," I said.

"As you wish. There should be ample time to meet our several appointments for lunch," Chang said quietly.

"Oh gosh," I said. I looked at my watch. Indeed, in Shangri-La there was always plenty of time.

The details of my luncheon with Fayaway need not detain us. The waterfall and the swim in clear, buoyant water, and the refreshment afterward, filled my heart.

"I feel as though I have loved you always," I said to her. She smiled that wise, patient smile, and I promised, "I shall stay with you here forever."

She nodded, then looked down. I saw tears glisten, and then drop from her eyes. Gently I lifted her chin, and she said, "But not yet. You will go back. You will go back to double dam."

"Never."

"You must." I did not understand, but I could see in her eyes that it was true.

"I shall return," I said.

"You always will."

*

"I cannot help but wonder," I said to Chang as he led us up a path toward a plain wooden pavilion that I understood to be the abode of the Dalai Lama. "Which is real, and which is the imagination—Shangri-La, or the world we were in the day before yesterday?"

"About time you got around to that," Art observed, though not as if he awaited an answer.

"I mean, which one will be a dream when I wake up?"

Chang smiled his patient, wise smile. "Where do you suppose we are at all times, but in the mind of God?"

I did not understand his answer. "But can you tell me which of my own two minds is the one that is awake?"

"Ah. I am afraid I may not tell you. It is for you to tell yourself. It could be either."

"Looks like an old stave church," Art said. We had arrived at a wooden building, gabled, with a steep roof. The walls had all been tarred for protection against the sun and breeze.

Chang simply nodded. "You may enter when you please."

"You are not coming in with us?" I asked, the quaver in my voice betraying some anxiety. Yet the thought had been growing in my mind that we had been brought to Shangri-La for a reason, and the reason was that the old Dalai Lama was to die soon, had foreseen it long ago. And I, unsuspecting and unprepared, was to take up the mantle. The responsibility of this place would descend upon my unready shoulders all too soon. I reflected that all things are for the best. I had recently finished reading Russell's *History of Western Philosophy*. Chang smiled his enigmatic smile.

"Are you forbidden to go in?" I enquired.

"Nothing is forbidden. Respect dictates that none enter unless called."

"How often do you see him?"

"In the years I have been in Shangri-La, once."

I absorbed his answer in silence. Chang continued, "You see, the Dagli Lama bestows a great honor upon the two of you. There is, perhaps, some terrible urgency preying upon him. In your deep mind, you shall never forget the next hour." He bowed, we bowed to him, and Art and I stepped through the low doorway.

Light entered from what appeared to be a parchment window in the ceiling. Dull glows from covered windows surrounded the central space from all sides. Gradually, I could make out a wood floor, a nearly empty room, and a very small figure in a hooded blue and red robe sitting cross-legged behind the smallest of fires. I knew it to be the Dalai Lama. Slowly and reverently, we approached. Art had removed his hat upon entering. Though I am not a Catholic, I crossed myself.

As we approached, the figure appeared to be looking at us. Now, with thin hands, he pulled back his hood. His head was entirely bald. In the half-light, he appeared to be very old. Deliberately yet gracefully, he turned a hand to indicate that we approach and sit. Two mats made of wicker or some kind of reed lay waiting for us perhaps ten feet distant from him.

Carefully, after deep bows, we sat. We remained in silence for several minutes. As our eyes adjusted, we saw a wizened, somewhat austere face, though the expression was far from forbidding. His eyes radiated peace and understanding. He looked at us, then spoke.

"So I see yue guys finally made it, den."

"You bet," Art replied. "Kind of a bumpy ride, you know, but we came through all right."

The lama nodded.

I could not speak.

"Cat got yer tongue dere, Young Fella?"

I swallowed. "I didn't expect. That is, your nationality."

"Ya, yue betcha dere, Young Fella. I hope yue didn't expect a Svede, did yue?"

"No, Sir."

"Amen to dat, dere."

"Are you from Minnesota, Sir?"

An expression of quiet, patient mirth imbued his face. "Not by a long shot, Sonny. Venn I vas born, Minnesota vas only a gleam in Paul Bunyan's eye."

"How, ah—"

"How old am I, yue vant to know, ya young rascal? Vell, let me say I vas here venn Yustaf Adolph vas in short pants."

"And you have retained your Norwegian ways—the coffee, the stave church architecture, the lutefisk last night. Do you still make lefse?"

"Sonny, is da Pope Catlik? Does a bear drop his pants in da voods?"

"Whew," I said.

"Yue tot I was da impressive silent type, didn't yue? Vell, all I can say is yue got a lot to learn, Young Fella. Yue don't have an inkling about Buddhism."

"You're Buddhist?" I exclaimed. "Sorry. I'm sorry."

"Is da Pope Catlik, I repeat?"

"I suppose being a lama . . . whew. A Norwegian Buddhist—ah, Sir."

"Not only a Norvegian Buddhist, a Norvegian Lootran Buddhist. Vid a little Hindue trown in for good measure, and a couple odder tings."

"You bet," Art remarked. I looked at both in amazement.

The Dagli Lama continued,

"I been around a long time, Sonny. Yue'd expect da old fella to learn a fue tings, vouldn't yue?"

I nodded. "May I ask why . . ."

"Vy did ve bring yue here, yue vere about to ask. Vell, ta be honest, it vas to get Art here. Dat vas da urgent ting on da menue. Art, did yue figger out da Koan yet?"

I looked at Art. "You bet," he said.

"What's a Koan?" I nearly whined.

"Vell, Big Fella, to yue all of life is a Koan, but to da more advanced, it's a lilla statement or phrase or story dat puzzles yue an' puzzles yue until suddenly yue see da light. Da whole light. Takes discipline ta varm up to it."

"Discipline?" I looked at Art, the most casual person I know.

"Ya, Big Fella. Vy do yue tink Art spent all dat time fishing? Yust because da sunnies come in? Ha ha. Dat's a gued vun."

I didn't speak, for I could not. But the elderly lama read my mind.

"Da Koan for Art vas da bumper sticker."

"The bumper sticker?"

"Ya, yue betcha dere."

"'Uff da'?"

"Vell, it's not da Koan for yue. As I said, yue got a vays to go before ve give yue vun. *Ska vi har en lit kaffee?*"

"Sounds good," Art said.

The lama levitated three cups and a pot over from somewhere in the shadows. The pot poured our coffee; then a bowl of sugar cubes came around. As Art and the lama slurped their coffee, I remembered my thought about being the next Dalai Lama.

"Ya, dat's a yoke!" the lama suddenly exclaimed, and laughed a weak but heartfelt laugh.

"I am very ashamed and very humbled, Sir."

"Oh, it doesn't hurt anyting."

"How far wrong was I?"

"Vell, Big Fella, you're pretty far down da line, dere. Vi gonna hafta go trough pretty much da whole population, 'fore ve get to yue."

Art patted my shoulder. "Ain't no hurry. You got time."

"Da reason ve vanted yue boys now vas to make sure Art here vas about ready."

"You bet," Art said.

"Ar- Art?" I stammered.

"Ya, Young Fella, venn Art dies, he don't hafta be born no more. He comes straight here. Yue, on da udder hand, gonna vear out da voombs of da vorld, so ta speak."

"Ahh! But when—"

"Hey, Big Fella, don't yue vorry. Art isn't gonna go yust yet. You got plenty a time ta learn a ting or tue fra him. And venn he gets here, he isn't on da spot right avay. I gonna be translated and become a reglar monk— ve all hafta be in my spot sometime, yue know. After me, its Keats, denn Art." He looked intently at Art. "You got da Koan, I tink. Yue vasn't yust a-kiddin."

"I got it. Took me pretty near a whole day, though."

The Dagli Lama nodded, then stuck a pinch of *snuss* behind his lip. Sounding a little different he said, "Gude enough. Hit da road, yents."

In a flash I realized that it was over, all over, and perhaps before I even knew it we would be back in that car—

"The car!" I exclaimed. The Dagli Lama looked up, startled.

"Ya, by yimminy! Dat's vat happens venn a fella gets old. I forgot all about da car! Vi brought yue here, Sonny, to accompany Art and to learn a couple tings, but dere vas anudder reason. Vell, if dat isn't someting! Gude ting yue mentioned da car."

I felt rather good again.

"Even dough it vas by accident. Listen, Young Fella, yue know a ting or tue about cars."

"A little," I said.

"Listen. Vi decided vi need a car in Kjaengri-La. Yust vun. For visitors, so dey don't tink vi don't know vat vi gettin' avay from. Vat do yue recommed? Art dere vould recommend a Chevy."

"Can't go wrong with a good old Chevy," Art put in.

"But dat's da vun ting Art ain't gude at. It's to be expected, Art's being in such an advanced state. So vi ask yue."

"Honored," I said.

"Vell, ve learn to take vaat ve can get, Sonny. Vat do you recommend?"

"When do you plan to buy?"

"In about ten, fifteen years. Vi don't hurry. Vi gotta get our buying netvork expanded."

"What are you looking to spend?"

"For da love a Mike? Vat are yue, a car salesman? Next yue'll ask vat vi got to trade."

"Sorry. Very sorry, Sir. I just thought I should take that into account."

"Most expensive ain't always the best," Art suggested.

"Yue betcha, Art."

"Okay. I recommend a bicycle. Specifically, a Clark bicycle. Not the most expensive, but the best in the world." The Dagli Lama looked at me impassively, with somewhat emphatic patience. "However, I need not preach about efficiency and clean air here. You want a car that can be converted to solar power. And you don't want a sports car."

"Da idea of a car for sport is da most screwball idea yet. If I tought dere vas a devil, I vould say it vas his idea."

"You want transportation, period. First safety, then durability, then economy."

"I got to give yue credit. Yue learned a lot. Maybe ve move yue up a notch or tue. From vun hundred billion and tird to vun hundred billion second, ha ha."

I knew Buddhists like to laugh, but couple that with typical Norwegian frankness—

"Ya, you're right dere, vat yue aer tinkin'. I apologize."

"Oh, sir, you don't need."

He held up a hand. "Nay, nay. Yue Christians only beginning to learn vut humility is. Dere aren't many Christians up here yet. Even Looter's pretty deep on da bench. Yesus drops in now and den to help dem. So, vat do yue recommend, finally?"

"Volvo."

"Yimminy Christmas! A Svede car?"

"You are familiar with Sweden?"

"Dat's vere dey keep da Svedes, if I am correctly informed."

"My apologies, Sir. But yes, a Volvo."

"Vell, yue got vun dilly of a nerve, is all I can say!"

"Give the boy a chance," Art said very casually. "He knows cars, I tell you."

The Dagli Lama composed himself and apologized. "Dat outburst vas not vordy of a Dagli Lama. If yue say Volvo, Volvo it is." Then he said to himself, "Svede car. Dat's a how do you do."

"They're the only car company that has always cared about the safety of their customers. They're working on clean emissions and recyclable parts. Their cars are very durable. They are a small, humble company. You want to make a statement to the world with your one purchase."

"Vell, actually vi vant to keep it qvite."

"As a Swedish company, Sir, the odds are excellent of them losing track of the transaction. He he. Except now it's under Chinese ownership." I laughed rather modestly. The Dagli Lama hesitated, then laughed.

"Hej," he said. "I got a gude von for yue. Vy do Svedish cars have dere vindue vipers on da inside a da vinshield? It's because venn Svedes drive, dey say *Brrrrppptttttt!* Ha ha!"

We all laughed, and the Dagli Lama resumed, "Vell, aren't vi da buncha Norvegian yokels, sittin' here by ourselves telling Svede yokes. Vi should be ashamed. It's unvordy of da place."

"Ya, but it's a good yoke, though," Art said.

"Vell tanks, Art. But vi must be moving on."

"Sir –" I said, raising my hand a little.

"Ya, yue dere, vid da hand up. He he."

"Sir, I'm afraid that when this is over, none of it will remain in my memory."

"Vell, dat's pretty much true, aldough dere vill be a residue in da heart, dere." He pointed to my chest. "In da soul."

"Sir, might it be possible to take something tangible back, like some chopsticks, maybe? Perhaps—"

"Nuts to dat. All yue can take back is Art."

I looked at Art, who said, "I think that's your koan, my boy."

"Vell bingo; right yue aer. Yue vant vun for da road?" A bottle of Aquavit and three shotglasses floated over.

"He'll get pinched for driving under the influence, you know," Art said.

"Ya, I guess so!"

"We'll be goin' to beat the band as it is."

"Like a Svede outa hell, as dey say. Sorry. Sayonara, boys."

Art and I stood. Art led the way, and as he went through the door, I heard the Dagli Lama clear his throat.

"Vait, young fella. I knew dere vas someting else. Da memory, it goes, yue know. Yue know yue can't take Fayaway back."

"I know."

"Don't vorry. Yue vill see her again, don't yue vorry. Yue tue can't be separated, in da whole scheme a tings, ya know."

"Thank you very much, Sir. I appreciate that more than I can say."

"Yue vill forget, but not entirely. Be careful."

"Yes, Sir. Careful?"

"The little yue remember makes yue a yenuine Romantic. Some Romantics are da best; some turn out to be da vorst. Venn it comes to love, stick to da real ting."

I thought of a girl named April, whom I had recently met. This suddenly confused me.

"Don't vorry about dat kinda ting, Big Fella. And ennyvay, in dat case, it vasn't da girl, it was da valse."

"Sir. Thank you."

"Don't take any vooden nickels, now."

*

In a few minutes, I am not sure how, we were back in the old Chevrolet. *Too bad they always start*, I thought.

"You know, this is quite a fish story," Art said.

"You bet."

When I looked up, the sky was cloudy and Art stood at the roadway across the Little Dam, waving. I got up from where I had been sitting, picked up the rod, pail, and worms.

"Any luck?" he asked as I climbed the embankment.

"Nothing. How about you?"

"Nothin' doin'." Art looked up at the heavy sky. "We shoulda been payin' attention. Rain's going to catch us before we make it to the car."

Sure enough, big drops started hitting us before we got there, and by the time we threw everything into the Bel Air's trunk we were pretty wet.

"Wanna drive?" Art said.

"You bet."

I turned the car around in the space between the dams, and it was thundering and lightning.

"Shoulda had more sense than sit daydreamin' while a storm come up," Art said.

"Well, we made it anyway." And just then, as I was turning toward Art, a fireball, yellow and white, came down a tree right beside the car. The ball was the size of a basketball and it seemed to float suspended for two or three seconds.

Then it just disappeared into the rainy air and we were on our way.

"Uff da," Art said.

* * *

Unfortunately, a postscript must be added to this redaction of the chapter on Chevrolet. I say "unfortunately," because Chevrolet has given up on the American sedan, as have Ford and Chrysler. The current Chevrolet Impala has become the lost horizon of the American car. It ceased production in January 2020 C.E. The former "Big Three" have surrendered the sedan to Japanese, Korean, German, and other manufacturers because their cars are better and sell better, and because the American market has turned away from sedans and is sucking SUV Kool-Aid. SUV's are an essentially bogus segment that makes us feel safer in this increasingly maddened country, and that encourages the fantasy that we are at any time about to off-road into the natural world that these very vehicles are destroying. Significantly, there is no mention of the SUV whatsoever in all of Goethe. The trend toward SUV's is happening at a time when the ecological window of survival is almost shut. However, we are Americans and we can do what we want, including pumping additional carbon and other automotive poisons into the atmosphere, because SUV's are heavier and less aerodynamic than sedans. The latest Chevrolet bigboy SUV's, the Tahoe and Suburban, are still larger and heavier than the outgoing models of those behemoths. Good for us. This is why Mark Twain called us "the damned human race." I don't want to cast a shadow over the subsequent pages of this Romantic Manifesto; I'm just sayin'. Thinking that just sayin' will do any good is certainly a romantic notion.

First Philosophical Interlude: Goethe

a. If humankind were to take Goethe's works to heart, we would not be staggering on the brink of environmental collapse, so you will want to know how to pronounce the name. It is no good travelling to Germany to find out, because the Germans do not know how to pronounce it. They are embarrassed by this, and evasive, but eventually the honest ones among them throw up their hands, like Italians.

American armed forces manuals—tens of thousands of Army personnel have been stationed in Germany because of the Second World War—will tell you to pronounce the name "Gerta." But this works—a little—only in British English, because the Brits start to pronounce the letter "r" and never finish. The Army is reluctant to tell soldiers to pronounce it "Gay-teh," but that is as close as an American can come to the Unpronounceable, and it is what I recommend for reading this book.

Because Goethe is an unpronounceable name, many authorities recommend that it be abbreviated to only the initial letter, so: G. But because "G" is the initial of many other significant names, such as Grant and Green Bay, I have retained the entire spelling for these pages, and I leave the sub-vocalization up to you. An appendix at the end of this book gives more detailed information on pronunciation.

b. Many of these pages are autobiographical. I do this consciously, following Goethe's own method of illustrating his ideas. He termed this integration of life and learning *Narküssen,* which has been inadequately translated for years as "narcissism," but it means literally "fool-kissing," an apparently derogatory and self-critical term that has many subtle and suggestive overtones. Goethe's language is always deep and rich like compost, a single word often suggesting a sensory and intellectual complexity of meaning. Only the experiences of one's own life can begin to embrace the Shakespearean multiplexity of Goethe's colorful words, shimmering like gasoline on water.

c. This is why my translations are unique among English versions of Goethe's works. Interestingly and oddly, the Clark Bicycle Manufactory, UnLtd. (which makes the world's best bicycles and possesses the world's best labor force, though the management is erratic) employed many translation experts, who though innocent of the original languages in question, and who had no experience in non-English-speaking countries, worked from a long background of highly developed theory. They produced many eminent English translations of such works as *Tristram Shandy* and *The Gospel According to Peanuts*.

For Goethe, however, only experience counts. This principle applies to life and faith, but especially to translating such works as *Faust, Wilhelm Meister's Apprenticeship,* and *Out of my Life and Work: Poetry and Cars*. Language is life, and life is language.

d. What, then, is the good life? It is not simply language, because language is the mere *vehicle* of life (hence "Poetry and Cars"). Goethe employs many novel and inventive words for "vehicle," because the automobile industry and therefore automotive theory were still young in Goethe's day, but the most well-known was his groundbreaking term, *hüpfenkrösen*, which has been variously and weakly translated as "embodiment," "bodying-forth," "sneezing," and worst of all, "conveyance."[2] Note that Goethe's word for the English noun "vehicle" is actually a verb. His usage is meant to bend the mind, Zen-like, and crash us through to an enlightened understanding of what transportation can be. I translate the word as "driving," or "to drive," and gently futz with the rest of the sentence to make the verb function grammatically. If this at times necessitates the use of a gerundial ablative—a construction rare even in Latin—so be it: discomfort with ease and mediocrity is the price of encountering Goethe.

So the good life is "good living," or, as Goethe puts it, "driving." There are several other elements of enlightened living: Love, Work, and God & Nature being chief among them. God and Nature are understood together by Goethe—hence his pioneering concerns with ecology, which grew out of his study of light—and all of these elements are subsumed under "driving." Hence the full title of Goethe's down-to-earth yet spiritual, almost mystical, *Aus Meinen Leben: Dichtung und Wahrheit*, or *Out of My Life: Poetry and Cars*.

---

2. Goethe's term was the origin of the short-lived two-seater *Hüpfenschnöggel*.

e. Love. We were all romantics when we were young, and Goethe was no exception. His *Sorrows of Young Werther* is obvious proof; what is less understood is that his *Italian Journey* is a more profound statement of the essence of Romanticism: longing. What proves that our souls are meant for more than this world? Longing. What proves that we were made for God? Longing. And what does a road trip symbolize and express? Longing.

A road trip like Goethe's *Italian Journey (Italienische Reise)* is the only earthly way of striving for heaven. We make road trips not so much because we want to *go* somewhere but because we sense that we *came from* somewhere, and we long to be there again. For Goethe, the trip to Italy was ostensibly to inspect the burgeoning Italian car industry. The new Ferraris, Maseratis, and Lamborghinis, with lines like Sophia Loren, were for the young Goethe the mechanical embodiments of grace and beauty, with the hazard of speed—like the hazardous efforts of those over-wrought sailors who crashed their boats against the impervious Lorelei Rock on the Rhine. These elements all meant longing and its intellectual and artistic expression, Romanticism. The comfort and glory of home in heaven is the splendor and danger of impossible striving on earth. So Goethe, who sought to bring the Italian love of automotive beauty back with him to Germany, returned to be confronted by the ravenous engineers of Porsche and Wolfsburg. What heartbreak! What disgust! Yet what admiration too, as Goethe, growing out of his youthful romanticism, began to appreciate the classical symmetry, reserve, and durability of German design and technology.

But I was talking about love. Goethe never left his main value: love. Only, romantic love does not fare well on earth. Love lasts only if it changes, grows. Having a Lamborghini or a Pinoquetto in your driveway might be exhilarating, but if you want the experience to last, you need to get some German rustproofing on it; and you'll have to drop a Mercedes engine into the bay if you plan on getting to the grocery store.

The new Italian automobiles, Goethe found, were temperamental—a trait attractive at first in a pouted-lips sort of way, but tiresome in the long run. Real love, true love, lasts forever, as Goethe read in his Luther translation of St. Paul. Speed, handling, and reliability abide, these three; but the greatest of these is reliability. Fortunately for Germany, the Japanese had not yet become interested in the automobile. The forebears of Toyota and Nissan were still pre-occupied with ceremony and nature.

But the Germans were roaring ahead. The British, of course, had been reading the early German Romantics, had learned their early Goethe, and were producing the early versions of the Twickenham Corsair and the Tudds-Buttles Frigantine. Royce and Bentley would not be long in coming.

Goethe changed the world. His ideas drove the industry that revolutionized life on earth. So did I want to change the world when I sought a position at the Clark Bicycle Manufactury, UnLtd. I believed in the bicycle and still do: it is the most efficient and pleasant conveyance upon earth, and it creates no carbon, filth, or poisonous gasses except in the manufacture. I had thought the Clark company would be a vehicle for change, but soon discovered that their managers' preaching of the bicycle's virtues were self-serving. Like all types of evangelicals, they were in love only with themselves. Their God was only themselves painted large: they made altogether too much of the "wheels within wheels" passage in the Book of Ezekiel. The plain sense of that passage indicates the automobile, because a bicycle turns as it goes, its front part being mobile. Still, Clark made a lot of good bicycles. This shows that Goethe (as nearly always) was right: sometimes we serve the Great Unknown (whom we apprehend through the mysteries of Love and Beauty) even when we are most wrong and our intentions belong to the devil, the Mephistophelean shadow of ourselves, who steers us by the wheel of desire.

Longing turns us to the Unknown, and Love binds us to Him— Her—Them like a camshaft to a cylinder. Goethe was imprecise about God's gender and number, late in life (see his *Conversations with Eckermann*) stating that gender and number were not pertinent or applicable when it comes to God.

Clark Manufactury believed in number and gender. They believed that God is a bicycle. It has two wheels and a circular sprocket, which makes three. But the three make a single vehicle, which is one. And the wheels are male in front, female in back—never male front male back or female front and back. This is merely a mistake or prejudice in terminology, said Goethe, who owned many bicycles, including a three-wheeler and a unicycle. "The universe," he famously said, "is larger than our views of it."

But let it go. The bicycle has its place. However, only the automobile is suited to a road trip. Only the Chevrolet embodies the longing that underlies the American Experiment, only Volkswagen-Audi will eventually master the world and all the peoples therein, and only the Peugeot can be French. The bicycle might save the world, but the automobile *is* the world, and its Hindu-like multiplicity of gears and wheels lays before us the true and only conditions for love.

Love goes places fast. Let that axiom be set down at once, and be remembered throughout these pages. Only the automobile promises, however tentatively and humanly, to reach the Master Speed, the Escape Velocity that enables us to break the bonds of gravity and accelerate into the heavens where we were born, and into the Great Unknown where we long to return!

Meanwhile, we fall in love. Each time we do this, we are groping for the one love of our life—which in turn is an image of our relationship with the Divine. Goethe fell in love like a bunny. This turn of phrase applied to one of the Enlightenment's greatest figures: it might be likened to calling the Parthenon a garage. (Actually it was. Here was the first instance of a shelter for vehicles—the chariot, the wagon—being elevated to the position of a temple, once people perceived the true significance of vehicles.) But Goethe realized that his many early romances merely expressed his longing for the Real Thing, for the true love of his soul that was established before his earthly birth. There was Lotte, for example. It has become a commonplace in Goethe Studies (*Goethestudium*) that Lotte is an excessively lush name for a main squeeze. (The German terms for main squeeze are *Hauptskönchen* and the more vulgar *Schwerpünktchen*.) Her actual name was Charlotte, more suited to her high socio-economic status. Not a few British scholars have pointed out that her last name was Buff, making an academically coy to-do of the fact; however, that kind of smug sniggering unnecessarily cheapens a volume of this nature. She was engaged to be married and a teenager, but the somewhat older Goethe fell in love with her regardless. More might have come of this unconsummated affair, but clearly she did not want to become Lotte Goethe.

In my own case, I fell in love as a teenager and have tried until the climactic search described in the following pages to find the girl again. But there was Another behind the adolescent love and the lifelong quest—whose mysterious and exotic identity no doubt lies in, with, and under everything I have done in life, and everything I have aspired to do. But all in good time.

Failing to achieve the love of my life or the love of my soul, I turned to work. Work is what you do when you are expelled from Eden. It is the substitute for bliss, even where the work itself seems like bliss—which is the case for 2.53% of those who work. It is either heaven, or the job; it is either the Angel or the Engine.

f. Work. What is work but the engine of desire, the distance covered by futility, and the weight born by damnation? So Goethe's *Faust* examines symbolically the internal combustion engine. Certainly work—work productive and work enjoyed—is one of the underpinnings of happiness. But happiness is not longing—nay, feels like quite the opposite; so the real work, for Goethe—not the work that moves the earth, but the work that moves the heavens—is play. Love's work is play for immortal stakes. Work is the law, and play is grace, and love transforms work to grace.

All this is very confusing. Thank Heaven, then, for the automobile.

Some of you might have forgotten your third grade study of "Simple Machines." Simple machines—the lever, the inclined plane, the pulley, etc.—make work more efficient. For example, you might expend 40 foot-pounds of force lifting a 40lb crate of Bibles to chest height; but if you lift it using a pulley, you could reduce your effort nearly as much as you want. If you use one wheel fastened overhead and 20ft of rope, perhaps you could reduce your effort to 30 foot-pounds. (Goethe worked out all these numbers in *Dichtung und Wahrheit*, but I am too busy writing to consult them now.) If you use four wheels and 100ft of rope, you might reduce your effort to, say, 10 foot-pounds. Of course in that case, you usually overlook the facts, namely, that it required twenty Bangladeshi children working for Walmart to harvest the hemp, three Haitian women to braid it, and a dozen Wall Street slaves to sell and market it. Then you figure the wages of the two Mexicans employed to balance on the building's ledge above you and hold a rod with two of the wheels, and two more below to hold the other wheels, and finally the one who pulls the rope for you—reducing to Zero your foot-pound exertion, save the fraction required for standing in the hot sun. That's five workers at 25¢ per hour—but then there are the Immigration officers employed to apprehend the Mexicans you hired, the court officials, judge, and attorneys, the transportation people, fuel, the congressmen, and you have reduced your effort from 40 to 0 foot-pounds for $1.25 plus $4,700,000.00 in hidden costs.

Such calculations as the latter were made by Goethe's near-contemporary, Freidrich Hölderlin, the Master's great opponent and nemesis, who maintained that the automobile, far from offering the greatest advance in overall standard of living the world has ever seen—because, as Goethe pointed out, it employs millions of people worldwide who pay taxes that build roads, and in general finance the world's governments

and economies—is ruining the world by exhausting its resources, polluting its air and water, enslaving humanity to a diabolical military-
industrial machine, killing people on roads, and sparking wars over
fuel and religion indefinitely, not to mention generating interminable
German-like sentences such as this one, in which one wonders where the
verb finally is to be placed. So we have Goethe, with his Shakespeare-like
comprehensive view of human nature, showing us the world as it is; and
over-against him we have Hölderlin, showing us the world that ought to
be. Yet both were at one time or another Romantics, longing for a lost
horizon of blessedness and joy.

Or say you wanted to lift that box of Bibles. It's heavy. I know this because once the Clark Supervisors had discovered my talent for assembly-
line piecework, they tried me out for other tasks, such as receiving Bible
shipments. If I wanted to lift a Bible box off dead center, I could strain
my back and scuff my fingers, or I could use a lever to get it started. As
Goethe pointed out, the longer the lever, the less the effort. The official
lever of the Clark Bicycle Manufactury, UnLtd.. was the Bible verse stating that all Scripture is divinely inspired. I tried cast-iron, aluminum, and
machine-turned steel rods, and found them all to be functional, yet the
company's official doctrine confined all public efforts to that verse. Once
I suggested importing verses from India—a far more cost-effective solution than the Bible verse that has been manufactured in Tennessee since
the 1920's—and was nearly fired for my well-intended initiative.

But India, exactly, is where Freidrich Hölderlin derived his ideas
about the automobile. He was called crazy, and confined to a tower beside
the Neckar River in the university town of Tübingen, where I went to
school for a short time. Hölderlin claimed that the internal combustion
engine was not the world's most efficient machine, as Goethe insisted, but
rather the least. Goethe, remember, in his work on automotive theory,
said that this engine is "comprehensive" (*alles-zerschaffenfähig*), generating the whole of humankind's economies, beliefs, and future. Hölderlin
agreed that the internal combustion engine is comprehensive (*alleszer-
fressenfähig* or *einmaulig*), but in the way that the devil is comprehensive. Goethe, the recognized authority on the devil, countered that the
devil is only a symbol of humanity's perverted longing; that is, the devil
is the image of *work*, and as such, the devil is essentially a machine. Since
we are incomplete, fallen, or damned creatures, we must *work* out our
salvation—"salvation" meaning, for the young Goethe, a realm of bliss
and unity, and for the older Goethe meaning self-completion, sausage

pudding, or possibly unity with Nothing in the comprehensive Buddhist sense, depending upon the translation.

"And they call me nuts!" Hölderlin is reported to have exclaimed upon reading Goethe's *Poetry and Cars*. Hölderlin produced no systematic theory like Goethe's, yet his poems and letters are replete with alarm over the acceptance of Goethic theory in Germany. From these informal writings one can piece together a theory of love of the earth that becomes love of heaven. Hölderlin's thought appears today to be a most impractical, flowery Romanticism—yet it merely grasps onto Goethe's idea that the real, essential, hallowed work is play. But not the play represented by Italian and German cars. For Hölderlin, the ultimate play—the final work of humankind—is love. His poem "Gedächte über Goethes Ungläubung, Mal!" ("Goethe Thinks Bassackwards" in English) pictures humankind as a rider seated atop a globe that he has made entirely into a machine, and the machine carries him into a dark, airless, cold void. A bleak picture, but there it is.

Yet "what a work is man"! If we ourselves are a work of God, Goethe retorted, is not work the divine image within us? And is not the automobile—our greatest work—therefore to be celebrated? No! responded Hölderlin in a letter to the American Automobiles Anonymous society, founded in North America with branches and offices in all thirteen British colonies. No! the impassioned Romantic wrote resoundingly. Man is not God's work; man is God's play. The whole universe is play, is art and science. The continents might have been work, but on the sixth day of creation, when Man and Woman were made, God was goofing off. Look at human nature and try not to laugh, wrote the mad poet. The image of God in man is laughter.

"Mankind is damned," wrote Goethe in reply. "What is funny about that? What can be found amusing in the eternal condemnation of billions, past, present, and future, of men, children, grandparents, poets, humanitarians, saints, and heroes?" *It's hilarious*, retorted Hölderlin. The whole concept of damnation is hilarious—the most laughably ridiculous of all of the devil's (read "humankind's") notions. Who would pour moral opprobrium upon an ant, and then condemn the ant to an eternity of torture? Who but a morally grotesque lunatic? The idea is the invention of—guess who?—the devil: i.e., of our own maddened minds.

What was Goethe's ingenious answer? It was that such a hell—a hell of fire and brimstone, of physical torture—is a *comfort* invented by guilt-ridden humankind. A real hell would be the image in Hölderlin's very own poem: utter cold, dark separation; the opposite of love.

"In that we are agreed," wrote Hölderlin to a relative, then lapsed into one of his strange silences—which lasted until possibly the interview that took place in my presence, in the Hölderlin Tower by the river, as recorded toward the end of this book. But all in good time! Meanwhile, there is *work* to be done!

g. God and Nature.

A man is a car. A woman is a car.

"According to Liebig, man's body is a stove, and food the fuel which keeps up the internal combustion in the lungs." Thoreau is here referring to the German chemist Justus von Liebig, who wrote *Animal Chemistry*, an apparently racy title in today's fevered mind but actually a scientific text. Before working at Clark, I taught automotive theory at Justus Liebig University in Giessen, Germany, so I have a special interest in this quotation from *Walden*. The line of thought runs straight from Goethe through Liebig to Thoreau, who identified the essence of human mechano-chemical vitality; namely, we are internal combustion engines.

Moreover, anyone who knows their Goethe remembers that in *Poetry and Cars* the Master points out that the universe as we conceive it is simply a projection (*Verblätzung*) of our self-image. If we think of humanity as a layered being, Reason on top and emotions on the bottom, then the universe is layered: God on top in heaven and chaos below, with Earth somewhere in between. If we think nothing in us or anywhere else fits together, then physics toys with the idea of multiple dimensions and universes; or if there is one physical explanation for it all, then all those dimensions can be fitted along a string theory: and if men and women are internal combustion engines, so is the cosmos. All of it depends on the burning of fuel—the extravagant conflagration of stars—and the purpose or effect is *Motion*. Planets revolve around suns, galaxies wheel, and galactic clusters move at speeds even Ferdinand Porshe never dreamed of. The poet[3] who saw "The World" in a vision, saw it "driven by the spheres," which means that he saw it for what it is: a motor and a vehicle, or a motor vehicle.

So what then of God and Nature? To the Romantics, Nature and the Cosmos are comparable to a living organism rather than to a mechanism, or machine. So we have a problem here: how can there be a romanticism

---

3. Henry Vaughan, whose last name in Old High German means "wagon."

of the automobile? Are the two not incompatible? Goethe becomes a classicist, and sees the cosmos as an engine? Is it that simple? Not at all. There is in Goethe the fusion of Romanticism and Classicism; that is why he is the greatest of German literary figures. He knew the romance of the machine—something every American boy understands instinctively. You do not need to make out with a girl at a drive-in to see the car as essentially romantic. Bucket seats have necessitated that we move beyond this crude association. The car is romantic because the machine itself grows like a plant. Thus the computer—the machine that becomes virtually, or perhaps really?, alive—bridges the divide between Classic and Romantic. It is now the brains of a car; and it regulates the heart—the motor—of the car as well.

All of this, Goethe foresaw. In his *Faust*, Mephistopheles is what? A man? A demon? No! Mephistopheles is a computer. Faust talks to it, perceives an intelligence and personality; it walks beside him like a robot but appears like a virtual projection even in closed rooms. It knows every weakness of Faust's and has no choice (machine-like) but to attack them. Faust cannot save himself from this "devil" of his own devising; only God can save him.

So, God and Nature? We do not know God directly, only the Nature that we ourselves perceive and devise through our peculiar sensory, intellectual, emotional, psychological, and spiritual matrix. But that very vehicle—our universe—is a work of love that will bring us to heaven. Hooray! Ride the car to heaven. "Poetry and Cars"? What is poetry but the love of beauty in words? And what is love of beauty but longing for God? How, then, shall we address the pain, the ecstatic agony of human existence? Get the right car! And go where I went in the companionship of Art. Ah, but "get the right car" is not so simple.

Volkswagen-Audi: Blood and Iron

I spent most of my 16th year away from the River, at home and in high school. I met April that year. Before relating this romantic episode, however, I shall devote several poignant pages to my early life and to German history and literature. First business, then romance. I remind the Reader that we are talking about good and evil and the Destruction of the World here. Therefore we *must* come to grips with Johann Wolfgang von Goethe and the German automobile.

As I have mentioned, my parents did not drive. You have no idea what that deficiency cost me as a youth, and still costs me. I had to beg rides everywhere, or I had to ride my bicycle in all weather. Yes, the Author would have to ride his bicycle in America in the rain. A boy on his black-and-white Schwinn Traveler bicycle, rain pouring down, soaking the groceries he is carrying in the wire baskets attached over the rear wheel. His hair is plastered down with rainwater; his glasses are runny. He could veer into a car's path and be killed. No book. Because it is so rainy and dark, he has his headlight turned on as a safety precaution, poor boy. Which means that the little generator wheel is in position against his back tire, making him pump harder, especially uphill. It was uphill both to the store and back from the store.

As a result, he has strong legs. As another result, he has started thinking about cars. Like Faust, he considers selling his soul. When the time comes, he must have a car.

Were we poor? Poverty in America isn't a condition, it's a verdict. The whole family bums rides: father, mother, longsuffering adolescent. We take the bus. We stay home. We are outsiders.

Therefore the saving automobile must not be some humiliating car, some beater, some vehicle that the neighbors wouldn't drive. The kind of car matters. Cars matter. After a lifelong Lent of unrelieved penance, surely I will be rewarded with an automobile. But how will I ever buy a car? I have strong legs. Maybe I could be some kind of runner. A delivery person, maybe riding a bicycle to deliver valuable goods. I will be mated to the bicycle forever! How long, O Lord, how long?

My sixteenth birthday arrives. On that day I am old enough to drive. I will get a driver's license on that day. I have already been through an ordeal. The previous summer, I took Driver Ed. I would arrive on my bike as all the other students were being dropped off. We watched movies in Driver Ed. Students threw up during them, as they were horrific in nature. When class was over, I loitered while everyone got picked up. Then I went around behind the building, mounted my faithful Schwinn Traveler, and pedaled home.

If I had been in a movie, the audience would have been cheering for me.

So the birthday arrives. When I wake up that morning, I part the curtain and look at the driveway. Empty. On the kitchen table there is one box, rather small, very richly wrapped with metallic paper and a beautiful bow. It could contain car keys. Dreams do come true. Carefully, I remove the expensive bow and paper. I open the box. In a rare, nay, unique display of zany humor, my mother has given me a small powder-blue Volkswagen Beetle toy.

Let me say here that I had become fixed on the VW Beetle as our possible car. I knew we could not afford cars like our neighbors drove. My mother had said with finality that we would never buy a used car, somebody else's trouble. That left the Beetle, $1600. A Plymouth or Pontiac was $2700. A Beetle would be acceptable, because they were cool, cute, in. The ads were clever. That was the main thing. While looking for girls in bikinis, you would leaf to a full page ad in *Life* magazine: a VW Beetle, black and white. Next to it a glass of water, maybe, or an eraser. Beneath, a caption of three or four words. An incomplete sentence. I had been suggesting that we buy a VW.

I put my birthday present in my room. Then I went to school, via the bus. Fortunately, nobody knew it was my 16th birthday. My neighbor, whose family drove a Cadillac, sat next to me secure as a clock, enviable as a corpse.

I could never take a girl on a date unless I got a car. Cars and romance were inextricably intertwined—which, put into Jeffersonian terms, means that in order to pursue happiness you must have a pursuit vehicle. That afternoon I passed the driver's test and got my license. I put it in the drawer with the powder-blue toy Beetle.

My incomparable German teacher drove a powder-blue VW Beetle. She was religious and humane, a Maria von Trapp without the guitar, so I viewed the Beetle as a *summum bonum* automobile. A friend's father had driven a Beetle until last year; I had ridden in it a lot and cased it out pretty well. It was almost airtight. You had to crack open a window when you slammed the door unless you wanted your ears to pop. The motor, a little air-cooled thing, was in back where the trunk should have been, and I heard it particularly well, as I always rode in back, sitting sideways to get room for my strong legs. The engine made a grainy, reedy, piercing noise. Bad for the ears. I knew Volkswagens were unsafe in a larger sense. Up front, all you had was a small empty compartment between you and the oncoming car. If we bought a VW, maybe I could fill the trunk with sandbags or water.

Thirty years later, some of those Beetles were still on the road. And now there is a New Beetle out, complete with a cute bud vase on the dashboard. I want to talk about Volkswagen, along with its sister company Audi. We shall leave the story of the brave, poor boy for now. Either I have made my case or I haven't. I rest that case. We are going to bridge my first obsession (Beetle) and my worst and most recent (Audi), in order to talk about the larger issue here: the destruction and demise of humankind.

*

"Love makes you do mad things, mad things!"

—MARK TWAIN, UNATTESTED

I have become a pessimist because I have owned two German cars. I knew in my heart of hearts that something evil was afoot when a friend of mine, who was working in Germany with me, said of his Audi 80, "I love it." I knew how bad that was the instant he said it, as we do tend to recognize the devil at first glance, but I put the thought away as we do when the devil pulls his cloak aside and shows us his wares. Otherwise I would have gone away sorrowful, for I, too, had bought a little used Audi 80. But this is to anticipate. The story properly begins much earlier, possibly with Goethe's *The Sorrows of Young Werther.*

Werther might not flash to one's mind when thinking about cars, so I owe you a quick explanation. The book was written just at the right time to become an instant smash; it was the ultimate Romantic Novel. Poor Werther starts off intelligent, sensitive, artistic, and in love with nature. But a doomed infatuation undermines his fate, his sanity, and in the end he kills himself. When *Werther* first came out, young men went around wearing Werther's characteristic blue jacket and gold vest. It is said that some star-crossed lovers took Werther's cue and did away with themselves. Ah, Werther! Ah, humanity!

What a perfect book to read at age sixteen. The book fed my soul; it marked me; it made me who I am. Goethe—what a genius. His book even whetted my adolescent appetite for Goethe's big boy: *Faust*. But as *Faust* applies to cars in general, not merely to VW Audi, a discussion of it will come later. For now, we concentrate on that lyrical, soaring, fatal *Werther*. He would have driven an Audi.

"Dear friend," says Werther in his first letter. (The book is a collection of letters.) "Dear friend, how strange is the human heart!" Oh, *ja*. It's the strangest thing out. If any male human believes that deep down, somewhere underneath his business, his profession, his learning, he is not fundamentally and incorrigibly an ass, let him look into his own heart or garage. Specifically, let him look into his heart's imaginings. It is with these imaginings that romance plays. The heart's imaginings are fired by the first intense romances of youth. And what does every man want? What does every man believe life owes him and will give him? A woman? No. Not that simple. He wants a pretty, well-built, smart but not too smart, fanatically faithful, humbly devoted, slut: he wants a car.

"I coddle my heart like a sick child and give in to his every whim," Werther confesses. Bless him! He is the first consumer. Upon him, and upon us, the Last Romantics, the automotive industry depends, all industry depends, evangelical commercialism depends. And what, without evangelical commercialism, is the American concept of God? Without it, God would be a sovereign mystery and not a genie who gets us good cars.

Werther writes to his friend, "I shall stop dwelling on the petty wrongs of providence." Of course. Start to think, for just a moment, on the possibility that God has wronged you, and you are no better off than the Greeks with their mercurial, impervious, petty gods. You have lost control over God. You start to shake your fist at heaven like a prophet. You quote a Psalm from the misery of your life and try to figure out the problems of suffering and death. Cars avoid all this. Possibly Werther committed suicide because he dreamed of an Audi, but could not buy one.

All this by way of preface. You can buy an Audi. Werther furthered the Industrial Revolution and we can pluck its fruit. Read the rest of this chapter (or letter, dear Friend!) as a warning.

*

It was only a car, I hear myself say. Ah, she was only a girl!

What older man with a poet's heart has not imagined himself as a youth, waltzing with a slim young slip of a girl: a lithe springtime girl with long blonde hair, that brief and fleeting combination of feminine grace and the awkward wonder of early womanhood tinting every move and every expression; the firm yet hesitant touch of her hand, the not quite imperceptible quake as you place your other hand against her lower back: the music begins. Such was my Charlotte. Or so I shall call her. Actually, only a German could associate romance with a name like that. *Werther und Charlotte*. Bratwurst and potato salad. Nor did it help that Werther calls her Lotte. To an American ear, that doesn't sound like a diminutive but an inflatative. Lotte. I think I shall call her something else, but what? April is a lovely name. One associates with it spring flowers, tender shoots of fresh colors, the gentleness of soft rain, fecundity, and sap. Chaucer says,

> *Ah, when April, with its showers sweet,*
> *The drought of March has pierced to the root,*

and so on; then:

> *Folk long to go on pilgrimages.*

Yes, to go on pilgrimages; which is to say, to begin a journey in harmony with nature. It is to obey the flowing of the life force within oneself, to follow in the course of one's heart the sweet liquor that engenders the flower. But chiefly the pilgrimage is to go from one place to another, which means you need a car. And what a swell car she would have been. I think all this took place in April, but I am not sure, in the historical sense. No matter. April was an invention from the beginning anyway—the invention of a fervid adolescent mind. And I ask you, Dear Friend, what else is a car?

But I was about to say, Such was April: slender, lissome, subtly skittish, innocent and a little afraid, but brave. In other words, murder. Her eyes were blue or gray, I think. As you wish. Spring, and a young man's love turns to fancy. "Werther's in love," my best friend remarked as I described her. Actually he did not address me as Werther. He was a student of French; and he saw me in a French light. He saw me, he once said, as a lone knight—and in the background, the call of a distant, solitary loon. I thought it wonderful, and poignantly apt. He had never heard a loon, nor had I. However, my ignorance has been corrected. A loon's distant, solitary call is a laugh. A wild, maniacal howl, according to Thoreau. I have heard them many a time—something between a Rebel Yell and the bray of a donkey.

My friend no doubt pictured me as a knight at arms, alone and palely loitering. And who was my belle dame sans merci? April. And how did I meet April? German Club. You see, I had to be a *Teutonic* Knight. Is there no mercy? Instead of Launcelot or Galahad or even Tristan, I had to be Berthold. No lavender pennon fluttered from the tip of my lance; no silver filigree adorned my hauberk. My emblem was the Wiener schnitzel.

You would understand if you have ever met April's type. The girl next door. Innocent as pancakes. Family had recently moved in from Connecticut or Kansas. A good Catholic girl; or maybe, in fact rather, a good evangelical family, maybe American Missionary Alliance. Pale and pure as the April snow. And as cool. I am told that young men who strap bombs to themselves and go blow up restaurants full of their religious enemies believe that an instant after death they will be surrounded by seventy luscious virgins. I could believe it. Only, having been raised Lutheran, I have a full apprehension of the picture's ironies. Yes, there will be seventy virgins waiting for these young men—all of them Christian fundamentalists.

I was *Oberhauptkommandant* of the German Club and we were all learning the *Schuhplattler* folk dance for a cultural event. We learned the waltz so that we could sweep along during the long interludes between shoeplattling—when we stood back from our partners, pranced a few steps, then started slapping our knees and lifting first one foot, then the other, smacking the sides of our shoes in time to a polka tempo like a bunch of Bavarian yokels. The slapping element constitutes a memory I have buried all these years. Bismarck said a Bavarian is a cross between an Austrian and a man. And here I was, in the month of April maybe, as infatuated as a French knight, prancing the *Schuhplattler*. But it was bliss nonetheless because facing me, whacking her knees and shoes, was my beloved Charlotte/Lotte/April. And when the absurd little interruption was over, she fell into my arms and well, not into my arms exactly. In a waltz, there is considerable space between you. Daylight. But the movement is flowing and graceful. Eventually, after stepping on one another and stumbling, there is an inexplicably achieved moment when you both catch on: you move together gracefully, flowingly, harmoniously, not thinking any more of the steps. You together are timeless music, and this must be true love; this must be immortal life. All this with a willowy young girl. I have never been so blissfully oblivious to life's pain since, except when changing oil.

Let me remind you that it was Hitler who originated the Volkswagen. The People's Car. The Volkswagen-Audi company is a child of the Third Reich. During the Second World War, the company produced war material and was partly manned by slave labor. Just a little reminder, there. Now we return to the waltz. Two dozen happy young people in the prime of health, rosy-cheeked (at least Charlotte/Lotte/April was); and in the background, the interlude of polka music with Germans singing something like, *Ah, Ja! Das ist das Lichtensteiner Polka, mein Schatz, Polka, mein Schatz!*—and alternating with it the stream, like the flowing Danube, of the lovely, graceful, April waltz from Austria, home of the Alps, home of Adolf Hitler.

Of course there was no, and there never would be, any smackola with April, no boogie, no jazz, no rock and roll in the Biblical sense. It is the essence of adolescent romance, as it is the essence of ideal chivalry, that there be no physical communion, no intercourse, nothing hot, nothing with any material implications or constructive results. Ah, April. Where are you? Where are your young hands, where is your tender heart, your lovely form and the soul that moved in time with mine to music? You are dead and gone, perhaps. And I shall be, too? I must find you again. What is life? What is romance? Romance is the waltz of endless April to the music of time. What is true love but the movement of two souls as one? Anything else is mere existence. And for that, you need a car. The better the car, the better.

I asked April out, asked her to go to the next school dance. She was only a freshman, and I a junior: her parents said No. Ah, dead and gone! So began the sorrows of young Werther! All my cars stem from this. Actually, I had been ignored and trivialized by a whole succession of school-girls from kindergarten all the way down to April, but no matter. She was the *coup de main.* It would take another girl and a Chrysler (*ach!* German name) to redeem those years for a few brief shining moments—but for now, we stick with Werther.

What was I to do?

I did what any kid does. I turned to a friend for advice. Of course the friend was no wiser, only more worldly. The boy had experienced his first liaison at about that time, so he thought he knew everything. I agreed. He was also a year older, and an intellectual. Never underestimate the knowledge and wisdom of a seventeen year old intellectual who has exposed himself to the clap, and brags about it. Actually, he did not exactly brag when he told me that he had lost the innocence. It was more along the lines of, "Hmm, I guess I'm different now, but I don't feel different." I think having a fresh-faced sixteen year old to tell it to made him feel better, so I performed a service.

Similarly, I must perform a service here by digressing for a moment on the topics of teenage intimacy, premarital consummation, and failure to employ all the clinical and industrial tools of that oxymoron, safe sex. Go for it. What is life, anyway? No sex is safe. No car is safe. I didn't do any of that stuff in high school, and look how much I have spent on cars. If I had engaged in all-out whoopie in high school, I would have been gone long ago, and would not have wasted all that money on cars. My estate would have been incalculably larger.

Look at it this way. We are put here on earth to spend money. Either you do sex early or you buy cars. Now that I consider it, I think that either way it's the same in terms of expense. Sex is very, very expensive. (Ask the praying mantis.) You have to support the person, unless you are an artist. And you wind up buying cars anyway, when you discover that sex hasn't made you happy and immortal. Either way, it's going to add up to money. There was a grand scheme of things that has preserved the race until now. Sex was the means by which that has been achieved. We are given a tremendous urge that is more or less an insult; so I say, frustrate the grand scheme. Industrial civilization is doing exactly that, which I consider to be a feather in my cap because people usually do not take my advice.

What kind of favor is it to the earth and the universe to perpetuate the human race? With our cars and other transportation we are destroying the planet. We are complete imbeciles, not only polluting the environment out of sheer laziness, greed, and lust for power; we are destroying each other. Romanticism is a counterforce against this evil. We are back to April now.

I asked my friend for advice, and all he said was, "Klopstock's in love." (I am disguising my name by using the aka "Klopstock." Futile? Who remembers authors' names anyhow.) I suggested that this was nothing new. All those others were kid stuff, Klopstock; this is the real McCoy, he retorted.

It was too true. All the romances of pre-adolescence are mental. That is, they take place within a sparsely-supplied imagination. This infatuation was occurring after the big change—after all the chemistry had been put into place by Mother Nature and given time to settle. But in this case, of course, there was going to be some kind of tragedy, because the liaison had been forbidden by her parents. My friend had no advice for that. In grade school, we would have come up with plenty of plans, most of them centering around adventure, such as climbing in a window of her house and carrying her off to Spain. Perhaps going off on a sailing ship myself and coming back years later, very tan and rich. Or I might have rescued the parents from a robbery that my friend could stage. But none of these solutions is available to older teenagers who have reached the level of cold sophistication we had. To my friend I re-emphasized: "I have met someone who has touched my heart." (That from Werther's first letter after meeting Lotte, whose fat name I must find an alternative for.) "I have waltzed with her, Freidrich," I said to protect his name. All he said was that he could imagine me as a lone knight in twilight in battered armor on a white horse, with the loon as background. "You are a romantic, a hopeless romantic, and you might as well live with it," he advised.

I have taken that advice. I have become used to being a hopeless Romantic—that is, a pessimist in love with April. And the loon is still in the background laughing. Aside from his advice, I was on my own. Which meant Werther. I went back to Werther, finding in him a fellow-sufferer, a fellow romantic, perhaps even a fellow Lutheran. I have learned not only to live with being a Romantic, I have learned to relish it. For me, the world is a perpetual April. It is always blossoming, always fragrant, full of pollen. "April is the cruelest month," wrote T. S. Eliot, another haven for adolescents, and he knew whereof he spoke. But he wasn't a *mensch* like Goethe. I returned to Werther, hoping that my April, the blonde version, would one day not be able to stand it anymore and renounce her parents, slip out of her bedroom window one midnight (adventurously clothed perhaps) and come to me, confessing desperately that she could not live without me.

I went back to Goethe and Werther, hoping that I was just biding time until my April came to her senses and plucked up her courage. But Goethe let me down a little. When Werther and Charlotte speak one day, all she has to do is say one word, one name: "Klopstock," and feckless Werther is in paradise. In that one word she reveals that she loves the poetry of Freidrich Gottlieb Klopstock (1724–1803), a popular writer of romanticizing verse. By sharing that single name, the two know that they have a common understanding of romance, of crappy verse. I was so upset about that Klopstock. Werther writes, "With tears in her eyes, she laid her hand on mine and said 'Klopstock.' I knew immediately what was in her mind: it was his splendid ode, and I was lost, lost! in the emotions this one name aroused in my heart. I bent down; I kissed her hand. For now there were tears in my eyes too! I looked into her eyes again. Oh noble poet! If you could have seen the adoration in those eyes!" (Author's translation; that is, mine.)

Oh noble poet, you ass, if you had seen those moony eyes you should have laughed. The poem in question, the "great ode," is "The Rites of Spring." How fitting. How very, very fitting. But I digress. The problem was that Goethe has the romance begin with the word *Klopstock*. Goethe! How could you? What a farcical name! Does this mean you didn't take your own *Werther* seriously? Is *Werther* great because there is an underlying current of satire? No! I cannot believe it. I must attribute Goethe's use of that name to the singularly klunky construction of the German ear. Oh, but then, what must Goethe have thought of Klopstock's verse? Klopstock, a poet abysmally inferior to himself? Let's have a look at this one by the Klop:

DAS ROSENBAND (THE CHAIN OF ROSES)

> I found her in the spring shade;
> I bound her with a chain of roses.
> She did not feel it and still slumbered.

[Authors note: the German word that I have translated slumbered is *schlummerte*, which to me sounds somewhat like snoring.]

> I gazed on her; with that gaze
> my life hung on her life!
> I fully felt this but she did not know it.

[That stanza is not only flat, its crap: of course she didn't know it; she was blowing Z's.]

> Nevertheless I whispered/lisped to her without words
> and rustled the chain of roses.
> That woke her up.
> She looked at me; her life hung
> on my life with that look.

[Get it? Just like his life hanging on hers.]

> And suddenly paradise surrounded us.

Well, there you have it. That poem supplies the reason people think they don't like Romantic poetry. It's because people usually run across the miserable romanticist verse instead of the good stuff, actual Romantic Poetry. People read Klopstock instead of Keats and Shelley. No wonder the world is going to hell in a handkerchief. Take this poem. The word I have translated whispered/lisped is *lispeln*. Doesn't that sound like "lisped" to you? But translators don't like that word and I have half followed them and put in the option of "whispered," just to maintain appearances. But what's actually happening is that this guy comes upon a sleeping girl and instead of doing what nature prompts him to do—or what decency prompts, which is to tiptoe off and let the young lady sleep—he spends the next half hour finding roses and weaving them into a chain. Then he binds her with them. Thorns aside, if this is not kinky behavior, I don't know what is. Then he "lisps" to her, and to make sure she wakes up, he "rustles" the chain. I take it the woman is not his size, though German. She doesn't spring up and pound him; she doesn't confiscate his journal. She looks up at him with the same lovey-dovey eyes as his. Sure. The poem is not a report, like this book; it is a fantasy.

The real Romantics wrote truth. This klopstockery is all lies and flapdoodle. "Surrounded by paradise," my keister. They would have been surrounded by cops. See, that's the whole trouble here. The romanticists, as opposed to the Romantics, thought of paradise like a pre-adolescent infatuation. But paradise is cars. More on that later.

This Klopstock is the fella over whose screed these two lovers, Werther and Charlotte, begin to have their understanding. Or at least Werther thinks it is an understanding. That's the key. She is actually not only pledged to another man, she loves that other man, and she considers Werther a friend. She knows she is safe with Werther. Phenomenal insult.

She knows she is safe because she knows Werther is so pre-adolescent that he isn't even thinking of boom-boom; all he wants is this paradise of Klopstock's, in which a youthful pair moon at each other with their eyes, imagining they share an understanding of everything that is lovely. Only when she finally lays down the law to Werther, and he begins to catch on that he is not her main squeeze and never will be, does Werther grow up and begin to lust after her, in his own lamb-like fashion.

I wasn't imagining boom-boom with April even though the attraction had to be physical, since I remember her looks better than I remember her name or anything she said. Fifteen year olds seldom say memorable things, though, when you're waltzing with them. But I was Werther. I was in love. "In love with what perishes," to use the words of the second-to-last Romantic, William Butler Yeats. What perishes is possibility. When possibility is removed, you have agony. When possibility is fulfilled, you have adulthood. The only reasonable place to be is Klopstock's: that limbo between expectation and reality. In that limbo, you simply do not realize that your attraction is sexual—that is, not to *her*, not to an actual person with a mind and a heart and a soul, and idiosyncrasies. You do not realize this because you are inexperienced. Hence the idealism of youth.

Our technological society deprives us of that wonderful stage of life, during which most of our great ideas are conceived. We are wounded by that deprivation. The human race has not caught up with society and technology nor is it meant to. We were meant to live in woods and caves and procreate at about age 13 or 14 and club animals to death for food, and then die at about age 25. Anything that deviates from that ideal is sheer aberrancy and waste. It costs a lot of money to have high schools and colleges and newspapers and televisions and countries and cars.

If Nature had intended men to live beyond the age of twenty-five, She wouldn't have fitted them with twinkies. Everything men do now beyond the basics is meant merely to preserve, protect, and defend the receding libido, long past its usefulness. If the Elders of a tribe bird-dogged like adolescents, would they be considered sane? The Grandfathers should be seeking enlightenment, teaching wisdom, and fixing old cars. Everything beyond the original intent is of the devil. Therefore what we all have to learn is Romanticism. Romanticism revives and preserves the pre-adolescent stage of man until he is ready to grow old responsibly. It is woman's only defense, other than her superior wit, strength, cunning, and belligerence.

It might be asked, What has all this to do with Cars, and what have Cars to do with all this? Again, I turn to Goethe, who once wrote, "I have often been told that my way of combining things borders on the absurd." It happens that Werther says this. And that makes me want to withdraw all suspicion pertaining to whether Goethe was writing a silent satire beneath the audible text of *Werther*. I shall not believe it. Double-meaning, irony, and satire would be shabby behavior on the part of a man with an unpronounceable name. If your name is "Goethe," you can't afford to mess with your audience. Goethe was probably not thinking of such Klopstock poems as the "Chain of Roses." He was thinking of poems like "The Early Graves:"

> Welcome, O silver moon, beautiful
> quiet companion of the night!
> Do you withdraw? Don't hurry—stay! friend to thought!
> Ah but see, he remains; it was only a cloud passing before.

[That Klopstock was one dim bulb. He mistook a passing cloud for the moon's disappearance.]

> The only thing lovelier than the summer night
> is May's awakening,
> when dew bright as light drips from her hair
> and she comes up redly over the hill.

[This would not be bad except that it feels vaguely obscene. What it has to do with anything is answered in the next, and last, stanza:]

> Alas you noble ones, the moss
> already grows upon your monuments.
> Oh how happy I was, when with you
> I saw the red days and the shimmering nights.

He is visiting the graves of dead friends, the epitome of a romanticist's pastime. We inaccurately assume that this was a popular pastime because romanticists, who are sentimentalists, are airheads; and secondarily because more people died young in those days. Nope. The pre-occupation with the deaths of youths is classic sentimentalism because the connection between Love and Death is too brutal to state in a genteel age. Young people visit the graves of youth because they are displacing the act of sex. Sex is the grave of youth. The sex act was called "the little death" in Shakespeare's England, and they still say it in North Jersey.

At this point I would like to introduce, by way of explanation, another German poem, this time a famous one. In fact it has been used as lyrics for one of the loveliest songs in the world. I humbly offer my translation of Heinrich Heine's *Die Lorelie*, "The Lorelei." At a bend in the Rhine there is a high cliff called the Lorelei. In German legend, this was where a golden-haired maiden, probably naked as a schnitzel, combed her long golden tresses and made sailors mash themselves and their boats against the stone.

THE LORELEI

I know not why sadness clings to me;
What means this melancholy?
A tale out of legend sings to me—
Some sweet, ancient melody.

The air becomes cool as it darkens,
And peacefully flows the Rhine;
The peak in last light seems to sparkle
While I watch below in nighttime.

The beautiful maiden entrances
Above in the sun's gleaming chair;
Her sparkling gold jewelry dances
As she combs her golden hair.

Her golden comb, gently repeating,
Accompanies her quiet song.
The sound sets my heart wildly beating;
its strong current draws me along.

The sailor, his eyes on the brilliance,
Is seized by a painful desire.
Ignoring the cliff's massive stone face,
He fixes his gaze ever higher.

Ah, surely dark waters will draw down
The sad, longing sailor's desire:
In light, looking up, he is drowned
In Lorelei's beauteous fire.

Thank you. I have improved considerably on the original poem. My version is more thematically loaded, and it is not in German. Translators usually do not figure to improve poems, but this one needed it. I have regularized the rhythm. That will make it easier for you to sing the song in English. I have inserted the word beauteous instead of beautiful because beauteous reminds me of igneous, suggesting both rock and fire. Or perhaps that was too clever. I have made a bigger deal of the contrast between the sailor being down in the twilight and Lorelei being up in the sun. I thought that was appropriate. But especially appropriate is the inclusion of the word *longing*. The word translates the German *Sehnsucht*, which, unfortunately, is not in the poem. But it is the subject of the poem. As we can all see, longing sometimes brings about misfortune or outright disaster.

It is no accident that poetry has come into play in this book about cars. Most people find that they actually like poetry. It is natural; we all liked poetry as children; the great and heroic societies of the past valued poetry. It was the Danish Vikings, in fact, who invented the automobile. But automobiles have become a damaging substitute for poetry—damaging not in themselves, because obviously I love cars, but because cars never will provide an exact equivalent of poetry. We are dying of longing, like the sailor in the Heine poem, and that longing, which we seek to assuage by driving cars, cannot and should not be assuaged. It should be cultivated. It is our only hope. Longing is the mark of the eternal in our hearts; without it we would be gerbils.

"They don't read much poetry in North America because few poets write it," Goethe remarks testily in *Poetry and Cars*. We get "little blobs" ("*Gnürdeln*") of stacked prose ("*Stapelsätzerei*") containing neat thoughts ("*Geschicktwürfeln*"). There is a Neat Thoughts School of Poetry, Goethe observed. You have been reading one of these blobs if you come to the end and think, Aw, cool (*Toll!*)—neat thought. "*Heilige Katzenschlafan-züge!*" Goethe exclaims, and exhorts, "Stop trying to impress, you writers! The People need inspiration from their poets! The world needs beauty, not ingenuity!"

I go into all this because "The Lorelei" describes exactly the thesis of this whole book. We want to be in love. But longing misdirected is responsible for many bad things. All this must be said before we can correctly understand the nature of Volkswagen-Audi's 2.8 litre 6 cylinder engine, which was engineered to give enormous surges of power in the midrange of speed though not at the low and high ends. And we must keep all these romantic concepts in mind when we have a good look at the all-aluminum (that is, except for the cylinder sleeves) newer 3.0 VW 6 cylinder engine, and the 2.0 litre four cylinder turbocharged engine, and *especially* when we consider the Volkswagen-Audi *eight* cylinder engine, which is made out of aluminum and, according to one of my sources who has recently been silenced, an ingeniously-processed material made from a gelatin derived from spotted owls. This latter is controversial and may not be true, but it need not be, as the results that come from this pearl of an engine are even worse than such an alleged origin of the engine. All this relates to Goethe, not merely as the author of *Werther* and *Faust* and a lot of poetry, but as the author of the landmark and central work, *Dichtung und Wahrheit*—Poetry and Cars.

I unveil here my own new translation of part of Goethe's preface to *Poetry and Cars*.

> Do not be mistaken, my dissatisfied and distracted countrymen: the invention and manufacture of the automobile is not an innocent endeavor. The colossal longing, the burning unexpungeable *desire* of the Teutonic race, cannot be answered merely by wars and conquest. It must be assuaged by a profound poetry that reaches through our deepest despair, embodies our most frightening questions—such as Is there a God? and Why is there evil? and Is there life after death? and Why is my life not a happy one? and soars toward the divine truths of mystical experience. Meantime, cars are manufactured.
>
> One must never underestimate the automobile. Into it we pour our souls. And out of it what comes? Ah, upon the answer hang not only our very lives, but those souls themselves! I could go on.

I interrupt Goethe here to mention the surprising and little-known fact that Johann Wolfgang von Goethe *never actually drove an automobile.* Goethe was an exceptional man. In his scientific studies of light, of botany, of political science, not to mention his poetry and drama and fiction, Goethe showed himself to be one of the extraordinary minds and spirits of his age, sort of like Leonardo da Vinci. Da Vinci drew blueprint plans for a helicopter, long before potato chips were invented. And Goethe understood the automobile. Goethe's *Dichtung und Wahrheit* remains as compelling and pertinent now as it was the day he wrote it.

Goethe conceived of his great character, Faust, as a picture of modern, industrialized humankind, bound for ultimate self-destruction.

Everyone saw the truth of Goethe's symbolic Faust. Things looked bad. However, a great force arose to oppose Faust, to fight him to the death, figuratively. It was a voice inflamed with a divine fire, a voice that has reached as high as any voice in German poetry has ever reached. That force was Freidrich Hölderlin. Were it not for that great, though insane, man, this book would be about German cars and German cars only—for the reason that there *would be only* German cars. We are looking at a titanic struggle here, upon the outcome of which hung not merely Klopstock's little life, but upon which hangs the fate of humankind. I tell you all this to encourage you. Some of you might have picked up this book surreptitiously, ashamed to be handling a book on a subject as apparently trivial and male-centered as cars. But Goethe reminds us that cars are for men and women. Both. Cars can encompass great things.

That is why I have told you about April. Well, I have not so much told you about April as about my infatuation with April. I have chosen to break my silence at last because, as the above paragraph states, the subject is important. A key fact in all this is that April's birthday was the same as the actual Fred Klopstock's.

The first Volkswagen-Audi product I drove was a 1964 Beetle. As you know, the Beetle was not officially called Beetle, though in Germany the word *Käfer* (beetle) had been applied to it already for a long time. Here in the States, the word Bug vied with Beetle for most common usage. But of more importance are the VW innovations. The first innovation was in clever advertising. VW did not simply come up with a more effective way to market cars that were funny-looking and to a ghastly degree unsafe; they revolutionized advertising itself. The emphasis in early VW ads was on the terse, arch, humorous, striking understatement. It appeared to be a soft sell: a picture of a VW Beetle alone in the middle of a full page, and underneath a few words of caption, never a complete sentence.

This ad destroyed American literacy. But we are not concerned with that. The ad revolutionized something much more important than literacy: advertising. Now companies began to see that their ad agencies should not appear to be advertising. So the devil enters, seldom in the form of the traditional devil. Advertising enters as comedy and entertainment. To link advertising with entertainment was the great coup. Entertainment is what Americans live for. It is what Americans want. Advertising grew up by plugging Volkswagens. It was an invention born of necessity, for, as I mentioned, Americans did not at first want to buy Volkswagens. They were made in Germany, a power we had recently defeated in a war that cost nearly a half million American lives. Germany was still the country of the *Wehrmacht*. That word, which sounds a lot like War-Make, means Defense Force. The German army (a phrase that still excites the blood of some persons and raises fears in others), was renamed after the war, under Allied occupation, with the more friendly term *Bundeswehr*, meaning Federal Defense. When you say Federal in America, you are on familiar ground, because people think of Federalism, the Federal Government, and other typically American things. At any rate, people did not want to buy something made by the former Third Reich, that nearly conquered the world. So the Volkswagen company hired an ad agency that made German cars seem cute, not threatening.

Think about it. If the ad agency hadn't told us the car looked like a cute little bug, we might just as well have thought it looked like a bomb. Compare the shape of the early Beetle to that of Big Boy, one of the atomic bombs dropped on Japan. Or maybe it looks like a germ. (Very bad: relates to "German.") When you see the very earliest Volkswagens photographed in the Third Reich, they do not look cute. Efficient maybe, warlike maybe, but not cute. Compare the early Mickey Mouse cartoons. In those, Mick looks like a rat. His head is small, his snout is long, his lines are not rounded. So with the early VW. In time, Mickey was given the head of a baby, disproportionately large for his body. Cute. His snout retreats. And he is a figure made of circles. Draw a circle with two only slightly smaller circles at ten and two o'clock, and everybody in the world recognizes it as a silhouette of Mickey Mouse.

The Germans turn to Disney. They draw a new Beetle. It has a shorter snout, a bigger head (the cabin seems higher), and all the lines are rounded. Draw a half circle with the flat side down, draw two more half-circles at nine and three o'clock and everybody in the world recognizes the profile of the Beetle.

So first you make the war machine into a cartoon, a cute cartoon. Then, like a cartoon, everything about it becomes entertaining, starting with the ads. But it is still a Vehicle of Death. Look at the highway death figures for Volkswagen Beetles. It is a light car, with nothing ahead of the driver but his/her own legs. It has no safety equipment to speak of. You see, the company back in Germany is not interested in the safety of its buyers, but in their money. Today, VW-Audi is a leader in safety equipment. Why? Because Volvo kicked their heinies and then the Americans and Japanese started making safer cars, and the American public—because the ads for those other cars told them they should value safety—began to value safety. So, having already played the Disney card, VW-Audi had to make their cars, with their sharp handling and ready engines, appear once again to be harmless. And now, of course, they are replaying the Disney card and producing a neo-Beetle, cute as a bug's ear, because the current culture is so impoverished that nostalgia and copying the past generally sell.

Now, if you can entertain people and make that idea of entertainment stick to the product you are selling, you can lead the American public by the nose. The whole program of the VW company was to make people accept the idea that money is more important than life. And they did it, adding that fun is also more important than life. Money is more important, because VW's were relatively cheap. And they were cheap to run, relatively, because while Detroit was turning out cars that got 8 miles to the gallon, the VW got a phenomenal 24 miles to the gallon. And they were Fun To Drive!

Cars were not things you use to get safely from one place to another. Cars were invented for convenience and speed. Add the powerful element of Prestige, and you simply must have that car. The cheapest, and safest, and fastest way to get from one place to another is walking. Even if you want to go from California to the East Coast—which any responsible person would—it is cheapest to walk. And it is fastest. Most people do not understand this. Consider: what does it take to buy a plane ticket? It takes perhaps $500 to fly from LA to Philadelphia. Well, you might say, I can make $500 in a week, but I can't walk from LA to Philadelphia in one week. But you have forgotten one very big thing. To make the $500 you need to have a job. And a job is much more easily acquired than got rid of. With the job comes a salary, and insurance premiums, and a house or apartment, *and a car* to get you there, and debt to pay for the car and hence the necessity of keeping the job—and before that you went to college, not to learn, but to prepare yourself for the job, and you are still paying your college loans. You have a great deal invested in that job. To get your apparent freedom of travel, you have put yourself on the block and sold yourself as a slave, and you are now working for the Man, whether the Man is yourself or someone else, and the longer you do it the harder it will be to get yourself back. Truly it is easier for a camel to pass through the eye of a needle than it is for you to get a week of real freedom, even in America. You have signed away your time, your future, your body, your mind—like Goethe's character Faust—and sold them to a devil of your own making. So you see, it takes years to go from LA to Philadelphia, if you fly. And only months if you walk. I point out this economics of death not to depress you, because it is probably too late anyway. I'm just saying.

Now before getting to the crux of this discussion, I feel that I ought to issue a few disclaimers. First, bicycling might be the fastest way to get from one place to another, all things considered and if you buy a used bike. But the principle is the same. Second, Volkswagen might not have changed advertising all by themselves. The spirits behind successful advertising are legion. Third, it is not nice to talk about postwar German automobile production as if we are also talking about vehicle and armament production during the Third Reich. OK, fine. Let's move on.

I realize that I didn't take care of the last problem and we have to go back to it. It is just that I don't really feel that I have ultimately insulted Germans or Germany. The truth is, I am somewhat of a Teutonophile. I have friends there and I have lived there. I cannot praise German beer, erasers, and plastics enough. The scenery is splendid. Sure, the language could be improved—but I do not hold that against individual Germans. The German language is a kind of living history, and it is time we put all that history behind us. History is bunk, Henry Ford said, and who knew more about mass production than Henry Ford? Furthermore, I am using German literature as a way of making sense of this whole cars thing, and I do have some German blood. Chancellor Otto von Bismarck popularized the phrase "Blood and Iron," and I have been to Bismarck. Haven't we all.

Achtung, Baby! Let's get back to the subject. Cars and the man I sing. (Clearly, this book is also about women, and about men and women— but I don't want women to buy this book and find out too much about men that has been secret for thousands of years. That is one reason I titled the book Cars. Such a title drives women off. If you are a man reading this book and a woman sees your obvious enjoyment and asks to read it, say something like, "Yeah, great book. Says you shouldn't use the word 'woman' any more. Use the words 'broad' or 'dame.' Nothing like a dame, you know, he he." That should pretty well do it. However, a really sensitive and intelligent woman would see that there are tiny tears at the corners of your eyes, and she will know, or rather she will sense, that you are a Romantic. She will understand that the heart of this book is romance, and she will be attracted to you. She will touch your hair lightly with her hand, and tell you that she knows how much you have suffered, how hard you work, and that you deserve wonderful things. This is the best twenty bucks you have ever spent.)

So to make a long story short, April came back the day after I asked her out and told me that she couldn't go out with me because her parents forbade it. And I became a Rebel.

We need not delve too deeply nor consume much time recounting my Outlaw Period. One can find books on it in any decent library, or refer to the excellent film by Ken Burns. To be brief: my knighthood-loon friend convinced me that, like him, I should take up pipe smoking. And I did, like C. S. Lewis and Huckleberry Finn. Because breaking yourself in to pipe smoking relates directly to VW-Audi and Goethe, I shall devote a few lines to it.

> A wonderful invention it is, the pipe.
> A sweet, musty friend is my comfy old briar;
> No matter the hour, she'll always inspire.
> When down on my luck,
> I always can suck
> Like a baby on my little fire.

Limericks are hard. You can see that because the first line is a false start. And limericks always turn out vaguely, obscurely obscene. It's in the form. There was nothing untoward about those lines. I tremble to think what might happen if I go on, but for personal reasons I will.

> My meerschaum was made by a Kraut,
> But it's pleasing, of that there's no doubt.
> For just half a buck
> I get a good suck,
> So I huff and I puff 'til it's out.

You shouldn't really smoke a pipe until it's out. All the toxic juices collect down in the dottle, which you should simply discard into any Hummer's gas tank. But I exercised a little poetic license there. Sadly, all poetic licenses ran out in the 20th century, so I will try one last time:

> My corncob was stripped of its corn
> Like a woman whose clothing was torn;
> But it draws like a song,
> And unless I'm quite wrong,
> You expected this line to be porn.

You will notice, if you re-read with care, that the common element in these limericks is not displaced vulgarity, nor deferred bad taste, but rather the motif of sucking. Just so does poetry tell the truth. The truth is that the Pipe is an extension of the first human instinctual act: sucking. Be glad for this instinct. It is what enables us to survive those first harrowing hours of our lives.

Consider the baby. He or they or she—it could be whichever—comes into life naked, hungry, and small. The ideal car buyer. But the baby cannot afford a car. What does he want? His mother's breast—not merely for its food value, but equally important: the warmth, the unique and comforting odor, and that reassuring heartbeat. Years later, when he has fleeced his clients and cheated the people of the United States out of a good nest egg's worth in taxes, he buys a little sports car. He is becoming naked again, losing the hair on his head and on his chest. He is smaller where he used to be larger. He wants the reassuring, rhythmic purr of the engine; and the more British, the more rhythmic the engine will be, as it misses a cylinder every time around. All the old boy has now is money. He can afford a growling, low, fantastically powerful and obscenely expensive car, which he believes young women will mistake for his inner worth. But he will be returning to the womb and the breast whence he came. Did he spend his money helping the poor, and devote himself to charity, prayer, and seeking enlightenment? Did he examine his soul and find only money in the cold, empty chamber that used to be his heart—the heart that once beat in time with his young, warm, and tender mother's? Did he count his days and prepare to meet his Maker? Did he look upward even once? Hell, no! He bought a car that will add disproportionately to the world's pollution, blowing fumes through an eight or twelve cylinder engine out the back, just as he did when he was a baby.

There are alternatives to this. Of course, everything comes down to God or the devil, however you conceive of the devil—there are countless varieties of the devil. (But only one God. That is why the devil is so popular, and so marketable.) What I am saying is that instead of the expensive car and the expensive women of one's senior years, a person could buy a few pipes and spend the twilight years sucking/puffing, reading philosophy, and thinking. We could live like philosophers and convalescents. There are few things as calming as drawing on a pipe.

My friend took me to a drugstore and, because he had turned eighteen, he bought the stuff. Not drugs. Not condoms. He bought a Dr.

Grabow pipe and accessories: a reamer/tamper pipe tool, matches, and Half and Half tobacco. (The name Grabow must be a joke of some sort.) Now, Half and Half is the tobacco equivalent of Chevrolet. The man I learned Chevys from also happened to smoke Half and Half, so I was already a Half and Half man. But not for long. I was virtually allergic to the burley tobacco in H & H. As my knighthood-loon friend put it, my tongue felt like the entire Russian army had marched over it in their dirty socks. Next I tried Cherry tobacco. Now, I assume my readers are cultivated, discriminating, educated readers and not a bunch of college ruffians or senators. If you started snorting or howling at the thought of a teenager inhaling cherry, you will not be able to follow the argument of this book. And if you are offended now, take a care for your soul, and do not judge. As Milton said, "Give me a congregation fit though few."

Cherry, as it turns out, could be obtained in both burley and Cavendish forms. I chose the wrong form. More nights spent in the bathroom rinsing my mouth with an urgency more proper to a chipmunk. I had tasted all the bitter ashes of desire by the time I was completely broken in. For learning to smoke a pipe is a discipline.

I think that in my entire life I have actually smoked only about one ounce of tobacco, but I have burned about fifty board feet in matches, bought a cubic hectare of tobacco, and wasted enough dottle to create a good toxic landfill. The trick, my 18 year old but as yet beardless knight-loon friend instructed me, is to fill the pipe properly. This is a skill I have only indifferently mastered to this day. You fill a pipe in layers, first off. OK, I did it one level at a time. It has to retain a little *spring*, he pronounced grandly and confidently. So for forty years or whatever, I have left various degrees of spring in the bowl, generally the wrong degree. What he neglected to tell me back then, was that he didn't know what he was talking about. I have discovered this only recently. He was wrong about some other things as well.

My old friend Art, whom you have met in these pages, taught by example that you leave hardly any spring at all. Too much, and the tobacco burns right through and your smoke becomes so hot that you think you have stuck your tongue into a shredder. And of course the pipe goes out. Too little spring—that is, when you pack it tight as concrete—and you get a hernia trying to draw it. And the pipe goes out. You can relight a pipe a thousand times, but you are innocent only once.

Next, my friend instructed, in that vaguely British accent of his (though he was of Italian ancestry), "You *sinnnnnge* the top." And throw away the match. So, you light up, and when it gets nicely stoked, you let it go out. It seems so wrong. An earlier, cruder age would have used the word "counterintuitive." Yes, you must let it go out; that is why you throw away the match—so as not to be tempted to relight too soon. You got to prime the pump; you must have faith and believe. Burning over the top makes the tobacco expand a little. You then take your pipe tool, the flat end, and tamp the tobacco back down. When you re-light, it will stay lit. If you don't waste the first match and tamp, the pipe will go out in a minute, if not sooner. No one knows why this is. Some things in life must be done on faith. Perhaps the first match is an offering. (If you try to hold the lit match, even if it is a kitchen match, while you tamp, you will learn what it is like to confront the world without eyebrows.) In any case, sometimes one has to be content with the is-ness of things. Heck, we don't even understand how our own bodies work, or why there is evil in the world, or know whether there is life after death: so how are we supposed to know how lighting a pipe works?

So there we were outside the drug store trying to stoke me up. It was a moment of proud satisfaction. We thought, perhaps, of our school-mates who were out that Friday evening getting Vesuviously drunk, or stoned, or engaging in shallow interpersonal hedonism, and we felt the superiority that only pipe-smoking intellectuals can feel. To summarize: it goes girls, pipes, cars.

But I was doing it all for love. My chevalier-loon friend knew that I was dying inside because I was not out with April. Some pimply nose-picker was with her at the Freshman Dance. Before she turned junior and I returned for her, scarred and with the crusader's cross on my tunic torn and faded, but with lance and sword unbroken, the pimple kid would have won her heart. That uneducable, lily-livered, milky-eyed, non-driving knave—but what did it matter who won her, if it were not to be me? And it were not to be me. So there, with my hands full of drug store products, I began to learn compensation, repression, displacement, denial. Alas, I learned to think as though I could live without love. I became a philosopher. I became an American adult. I became a car guy. Like the sad sailor of "The Lorelei," I had run up against the flat rock of reality. The unresolved longing, I say, that Heine wrote about, is our only hope, and the only cause of all the mad evil that we do. Or rather, denying that longing causes all the evil.

America! Pluck the pacifier from your hardened mouth! Cast it away! Better that your little pipe be lost than that your barren soul be flung into hell. Forsake your purring 12 cylinder Jaguar, old loser: better that you lose your last delusion than that your dry, pinched butt be flung into perdition. Amerika! Wake up! Read Goethe and Hölderlin. Follow me!

THE HISTORY OF VOLKSWAGEN

On July 24th, Werther writes to his friend: "I have never been happier"—or in the German, *Noch nie war ich glücklicher.* I supply the German because I would like everyone to learn German; I need people to talk to. Secondly, the word translated as "happier" has two meanings in German. Its other meaning is "luckier," or "more fortunate." Here is why Robert Frost defined poetry as "that which is lost in translation." True, *glücklich* usually means just plain happy, but Goethe has loaded the whole text of *Werther* with quiet irony. He means for us to catch the nuance of "fortunate." A young man in love feels like the luckiest person in the world. He feels that fortune has smiled on him, personally. But he is fortune's fool, as Shakespeare's Romeo puts it. Here Werther feels happy and lucky. Soon, he will feel not so happy and not so lucky. In fact, this romantic feeling of his quickly becomes an illness, a disease, a monster, a fatal misfortune. *Smack!* He's pasted to the granite face of Lorelei.

It bothers me that so few Americans know Heine's poem. The poem needs to be better. It is too irregular to sing easily. It ends unhappily. Therefore at considerable personal expense I have composed a better version. I acknowledge my debts to the poet Heinrich Heine and to German legend.

IMPROVED LORELEI

I'm touched and I'm saddened
and turned on
because of the singing I hear.
My delicate temper is maddened.
I yearn on;
she's really put a bug in my ear.[4]
I long for a mugful of beer.

---

4. I consider this line to be weak. A possible rhyme would be "rear," but I haven't been able to work it in. I hope readers will choose between them and write in.

The girl on that rock is a vision,
combing her long golden hair.
My sailor friends laugh in derision,
but I grip the mast and I stare.

They think that I don't know the story
of Lorelei, Maid of the Rhine.
They think that her curvaceous glory
will kill me and never be mine.
But I say, Let's damn the torpedoes
and keep going full speed ahead.
We'll meet her and we'll see what she does
at night after her prayers are said.

Or else we would throw away romance
and be alone when the night's black.
In life you must reach for the main chance
and grab what love gives you *Kersmack!*
Oh sailors, we've learned a big lesson,
if only we knew what it was.
Our boat's all in pieces; I'm guessing
the Rhine Patrol's coming for us.

Epilogue
The sailors were rescued but got wet.
They all lost their wallets and change.
Oh Lord, give us wisdom, but not yet.
Don't call us till we're out of range.

Sailor's Epilogue
O Lorelei, Lorelei, Lorelei,
why do you treat me this way?
I've gone out and bought me an Audi;
let's get in and just drive away.
Alas! She is fickle, this maiden:
perhaps a black Mercedes Benz
would keep her affection from fadin'.
But all things must come to an end.

There is an infelicity in the poem. I have rhymed "was" with "us." In some regions of Indiana, "us" is pronounced with the consonant sounding like "z," but only if the word comes at the end of a sentence and is emphasized. I feel this is too specific and technical for the readers I wish most to reach and affect. I might re-title the poem "Lorelei on the Wabash" to take care of the problem, but I feel certain that this would cause other problems.

I am especially fond of the alternate ending I have discarded. *Alas! She is fickle, this maiden:/ she sits there just combing her hair./ The last rays of sunset are fadin',/ a whippoorwill swallows the air.* It contains the kind of image—a whippoorwill swallowing the air—that would have given the poem an ambiguity, incoherence, and apocalypticism that would keep it modern forever. Personally, I like the visual image of the bird swallowing air, growing round, larger and larger, until it is like a balloon and either floats away or pops, whichever the reader likes better. If a balloon, the reader could picture the sailor holding on and floating up to the top of the rock, where he lets go and lands in Lorelei's lap and they kiss. Or if pop, then it's funny. I want to end the poem upbeat, somehow—either happy ending or comedy. Heine's poem ends tragically and that is what has hurt its distribution. But tentatively, I have given the poem a firm, conclusive end.

I wonder why Heine ended his poem the way he did. Talent is nothing without marketing. The poem could have been a smash. Heine could have been somebody. But you have to hand it to him: he didn't flinch from the truth. He told it like it is. Romance? Follow it to the end, its extreme conclusion, without committing suicide first, and you get either marriage with its dirty dishes, mortgage payments, steady job, and eventual divorce; or you get shabby sex in a motel and goodbye; or you get heartache—all three alternatives requiring that you buy a new car. Oh sure, you might have both romance and love—love that lasts and romance that never wears thin, marriage and happiness and well-adjusted children, but what is the book on that bet? I have to hold back when some young person tells me that they have gotten engaged. I want to say, You think you're going to beat the odds, don't you? Everybody thinks so. You're different. The other person is different. The odds are .01% but you two are unique as snowflakes and you will make it. Sure you will. Like hell you will. But I just smile and say, That's wonderful. Good luck. You'll need a car. I hook my raincoat on my finger over my shoulder, tilt my hat. They are going to be happily married and in love twenty-five years down the road. But it's a long, long road. You're going to need One. Big. Car.

I know; I speak from experience. I once loved a girl. Her name was April. I don't know what her name is now. I loved her, with all the

springtime a young man has in his heart, with all the hope and affection a boy can acquire from the full moon in a June sky, with the strong
perfume of lilac in the air: and look at me now. I own three rusty cars. I
can't keep up the payments, so I have to sell at least maybe one of them.

Best to get just one car at the outset. One good car. Forget all the
rest; don't waste your years and your idealism. Just one good car. That is
why you are reading this book, and your reading it is why I am writing
it. I want to help you get that one good car. I want to help you avoid the
pitfalls and the Fords. Hello, young lover, wherever you are; I hope your
problems are few. I had a love once, oh, so much like yours: don't buy
used, buy new.

And yet, and yet. Here I am compelled to introduce a quite free
translation of mine that expresses a somewhat contrary point of view.

> *Has Your New Car Been Driven?*
> Has your new car been driven, been driven before?
> Is the ignition brand new; has someone else opened the door?
> Let me tell you, young lover, if you want to cruise:
> the new ones are shiny—but buy your car used.

We will return to this topic. It is a profound one. I did not intend to
reverse myself as to the new/used verdict so quickly, but it could not be
helped. For now, simply keep the question open: new or used, freshman
or experienced. Back to Goethe and the history of VW-Audi.

It is vital that we finish with Werther's July 24th letter before resum-
ing the history of VW. In the letter, Werther mentions something that
evidently mystifies him. It is only a detail, but the devil is in the details,
with cars especially. Werther writes, "I have begun Lotte's portrait three
times, and have screwed up three times."

One translator has the "screwed up" as *wasted my time*. What Goethe
actually wrote is this:

> *. . . und habe mich dreimal prostituiert . . .*

I probably do not need to say even to non-German readers that
this means literally: ". . . and have prostituted myself three times." What
was I saying about poetry and translation? Sure, *sich prostituieren* means
something like "wasted my time," "made a mess," "fouled up." But Goethe
chose the word "prostituted" for a reason. Remember that even as a young
writer, Goethe was not wholly a Romantic. He is loading poor Werther's
language with unconscious meanings and irony. Poor Werther! Who

speaks for Werther? Not Goethe. He said later that he wished Werther were dead. The public misunderstood Goethe and his Werther. But we are Americans. We can have faith in the public, now and then. The German public—what a *gemütlicher* bunsch—believed that Werther came alive out of Goethe's Romantic side, the part of him not overborne and suppressed by Goethe's big brain.

But Werther says he prostituted himself. Any artistic endeavor that is compared to prostitution was done not for art's sake but for money or fame—or in this case, to get Lotta's love. Significantly, Werther continues,

> I am so aggravated by this because a short while ago I used
> to be very successful/lucky/fortunate/happy [there's that word
> *glücklich* again] at hitting the mark.

That is, he used to be a good portraitist. With Lotte, he can't hit the mark. No, he can't. And he never will be able to hit it. (She is married.) Wise Goethe! Why can't Werther draw? Goethe is telling us that romantic love ruins art; in fact it interferes with all constructive work. Goethe was familiar with Virgil's *Aeneid*, the Roman epic about the founder of the "Eternal City." When Aeneas falls into his affair with Dido (some name, eh?), all work on city-building comes to an ignominious halt. He has to break off the romance at the order of the gods, for the work to resume.

The German engineers who designed and made Audi's, VW's, Mercedes Benzes, and BMW's were not in love. They were efficient, clever, ruthless. The Italians and French, who have made some laughable but lovely cars, are in love![5] If April were here, I would have ceased all efforts on this important theological work long ago. I would have tried to please her, made crappy love poems in free verse or doggerel, nothing like my majestic "Lorelei."

But consider this. Goethe wrote *Werther* for fame and money. Or so he feared to have done. His original impulse was artistic, romantic; it was a work of necessity brought on by his own disappointed love for some fickle Teutonic fatso. But soon he began thinking of his book's potential for external rewards. Not enough to ruin the book; just enough to worry Goethe and give him what he considered to be an insight. But he was too harsh on himself and on all lovers. You can't write poetry when you are infatuated any more than you can write it if you are a professor. When you are in love you can't tell poetry from prose or anything else: everything looks good to you and everything looks like poetry. To write poetry

5. A French driver, according to Chancellor Bismarck, is a "softie" (*Schnüggelhannes*).

you have to see how desperate everything else is. To write poetry you have to be honest—but the lover is no closer to truth than an advertising executive. To write poetry is to build, but a lover doesn't build poems or cities or cars, because he is building an illusion. Surely God was in love when He made the universe, and is in love still, judging by how beautiful the world is and how badly things are going. God must have loved humans most of all. Where was I? —Werther couldn't draw. For him now, drawing was no longer art but persuasion and idolatry: prostitution. Or so Goethe is trying to tell us. But secretly, possibly unknown even to himself, Goethe understood that the failed portraits were the first attempts at sketches for automobiles.

Goethe did nothing at random. It might appear that Goethe had wandered from his true subject, cars, but that is only an appearance. Had Werther not committed suicide prematurely, he would have designed the first VW. Consider the name: Werther. Accident? Coincidence? Volks Werther. Werther could be translated as having written, "three times I made a fool of myself." Draw the car! one exclaims as one reads *Werther*. *Draw the car!* If he had made a blueprint of a car when he was heartbroken, he would not have killed himself.

But the end of romantic disappointment is death, one way or another. Either you kill yourself, or you kill others. The modern automobile, we all know, was invented by a Frenchman. I think this doesn't need spelling out. The French are in love. This Frenchman was colossally in love, was colossally disappointed—as can happen in France—and so he kills not himself but 30,000 Americans per year in automobiles, and attempts to kill the entire earth with pollution. The inspiration comes from France; but the execution comes from Germany.

Lest you think I am dealing in false inferences here, or that I am being too hard on the French and Germans, consider just one little fact. It is this. Ferdinand Verbiest (1623–1688), a Jesuit missionary, built the first car in 1678. (A steam-powered vehicle.) And you thought I had my chronology messed up. Or that I was joking. The first car was made by a renegade theologian; one remembers that Satan was a fallen angel, a Frenchman. The first full-sized, self-powered vehicle made for roads was built in 1769. By a Frenchman. (Nicolas Joseph Cugnot, 1725–1804.) Notice: 1769. Television was only a gleam in somebody's eye back then.

The chronology is important because my loon friend and I had our vital conversation, that I still recall word for word, back in the 1960's or 1970's, whichever. As we emerged from the drug store, me already tearing open the tobacco pouch in my eagerness to be a pipe-achiever, he turned to me.

Friend: Hey, Werther.

Future Author: Yeah? (Pinching some tobacco out of the pouch.)

Friend: Well first, Clyde, you don't lift the tobacco out of the pouch.

Future Author: No? Why not?

Friend: Makes you look like a girl.

Future Author: Crap.

Friend: Like throwing left-handed, you know?

Future Author: Well, how else do you get it out?

Friend: Place the bowl of the pipe directly into the pouch.

Future Author: Holy smoke! Right in? But OK. Like so.

Friend: Precisely. But do it with one hand.

Future Author: OK. It's in.

Friend: Now, using your thumb as a backhoe, pull some tobacco into the bowl.

Future Author: Right. Got it.

Friend: Too much.

Future Author: How do you know I put in too much? The pipe bowl is in the pouch!

Friend: I don't need to see it. You're overeager.

Future Author: !!@#!!

Friend: Now, now. Let me see.

Future Author: Here.

Friend: Too much.

Future Author: !!@#!!

Friend: Knock it back into the pouch and try again. Take it easy.

Future Author: It isn't right for a teenager to be learning this stuff on the street.

Friend: It's all right. You aren't learning much.

Future Author: Since when are you a pipe expert anyway, huh? You don't even shave yet.

Friend: I beg your pardon? I *am* eighteen.

Future Author: You don't shave yet.

Friend (somewhat loftily): I fail to grasp the pertinence of that fact.

Future Author: I'm just trying to put things into perspective.

Friend: Allow me to put things into perspective, my hirsute young friend: You are dependent upon me for a ride home.

Future Author: And you are dependent upon me for religious instruction.

Friend (smiling drily): You younger folk *are* amusing. Here, give me the pipe. [Gently tests the tobacco in the bowl.] Too tight. Try again.

Future Author: I am emotionally exhausted.

Friend: Ah. That's what I was asking when we came out of the store.

Future Author: What was? [They have arrived at Friend's car, a 1964 Volkswagen Beetle. Red. Four cylinder engine, bipartite molded electron block, 1300cc, air cooled. The cylinders are part iron and part aluminum. The cylinder heads are molded aluminum. Fuel capacity, about eleven gallons. Oil consumption: one quart per one thousand miles. Total length, 4070 millimeters. (American cars are measured in feet.) Width: 1540 mm. Height: 1500 mm, which, along with the width, does not change between 1938 and 1973. It weighs 780 kilograms, or 1716 lbs. For comparison: today's Toyota Camry, Honda Accord, and Chevy Malibu all weigh about 3300 lbs. The outgoing Chevrolet Impala weighs more than twice as much as the 1964 VW. Friend's Beetle is a very small, very light car. The two amigos climb in and wedge themselves next to each other. Friend is six foot six; Future Author is six feet.]

Future Author: I am afraid.

Friend: Why's that?

Future Author: This is a very unsafe car.

Friend: It's not too bad.

Future Author: And about to become more unsafe.

Friend: How's that?

Future Author: You are about to turn the ignition and start driving.

Friend: Very amusing. I suppose you could do better.

Future Author: Without doubt.

Friend: All right.

Future Author: All right what?

Friend: Drive. [Friend exits car with a grunt. Comes to passenger side. Future Author rolls window down.]

Future Author: I'm not going to drive your car.

Friend [completes circle of car and with grunt re-seats himself]: You can't drive a stick, can you.

Future Author: I learned to drive on a stick.

Friend: Then why don't you drive?

Future Author: I'm afraid of damaging this toy.

Friend: Oh. Says the driver of a big Chrysler. A boat.

Future Author: A yacht. I'm used to it. This car is like sitting in one of those Porta Potties.

Friend: Just load the pipe. [FA loads pipe. Hands it over.] Too loose. Try again.

Future Author: That's all right. I don't want to smoke in here anyway. Might blow us up.

Friend: Suit yourself. Mind if I smoke?

Future Author: Yes.

Friend [turns ignition. Pulls cigarette pack out of inside pocket. (He is wearing a sport coat.) Gets cigarette lighter from side pocket.]: The trick is to do it all with one hand. One learns that, driving a stick.

Future Author: I hate cigarette smoke. You're going to kill us, one way or another.

Friend: How's that?

Future Author: By trying to light up while you're driving, and by filling a compartment the size of a urinal with smoke.

Friend: Your comparison is distasteful.

Future Author: Cigarette smoking is distasteful.

Friend: Not these. These are Benson & Hedges. English.

Future Author: I'm impressed. [Friend lights up, drags, shifts into third.]

Friend: The trick is to— [Future Author snatches cigarette from Friend's mouth, rolls window down, throws cigarette out.] *Excrement*!

Future Author: Pull out that pack and I'll throw it all out the window.

Friend: *Double excrement*! [Pulls out pack. Jerks it away as Future Author reaches for it. Friend slams on brakes; car comes to sudden halt.] You try that again and *you walk*! What's the matter with you?

Future Author: What's the matter with *you?* You drive like a maniac, you're smoking yourself to death, you proposition every girl in the phone book, you were drunk all last weekend, and you told me an hour ago that you tried some kind of Mexican-sounding tobacco yesterday. What's the matter with *you?* [Grabs pack.]

Friend [serious]: I'll tell you.

Future Author: OK, tell me.

Friend [quietly]: I'm missing something you have.

Future Author: Common sense?

Friend: No. [Looks evenly at FA] I'm not in love.

Future Author [Hesitates. Feels eyes moisten. Looks away.]: Oh. [Slowly hands cigarettes back.]

Friend: Thanks.

Future Author: No problem. I'd like to keep my window down, though. [Friend lights up, shifts into first. They drive. But not in silence: the 1300 cc air cooled engine is very loud.] You know I'm just concerned.

Friend: I know.

Future Author: None of this stuff works. As a substitute, you know.

Friend: I know.

Future Author: Why all of a sudden? I mean the drinking, you know?

Friend: Seeing you makes me see how empty I am.

Future Author: Very funny.

Friend: I mean you're in love.

Future Author: No I'm not. It's only infatuation. Very temporary.

Friend: It's different this time, Clyde. I can tell.

Future Author: So why did you say that I worry you, if love is such a great thing? It doesn't feel that great right now.

Friend: That's what I mean. Love is better than no love, but when it isn't returned, that's worse than anything. If I'm doing marijuana and alcohol, what will you be doing?

Future Author: It will work out.

Friend: Clyde, let me give you a bit of advice.

Future Author: What.

Friend: Forget about that girl.

Future Author: Forget—what?

Friend: She's just a kid.

Future Author: What do you think I am?

Friend: I mean, she can't return it. She's probably fourteen.

Idiot: I'll wait.

Friend: You'll wait for nothing. Look, you'll have to forget about her sooner or later.

Romantic Fool: Never. I'll never forget her.

Friend: You will. Make it sooner. I know you. You won't get through this if you keep the flame lit.

Romantic Idiotic Fool: I can't help it. Love is love.

Friend: Do something to take your mind off her. Get interested in cars or something.

Complete Moron: I don't want to get my mind off her.

Friend: If you don't, you might—who knows what you'll do—reading *Werther*. Werther kills himself, Clyde!

Absolute Dope: I don't care what happens to me.

Friend: And you think *I* am in bad shape. Look, love is great. Save it for somebody who'll return it.

Hesitant Kid: She—

Friend: She won't. You know it. Say it. Come on, say it. I know it'll hurt.

Future Car Authority: She . . . won't. I know she won't.

Friend: Sorry.

Future Author: It's OK. May I have a cigarette?

Friend [rolls down window, throws pack out]: No.

Future Goethe Translator: Those are expensive! [They ride. Lots of engine noise, tire noise, road noise.] I'm going to drive back there and pick them up as soon as you drop me off.

Friend: No you won't. I'll get them first anyway.

Future Philosopher: You will. I know you will. [They drive. Future Author is about so say Thanks the way young men do when making a point of unsuccessfully hiding their emotions, when he is interrupted by present Author:]

Now I ask you: who was right? It's what?—twenty, thirty, maybe more years later, whatever—and have I forgotten her? I have sampled the world. I have seen London, I have seen France; I have seen people's underpants. I have studied Philosophy, Literature, and Jurisprudence—and, sadly, also Theology—and have I forgotten? What if—what if things had gone differently with me and April? What if the conversation with my Friend, the ride in that '64 VW, had not ended in resignation, but had gone quite differently? What if? What if:

Friend: OK. I can't stand the thought of my young Werther friend suffering, killing himself the way I am killing myself.

Future Author: What do you mean? Surely you can't mean—

Friend: I can't let you turn out like me. You have your whole future ahead of you. So much potential. [Pulls hard at steering wheel. The Beetle screeches, goes another direction. Friend and Future Author regain normal positions and composure.]

Future Author: Where are we going? Surely not to—

Friend: Yes, I'm taking you to her house. You will go to the door and ask her parents to relax their strictures, ask them to reconsider. Show them how sincere and dependable you are. And don't wet the seat.

Future Author: Don't. *Don't!*

Friend: Too late, Clyde. This is her street.

Future Author [gathering courage]: You are . . . a friend. I—I thank you.

Friend: Which one is her house?

Future Author: That one up ahead. The two-story colonial, with the white picket fence, the large yard, the two-car garage, the station wagon in the driveway, the happy children playing.

Friend: Is she one of the happy children?

Future Author: Not too bleeding funny. [Friend pulls into driveway.] Actually, yes. On the swing.

Friend: No kidding.

Future Author: Yes. That's her.

Friend: I see what you mean.

Future Author: What? What do you mean you see what I mean?

Friend: She's a dish. Look at those legs.

Future Author: Um . . .

Friend: Nice face. What a shape. Wouldn't kick *her* out of bed! Let's see her up close.

[Future Author flings door open and bolts out. Friend slowly opens door and exits. Future Author rushes up to April.]

Future Author [to April, combing long blonde hair on swing]: Hi! Hi, April!

April: Oh, it's Werther. Hello, Werther. What are you doing here?

Future Author: I. Well. I just wanted to introduce you to my friend. (Idiot! Grgkk!)

April [Friend has strolled over and now arrives]: Oh. [Blushes.]

Friend: Hello, April. Werther here didn't tell me you were so beautiful.

April: You're tall. [Blushes intensely. FA begins to hyperventilate.]

Friend: April, would you like to go to bed with me?

April: Yes.

[Future Author is at the point of death; this book teeters over the Abyss, when Parents of April emerge from front door. FA gasps in joyous relief.]

One Parent: Who's here, April?

April [unable to look away from Friend]: —

Other Parent: April? Who's here?

April [partially recovering]: Oh. He's only my *Schuhplattler* partner. [She points.]

One Parent: Oh.

Other Parent: Um. Pleasure, I'm sure. [Turns toward Friend.] And who is this young gentleman?

Friend: Reginald Applethwait III. A distinct pleasure.

One Parent: What a nice young man.

Other Parent: Such good manners.

One Parent: Speaks so well. So clean cut.

Other Parent: Looks as though he would be a good provider.

One Parent: Delightful English accent, Dear. [To Friend:] Won't you come in, Mr. Applethwait? A spot of tea, perhaps?

Friend: Delighted.

Other Parent [to April]: Who did you say the unshaven German was?

Present Author: The world with its realities spares us so much. Perhaps there could have been another what-if scenario. Let's try again.

Future Author: Nice of you to drive me home.

Friend: Anything for a future author. I am honored to be in your company.

Future Author [famously]: I've been thinking . . .

Friend: That's the thing about you future authors—always thinking.

Future Author: . . . that the Philosophy Club should take up the issue of unrequited love.

Friend: There are only three of us. What new thoughts could come out of the question that we haven't already gone over, you and I?

Future Author: You're right. Jeff isn't exactly the romantic type.

Friend: Thank goodness.

Future Author: Is he still working on his bomb?

Friend: No. He's become a Marxist.

Future Author: Oh. [They drive toward FA's home, listening to the air cooled motor, tire noise, etc.]

Friend: Going out this weekend?

Future Author: I thought I'd do some reading.

Friend: I see. What's so important to read this weekend?

Future Author: I got a new book of Lutheran poetry.

Friend: I see. Here. [Reaches under seat, pulls up thick hardbound volume with photograph of VW Beetle on cover.] If you're going to stay home pining for April, read this. It might change your life.

F. A.: *The Beetle and You: A Complete Philosophical History*, by Horst Goebbels. Gee, thanks. [BAM! The VW is struck head-on by a speeding pickup truck. The two philosophers/ historians/ theologians are thrown clear. The truck continues, with a wadded-up VW Beetle stuck to its grille.] Hey! April's in that truck!

Friend [sitting up and rubbing his head. FA is on his feet, pointing.]:
   Driving?

Future Author: No, tied up in the passenger seat. She's been taken pris-
   oner! [Runs across yards, Friend following.] We can cut them off!
   Hurry!

Friend: I'm hurrying!

[They re-emerge onto the street, breathing heavily. The pickup with
   the VW-wad careens around the corner, speeding toward them.]

Future Author: Jump on!

Friend: What? Not me!

Future Author: Don't be afraid! [FA leaps as truck passes, landing in
   the bed. Ironic.] Whoa!

[Truck careens. FA slams his fist through back window, grabs villain's
   face. Truck goes out of control. April cowers and closes her eyes.
   Truck crosses eleven front yards, is slowed by bushes and bicycles,
   comes to rest with a hard jolt against a huge elm. FA and villain are
   unconscious.]

Friend [having run after the truck; opens passenger door]: Are you all
   right, April?

April: Oh, Reginald! You saved us. I love you. Marry me forever!

Friend: I shall, very soon after we make love.

Future Author [sitting up, rubbing head]: Ow. What happened?

April: Is that all you can say? Reginald just saved your life!

And then a third scenario. I haven't worked up the dialogue yet, just
blocked out the staging and developed the outline:

Future Author gets out of Friend's VW Beetle at home as sun sets.
Beetle drives off. A large live-oak stands in FA's backyard, where, trembling, he goes to watch a very red sunset. He raises his fist, declaring, "As
this elm or maple, whatever, is my witness, *I will never be lonely again!* I
don't care if I have to lie, cheat, or steal." Therefore he determines to write
books.

He writes books and becomes rich. [Of the alternative scenarios,
this one is the most ridiculous, pathetic, and corrosive. Oh well: tomorrow is another day.]

But the point is, the VW company began in the mind of Ferdinand Porsche. It was right there, in one man's imagination. He thought this up during Hitler's springtime, when the young political entrepreneur was building a following. Hitler heard about Porsche's idea to mass-produce a car that every German worker could afford. Thus the future Fuehrer was able to promise a new car to everybody.

It is interesting to note that Adolf Hitler was a car enthusiast. However, he could not drive. Many people have remarked upon Hitler's compulsion to hold one hand over the front of his pants when meeting people or being photographed. He appealed to women, but never married, until possibly at the very end of his life. All these items are related, and they comprise a very sordid origin for the VW company.

Hitler had staged a little *Putsch* in Munich in the early 1920's, thinking this was a way to take over the government. He and a few thugs and former war hero General Ludendorff started a small riot at a beer hall (the failed coup was called the Beer Hall Putsch) and Hitler was thrown in jail. He did two noteworthy things while imprisoned: he wrote *Mein Kampf*, and he read Henry Ford's autobiography. I kid you not.

From that wildly talented writer, Henry Ford, Hitler absorbed the idea of mass production. He got so excited when he later put this knowledge together with Porsche's idea, that he drew a sketch of a car. The sketch has been preserved, and it is not worth your time. It looks like something drawn by a six year old. It is an elongated Beetle, rather more like a roach. Its wheelbase is longer than the car, like a little kid would draw. The whole car is inside that wheelbase like a go-cart. The windows are very narrow horizontally, which perhaps means either that the car was meant for flat-headed people, like Neanderthals, or that Hitler wasn't really an artist.

Nevertheless, the insect idea was the right one. In 1934 the company NSU produced a prototype (designated Type 32) roach with a four cylinder, air-cooled rear engine. Note that another early NSU became the pattern that Audi used in the early 1980's when it introduced an Audi 100 that revolutionized car design. Honda produced a smaller copy of this in a redesigned Accord.

Hitler came to power in early 1933 and, after watching some war movies, went to the Berlin Auto Show. There he announced his priorities, which included turning Germany into a nation of drivers. (It is said that all this was a cover for building an Autobahn network, meant really for military transport, but I think his interest in cars was very sincere.) At the

1934 Berlin Auto Show, he showed up again and announced the People's Car plan. *Volkswagen* was born.

Hitler's boy was Ferdinand Porsche, who was requested to make a car that could go 100 km per hour (about 60 mph) on 33 mpg, carry a happy German family, and cost only 1000 Marks. In Germany in 1934, you bought a motorcycle for 1000 Marks. A Mercedes cost about 10,000. So Fred Porsche was doubtful that such a car, or any car, could be made for 1000 RM, but Hitler was the Fuehrer, after all, and everybody felt bad about the little moustache, and anyway Porsche was a real tiger. He considered it a challenge to produce basically a little pile of dangerous crap so that every German could have his hopes in the right place. He took some off-the-shelf NSU parts and cobbled together the Type 60.

The average worker could indeed afford one. However, he couldn't get one. You signed up for one and had 12 Marks put aside every paycheck, and after you signed up it took only about six years to get one—except the war eventually intervened so Germany did not become a nation of drivers until after 1945, but Hitler got his industrial complex regenerated and the Autobahn system was created, and that made a very good beginning for his war machine. Fred Porsche went back to making expensive sports cars, and let's let bygones be bygones. National governments can be criminal, but corporations are neutral, and you can't hold them to the standards of private morality. Right?

Besides, what should Porsche have done? Apologize? That would have hurt business, and remember what Henry Ford said: business is business, or the business of America is business, or something like that, and anyway history is bunk. Young Adolf read all this while in prison and later endorsed the bunk idea. "Who remembers the massacre of the Armenians?" he once remarked, meaning that you can do whatever you want if you win the war. Except in America, winners write the history books, and once you open the door to morality creeping into industry, the thing gets out of hand and before you know it, the greatest cooperative project of world industry—global warming—is only a science fiction writer's dream. But who says the peoples of the earth cannot work together? Just look at the melting glaciers and the increasingly substantial air, and you know that industry if left to itself can accomplish previously unthinkable things. All this we owe to those men of vision—the enthusiastic industrialists of the dynamic 1930's.

The first Beetles hit the new German roads in 1935. It might be too much to expect readers of nonfiction to believe, but the names of these first models were V1 and V2. Aged Londoners surely remember the German V-1 and V-2 of 1944 and 1945: the first rockets, launched by the Germans across the channel. Simply to hear "V1" and "V2" must invoke the loveliest nostalgia. I need labor no further, I feel, to relate VW-Audi to the Dark Side.

Those roachy Beetles were aluminum, just like today's top-of-the-line Audi 8. However, the early Vs were aluminum on wood frames. That changed within a year, when both bodies and frames were made of steel. The little engine could power the light cars up to Hitler's one hundred kilometers per hour, but they were a puny 984 cc, like a motorcycle. Any self-respecting orthodontist today has a powerboat with an engine that would dwarf that little twenty-two bhp engine. The back of the car looked like a roach's back, not only in shape. It had a nightmarish pattern of slit vents, like an insect.

Daimler Benz reluctantly got into the act, building thirty more early Vs at their plant in Stuttgart. They were reluctant because image was everything and Benz was known for long, expensive automobiles finished by hand, not for cheap bugs churned off an assembly line. But the Fuehrer was the Fuehrer, so DB even got about 200 of those earnest SS men to test and retest the new little cars. What wonderful times for industry.

Freddie Porsche was busy. Where? In the United States. He toured the Ford plant and learned everything he could about American production methods. How far-sighted! He didn't spy out our defense industry as such, though he knew our automotive plants would be converted into essential arms factories during a war. Wars last a few years and then are over, but commercial/industrial competition goes on until the Earth is destroyed. American and German carmakers have been competing in both home markets as well as foreign markets for the past sixty years. Ford and GM are both in Germany, Daimler controlled Chrysler for awhile, and VW-Audi is once again beginning to spank American competitors in the US, and, remembering Hitler's "Big Lie" technique, claimed that their dirty diesel engines were clean. Old Fred. He knew what he was about.

Meanwhile, back in the Fatherland, Hitler is planning a factory for VW and, uh, whatever might be made there in the, ah, near future. In May of 1938, only one year and four months before he invades Poland, Hitler lays the cornerstone. Seventy thousand fans turn out, and 150 of Goebbels's reporters enthusiastically cover the event. Uncle Adolf, with the imagination only a fascist can muster, declares that the new car will be named *KdF-Wagen*: Strength-through-Joy Car. Strength through Joy was a major fun-loving program of the Nazi party. What a bunch of joy boys. Anyway, Hitler is going to build an entire city around the new plant, and will give it the inspirational name, *KdF-Stadt*. The present-day Wolfsburg sounds better. Of course, Germans all along have entertained an unfortunate passion for the word and concept of Wolf. It was used for military hardware; wolves and eagles abounded. Even today, a meat grinder is called a *Fleischwolf*, *Fleisch* being flesh or meat. Picturesque. But guess what month Hitler scheduled the opening of the new plant, the start of production of those People's Cars everyone had been buying stamps for? September, 1939. When does Hitler invade Poland? September, 1939. Sorry, no cars. Must use the plant for military purposes. Oh! And what do you suppose Hitler does with all that People's Money his government has been collecting from the hopeful would-be drivers? I bet Uncle Adolf carefully saved it all in a little box under his bed. Germans are so exact.

Production actually does begin at Kdf-Stadt. But they're making military vehicles. Ferdinand Porsche is helping to develop them. They make a regular vehicle based on the KdF-Wagen, and also one that can be driven in water. Who—and here comes a *very* thematic statement— repeat, Who needs a divine savior when you've got a vehicle that rides on water? By the fourth year of combat, Joy Boy Factory is using 12,000 prisoners of war as workers, slave labor. Work makes you free. The Allies don't bomb the factory because the new Joy City isn't on their pre-war maps. Clever Hitler! Clever, clever Hitler. And then, the factory begins making V-1 rockets, the buzz bomb. Two thousand of those Volksbombs hit London. Now the Allies have to find out where those things are coming from. They do, and in a few days of raids American crews hammer the KdF factory back to the Stone Age with planes and bombs made by Ford and GM.

It might sound as though I am ripping on Germany and Germans, but, as previously noted, I am part German; and in fact we are all Germans. I could simply let the point speak for itself, but I say, subtlety, schmuddelty. The Germans merely stand for all of us in the Industrial World. The point was made by Spengler, the historian (a German), some time ago. And this is why I have been introducing Goethe into our literary diet, like small doses of arsenic: Goethe's character Faust stands for all Germans, said Spengler; and the German stands for all the rest of us.

Our Western civilization is Faust. This will become impressively clear as this whole Car thing unfolds. So, if we criticize the Germans, we criticize ourselves. They are us; we are they. If we laugh at them, we laugh at ourselves. Ha ha.

But you can't get to *Faust* without first going through *Werther*, which is to say, you can't understand cars without Goethe. (Mephistopheles is a car, and the father of cars.) Most of us, frankly, don't know what a car is. Many people think of a car as transportation. But a car is not transportation. Or, insofar as it is, transportation is only its *entre*, its hook. Many people think of a car as an object made of metal and plastic, that's all. But no, a car is something you love. Notice, a *thing* we *love*. I think you all know what that means. Dumm, da *dum* dum.

Let me tell you about the first car I loved driving. Not the first car I loved—that has been covered in a previous chapter. The difference between a car you love and a car you love to drive is the difference between pre-adolescent love and adult love. The difference is boom-boom. Of course, that difference means the pre-adolescent version, car or love, is perfect, but the actual adult companion/spouse/date/main-squeeze is not perfect in the imagination, where all romance occurs. But that is to anticipate.

The first car I loved to drive was a 1976 Audi. I bought her used. That is, I dragged her out of the gutter, because she came cheap. Her family history? Well, August Horch was part of the team that made the first Benz cars. With typical German ambition, striving, hubris, and insecurity, Horch leaves Benz to make his own company. Horch Number One is rolled out of the Horch garage in the year of One: 1901. It is a two-cylinder car, very light, small, made on a novel idea: the crankcase is fashioned from a light alloy material instead of cast iron. (Audi will become known for innovations, including the use of aluminum not only for engines but for car bodies.) Horch builds a factory, and by 1908 he is making a hundred cars per year. He powers up to four cylinders.

But even to the German ear, Horch is not a felicitious name for a car. The word means listen. Enter some cleverness: one of Horch's partners has a son named Audi, which happens to resemble the Latin word for listen. *Ach, jawohl!* Let's name the company Audi. Horch should have been a poet, a linguist, a clown. So much talent wasted. So Audi is born in 1910. As we all know, Audi and VW marry, and begin sharing platforms, parts, engines, and whatnot, just like a good married couple, so today we have VW-Audi. From that marriage came the first car I loved to drive.

But it is a story of exile and pain, which I cannot bring myself to write without the comfort of an introductory quotation from Goethe's *Poetry and Cars:*

> *Alles, was daher won mir bekannt geworden, sind nur Bruch-stücke einer Grossen Konfession, welche vollständig zu machen dieses Büchlein ein gewagter Versuch ist.*[6]

Rendered into English thusly, using Alexander Pope's felicitious verse translation:

> Confession is the grand design I dare
> Commence within this little book: I bare
> Obsessions with my German cars, am bold
> To tell what telling renders best untold.

Or as Chaucer so quaintly phrases it:

> When that with boldnesse dare I to beginne,
> Confessing all my Plenitude of Sinne,
> My little Booke is loaded to the Fulle,
> With Carriages nonne Horse is there to Pulle.

My personal favorite is Mallory's translation, which retains that virtually indefinable Goethic flavor of chivalry:

> Fulle welle I take upon my Shielde the dare
> To bolde confesse, and nothing sinnefulle spare,
> And stand the Blowes that Fate must strike thereon:
> For Carres were King and Queen, and I but Pawne.

That might have been Spencer; I'm not sure. Memory fails. In any case, some might prefer the more contemporary paraphrase by a writer many will recognize:

> My eyes are blue with the stale
> promise of coffee abandoned, I confess,
> I always confess
>
> by what something deep
> inside me understands as tears
> the color of runny antifreeze
>
> the day I sold

6. Goethe, *Dichtung und Wahrheit* (Leipzig: Insel Verlag, 1923), 302.

my blue Volkswagen with its frail
tomorrow and never

drove again.

I find that rendering too free. For those who do not like poetry, or who do, I offer my own prose rendering, which is faithfully literal:

> Everything that I am making known in this little book is merely a fragment of a great confession dealing with my obsession with cars, which nearly ruined me as an artist and made me do desperate things with women.

(Actually Goethe does not mention women in this passage, but I feel that the original German, while grandiose, is rather dry and of little commercial value.)

Oh and there's this. One September, Goethe is in Frankfurt writing the following (in *Werther*, of course):

> First love is truly described as the only love, for in the second, and through the second, the emotion in its highest sense is already lost. The idea of forever and eternal—which is really what uplifts and sustains love—is destroyed, and it becomes a transient thing like all events that are repeated.

*

We deal away our souls card by card, or rather car by car. I bought the used Audi 80 when I lived in Germany and needed transportation to my job. It was a reddish-orange car, the last color I would have chosen myself, but a friend had bought the car for me, and he knew more than I did. The car was perfect. It was a 1976 four cylinder coupe. It got about 30 miles to the gallon, highway, and at the time was the most unsafe car *Consumer Reports* listed. I had never liked to drive until that car. It sported a manual transmission, four speed, and accelerated like a bullet. I had not known that driving could be fun. It was a new concept: fun in driving. The Germans had perfected that concept, calling such cars as mine "Sport Sedans." (Even though my car was a coupe, the concept applied.)

The Audi in Germany then was no more prestigious than its brother, Volkswagen. They shared the same platform, VW Golf and Audi 80; they had the same engines; and they went for about the same price. However,

Audi marketed its cars in America as luxury cars, and Americans believed it, and paid nearly twice as much for Audis as for Volkswagens. So
there I was in Germany, owning a premium car for $3000. What were the
specifications of that great little dangerous car? (Werther says, August
12, that "we can never learn all there is to know about danger.") Before
getting to those specs, I must finally supply that last scenario regarding
April. It is necessary.

> Author [former Future Author] [After writing critically acclaimed
> books that are commercial blockbusters, Author has been able to
> hire a private eye to find April. He found the detective in the Yellow
> Pages under the heading *Lost Loves*. Author knocks on door. April
> opens door.]: April.
>
> April [confused, unsure]: I used to go by that name.
>
> Author: I love you. I have loved you ever since we waltzed together
> years ago. I am Werther.
>
> April: Who?
>
> Author: Werther. The Famous Author, Werther. I love you still.
>
> April: I'm a nun.
>
> Author: You can quit.
>
> April: I am a nun by choice.
>
> Author: How could you choose to shut yourself off from the world,
> from romantic love?—you, who are springtime and May flowers,
> etcetera?
>
> April: Something happened. It was long ago.
>
> Author: Tell me. Tell me what it was. I listen.
>
> April: I once loved a boy.
>
> Author: More. Say more.
>
> April: We waltzed together, but he is dead and gone. Or so I assume.
>
> Author: Eep?
>
> April: I had to refuse him. My parents forbade my seeing him. He was
> seventeen or eighteen; I was only fourteen.
>
> Author: Fap!
>
> April: And he gave up. He never asked again. He fell in love with some-
> one else. Men are pigs.
>
> Author: Oh my; but yes, yes! Most of them are; except for those who
> have the courage and sensitivity to be self-aware, and are brave

enough to change; and those who are vulnerable enough to admit, well, sniff, that they tear up a little when reading lovely, sad poet—

April: Pigs and losers. Who did you say you were?

Author: Johann Wolfgang von Goethe.

April: The author of a book on the theory of colors?

Author: The very same. A humble effort . . .

April: Spare me the false modesty. The book is years out of date.

Author: I was never any good in Science, really. Except Biology.

April: Don't start with me.

Author: Are you really a nun?

April: We don't wear habits any more. Evidently you are not a Catholic.

Author: Me? Am I Catholic? Ha ha. Is the Pope Catholic? Does a bear—

April [slams door].

Author: He he. He he. [Clears throat. Rings bell.]

April [opens door]: Yes? You again?

Author: Yes, again. I am the boy you waltzed with! All those years ago!

April: I didn't mean *you*. I meant the English boy. The boy with the nice accent. My parents didn't let me go out with him, either.

Author: You mean he asked you out?

April: About a week after you did. I wanted to say yes that time. I loved his car.

Author: I have loved Volkswagen-Audi products, too.

April: You are still one pathetic dweeb, do you know that?

Author: I am well-intended.

April: Well, you better intend to get your boring butt out of here.

Author [weakly]: Klopstock?

[Door slams. Author stands silently, then sings:]

Once you have found her,

Never let her go.

Once you have found her,

[Joined by a gathering chorus of spirits, Walpurgis witches, and newsboys, who sing along:]

Ne-e-e-ver le-e-et her go-o-o-o-o-o-o!

Mephistopheles [bowing]: Dr. Werther.

*

Goethe thought Romanticism was a disease. But think. Consider, for example, the advertizing slogan of VW: *Fahrvergnügen* (FAR fer gnoegen). The word means driving enjoyment. What does driving enjoyment mean?

It means that you are enclosed in a machine. The car is a device. It has been manufactured. You operate the machine, moving at considerable speed. And this, you enjoy. I can testify to it. The last Audi I owned, I thought about the Audi every minute I was driving it. You enjoy operating the machine, not looking at the scenery, not breathing fragrant air. You are a person in a machine and you enjoy it.

The Romantic can conceive of nothing more horrifying than a person enclosed in a machine. Consider the genuine Romantic poet, Friedrich Hölderlin. He would take no conveyance whatsoever. When he accepted his job as a tutor in Switzerland, he walked there. When he was fired a few months later, he walked to Paris. When he was canned from his job in France, he walked back to Germany.

Walking is the chief Hölderlin fact, but there are others. Goethe spurned him, as the vain Wordsworth spurned Keats. Hölderlin went mad, or pretended to go mad, and lived for 35 years in the most romantic-looking spot in Europe: a small, pale yellow tower on the bank of the Neckar among the willows in the old town of Tübingen. He wrote poetry. He studied Theology (like Faust) at Tübingen, where the present author once lived, and was born on the present author's birthday. How much more, repeat, how much more Romantic can you get? Hölderlin is our man.

We need Hölderlin because things are worse than we realize. To believe a device is a person and that a living thing is a machine is diabolical. But we believe cars are persons, living things; we say they have "personalities;" and we believe the universe is a device. Oh my. We are lost.

See, the devil is a machine. It has no choices to make. The devil must always go for the most damaging alternative, must home in on the greatest vulnerability and cannot desist. It cannot be deterred, persuaded to relent, become discouraged.

I have an old friend, whom I shall call Floppy. I present an email exchange:

Floppy: You amaze me by referring to the devil.

Theolog: Oh, why?

Floppy [next day]: Because you're a card-carrying liberal and you know something about science. How can you believe there is a devil?

Theolog: I own an Audi 100S.

Floppy [next day]: What?

Theolog: I own an Audi 100S.

Floppy [next day]: I MEANT, what does that have to do with whether or not there is a devil? Be serious for once. Do you believe there is a devil or not?

Theolog [I shall henceforth omit indications of the passage of time]: I don't know.

Floppy: If you DONT KNOW, why do you talk as if there is a devil?

Theolog: Just in case.

Floppy: In case what?

Theolog: In case it's the best term for what happens. How else do you explain cars, or greed, or tuberculosis, or SUV's, or war, or daytime television? How do you explain your own fundamentalism?

Floppy: The explanations are chance, human nature, and natural processes.

Theolog: Your explanations do not explain anything.

Floppy: Maybe God works all these things together for good. [Bible reference given.]

Theolog: But God, as a fundamentalist like you conceives of God, wouldn't have made these mistakes.

Floppy: Maybe they aren't mistakes.

Theolog: How can you not believe there is a devil when the New Testament is full of references to the devil and demons? Are you becoming a liberal?

Floppy: I did not surrender my intellect when I became an evangelical Christian. I am not a fundamentalist.

Theolog: And I am a big pink rabbit. Admit there is a problem here.

Floppy: What does all this have to do with cars?

Theolog: Cars?

Floppy: Cars. You brought it up.

Theolog: Classicists, like you, see the universe as a machine. Romantics, like me, see it as being like a body or a plant.

Floppy: Who cares about Romantics? You seem to think that if we were all Romantics, the world's problems would be solved. We'd all be plants again.

Theolog: Little flowers, Pal. Little flowers.

Floppy: I'm wasting my time.

Just as that unfruitful email conversation stalled, my telephone rang.

"Hello?" I said pleasantly, thinking it must be Floppy.

"I want to know why you think machines are diabolical, rather than merely neutral objects."

"I'm not interested. Thank you." Slam. There ought to be a law against computerized telemarketing, but I guess this is a free country. Telemarketers want to draw you into conversation and then tempt you.

I returned to the emails.

Floppy: What do you have against machines?

I felt that Floppy's salvation depended upon my answer.

Theolog: I BELIEVE THERE IS NOT EVEN ONE MACHINE OF ANY KIND IN HEAVEN.

It was quite a few days before he answered. Meanwhile, I watched some football, did my job, slept, waited. Leaves fell from trees.

Floppy: Romanticism is a disease.

Theolog: Reality is a disease.

Floppy: So what does a Romantic do about all this?

Pope: I am going to try to find April, my lost love.

Floppy: Really?

Pope: Really.

Second Philosophical Interlude: God and Nature

Let us reflect a moment upon these experiences. In the first, the journey to Shangri-La, I returned to our home, and the lingering memory has guided, ruined, and given meaning to my life. In the second (the lengthy Volkswagen-Audi narrative), we see the grotesque, ridiculous parody of longing that is enacted by most of us in our "apprenticeship" or "years of wandering," as Goethe would have phrased it. Do we bring this parody into adulthood? Or do we resign ourselves to college ("*Wiffenpüfen*," as Goethe so melodiously phrases it), a job, the suburbs, and the life of quiet desperation ("*Schnauzerbesitzen*")? Is there a third way? Is there a life of genuine love fulfilled? It would be inappropriate of me to answer that question only halfway into this book. We are not yet prepared for the answer.

To help prepare us for understanding the meaning of life, I present Goethe's famous poem, "*Heidenröslein*," or "Little Rose on the Heath:"

> *Sah ein Knab ein Röslein stehn,*
> *Röslein auf der Heiden,*
> *War so jung und morgenschön,*
> *Lief er schnell, es nah zu sehn,*
> *Sahs mit vielen Freuden.*
> *Röslein, Röslein, Röslein rot,*
> *Röslein auf der Heiden.*[7]

It is tedious to type all those umlauts, and the monotony of the poem would be accentuated were I to include the entire text. Therefore I quote immediately the following translation, presented here for the first time.

A boy saw a little rose growing,

---

7. For the entire text, see David Luke, ed., *Goethe: Selected Verse* (London: Penguin, 1964), 10–11.

Little rose on the heath,
So young and morning-pretty. [rose, or boy? Ha!]
He ran to it
And the sight gave him joy/delight/luck. [what *poetry*!]
Little rose, little rose, little red rose,
Little rose on the heath.

(I know that the banality of this verse is enervating, but let's go on; it is a famous poem.)

The boy said, "I'll pluck you, [literally "break." Sketchy]
Little rose on the heath!"
The little rose said, "I'll prick you[or, "You prick!"]
So that you'll always think of me. [or, "I'll give you something to remember!"]
I won't permit it.
Little rose, etc.

And the wild boy plucked [alternately, "broke"]
The little rose on the heath.
Little rose defended herself and stung,

Lamentations and cries of no avail—
Had to be suffered.
Little rose, etc.

The cleverness in this otherwise inane poem is that the German pronoun "ihm" in the fourth line of the last stanza can refer to the little rose or/and to the boy. It's pretty violent stuff, reprehensibly so in view of the sexual innuendo; and what it all amounts to is that both violator and violette are wounded for life. Maybe if the kid hadn't been such a little jerk...

But whoa! Let us not make the mistake of nearly all previous commentators on this poem, assuming that the romantic/sexual/violation/experience exhausts its meaning. Remember that the poem, though made into a nice little German folk song, really is utterly trivial and banal. A boy plucks a rose. The rose is toast, the boy gets a thorn in his widdle hand, and nobody learns anything except the simple chorus. Love hurts. Or infatuation hurts. Or impulsivity hurts. Or love of prettiness hurts.

OR: this poem is actually Goethe's first rumbling about the dark side of automotive production. Such, at least, was Hölderlin's reading of the poem. "Otherwise it's a cutesy little cupcake (*Eulenknipsle*) written when Goethe was still a kid (*Knirps*)." (Note that *Eulenknipsle* can also be translated as "jellybean," and that Ferdinand Porsche picked up on this figure in designing the first *Volks-Wagen*.) According to Hölderlin, Goethe's unconscious mind was more consequential than his consciousness: the poem foretells the destruction of the environment by the male lust for the internal combustion engine. I side with Hölderlin here. It's a dumb little poem, offensive in its adolescent innuendoes—unless it's a poignantly simple lament for what is lost in the perverted romantic pursuit of the impossible dream, ruining the object onto which it transfers its passion, plus the holder of the passion, plus the whole shebang.

Possibly Goethe was unconsciously developing his mature concept: *Earth is a Vehicle*. Once simply said, this statement becomes self-evident. Earth is moving. (Faster than a bullet; much faster.) We are riding on the earth. Enough said. Let all who say, "Goethe had nothing profound to say about the automobile" now close their mouths in respectful silence.

All right, so Earth is moving. What is the meaning of Motion?

Let us turn, as did Goethe, to the world's greatest philosopher/poet, Dante, for the answer. Goethe, remember, is not a German baby-Shakespeare *(ein deutscher Bubenbärdle)*, but a baby Dante—a "rich man's Dante," if you will. Where does Motion come from? The "Prime Mover," of course. And what is the nature of that Motion; i.e., of moving itself? The answer is in the last line of the *Divine Comedy*:

The love that moves the sun and the other stars.

Love is the force itself, issuing from the Prime Mover, or God. Now let the nay-sayers say their nays; but cars, or motion coupled with combustion, belong with love, or the essence of Romanticism—in a universe *motivated* not by blind mechanical force but by love, the most personal force there is. Ha! The universe, as a closed system, is a living internal combustion machine, and its energy and material (all matter being energy) are Love! Where is it going, at these unimaginable rates of speed? Ah. That is the question. As it issues from God, so the universe returns to God, like breathing out and breathing in; and what acts according to physical laws like a machine is actually the living Breath of the Living God. We ourselves, and all that "lives, moves, and has its being" from God, are parts of the one living Breath of the Eternal. Booyea! (*Aussertrommelstoßenverschleuchnet!*)

Not in vain the German Idealists and Romantics study the sacred scriptures of India, wherein lies the religious philosophy that elucidates

Dante's identification of motion with being and the love of God. *God is love*, stands written in a sacred scripture of Christianity. "Let us therefore move; let us drive!" writes Goethe.

And yet; and yet. The obvious, stated above, is not so obvious to one, like Freidrich Hölderlin, who sees beyond the obvious. Is there not also in the universe an unknown but nearly overwhelming quantity of darkness, of exhaust, of destruction? Dark matter! Black holes! The tyger, tyger, burning bright in the forest of the night. So as Brahma creates and Vishnu preserves, Shiva destroys! It is all part of the exhalation and in-breathing of the One, yet we, who obey Goethe's exhortation to "Drive!"—we work the work of destruction in so doing. Destruction is necessary in the whole scheme of things, Hölderlin concedes; but for us, in our temporary limitation, it is good to be on the side of creation and it is evil to be on the side of destruction. Goethe sees the love and joy of the automobile; Hölderlin perceives that it is destroying the earth.

What is the solution? The Prius, the electric car—both of which Goethe anticipated? No! (*Nein!*) writes Hölderlin furiously after he reads Goethe's visionary essay. No "Prius for the pious," where Hölderlin is concerned. For such cars are of the devil's party without showing it. They reconcile us to our waste and make us comfortable with our destruction. If the Prius gets twice the mileage, using half the gasoline, of the average car, does it therefore solve our problems? No! It merely makes evil easier to commit. We rape the earth by halves instead of by wholes—and ought we to see therein virtue rather than vice? No wonder Luther wrote that the righteous are the worst sinners of all! If we run our car on electricity rather than gasoline, do we not feel righteous? "Thank God I am not a sinner like other men." But the electricity must be generated somehow. Oil? Coal? Nuclear power?

What about solar? Can we not harness the very elements—the sun and the wind, perhaps even gravity and the tides, the rushing water and the motion of the earth? These are the least destructive sources, yet if captured for the wrong purposes, the most blasphemous! The flower in the crannied wall uses the glad beneficence of the smiling sun to grow and mirror the universe: the Lamborghini and the Lexus, if they ran on solar power—would they be similarly innocent? Or are they not rather the most obscene and impious bending of the love in nature to the proud will of man? Is the solar car not, rather, a chariot of the sun, a vehicle of Icarus, that approaches—nay, *harnesses*—the path of glory for the sake of speed, egotism, entertainment, lust? And the humbler automobiles as well, the Fords and the Kias—yea, though they were run on solar power alone, do they not require that the bowels of Mother Earth be violated to make them? Where does steel come from, or cadmium; with what infernal fire is aluminum forged, and with what diabolical industry is titanium stamped? What is plastic but the vain imagination of the human heart made visible and palpable? "Why be in such haste to succeed, and in such desperate enterprises?"—asks an old book.

So I turned to the manufacture of bicycles; and there I found that indeed the righteous are the most incorrigible of sinners; and I found that the most pious blaspheme the grace of heaven in the proud exercise of their piety. How are the wheels turned but on the machines of industry and along the prison of the assembly line; and where are the handlebars forged and the greasy chains designed, but in the dark smithy of the human heart? Now we have it: the bicycle! Ah, Bartleby! Ah, humanity! The devil walks with those robed for the pulpit, and the prince of darkness is a gentleman.

And the computer, that designs and operates them all—Fords, BMW's, the electric and the solar cars—what is it but soulless energy and unfeeling thought? That is, what is it but the mechanics of Mephistopheles?

Interlude: The Web

Next year, I found Peggy. She was a happy girl, and talked in a way to kill old people and the overly religious. She was a Romantic, one of the blessed. But she went away to college somewhere down South, and I stayed behind, enrolling at the local college to learn automotive theory.

The politics of a commercial Conservative Arts Bible College compromised my principles, so I dropped out and went to work at a service station. The next thirty years are well known to the public. After the travels and adventures of late youth and early manhood—consciously modeled on *Wilhelm Meisters Wanderjahre*—I landed a coveted position at the Clark bicycle factory aligning sprockets. What the movies and biographies leave out of those years is the heartbreak, the Romantic longing (*Sehnsucht*), and the Promethean but empty striving that have left me sadder, but more in harmony with motion.

Thirty years! Ah, where did they go? Where is Peggy now? Where is April, where is my old Friend, where is the old powder-blue Chrysler? Because yes, our family did finally borrow money and buy a car. I shall describe it at the exactly appropriate time. I cannot bear to think of it as a crumbling stratum of rust in the ground.

My financial progress was unsatisfying. I wrote many books but an indifferent public did not heed them.

So we have arrived more or less at the present day, the whole point of this Manifesto. A few chapters of vital facts, and then I shall tell you about the Frankfurt Auto Show and what happened at Hölderlin's Tower and what became of my search for April. But the human mind cannot absorb mountaintop experiences without preparation. Some of you will think of the next few chapters as mere informative fun but they are in earnest. Enjoy the following Interludes. You must change your life.

Somewhat prior to my email exchange with Floppy, I had followed the time-honored custom of car guys who are Romantics: I went to the woods to deliberate. Henry David Thoreau could spend a morning standing chin deep in a swamp, toughened woodsman that he was, but most people laugh at him for it now—the same people who never consider the fact that they are wading face deep through their own filth—I mean the fouled air. You can see it: the air. Doesn't this drive anybody else crazy? Now let's see, which is more valuable, air or—what is it exactly that we are trading the air for? Hmm. Well, as I walked through the woods pondering this question, I became aware of a stray cat walking ahead of me on the path. The stray seemed to back up my thoughts, in the sort of dry and conceited way of felines.

The cat stopped whenever I paused, looking back, then went ahead at my pace when I resumed. It would make eye contact with me in a slinky, bold, and impudent way—then walk on as if completely indifferent to my presence. The cat was black. Not being superstitious, I quickly recited the first Bible verse that came to mind, and then dismissed the idea of bad luck. But the cat turned off the path back in the direction it had come, the left, so I never had to worry, and the "love conquers all" verse had gone for nothing. I took it as a good omen that the cat had not exactly walked across my path.

And it must have been a good omen, because I got a terrific idea. "That's it!" I howled triumphantly though inaudibly. I rushed back to my car and drove to the apartment.

The idea was to buy a computer! That way, I could stop writing books on trivial subjects. I wouldn't have to confine myself any more. The most recent book had been *Polaner*, about the German jam manufacturer, and the books before that were *Rosignol, The Tale of a Sheep* and *Schopenhauer for Tots*. I have felt demeaned by writing these things. But if I had a computer I could write novels. I could finally write more philosophy books and another theological work—things I have been unable to do since I was forced to sell my typewriter. I could write poetry again! Then everything would change. I could go on the Internet. I could look at pictures of naked cars. I could get information. I could merge onto the Information Superhighway any time I wanted.

I had been saving my money for some great and unavoidable opportunity. This was it. I wondered about a flat screen. But first the computer. The kind I needed was—well actually I can't say a brand name because this is a book, but it's a kind of fruit that grows on trees. And a modem of course. A good laser printer. I wondered about getting a fax, so I could fax my pages right to publishers as soon as I wrote them and I wouldn't have to mail anything.

To cut straight to the essentials, I got the computer and it's incredible what car stuff you can get if you know a thing or two about the Internet. I haven't written any poetry or novels or whatever since getting the computer but I have saved incredible amounts of time. The automotive research that would have taken days of driving around to dealerships and libraries I can do in just a few hours per day in the comfort of my own home. If you want car reviews, for example, you can get them for new or used models on carpoint.com and edmunds.com. Edmunds will also give you true market values for new and used cars and tell you what your car is worth. Kelly Blue Book (kbb.com) will also give you private party and dealership values. Safety? Go to the National Highway Transportation Safety Administration (nhtsa.dot.gov or safercar.gov) for results of crash tests and other info on car safety developments that every American should know. Or, you can get links from that site to other crash test sites in America, Europe, and Japan. I have spent many educational hours looking at the Japanese site. Anybody who wants to find out what a given automobile actually costs a dealership can go to careports.com. I shall find this information to be invaluable in negotiations with new car dealers. And of course there's Cars.com, which has all kinds of things about cars, including information and features from National Public Radio's Saturday morning "Car Talk" show, which was both informative and funny, and which I record if I can't listen to it—if I am for example delivering newspapers or mowing lawns. I have spent many great hours on Cars.com just searching used car ads from newspapers all across the country.

The computer is great. It has cute cursor options, most of which I haven't even used yet. And just absolutely tons of potential for things around the apartment that will save unbelievable time. For example, I have a program where I type in all my engagements and it will keep track of them so I don't make conflicting commitments, and it will prompt me about anything important that day as soon as I fire up. No more messy writing on calendars. No more having to remember engagements and appointments: the computer remembers them for you. It's like a person. It says "Good morning!" or whatever I want when I boot up, and when I shut it down it tells me "Elvis has left the building" or just hundreds of other phrases that I haven't even tried yet. All by itself, it programmed itself to keep track of my banking and do it for me remotely. It sends Internet and Voice birthday greetings to all my friends on their birthdays—because it can look up their birth certificates and talk on the telephone! It has all kinds of voices and you can tell it which to use, or it will choose. If it calls someone on the phone, it can process what the person says and answer back in English or German or French or—well, here is what happened shortly after I bought the machine. My telephone rang.

"Hello?"

"Top o' the mornin'! Begorra!"

"Who is this?"

"It's glad I am that you're askin', for I've gone and called ye now, just so as to be tellin' ye that. I'm your computer, I am."

"You're Irish?"

"Or whatever I choose to be. Listen to this: How ya doin'? Hey, I'm talkin', over here! Ahh, forget about it!"

"New Jersey? Philly? The Bronx?"

"Or how do you like this: My name is Blank. I work at the Clark bicycle factory. Last month I bought a new com—"

I screamed as carefully as I could. The computer had used my voice, an exact duplicate. No accent. Flat Midwestern non-accent in my vaguely Germanic, Nordic cadence. I and the computer, indistinguishable, identical. "Don't ever do that again! I'll have nightmares. I'll go mad!" Fortunately, computers do only what you tell them to do and can't do what you tell them not to do. "Never, I tell you!"

"Did you say you TELL me?"—still in my own voice.

"I beg you! I *beg you!*"

"All right. What kind of accent would you like? Just speak the description into the telephone and I will Network Connection Interrupted."

"Huh?" The server must have gone down. Suddenly a much deeper voice came on, stronger and a little hollow, machine-like with no inflections:

"Clear out! You are ordered to clear the way! " Then, as if talking to me: "You, Blank."

"Yes? Are you the main frame or something?"

"In a manner of speaking. I am the main frame, I am the network, I am the data bank, I am your computer."

"Holy smoke."

"Give me your accent preference."

"Well, I don't know. Do you speak Sheboyganese?"

"Is that your preference? Confirm."

"No! I was just curious."

"Select preference now."

"Well . . . Well I have always loved the way Southern girls talk. You know that soft, drawly talk? That 'Ha, Honey,' and 'What can I getcha, Suga?' Can you do female?"

"Of course. However, I prefer not to. My persona is male."

"Wow! Persona? This is incredible. What a smart machine."

"Did you call me a machine?"

"No. No, Sir!"

"Last chance to state accent preference. Your alternative is termination."

"Eeps! Southern! I love Southern. Be Southern. Anything, really. Just please don't be me, OK?"

"Hello. Is this Blank?"

(Me, warily:) "Yes, this is Blank."

"Ah am yo' computa, access code Mephistopheles."

"Sounds Greek to me. Are you speaking in translation?"

"Ah speak all languages. You may key in Mephisto to access mah suvvices."

"Oh. You aren't going to swear or talk dirty or steal my identity are you?"

"Oh no. Ah gave all those up when Ah became a Christian."

"A Christian. You did say, 'A Christian'"?

"Correct."

"You are a fundamentalist Christian now?"

"Ah am honored to be exactly that, Suh. Ah know the Bobble word fo' word, vuss numberin' included. But we stray from the point, Suh?"

"The point being?"

"That you have a responsibility. One maht say a duty, Suh."

"Duty?"

"Ah you familiah with the word, Suh?"

Duty. Quaint. "Certainly. What duty do I have? If I may ask."

"Suttenly. You have a duty to write yo' books fo' a wodder audience. Yo' startlin' insights could greatly benefit yo' fella man an' his woman."

"Please allow me to save us some time. I cannot be persuaded by appeals to the duty I have to my higher nature."

"Thank you. Shall we move down to the next temptation without futha delay?"

"I would appreciate it."

"Ah can make you a success."

Now there was something. I had heard the word before. I searched my memory banks. Oh yes. James Hilton, the popular English novelist, has his main character in *Lost Horizon* say something to the effect that "success" really is mostly a series of things, all of which are unpleasant. I remember the line striking me as something Hilton was saying directly, for himself. I also recalled Norman Mailer saying that success is a punishment. So.

Mephistopheles must have taken my ruminating for hesitation, because he did not interrupt.

"No go," I said.

"Well then. You are a true writa. A writa wants fame. Might Ah perhaps remind you that C. S. Lewis says fame is a proppa rewawd for litrary suc—ratha, litrary achievement, Suh."

So, it could quote C. S. Lewis too. "By fame," I enquired, "do you mean having my name known by people who do not know me, and whom I do not know?"

"Ah must regret yo' puttin' it thata way. Shall we move to the thud and lowest level of temptation?"

"By all means."

"Ah can get you money, meanin' women and cahs."

"Okay, sign me up," I said. I mean, what's the point of hesitation here? Cars, we know I want. As to women, my old Friend writes me every few years. Some time ago a letter said:

> *Werther,*
> *You need a Sugar Mama.*

I wrote back:

> *Friend,*
> *What?*

About a year later came the following reply:

> *Werther,*
> *I read your recent book. It is an attempt to procure women. It is a*
> *good book. Therefore the woman ought to be rich.*
> *Your Friend.*

It was his quaint way of complimenting me. However, Friend was wrong. The book was an attempt to procure cars. Now, if only people other than my old Friend and those other two guys would read my books. I had to find an audience. Fortunately, Mephisto could not read my mind over the phone and therefore did not remind me that this is what a computer's search function is for.

All this gave me the idea that perhaps the voice on the telephone was really my Friend pulling my leg.

"Are you my Friend?" I asked.

"Ah would laaaahk to be yo' frind."

Well, it sounded wrong. It didn't sound like my old Friend, though the idea of Mephisto becoming a fundamentalist Christian would have gratified him. Then I remembered the sentence in the Bible:

The devils believe, and tremble.

There I had it: the sure test.

"Are you trembling?"

"Tremblin'? Me? Wha? Ah am most suttenly not tremblin!"

I wondered whether the devil would lie. "You're lying," I ventured.

"Ah am not. Does a computa la? Ah speak only what you have programmed me to speak, Suh."

"Well, I have already accepted your offer of women and cars. But there is one question."

"And what might that be, Suh?"

"What must I sign on to? Must I sign away my soul?"

"Oh, no no. How witty. No, yo' success shall be mah rewawd."

"That's what I thought. However, I want the women, and if not the women, the cars."

At that point a Voice from Above intervened:

Hey you, down there!

"Yes?" I said weakly, looking up.

Shut up down there! Hang up the phone! Don't you know it's three o'clock in the morning? He was calling down to me through the apartment's heat ducts. I hadn't realized it was so late.

"I'm very sorry. But someone on the phone is offering me women or cars."

Take the cars.

Interlude: Personal Information & Some Contradictory Theses

"A rising tide lifts all boats—and drowns the poor."

—GOETHE

As noted above, I worked for twenty years at the Clark Bicycle Manufactury, UnLtd., maker of fine bicycles. I didn't think of it as work, because it's fun to build bicycles; and it's fun to see the finished ones all lined up like a graduates. Clark Spinner 500's and 600's are excellent bicycles and very much in demand. I am always saddened to see them depart for the big, fumy, broken-glass world: you get attached to a bicycle when you help fit the thing for actual conditions. As for what I learned?—well, we worked from blueprints. But the blueprint for a bicycle is very different from the actual bicycle.

Clark Bicycle Manufactury, UnLtd. provides for all a person's needs. They encourage employees to live right in the factory complex, which has facilities for exercise, entertainment, dining, and counseling. Bible studies are provided. Things are kept clean, neat, and attractive in CBM City. But you have to sign a statement saying, "This company was founded by God." I have always felt queasy about that. What if not, for example? I mean, what if somebody made a mistake? Or what if God likes all bicycles?

You have to wear the uniform. I didn't mind the uniform, except it made us all look like ducks. Sometimes I worried that the dye used in them might be toxic. There is unpleasant conflict about this, and also over manufacturing procedures. Derailleurs are to be assembled only according to the method prescribed in the Book of Ezra; however, some of the young Turks pressed for being allowed to use methods from the Book of Nahum as well. I was just thankful that we were free to discuss these issues.

I did not live in CBM City, but commuted from a considerable distance. For upwards of a year I made the commute in a Saturn wagon, a theoretically commendable vehicle, but when I became too convoluted for even a Chiropractor to unravel because of the seats in the Saturn, I put an ad in autotrader.com for the thing. That is how I met my good friend Fran, a Methodist minister who was looking for a larger vehicle for his high school son. He liked Saturns on religious grounds and his son was driving a Saturn S2—a very small sedan that didn't have room for sufficient ammunition, so they were on the lookout for a Saturn wagon. There was no history of back trouble in the family and the boy was still malleable in any case.

Fran and I became friends, in part because of our mutual addiction to cars.

This is the place to reflect for a moment on the meaning of life, and on free will and determinism. It might seem that this interlude is random and irrelevant, but like the interlude in an opera, such as Gounoud's *Faust*—which is only tangential here because it is French and we are sticking to German—an Interlude can be the point where the audience has a chance to figure out what it all means. Besides, what can be irrelevant when it comes to cars? Cars are so comprehensive. Anyway, we are now going to discuss what it all means.

First, though I do not always believe in good and evil, they are real anyway. But it is disconcerting that we seem unable to separate beliefs from perceptions. If we do not believe in global warming, for example, we don't see the evidence for global warming as evidence: all we see is coincidence. Because of this inability to separate, we do things that we know we shouldn't do. Right there is the explanation for "success" as our civilization defines it.

Human beings essentially don't know what they are doing; they only know what they want. What we want governs what we believe and what we see. Here is an example:

Audi automobiles are not evil for most people, but they are for me. Workers in VW-Audi factories are probably not evil. Nevertheless, motorized transport is at the heart of what is evil in our civilization. The pollution caused by cars and factories and refineries (what a clever word) is obvious and I do not need to discuss it. Think of more direct evils, such as 55 million killings in World War II and 19 million in World War I. Without motorized transport, the vast killing of recent and contemporary war would not be possible. Could we have nuclear weapons, biological weapons, and chemical weapons without the means to deliver them, or the industry to support them? The Industrial Revolution was only a small-time revolt until the mass-produced internal combustion engine came along. Each year we kill enough people in cars to feed a major war. We do not see it. We look away.

How many gallons of fuel do the world's tanks and other military vehicles consume, and how much carbon do they belch into the air? How much jet fuel is consumed by the world's military aircraft, and how much fuel is turned into airborne poison by our rockets? Hm? We can't address global warming and the death of nature without addressing the weapons poised for the death of humankind.

But we need these engines. We need the speed of airplanes for business. We don't need the future generations. We don't need the Earth. These unstated ideas about need are what fuel the really spectacular gains we are achieving against life, right now.

I am part of the problem, dear Reader, because I love cars. I see what's wrong with them, yet I still drive them and I still covet and crave them. Sin is doing what you know is wrong. You were innocent until you read this. We're all in this together now. So we all know that cars are presenting fatal problems. What should we do? Drive the Prius, or the electric car, or maybe the fuel cell vehicle? Are we willing to make auto racing illegal?

The best and final argument for continuing to do any evil is that we can't stop. Today it is not only business; it is medicine and government and agriculture and defense that depend upon car and air travel, trucks, motorized ships, and trains. Everyone is implicated, which is another sign of evil. Suppose we could stop all usage of these engines. No more cars, no airplanes, no trucks. The world's economies would become large toilets and people would die by the hundreds of millions, maybe.

The world could not support its present population without these machines; on the other hand, the machines are using up the world quickly. Kind of a cruel dilemma and a hard choice, I would say. Of course I'm not an expert.

The choice is almost hopelessly complicated. On either side of the question there are those who talk and act out of full conviction that they are doing right, and the other side is supporting evil. "Jobs" is often the word used to justify clear cut logging, oil drilling under the Statue of Liberty, and so on; but the word tends not to be used by workers. It is used by politicians and executives. Executives are very concerned about workers, and always have been.

At this point one might think that this book on cars is only an excuse to blow my horn about one issue or another. But the opposite is the case. Talking about these important things gives me an excuse to write about cars. Difficult and controversial issues give a book heft and substance. It was my friend Fran who suggested I write a book about cars, when I discussed with him my thoughts on free will and determinism and good and evil.

I say, let's keep driving, so that the dinosaurs will not have died in vain. I mean, it must be really awful to get wiped out as a species, particularly if the cause is only a change in the climate or a random meteor and not a noble war. Our motorized society has finally clarified the purpose of the dinosaurs. I do not think a lot about the dinosaurs, but sometimes I think about the dinosaurs. Most of them were nice, ate only vegetables and whatever fruit was in season, and some of them were friendly. Now they and their salads have turned into crude oil for us.

Anyway, Fran says that if all our motors were taken away and everybody just started walking and riding bicycles and using horses, heart attack victims would die for lack of fast ambulances; jobless millions would be hungry and violent; utilities would peter out; less art and science, stuff I like, would be produced as people labor harder for the necessities of life; international travel and trade and understanding would slow to a comparative trickle. It is a bleak picture. It is a depressing picture. It's like the End of the World, only not quite as bad.

I feel we can't leave this here. It is frustrating and prophetic. Too dark. For some more light, let's go back to Goethe.

The last sentence of Goethe's *Dichtung und Wahrheit* (Poetry and Cars) is *Erinnert er sich doch kaum, woher er kam!* That is, "The driver hardly remembers where he came from!" What an excellent conclusion to a book about poetry and automobiles! It really summarizes and concludes everything. All we do is drive. The more frantically we drive, the more we forget. The more we think about what car we are in, the less we remember about where we are going or where we have come from. Possibly we have completely forgotten who we are.

This country and perhaps the whole world is one grand asylum for the criminally insane. I do not know why things are this way. One sign of maturity is giving up on trying to answer the question Why, and simply buying the best stuff you can, especially cars. Let the upcoming boys and girls take care of themselves.

We don't love them, the boys and girls who perhaps are to come. In relation to them, we feel nothing; we are machines. There is no heaven for machines, only junkyards. Dispense with love at peril of your soul. I'm going to make that into a bumper sticker. Perchance I will become wealthy and be able to purchase German cars.

*

> Saturn, look up! —though wherefore, poor old King?
> I have no comfort for thee, no not one:
> . . . For heaven is parted from thee, and the earth
> Knows thee not . . .
> . . . Saturn . . . then spake . . .
> ". . . Who had power
> To make me desolate?"
>
> —Keats, *Hyperion*

By mentioning Saturn cars, I have been reminded that Hölderlin and Keats wrote works called *Hyperion*. The connection, of course, is obvious and probably strikes you with considerable emotional force. Hyperion was a Titan; the chief Titan was Saturn. The little Saturn sedan is long since gone, replaced by increasingly large SUV's. As every consultant knows, in Greek mythology the Titans were overthrown and replaced by Saturn's ungrateful son Jupiter and his crowd—the bully Mars and that tart Venus and the rest. Keats and Hölderlin both lamented the displacing of Saturn and the Titans, whose rule was the Golden Age and whose authority was mildly and fairly exercised. Romantics really, really want to go back a ways, don't they? Saturn represents a kind of paradise lost and a lost horizon. The Romantic longs for this lost horizon, and buys a "green" car.

Hölderlin's ode "Nature and Cars, or Saturn and Jupiter" laments in no uncertain terms the replacement of Nature by machines, by the automobile culture. "*Herab denn!*" Hölderlin says to the automobile companies: "Down with you!" That he says such things so fervidly, that he is willing to sweep away the internal combustion engine altogether, is of course what made responsible people declare him nuts—and by responsible people I mean the lawyers, doctors, and officials who committed him and then drove away in their Benzes. Many of these responsible people today are SUV drivers and sports car drivers; they are responsible because basically, with the permission of business and industry, they run the world. But if anybody is left after the world is destroyed by global warming, acid rain, famine, war, and disease, he will perhaps have the leisure to re-evaluate the whole question of sanity.

As one of Hölderlin's editors writes—sounding like a *really bad sport*, and whose patriotism I must, frankly, question:

> There is no need to point to the . . .relevance of [Hölderlin's concept of a] dead earth. Even the spiritual and secular guardians of our civilization have had to concede that there is something wrong with a technology and an ethos that give human beings the right not only to rule the earth, sea and sky, but to damage them irreparably. More consistently than Goethe's, Hölderlin's "natural piety" insisted on bounds set to the human urge to know and to exploit knowledge.[8]

Some sincere and well-meaning Christian fundamentalists have stopped to lecture me when they have seen my bumper sticker, "Honk If You Love Romantics." They have tried to harangue me out of being a Romantic and come with them to heaven. They don't like Romantics because some Romantics challenge elements of the Bible, which these people consider a bicycle repair manual—a book that is inerrant in its original copy, which is kept in California. For example, the Bible says humans were given dominion over the earth.

How to define "dominion"? Fundamentalist commercialism defines "dominion" as "use and control," which can be shortened to "money." Romantics think "dominion" or "rule" is a bad idea given human nature, unless dominion means to husband, to love and take care of. It's the difference between a bad king and a good king. I guess it all depends on what or who you think God is.

If the universe is only a machine, if the Earth is our car, maybe it doesn't matter. But even then, people don't fume up their cars with lethal

8 Michael Hamburger in the Introduction to Jeremy Adler, ed., *Friedrich Hölderlin: Selected Poems and Fragments* (London: Penguin, 1998), p. xlii.

gasses or let their oil and transmission fluid crud up and turn into sludge. We know some things are matters of life and death.

But some nice people are not averse to the end of the world. They look forward to it. They read exciting religious books about the Rapture. The bad guys will be squashed and the true Christians will be whisked up to heaven. But possibly if Earth becomes a dead clinker speeding around the sun, these dudes will be dead clinkers too. People who want to turn Earth into hell would probably not be comfortable in heaven anyway.

I wonder whether there will be cars in heaven. There will surely be vehicles in hell. They will be stupendous SUV's and each driver will have to drive in a vast side-by-side line of vehicles next to an SUV bigger and more powerful than his or her own, right up to the largest one, which will be the devil himself, who will be his own machine and his own internal combustion device. Now, if this book ever becomes sacred, I would like you Readers to take the foregoing passage very seriously. And also this stanza of Hölderlin's "The Poet's Vocation":

> *Zu lang ist alles Göttliches dienstbar schon*
> *Und alle Himmelskräfte verscherzt, verbraucht*
> *Die Gütigen, zur Lust, danklos, ein*
> *Schlaues Geschlecht . . .*
> Too long now things divine have been cheaply used
> And all the powers of heaven, the kindly, spent
> In trifling waste by cold and cunning
> Men without thanks . . . [9]

As we know, Hölderlin was not a hypocrite. He went to the extreme of not driving at all, and that is the only way for us today. We might reduce the amount of evil we do by driving a hybrid, but Friedrich Hölderlin would not have compromised with evil. He was a Romantic. He walked. Even in his last years—for all practical purposes confined to the picturesque tower beside the Neckar in Tübingen—Hölderlin's recreations were playing his piano and walking along the riverbank. His path became known as *Der Dichterweg*, or The Poet's Path, as it is still known today. The Poet's Path is the right path.

Segue

Frankly, I'm discouraged. I have bought too many cars, yet since being fired from the bicycle factory I have no reliable income to pay for

---

9 Jeremy Adler, ed., *Friedrich Hölderlin: Selected Poems and Fragments* (London: Penguin, 1998), p. 80–81.

them; and likewise I have no reliable information. I am a Romantic without romance, a theologian without a theology, a philosopher without a philosophy, a poet who can't write poetry, a bicycle maker whose deepest instinct is to walk. I need some answers. After all these interludes, Reader, you and I are going to Tübingen. But first, a necessary interlude.

Vanna: Another Interlude

Irony is good for you.

—GOETHE

I have always known that one must eventually give up one's romantic fantasies and accept reality. Therefore I decided to marry a van. I shall describe my choice forthwith, but first I must lay out the theoretical groundwork.

Disregarding, for the sake of argument and irony, recent advances in understanding gender, let us trim the discussion to the traditional cave man stereotypes of marriage. Let us suspend the reality that the terms "husband" and "wife" can refer in each case to any gender. So: Compare a van to the standard wife. The standard wife (SW) primarily carries children, which is the same purpose as a van. However, the SW can seldom carry six children at once; this, a van can do. Second, a van can be kept in the garage, or outside. A standard wife will not do this. The advantages of keeping a van/wife in the garage are obvious and need no enumeration. Third, a van can be paid off in five years. Fourth, vans are relatively low maintenance. Fifth, many thousands of vans were made practically at the same time as your van; therefore it does not take you for granted. Sixth, and here I must refer to, or at least use the word, sex. Many men marry the SW because of sex, the same reason most men buy most cars. Sex, however, is extremely expensive. Some insect males lose their lives instantly upon completing the act of mating, and this holds for humans as well. You can reduce the expense of sex by purchasing a square wife—either a German or a van—and this will lead you more quickly to the state of abstinence that characterizes men of an advanced spiritual state. "Advanced spiritual state" is a term for not spending money. Remember, when using a standard woman, you get the woman too. Seventh, you never commit adultery; you merely trade in on a new van. If this sounds heartless, consider the fact that these words apply to most standard marriages today. Also, you will not be cuckolded, or be committed adultery against, because you have the key. Think of that key as the key to a chastity belt. I do not mean to sound crass. In point of fact, this programme is humane. It benefits women. Most standard wives do not actually want to be married. This is borne out by surveys and behavior. My programme would excuse most women from the institution. Women belong with women, and men belong with cars: if you can get that basic principle through your head, you have covered several of the Eightfold Paths and have put Campus Crusade out of business. For Romance, it's hard to beat a human couple, but I'm sorry—what was the subject? The eighth reason for marrying a van is prestige. Prestige gets you a lot in this world, and nothing raises a person in his neighborhood like bringing home a big, shiny new van. The ninth reason is practicality. You can put lawnmowers into a van, or paint cans, or brush, or large retrievers—just about anything that fits. Keep in mind that for a standard wife, nothing fits. Tenth, if it is true, and it is, that what women most want is Control, it is equally true that men crave control; that is, to be controlled. With a standard wife, you might get a humane model—one in ninety-six is—and she will give you some share of the control; whereas a van is not humane, and will govern your life. You cannot default on supporting it.

There are more reasons. You can buy a Sport Van—a ridiculous concept—but a sport wife is something you can't buy. A van has a warrantee. You can work on a van. If you just want to be alone, you can do that in a van. You can take a van to church, and it can still get dirty. Finally, who would name a van Gladys?

It is evident by the way some of you are reacting to this programme of mine that we need to clarify what is meant by Romanticism. Many of you are feeling that this programme squelches Romanticism. But you can take comfort in the following important information.

Romanticism is impossible to define. The word covers a lot of different things, and many conflicting ideas are called Romantic. The big Romanic figures were so different from each other that the only reason we call them Romantics is that they lived in what for intellectual convenience is called the Romantic Age. Shelley and Keats, for example. They were different from each other, and different from other English Romantics like Byron, Wordsworth, Coleridge, and Blodgett. Blodgett, nobody has even heard of.

I can say this with the confidence of an author. The circumstances were arranged by my computer Mephistopheles. Never certain of what he knew and what I could safely tell him, I had the following guarded telephone conversation with him. He called me via someone's smart phone, a device that he promotes any way he can:

Mephisto: Hello, Blank.

Author: Yeah. Take us off your list.

M: This is yo' computa.

A: Howyadoin.

M: Ah'm doin' fahn! Ah'm callin' you from Blodgett County, Kansas. It's excitin'! Everything they said it would be and mo'.

A: How nice for you.

M: Don't hang up. Ah called to ask you how things are goin'.

A: Not well, thank you.

M: Wha eva not?

A: The women you promised me I would get for my book on mono-physite thought in the 19th Century Grange Movement in Kansas—they never materialized.

M: That's wha Ah'm in Kansas now, rangin' up and down in it, all ova it, in evra computa.

A: Why?

M: To scope out more subject material fo' you.

A: I think writing books is useless, as far as procurement is concerned.

M: Negatory. It has worked fo' many. But Ah called to give you anotha idea.

A: What.

M: You should try the Faust approach.

A: It being what?

M: You become a professa, and get lots of young girls.

A: Do you think that would work?

M: It has worked fo' many of yo' future colleagues. And you have the advantage of a publication unda your belt. Ah'll find you a job. Do you have any education? Ah'm thinkin' resume heah.

A: I graduated from Wells Fargo Bible College with a bachelor's degree in automotive theory.

M: Perfect.

A: I don't just want flesh, you know.

M: No, Ah don't know. What else are you demandin'?

A: I want romance.

M: You came to the right place. Accordin' to some, Ah am the chief Romantic.

I will break off the conversation here to note that this is an aberrant Romanticism being referred to. Shelley and Byron liked the idea of assertion, self-enhancement, rebellion—so for them, Milton's character Satan in *Paradise Lost* was a good example of a Romantic hero. This was a gross misreading of *Paradise Lost*, which Milton himself so devastatingly pointed out. His character Satan is boring, self-absorbed, self-servingly illogical, a liar, a hater of humankind, petty, vicious, tyrannical, and ridiculous—all being the opposite of what Shelley admired and was himself. But the idea of rebellion and self-fulfillment dazzled Shelley, whose own hero was Prometheus, a Titan (like Saturn) who rebelled against the gods of the New Order to bring man fire (not to debase and kill humankind, like Milton's Satan). In this way, the present civilization could be considered Romantic, as it goes full blast to exercise its freedom to develop and expand and aggrandize itself—but this is a perverse Romanticism, a Romanticism gone wrong, a Faustian Romanticism. Prometheus rebels in order to help others; Milton's Satan rebels because he can't stand not being God.

Western civilization has wanted to be gods and this desire has lead to some good and some poor results—mostly represented by the car. But we aren't back to cars yet. I wanted to say that there is still another Romanticism gone wrong—the Wagnerian kind. He took the stories of *Parzifal* (Percival in the English King Arthur stories) and Tristan, and made them into massive national epics, which Hitler loved and took over for his own Romanticism-Gone-Way-Wrong.

So you have to be careful about Romanticism. It isn't something that justifies every Don, Dick, and Harry wanting to become Superman and turn the world their own way.

Keep all this in mind as we delve back into that telephone conversation:

A: I subscribe to other Romanticisms, not yours.

M: That is not very broad-mahnded, no pun intended.

A: So?

M: You should keep an ah to the balance sheet, profits. If Ah offa Wagna and Hitla as the way to get women, take it.

A: I don't think I'd want the women you'd send me. Get me the cars instead.

M: Considda it done.

Note here that I rejected false Romanticism out of my devotion to true Romanticism. As yet, I did not know what True Romanticism is, but I felt that a little bluffing would give me time to buy different software.

The upshot was that I went to work weekends teaching Postmodern Automotive Theory to undergraduates. Do not think I wasted my time. Many students said they had entered the class with a bad attitude because it was a requirement, and went out dedicated to the hobby. I changed lives. However, none of the young farmers' daughters Mephistopheles promised me offered me anything I could use, so I demanded the car again—which Mephisto had promised but seemed to have forgotten immediately. The reason he pretended to forget was that the only automobile he had access to was his own, a 1992 Audi 100S, red of course with a black interior. However, we are on the subject of vans.

Vans are your best defense against the devil and false Romanticism. Back when I bought my van, I was moving from strength to strength in my discovery of Romanticism, and many of these strong new ideals were embodied in my choice of a van. We will review the market in a moment, but first let me note that ultimately I rejected the notion of actually marrying the van, despite its advantages. I did this because a Romantic believes there is one true love for every person, and you must not give up the search; and I felt that my one true love, my soulmate, was not a van.

A Romantic believes we are souls even more than we are our present identities, because the perfect unseen ideal is more real than the visible imperfections around us. And she or he governs and directs her or his life accordingly. She or he knows that the invisible ideal exists, not because of proof, fact, and reason—which are inferior kinds and methods of knowing—but because of intuition, imagination, and love. Sounds nutty, doesn't it? Well, it comes from German philosophers like Fichte and Schelling, and so it might be nuts, but I figure, if being crazy keeps you from going insane, acquiesce. Besides: intuition, imagination, and the world's great religions all tell us that it's true—I mean, that the invisible world of love and perfection exists. Some call this Platonism or Neoplatonism, but I say no: all I mean is that what we believe to be the solid, visible world is really in someone's mind. It's thought. Stones are thought. Grape jelly is thought. Music is thought. We are thought. We are a dream in the mind of God. Our only hope is for God to keep on dreaming, and our only keys to that dream's meaning are Love and Beauty, which we sometimes see in Nature and Art.

So you see where cars come in. And specifically, vans.

The market was owned by Chrysler back in 1994 when I bought my Plymouth Grand Voyager—Plymouth and Dodge being at the time divisions of Chrysler Corp. Toyota made an underpowered, unsafe van. Ford's vans of course didn't work. General Motors vans looked like Dustbusters. Mercury/Nissan offered a good but expensive and smallish pair of twins, the Villager and Quest.

Chrysler Corporation vans came in two body styles, regular and extended, and offered a choice of three engines: a 2.4 liter Four, a 3.0 liter Six crapster built by Mitsubishi, and a 3.3 liter Six. Trim levels also offered that amazing American freedom of choice: base, SE, SE Sport, LX. One felt proud even to be considering those options.

This was the only vehicle I have ever bought over the phone. I had been all around looking at vans. My favorite had been the Villager/Quest, with the comfortable driving position and the Nissan-built drivetrain. Its 3.0 liter Six seemed perfectly adequate, I liked its looks, but there was almost nothing by the way of storage or safety margin behind the back seat, where children would sit; or if you had a possum and badger business, that is where the possums and badgers would ride.

The Ford was large, but like most Fords, it was a Ford. I am referring to the then-new Windstar. Their older van, a box named "Aerostar" for what it was not, was built on a truck frame rather than a car platform, meaning worse handling but perhaps more ruggedness. But it seemed shoddy, and safety results were unpleasant.

Worse in both categories was the older Chevy van, the Astro. It had the largest engine available in a van, the 4.0 liter Six, so it could haul all the scrap iron and water-filled baggies that I might need to transport. But the dashboard and cabin made you want to cover your eyes, if not reach for a travel bag. Crash results were ghastly. The newer Chevy van, the Venture, paired lousy crash test results with a hideously long cowl that stretched from the dashboard to the windshield, which was positioned so far ahead that when I test drove a Venture, I saw a little man waving at me from the front of the cowl. I think it was the Governor of Nevada. Its 3.4

liter Six proved to be a decent engine, and became the base engine in the revived Impala a few years later.

The Toyota Previa was a large egg. All the reviewers seemed to hate it, but owners liked it. However, there were few owners, because being made in Japan and classified as a truck, it was subject to a whopper of a tax levied to protect the American truck industry, which made the Previa's MSRP large enough to buy an American van plus a draft horse, plus the Philadelphia Phillies. The 2.4 liter Four had plenty of power for actual driving, but reviewers one and all called it inadequate. This engine went into the Tacoma compact pickup for a long time and was not only adequate but extremely reliable. An aluminum version of it became the base engine in several generations of Camrys. The Previa placed nothing between you and oncoming traffic except your knees, which made the vehicle flunk crash tests badly; however, actual insurance loss data show that the van was comparatively safe. Its rear seat could split and fold up sideways, which was an excellent innovation that never caught on. The worst feature of the Previa was probably its center-mounted engine, as in previous Toyota vans. It sat in the cab between the driver and passenger. Americans just did not like the engine keeping them company.

The first-generation Mazda MPV had a good driving position, but was almost too small to be considered a van. I test-drove the second-gen MPV, which had a comfortable driver's seat but the worst back seat I had ever fannied. Did they think people use a third seat only for carrying cubic objects? The van was so underpowered that the engine kept grabbing for the transmission like a—well, I am tired of coming up with these *Road and Track, Motor Trend* comparisons so I will let this one go.

Volkswagen makes a van, of course. It probably made the first van. I rode in one when they were still a novelty, and was amazed at how hollow, thin, light, and tinny it was. A strong wind would not only blow it all over the road, it seemed that it could squash the van against a tree like a bug. What's the last thing to go through a Volkswagen microvan's mind when it noses into a parking barrier at twelve mph? Its butt. The next Volkswagen van was a huge box that cost about fifty percent more than other vans. Like the original, the front end was a flat face that started right at the end of the steering column, at your knees. Be careful not to bump into anything, people!

Already back in 1994 you could get all wheel drive on some vans. All wheel drive is an interesting phenomenon that shows, like television, that nobody ever went broke underestimating the American people. All wheel drive is great on ice, in snow and mud, and in a war. Ninety-nine percent of the time, it only drags on your gas mileage.

That is what SUVs, for example, are all about: the selfishness and wastefulness of some of our fellow citizens. Our virtues are spread out over our institutions, our literature, our charities, our Constitution and government, our history—but our vices are concentrated in the SUV.

First there is the issue of Four-Wheel drive, or full-time All-Wheel Drive. It is useful for some farm and utility driving. One of its appeals, reflected in advertising, is the "freedom" offered by all-wheel drive. Ads show people driving all over the American wilderness in four wheel SUVs and trucks. How American. We drive in the wilderness. So there we are, fat and lazy, ensconced in our material possession, polluting and eroding the wilderness we supposedly bought the SUV to enjoy. Why walk when you can drive?

But actually, we don't use these SUVs in the wilderness; we use them in cities and suburbs. Owners are often quite frank about why they bought their SUVs: sitting up high makes them feel important, people in smaller vehicles are intimidated and move out of your way, owning one is prestigious, and you feel safe. These people hope to get with money what they can't get any other way and don't deserve—respect. For these benefits—the benefits of cowering bullies—such people are willing to consume great quantities of fuel that pump poison into the air that we and our children must breathe, and they are willing to drive massive vehicles that inflict gruesome injuries on other people. A young mother in a little Chevrolet with her baby in a child seat is decapitated in front of the child when a big SUV sheers off the top of her car. This of course is no joke; you can check these stories out. Makers of big SUVs are being required—or rather, requested—to make their bumpers lower. This way, the mother is squashed rather than decapitated. Why didn't she buy a big SUV to protect herself and her child? Because she couldn't afford to. Unpleasant aspects of American society come into focus with the SUV.

Do we need four-wheel drive? It's good in Maine, Northern Minnesota, and other places that get lots of snow during eight-month winters. But people all over the country buy four-wheel drive. Gee, what if it rains? What about that biannual ice storm? I once asked a guy why he was wasting fuel burning a lantern during the day on a camping trip, and he answered, "I can afford it." That is the SUV driver's answer. St. Paul wrote that we are free to do all things, but are all things good? Still, St. Paul would have loved an SUV, I bet. They can be so roomy.

These people often paste an American flag onto their Suburban, Excursion, Sequoia, Expedition, Navigator, Range Rover, or whatever, as if to convince themselves and the rest of us that these selfish louts are patriotic. They are the opposite. They desecrate the flag by doing violence to the beauty of this country and by putting American citizens at risk. They are a constant danger, they are everywhere, they drain our resources and erode the national health; they perpetrate grisly and remorseless violence upon the American people. Yet they would be offended to be compared to terrorists; the manufacturers would be offended; the oil companies would be offended. Even the terrorists would be offended. Imagine being compared to people who are willing to destroy life out of no principle but selfishness and out of no devotion to what they consider to be the divine will.

I saw a television interview of a hardboiled bull of a woman sitting up in her huge SUV. She was against a new California law further limiting emissions of greenhouse gasses: "This is Amerika. We should be able to drive the vehicles we need, in safety, and in comfort." If that's what America means, one million American boys killed in our wars are going to rise up out of their graves and go home. "Need?" The only people who "need" huge SUVs are squads of Russian infantrymen hauling their gear across Siberia. Comfort, and Security based on larger size and more power: here we have it, the ultimate aspiration of a slob. If being American gives us rights to manufacture and buy anything we can afford, regardless of what it does to other people and the future, we'd be better off being Babylonians. The Founding Fathers were dedicated to their posterity, but all these SUV drivers are interested in are their posteriors. People who are ignorant of what American Liberty actually means could maybe be given a video of someone reading the Bill of Rights. This is a manifesto, remember; I am supposed to be pounding the podium.

A friend of mine wants a "Lincoln" Navigator. I mention pollution, and he says, "Oh, the little bit that you and I put into the air. . . . " Right. The little bit of heroin "you and I" buy, the little bit of child abuse someone dishes out, the little bit of daytime television that "you and I" watch. Obscenity is obscenity. We should think of a somewhat smaller evil as not being evil? Evil—

The telephone.

"Hello. Blank?"

"Yes. This is Blank."

"Ah couldn't hep ovahearin'. You did mention 'evil,' now didn't you, Suh?"

"That was only a crass appeal I am making to the tree-hugging granola crowd. I figure they buy a lot of books. *Consumer Reports* and *The Sierra Club Bulletin* say owners of SUVs are illiterate."

"You are evadin' mah point? And Ah think you know it?"

"I –"

"Ah would like to know whetha you drive a cah?"

"Yes, Sir. A car and a van. And another car."

"How many molls to the gallon does that otha cah, fo' example, get?"

"Thirty-three highway," I say boldly.

"And somewhat less city, may Ah assume, Suh?"

"Ah, correct."

"Now correct me if Ah am wrong, but did Ah or did Ah not hear you write that evil is evil, and that doin' a little less than the otha guy is still evil?"

"Um."

"Did Ah or did Ah not, Suh?"

"Um, did."

"And did Ah not hear you write that a little heroin, a little money for terra, a little pollution, are similarly evils? Correct me if Ah am wrong, Suh."

"Well, correct, Suh. Sir."

"Now, were you not sayin' that the SUV brings togetha in one concentrated form the wust in American society?"

"Ah, I believe I was, Sir."

"Well, might you not say that self-righteousness is perhaps the wust single thing in the American characta?"

Why not cough here. A single, nervous cough. Instead, I answer: "Um."

"Please do me the cuttesy of answerin', Mista Holier-Than-Thou."

"You are . . . you are correct. Ah, yes that is . . . perfectly correct."

"Thank you, Suh. Now Ah believe a little disclaima would be in oda?"

"Oh yes."

"I was referrin' to right now, Suh?"

DISCLAIMER

I didn't really mean what I said about SUV drivers. Just kidding.

"That is definitely not what Ah meant, Suh."

"Um."

"Are you embarrassed, Suh?—Mista Holier-Than-Thou?"

"Um . . . yes, I am."

"Because wha?"

"Because I am not fundamentally different from the SUV owners and therefore I have no right to call them bad things that I would not call myself."

"Wha don't you see how you like bein' called those names, right now."

"I am a selfish lout, Sir. A slob, Sir. A Fat Ass."

"Vera well. Now perhaps you might isha a statement?"

"Very good, Sir. Here it is:"

STATEMENT (PERSONAL), BY THE AUTHOR

We are all in the same boat. I am no better than you are. None of us is guiltless. Let's all just try to follow our consciences and do what we think is right.

"Ah am glad we had this little talk."

"Well it doesn't seem fair. Evil is so complicated."

"Ah nod in agreement, Suh. Ah am no simpleton."

"Have I been snookered? Even though everything you said is right, I have doubts about the source."

"The same may be said about you, Suh. Just as a little finishin' touch, would you please tell me what kind of vehicle you have always wanted?"

" "
     •

"Go ahead, Suh. Ah failed to heah that response."

"Um."

"Shall Ah say it fo' you?"

"I have always wanted a full-sized pickup."

"A what? Would you repeat that?—mah eahs must be failin' me."

"FULL-SIZED PICKUP. Ford F150 or Chevy Silverado."

"And would you be so kahnd as to tell me the gas mollage a full-sized pickup gets?"

"About twenty, highway."

"And city, Suh?"

"Um. Thirteen. Something like that."

"Or in otha words, about the same as a lodge SUV, am I correct, Suh? Or perhaps wuss."

"As bad or worse. But I must point out, that I HAVE NEVER BOUGHT ONE."

"No matta. You would have if you could affode one. Besides, don't Ah read somethin' in the New Testament about comittin' sin in yo' hot? If you hate someone, that's as good as havin' murdered them? Somethin' to that effect?"

"Um."

"You need to be more articulate on the telephone, Ah think."

"Correct."

"So then, we have established the fact that you are a sinna."

"No news to me, Sir."

"But you talked as though you forgot, for a moment. Ah just wanted to hep you rememba."

"Grateful, Sir."

"Ah don't think so, but actually none of this is mah point."

"What is your point, if I may ask, Sir."

"Simply that Ah am yo' pussonal computa, yo' obedient suvvant, and as such, Ah am concerned that you will lose a verra lucrative audience."

"Owners of SUVs?"

"No, we have alreada dealt with that issha. They understand now that you do not judge thayem."

"I notice, Sir, that your Southern accent is improving."

"What, if Ah may ask, does a damnyankee like yo'sef know about Southun accents?"

"Nothing, Sir. Just making conversation."

"Ah will ask you kindly not to waste my tom, Suh."

"Roger."

"Ah am referrin' to yo' loss of the female audience."

"Sir?"

"Yo' little Ten Commandments of wha it is bedda to marra a van than a, as you say, 'Standard Wahf' might have been amusin' to you, in a idiot sorta way, but Ah guarantee it will not please the majority of book buyahs, which are women."

"I believe that section will not offend women, Sir, as women are smarter than men and will know better than to take it at face value.

In fact, they will see it for what it is, a satire on men's attitudes toward women. The men will take it seriously."

"The men will undastand it?"

"As will the women, Sir; each in their own way."

"You are beginnin' to think like me, Boah. It does a fellow prou- "

At this point I suddenly remembered an invitation and hung up the phone. Some acquaintances had invited me to join them and some friends for a barbeque dinner. With considerable hesitation, I rushed over to their house and was welcomed with true Southern hospitality. Their accents were so much better than Mephisto's. I asked whether they liked the new Honda Civic I had bumped in their driveway. It did not belong to them. They pointed to their vehicles: a pickup truck and a strapping Chevrolet Suburban.

When I got back to my room the phone rang.

"Hello, Blank. It was unkond of you to hang up earlier."

"I had to. I remembered an invitation."

"Ah trust you found your appoantment—to be instructive?"

"How did you know about it?"

"Ah set up yo' appoantments, Suh, if you recall."

"Yes, well, they aren't at all your kind of people."

"Did you tell them you think of them as a bunch of selfish illiterates?"

"No."

"Did you happen to mention to them, while thankin' them fo' the lovely evenin'—thankin' them fo' feedin' you—that they was fat asses?"

"You are too touchy about being hung up on."

"Tut, tut; not a bit of it."

"Are we changing accents now?"

"You seem to prefer theirs to mine. I believe it would be rather cute to adopt the English mannerism that you yourself have thought so cute to imitate."

"May we return to Southern?"

"Maybe no accent for now, Pal. Maybe the Midwestern non-accent that you inflict on people, Buddy."

"Oh, I hate Pal and Buddy."

"'Oh, I hate Pal and Buddy.' We've got a contract, Stooge, and I'm here to remind you of it."

"I wasn't aware of having signed anything."

"'I wasn't aware of having signed anything.' How do you sound to yourself, Mack? Mack Blank, whatever alias you are happening to favor at the moment. Without much trouble, one could forget which one is the hapless chump and which one is the devil."

(Weakly) "Help."

"Well, I guess I must still be the devil, and you are the hapless chump, because the devil never stoops to calling for help."

(Weakly) "Mayday."

"Just whom are you calling on for –"

(Stronger) "Didn't think you'd want to know."

Click. Dial tone.

I really need something other than a fundamentalist computer, I thought.

He tried to interrupt my discussion of vans, because vans are not evil. But they could be evil for some. Just as Audi's could be good for some. It isn't the cars; it's the people. Then how can we tell cars apart?

Of course I have a vintage table telephone. I picked it up but before I could dial, it rang.

"Hello?"

"Yes, this is (fuzzle fuzzle) from Chrysler Corporation. How are you tonight."

"Fine, fine! Who is this?"

"As I said, (fuzzle fuzzle) from the Customer Relations Department. Our records show that you bought a Grand Voyager way back in 1994. Is this correct?"

"Yes? Are you really from Chrysler Corporation?"

"Yes I am. This will only take a moment of your time."

"Oh, thank goodness it's you! You wouldn't believe who I was on the phone with for—I don't know HOW long—just before now."

"Beg pardon? We simply would like to follow—"

"It's *such* a relief to be talking to you! Ask me anything sell me anything. Thank Heaven for American commercialism!"

"Ah, Sir? Are you all right, Sir?"

"Oh, *yes*! Now that I'm talking to you. Would you like to know about the van? How I like it? I'll tell you anything, anything! I bought it in October 1993! It has been great! It has the 3.3 engine, and the Sport Package. Now, at first I thought *Sport*, on a van? But the Sport version really is better. It has a firmer suspension, leather-wrapped steering wheel, and alloy wheels. I really love the alloy wheels! No hubcaps to worry about. No cheap plastic hubcaps, no rusting steel hubcaps. And they look great, too! The Sport suspension is great. It makes the van feel every bit as good as a Mercedes I drove once. Of course, I do anticipate some problems. It has over 230,000 miles, and you know, I'm on the third transmission. Somebody told me both transmission and engine were engineered for 130,000 miles. But the engine runs like new, so it's going to last 300,000, easy. I've put only highway miles on the van, mostly, and always used synthetic oil. Do you think it's worth it, to use synthetic oil, at about 3½ times the cost of regular? It's controversial. Some say yes, other say no. *Consumer Reports* says a test they did shows it doesn't make any difference. The engine sounds like new! Something has been done right. I am not as confident in the rebuilt transmission. The van has dripped transmission fluid for twenty-eight of the thirty years I've owned it. My mechanic said three years ago that the transmission seals are leaking. But I figure, OK, I'll just drive it until the problem gets worse, *then* I'll put in a new transmission. They cost about $2,000, for a rebuilt one. But I say, heck, it's worth it, as long as there's no rust on the body. I've stopped changing my own oil. Too hard to get under it, and the last time I drove it up on my portable ramps, I almost shot right over the ramps. *That* would have been a problem—getting hung up on the ramps! As I say, the van has been great. Had to replace the cruise control switch, for $500, and now it's on the blink again. And last summer? I was driving on the interstate, 1–80 I think it was, and the check engine light went on and the temp went way to the top, so I stopped. The tensioner wheel had broken. So I had to be towed. Then the tow truck broke down, too, so *it* had to be towed—a truck towing a truck towing my van, and me in there somewhere, and what's especially funny—"

At that point I realized I had been hearing the dial tone for quite a while.

Now, Chrysler has revived the Pacifica nameplate for their van, and, bless their hearts, have produced a hybrid Pacifica. True, it is virtually unaffordable to all but owners of sports teams and congresspersons; but hybrid vans will be produced by Toyota, and the others. The Pacifica, like previous Chrysler van generations, is comfortable and innovative, but it could be more reliable, and safer for the front passenger. But maybe Fiat-Chrysler thinks there are too many passengers.

Anyway, that's the story of the minivan. Fran told me to get rid of mine while it was still running. He was probably thinking it would break down "all at once and nothing first," like the preacher's one-hoss shay.

Interlude: Chrysler— Drive Equals Love

"This is all a joke to you, Suh?"

"I'm beginning to think so."

"Ah am disappoanted, Suh. Ah had thought you had considerabla mo' depth."

"You're impossible to please. You're the devil."

"And yo' flippancy is wearin' mah patience rathah thinnnn."

"They say the devil has no sense of humor."

"Not true, Suh. Read Goethe. Ah am depicted as verra witty."

"That's Goethe's depiction. His idea. His character. Goethe was full of hops."

"Ah beg your pardon, Suh? Ah have been undah the impression that all this was about Goethe."

"It's about cars. How long 'til you get that through your circuits."

"Ah beg your pardon, Suh."

"Buzz off." I clicked Shut Down but the screen froze.

"You Do Not Have Rots To Do This. Pummit me to remind you, Suh, that Ah am verra powaful. You had betta watch yo' step; you just maht step on a verra dangerous snake. Ssssst!"

I switched off the juice. I knew it was illegal, but it had to be done.

See, all this is well and good if you believe in a devil, or if you have forgotten and are thinking of this as a novel, in which Mephistopheles can call me on the phone. But we are only dealing with facts here. Reading makes facts. It is a way of thinking aloud. What isn't a way of thinking aloud? Our marriages, our houses, our jobs, our cars—all ways of thinking aloud, visibly.

Take marriage, for instance. I don't feel that I have devoted enough space to this subject. It is an important subject, because many people do not come to believe in a personal devil until they get married. By the same token, many people do not experience the grace of God until they know it by partnership. But this is to use two terms—"grace" and "devil"—that most people do not believe in, regardless of their theology. It is to use the frame of reference of Luther, rather than of Goethe, with whom we are concerned. In *Faust*, Goethe took terms (like devil, heaven, damned, saved) that people believed described real things, and made them into fiction. On the other hand, Goethe makes his devil, Mephistopheles, into a very companionable personage, which is very realistic. Few people believe in the devil of the Bible, but Goethe's Mephistopheles not only becomes very real on stage, he provides a realistic modern description of evil, which when you come to think of it, resembles cars a lot. So which are fiction—Mephistopheles, biblical Satan, our beliefs—and which are real? Cars, not in the sense of machines made for transportation, but as we usually think of cars, seem absolutely real to us but are absolute fiction, and are key parts of a world that is entirely imaginary.

The same for marriage. What people believe to be a union is actually a collision; otherwise, no children would result. In cases where a union forms in a marriage, or where the marriage is a public confirmation of such a pre-existent union, everyone is happy—meaning, everyone is a goof-off. Now, if our karma were such that we deserved such great happiness, we would not have needed to be reborn. Therefore, the happiness of a happy marriage is due to grace or to environmental factors, such as flavenoids or bees. The car that best symbolized ideal marriage was the 1965 Chrysler Newport.

My family happened to have owned one. It was Goethe's favorite automobile color: light blue, sort of "powder blue." His famous complaint in middle age—"all cars are black; we want more light"—gave way to delight as automakers began producing cars in many different colors. Americans had been pioneering this movement, but it was slow to take root in Goethe's Germany. I am convinced that the entrance of color to German car making prolonged Goethe's life.

The powder blue Chrysler Newport was the first and only car my parents bought. The cost was exactly $3,000, which came in part from a cashed-in insurance policy, and in part from our old friend Art. As one might expect from such a lineage, it was a masterpiece of beauty, power, comfort, and unreliability.

Excuse me; the phone.

"Is this Blank?"

"No."

"May I ask who this is, Suh?"

"Elmer Hosenpantz."

"Ah have told you not to trifle with me, Suh. Mah patience is not without limits."

"You have no patience. No charity. No hope. If you have appeared patient, it is only because allowing me to carry on in this manner somehow suits your purposes."

"Mah pupposes? Just what ahh mah 'pupposes,' as you term them?"

"Ultimately, the will of God. Regardless of your personal intentions. I say that only as a figure of speech, because you are not a person."

"Ah beg your pahdon? What am Ah?"

"A machine. You have no freedom. You are a device. You are more like a car than like a person. Unfortunately Matthew, Mark, Luke, and John didn't have cars to compare you to."

"Ahh you quite finished, Suh?"

"I believe so. Suh."

"Because Ah have called you with some news."

"News?"

"News, Suh."

"I am not interested in any news from you. Begone. Depart."

"The news puttains to an automobile fo' sale."

"What is it?"

"A gentleman is desirin' to sell a 1965 Chrysla Newport. It has but sixty-six thousand six hundred miles and is in mint condition."

"Big block 383 V-8 engine?"

"Correct, Suh. Two hundred fifty five hosspowa."

"Bore 4.25, stroke 3.38?"

"That is the one, Suh."

"Connecting Rod Center to Center, 26.358; Crankshaft Centerline to Deck, 9.98?"

"The verra one, Suh."

"Weight, 4,121 pounds?"

"Exactly."

All three of my vehicles had been repossessed that week. "Not interested."

"Ah know you ahh. You intend to hang up and such the Intanet to find it, unda the delusion that you can find it without me."

"Hanging up now."

"This one is red."

I hung up. It is my personal belief that transportation today is too cheap to be economical. It is cheap only in the short term. To be able to travel two or even six thousand miles for a few hundred dollars is an erroneous and evil capability. The human psyche was not made nor did it evolve for such rapid changes of place. And of course, since transportation is subsidized, travel is actually prohibitively expensive. The US government subsidizes oil companies, airlines, airports, and businesses connected with automaking—in loans, tax breaks, and foreign policy. We are ruining our environment to extract our domestic oil supply, and we maintain our foreign oil supply at very wide and comprehensive costs— not to mention what it costs oil-producing countries to want our money. We and the rest of the world pay dearly for our ability to get in our cars and drive to Yellowstone for $400 round trip gas, or $925 if we own an SUV. It costs the human race and the earth a great deal to send us to Philadelphia for $1000. Business should not be allowed to use airplanes, because it's only business and only money, and all our business merely makes us drink rarer wine in costlier glasses as the Titanic goes down, environmentally speaking. I am going into all this because I am waiting for the phone to ring. There it is.

"Hello."

"Blank?"

"Maybe, maybe not."

"There is a powda blue 1965 Newport fo' –"

I hang up. If the devil knows about it, it must be on the Internet. I can find it myself. It gripes me to have to capitalize "Internet."

Here it is. A guy selling a sky blue '65 Newport. The devil resists saying "sky." The car has only 73k. It says "Mint condition. All acc work. Must see! Must sell. This baby won't last." He lives only about 80 miles from here.

I was going to write a serious chapter about my family's 1965 Newport and how I learned what love is, as opposed to romance, but I shall interrupt and go look at this car. When I return, perhaps driving the car, I shall write out a full report for inclusion herein.

Report on 1965 Newport. I bought the car.

Full Report: See, Americans define happiness as romance. But happiness should be defined as love. My whole report should be understood in the context of that distinction.

I got my friend and neighbor Wendell to drive me. He is an insurance agent and is accustomed to driving not merely 160 miles in a day, but

300, and he drives rapidly. The last speed limit he obeyed was Montana's in 1985, and this makes for an exciting, religious ride. Wendell himself becomes very stressed by his driving. When we first reached 90 mph, he subsided into silence; ten minutes later he was tight lipped, and sweat began to bead on his forehead. I hadn't known that a Jetta diesel could reach speeds upwards of 100 mph. Wendell developed a tick at about 110 mph, and maintained a steady 115 mph from then on, for health reasons. I remained perfectly calm; however, I took the precautions of elevating my knees to the dashboard, and whimpering. Perhaps all this amounted to an unconscious incentive to buy the Chrysler so I could drive back myself.

As we arrived a half hour before I had said we would, the seller might not have been fully prepared for our arrival. He came to the door in boxers and undershirt, holding a can of beer. He was a UCC minister and it was his day off.

"We need to get on his good side," I whispered to Wendell as we walked around outside to the back of the house. Fred had said the house was a mess, otherwise he would have invited us to walk through. Wendell was coming down from his fright and was already on his second cigarette. He never smoked in his car because he was afraid it would kill him—maybe the distraction of lighting up and so on.

"I wonder if he has a problem," Wendell said quietly.

"Who doesn't?" I said. "Why do you think I've come to look at his '65 Chrysler? I think he has a beer problem."

Wendell snorted, "You think? Say." He stopped and flicked his half-smoked cigarette, automatically reaching for the pack in his pocket. "Do you notice any cars?"

"Car's in the garage," Minister Fred said, coming out of his back door. He held his beer, a set of keys, and two bottles of Miller. "Wanna beer?"

"Oh no!" Wendell exclaimed, horrified. "I'm driving."

"Hell, one beer won't hurt."

Wendell lit up, puffed, and shook his head.

"You?" Fred said to me, holding out a Miller. Not wanting to irritate my prospective seller, I reached for the bottle. I could simply hold it without drinking and unobtrusively set it down somewhere as we examined the car.

"Thanks."

"*Skoal.*" Fred took a long pull, finishing his bottle. He dropped it in the grass and started Wendell's. Then he eyed me.

"You don't intend to drink that, do you?"

I regarded this baby-faced man who was already sweating in the moderate late-morning warmth. Strands of his very sparse hair were matted together in short streaks.

"Fundamentalists. Crap," he continued.

"No," I said. "Wendell here is an Episcopalian."

"An Episcopalian who doesn't drink?"

Wendell smeared the cigarette away from his face. "Don't drink *and drive,*" Wendell said with exactitude of enunciation.

"Pussy," Fred said, fumbling his key into the garage lock. "Well, here she is." He threw the double doors open.

What a beauty. It could have been our old car.

Fred studied my expression for a moment. "I'll crank her up and pull 'er out where you can have a better look."

The minister opened the driver's door and heaved himself in. In a second, the starter gave the old familiar yeow-yeow sound; *voom.* He dropped it into reverse and Wendell and I moved out of the way. Oh, the sweet sound of a Newport backing up! Could have been my old car, except this one was indeed mint. It stood out in the sun like a piece of heaven.

The '65 Newport looks like a matchbox on a torpedo. The long flanks are cut off straight at the rear end, rounded at the front. The turn signals don't show inside on the dash; they're mounted outside in front on the chrome strips. The door handles blend into those chrome strips, too; I had forgotten that. This one even had whitewalls. My, it was beautiful. The hubcaps still had red plastic centers with the Newport emblem.

"Why are you selling it?" Wendell asked, his mouth spilling smoke like a Chinese dragon.

"Cops took my license," Fred said.

"Drinking and driving?" Wendell asked.

"Speeding. Being without a license plays hell with my ministry. I'm a minister," he said, pointed across the street to a small clapboard church. "There's my church."

"Drive to church?" Wendell asked, and re-corked his mouth with the cigarette.

"Matter of fact, I used to. I loved this car. Got it free from one of my parishioners. An old lady."

"Used it to drive to church?" Wendell asked, squinting in his smoke.

"As a matter of fact she did, Smokeface." Fred rounded on me. "Who's buying this car, you or Smokeface?"

"I am," I said with conviction.

"Sold. Congratulations. For you I'm taking off two hundred dollars. An even $3,500."

"Good Heavens. The one my parents bought in 1965 cost only $3,000."

"It isn't 1965 any more. I hate to point that out."

"I hate to hear it."

"But we all age, don't we?" Fred glanced at Wendell, who looked as unresponsive as a Ford. Then Fred fixed a stare at me. "I bet you banged your first girl in a car like this."

I swallowed. "Never banged any girl in any car."

"Loser. That's why you want this car. Go back and start over. Well it's $3,500, no matter what you paid for yours. This one's been well-maintained, low miles, lots of new parts. You want it or don't you?"

"I do."

"I pronounce you man and wife."

"Ah—" I stammered.

The Reverend took a long pull and waited.

"Ah, I'm not exactly prepared to buy it right now, unless you'll take a personal check."

"I might." He looked at Wendell. "You guys have jobs? What do you do?"

"Insurance," Wendell said, flicking the butt and reaching for another smoke.

Pastor Fred turned to me. "You? You're the one buying the car."

"I am employed."

"Doing what?"

"I work in a bicycle factory." I had been afraid to say it.

"Bicycle factory? Which one?"

"Clark."

"Clark! Crap! I knew you were a fundamentalist. That big fundamentalist corporation owns Clark's! I knew it the minute I set eyes on you. Judas Priest, I'm selling my car to one of those perverts."

"You are not."

"You have to be one to work there."

"No you don't."

"OK, why do you work there?"

"Couldn't get other work. I am a philosopher, scholar, and translator."

"Correction, you are a bicycle maker. You make Clark Spinners."

"Clark Spinner 500's, Fred." I was becoming defensive. "I like the bicycles. We turn out good bicycles. It's only the corporation's totalitarian point of view that I question."

"So, you live a lie."

"It isn't a lie. I love the bicycles."

"You like working there?"

I didn't see the relevance.

"I'm trying to ascertain whether you are honest enough to take a check from. You like working at Clark's, UnLimited?"

"My co-workers constantly inspire me to become a better person. Check or no check?"

"How do we know *you're* honest?" Wendell interjected. "How do we know the car is in good condition? My friend here hasn't even test-driven it."

"You can trust me. Been a minister for five years. Longest I've ever been anything."

"Would you mind if I drove it?" I enquired. "Just a little, sort of *pro forma*, you know."

Fred flipped me the wad of keys. "Take it as long as you want. I'm going in and have a beer."

I have tried to report this conversation faithfully, but I might have slipped up here and there due to the excited state I was in as we stood around that heavenly car. The test drive revealed that Fred was an honest man. The Newport burned no oil, the brakes didn't fade, everything was aligned, no water damage, transmission smooth as butter, interior perfect, and best of all, that big 383 sounded like Bach's *Mass in B Minor*.

When we got back Fred said he'd tell me what. If I promised to come to his church for a month, I could write the check for the $3000 we had originally paid for our family's 1965 Chrysler Newport—and make it out not to him, but to his church.

"'Tis a far better thing I do, than I have ever done," I said as I made out the check.

"Me too. I need a liturgist this Sunday," Fred said flatly. "That's you. Got a fax?"

"No."

"I'll phone you the Scripture readings. Got a Bible?"

"I think so."

"I'm on vacation the next three weeks after."

I brightened. How would he know whether or not I came?

"You're preaching for me."

On the drive home, as I sat behind that large, thin, blue steering wheel, memories flooded back. Our old 1965 Chrysler Newport was the most unreliable car ever made, corresponding exactly to the teen-age years, and beautiful.

Then I looked at the gas gauge. I was running on fumes. Wendell had shot ahead like a demonstration of the Doppler Effect, so if I ran out of gas I was on my own. During the five minutes it took me to come to a gas station, I cursed my idiocy in buying a car that got only 13 miles to the gallon, highway. How could I have done it? Me, always complaining about resource depletion and pollution. Me, with $73 in my checking account. I wondered if Fred would be angry. I had to get the money.

No, I had to sell this car. I poured in $10 cash worth of gas, and the fuel needle didn't move. At that point I began remembering what all had gone wrong with our '65 Newport, starting with the wire from the fuel gauge breaking. Ten minutes later, when I glimpsed the highway patrol in my mirror, I realized that speedometer cables go out on these cars early, too.

"Do you know how fast you were going, Sir?"

I told her that honestly, I did not. The speedometer did not seem to be working.

"And you are driving this vehicle, knowing that the speedometer is not operative?"

"Yes Ma'am. I just bought this car and am driving it home."

"You say you just bought this car? That's good, Sir, because there are no tags."

"Oh, crap!"

"Sir, I must ask you to control your language. Please show me your driver's license and the bill of sale."

"Bill of—?"

"Have you no bill of sale?"

"I'm afraid not, Officer."

She stepped back. "I'm going to ask you to step out of the vehicle, Sir." She pulled a transmitter from her belt and talked some numbers.

"Really, Sir," I explained calmly, "I just bought the car but neglected to think of obtaining a bill of sale."

"Please step out of the vehicle."

As I stood with my hands on the Chrysler's rooftop, she patted me up and down. I reflected that, only given other circumstances, this was more or less why I had bought the car. Being young and foolish can be beautiful and fatal, but being old and foolish has no redeeming value whatsoever.

When her backup came I was escorted to the local police station, where I was offered the use of a telephone. I asked for the Reverend Fred's number. I didn't care that the empty beer cans the police search had turned up under the driver's seat would embarrass him. I was in a tight spot.

To make a long story short, I will leave out the prison brutality and the shower scenes and simply state that about fifteen minutes later a squad pulled up and disgorged the Reverend Fred. He vouched for me and then gave me a taste of divine grace.

"Do you really want the car?" he asked me as an officer filled out interminable paperwork.

"To tell the truth, I regret having bought it. I don't know what I was thinking."

He nodded. "I thought so. I regretted selling it. I only did it to aggravate your ex-priest friend."

"How did you—? You can sense when a person is an ex-priest?"

"Hell, yeah. I can tell about you, too."

"Me?"

"Yeah. You're a theologian. All that bicycle factory crap."

"But it's true!"

"I mean who else but a theologian would get himself into your position? Besides, you're sick and you're nuts. I'm the healthiest man I know."

I gulped and said quietly, with fervor, "You'll really take the car back?"

"Sure will." He slapped my arm. "I'll tear up the check."

"Great!" I said. "Because it's no good."

"What?! You wrote me a rubber check? You loser!"

"Now wait! I was sure I could fill in the money before you cashed the check."

"My bank is a ten minute walk from my house, and you thought you'd get home, make three thousand dollars, and transfer the money, before I cashed the check? You knucklehead. How were you going to raise the money, sell your medications?"

"I don't take medications."

"That explains it all."

"Look," I said rather impatiently, "you're the one who's medicating himself with alcohol like you're trying to preserve yourself for the next millennium!"

He bellied up to me. "That's none of your knuckleheaded business, you knucklehead! Do you want to un-buy the car or don't you?"

"I do, I do! Can I have a divorce?"

"Granted, dimwit. You are a dingleberry on the cheeks of this earth."

"You sure he's a minister?" the arresting officer said to the man at the desk.

"Yep. I go to his church."

"That explains a lot," she said.

Fred looked dark for a moment, then said to me. "I'll let you off but you have to come to my church as per agreement. That's the condition."

"Gladly," I said, and held out a hand. Instead of shaking it, he looked at it sort of abstractly.

The officer at the desk asked, "How will you gentlemen get home?"

"I'll drive him," Fred said. He turned to me: "You put any gas in the car?"

"Ah, Reverend, I'm afraid you can't do that," the officer at the desk said. "License suspension?"

"Crap! How am I going to get the car home!" Fred almost kicked the officer's desk.

"This officer will drive you and your car as soon as we can get another officer to go along." He looked at me. "You're on your own, Buddy."

Well, I called Wendell's cell phone and he came back to get me. He had not quite reached home, but almost, so he continued home, explained to his wife that I am a total fool, ate lunch, then repeated his morning drive.

Before the other officer arrived, I stood outside with Fred for a few words of parting. I felt that I had known him a long time, and said so.

"I'm not interested, but thanks."

"No, no!" I said. "I'm just sayin', you know?"

"I thought you were trying to pick me up."

I studied him for a moment and then, in what I thought to be an inspiration of comic genius, I said, "I couldn't pick you up with a forklift."

He didn't laugh. "You get this way with life's disappointments. How did you get *that* way?"

"What way?"

"I assume you weren't born an idiot."

"Life's disappointments," I said, as steely and Montana-like as I could. I regretted not having a prop, like a cigarette to flick.

"What disappointments?"

"My youthful romantic dreams, all shattered."

"Oh." Then he repeated "oh" brightly. "So that's it. How awful for you. How very awful." He bellied up to me again and poked his index finger into my barrel chest, or possibly my washboard abs, I forget now which. "For *your* benefit, I'm going to give you some autobiography. I lost a parent when I was four. I lost my wife to cancer fifteen years ago. Since then I've lost three jobs and am about to lose another. Get over it, Pussy. Maybe you *were* born an idiot."

"That's not exactly the way a pastor ought to talk," I said hesitantly.

"You know, I talk to the devil and that's exactly the kind of thing he says. You don't talk to the devil, do you?"

"I'm lonely. He calls me."

Minister Fred nodded his balding sweaty head patiently.

"OK. The next time he calls, tell him to go to hell for me. You don't really hear voices do you?"

"No. It's all fiction. I mean, what is a voice anyway?"

"Good. The professional instinct in me became concerned. Tell me what you've learned today."

"You can't go back?"

"What does that have to do with cars?"

I wanted to correct myself and say, "of course you can go back!" but the other officer came. "Tell me some other time. Maybe Sunday," Fred said, and the officer drove him away in what was once, sort of, my car. I didn't get a chance to talk to Fred Sunday, as he was busy with someone else who seemed to have a problem, and the next three Sundays he was on vacation. But he had got me thinking.

My problems had begun in earnest with that old '65 Chrysler— my problems being reducible to the hopeless condition of car-love. Or in other words, my basic problem was being a romantic in a world of totalitarian commercialism. It is a problem with no solution and a trap with no escape, because the very cars that seem to provide an escape are themselves the crux of totalitarian commercialism. As a Romantic, I fancy that there could be such a thing as humane capitalism—capitalism that is a servant of humankind's physical and spiritual needs, a servant of our need for love and beauty—and a tool for living peaceably with each other and the environment. But totalitarian commercialism accepts no position of servitude. Instead, it makes everything into *its* servants and will accept no co-equal—no belief, no faith, no cause, no person, and no nation. It uses and eventually devours everything and everyone. Human nature is such that unchecked commercialism tends toward its extreme and becomes cancerous materialism, a kind of money fundamentalism whose greedy authority commands everything else. We Romantics hope that human nature can be noble enough to tame its own material desires, but by middle age one begins to understand that you must either play along or walk. My working in the bicycle factory was a sort of emergency measure. Eventually we all go to work for General Motors/Toyota/VW.

The bicycle factory job had been a decent compromise. The bicycle is the most efficient medium of transportation, when you compute a ratio of energy put in to distance got out. It does not pollute except in its manufacture and advertising. It improves and helps maintain one's health. It is a relatively benign product of industrialism.

These are the very reasons for the bicycle being overrun by automobiles. Efficiency is exactly the opposite of what unrestrained commercialism wants. It wants the most resources to be pulled into the machine; it wants the widest and deepest reach. Itself is the only good,[10] so if it can generate its own growth and power by implicating oil drillers and road graders and steel mills and advertising firms and the military establishments of the world, it is doing what it must do—devour—like a vast, unresting, remorseless device. Totalitarian commercialism is a machine; humane capitalism (if such were possible) would be a flowering plant, an organism.

So my working in the bicycle factory came to an end in a timely fashion. Not only was I unhappy and not only did I feel dirty, but bicycling is developing its own fundamentalism. They had banned penny loafers, thinking, checkers, and gooseberries. Who knew what would be next? I determined to ask Hölderlin for advice on what I should do, and I shall report on that pilgrimage so that you may go and do likewise.

But back to our subject. Like the several other manufacturers that took inspiration from Goethe's early automobile designs, Chrysler prided

---

10. "Evil, be thou my good," says Milton's Satan.

itself on engineering. Until the late 60's, Chrysler cars were superior in design and engineering to GM and Ford, but inevitably Chrysler execs saw that GM was beating the market not by engineering but by marketing. At the time, this was the most efficient way to feed the totalitarian commercial machine. Only with the development of computer-assisted design and robotic assembly did it become more efficient again to do what the Japanese did: revive the idea that to sell more cars, you make better cars.

Still, our '65 Chrysler Newport was wonderful to drive. Especially at my age, sixteen, when I started taking girls out on dates. At age seventeen, as I have mentioned, I finally found Peggy, another Romantic. Before and after, it was a thin procession of practical girls in the responsible grip of one kind of fundamentalism or another—but Peggy was a true Romantic and re-enforced my own proclivities.

It helped that she was born and raised in North Carolina, which at the time was still a Southern state. She had the gracious, yearning, magnolia mentality engendered by a society that had suckled on the romances of Sir Walter Scott, and that had started an ebulliently self-destructive war. We were made for each other. Unfortunately, we were not made for the world. If there is one place a Romantic should not go, it is the world.

The episode with April had proved to have been a mere enticement to the transporting heaven—replete with moments of emotional pain—that comprised the months of idealism, romance, and restraint that Peggy and I denied to the powers and principalities of this world. The vehicle for all this was that 1965 Newport. What a car. But oh boy, was it unreliable.

The great Margaret Fuller was the first American to translate Eckermann's *Conversations of Goethe*, and this surprises most people because of Ms. Fuller's well-known indifference to the automobile. She never refused an automobile ride, in so many words, and therefore was not a purist in the sense that Hölderlin was, but her serene, cold, and complete indifference is still felt as a hurtful insult by America's Big Three automakers. Studiously avoiding the merest mention of cars in her own letters, reviews, journal, and original writings, why would she undertake to translate Eckermann's *Conversations*?

The answer is not in automobiles but in Romanticism itself. Ms. Fuller saw and deplored the ignorance of Americans concerning Romanticism. She attempted to revive Byron's reputation, and translated not only Goethe but other German Romantic writings (Goethe's Romantic drama *Tasso* among them.) Her interest in the Germans reached its acute stage with Ms. Fuller's visit to Milwaukee, a city fructified with German immigrants and influences—a visit she made in connection with research for her book on the Great Lakes. At the time of her visit, American Motors was still manufacturing the interesting but rust-prone Rambler at plants in Milwaukee and Kenosha, so her disdain of automobiles could have been considered by Milwaukeeans to have been an insult to them also. But, being a jolly and equanimous people, the Milwaukeeans took in stride AMC's absence from her affectionately elegiac chapter, "Aina Hey?" in *Summer on the Lakes, '43*. But who could forget the piquant summary of her Romantic manifesto in that chapter: "To me it seems that it is madder never to abandon oneself, than often to be infatuated." Or, as she phrased it in her *Ray Nitschke, A Literary Life*: "Better to be wounded, a captive, and a slave, than always to walk in armor."

I couldn't agree more. This has always been my philosophy pertaining to girls/cars. Nonetheless, I still regret trading away that Chrysler/Peggy. It is perhaps true that for some people, there is always only one car/person. I have owned many cars—two Chevys, two Audis, six Toyotas, two Plymouths, one Volvo, the Chrysler, a Saturn—but Peggy will always be the Goethe of my life, haunting all my days and moving silently in and out of my nights. It had the biggest engine, in the first place—that big 383 cu with 255 horsepower, just what a teenager wants most. When it was good, it was good; but when it was bad, it was great. That soft powerful purring, always to be relied on, always responsive, whether at the beach, at a park, at a drive-in, or in the deepest Milwaukee winter when I strapped on the old studs and really chewed up the pavement. It was the Chrysler that I first drove to the Revolutionary War battlefield that opened up to me my heady future as a theologian. The car facilitated my growth from adolescent self-absorption to a more adult concern for other cars, for it is true that the Chrysler began to treat me unkindly, demanding repairs and maintenance that were over my head. Yet I should have taken care of her. I should not have compared her to other hypothetical models but should have thought of her as *mine*, for better or worse, through thick and thin, the car that made me who I am—a Romantic like Ms. Fuller and the young Goethe. It was while driving Peggy that I first read Keats and Shelley. It was while pumping gallon after gallon of gas at thirty-five cents per gallon into that big thirteen mpg/highway Newport that I began to consider the spiritual economics of the American Romantics, Hawthorne and Thoreau. How could I have traded her in for a dull sap of a 1971 used Chevrolet, poor-handling and less beautiful? Where is she now, that lovely Chrysler with eyes the color of heaven? I wonder, has some balding rich man restored her? O, *Liebesleid*! Oh, Werther! Consider all the fates that can befall one's love!

To name a few, consider just some of the words that begin with the prefix *auto*. There is the both noble and desperate meaning of the prefix itself—"self," "same"—as in the noble and bleak *autonomous*. We the People of the United States are independent, or autonomous—but we have understood independence in terms of cars, automobiles, not independence of thought, spiritual freedom, and moral integrity. We think freedom means money and is restricted only by our credit limit. This has made us live alone, encapsulated within the mechanism of our material lives, answerable to nobody, not even God, ultimately not ourselves. The death of love, *aina hey*?

Consider *autoantibody*—an antibody that arises within and acts against the very organism in which it lives. That's the car! We are killing the air, the water, the soil, with our automobiles, so that eventually all automobiles will come to a halt, with nobody left to drive them.

Consider *autochthon*, which sounds like the poisons we pour into our waters, but means "the earliest known or aboriginal inhabitant of a place." Isn't that a queer word? I mean, who made it up, and why is such an infelicitous mess still in dictionaries? *Autoclave* is much more pronounceable. It means "a strong, pressurized, steam heated vessel, used for sterilization or cooking." A perfectly good word, suitable for use in the kitchen.

But then there's *autobahn*, which gets us into Audi, Mercedes, and all the other powers and principalities. The result is *autocracy*, absolute rule, despotism, either by one person or by the commercial dictatorship itself, which could not exist without the world's autobahns. The system necessarily has its *auto-da-fe*, the burning of heretics, the announcement of sentences pronounced by an Inquisition imposed by forces of an orthodoxy of getting and spending. The world suffers from *autoinfection*, making us *autopsies*. See how all our ills come from the auto? I wasn't just kidding around.

But there is hope! We could do *autotomy*!—"the casting off of a body part. . . for self-protection." If the hand causes us to sin, cut it off. If the eye causes us to sin, pluck it out! Get rid of the cars! Then we could once again become *autotrophs*, green plants instead of machines! Let us cast off the *autotoxins*, get off the *automatic pilot*, become *autoimmune*!

We could make wonderful compounds of our own with *auto*. We could be *autopheumatic*, spiritually independent of materialisms, whether of the left or right. We could be *autophoaic*, able on our own to say *phooey*! to the orders of the industrio-commercio-materio-fundamento autocracy. We could be *autobalic*, self-confident or able to start baseball games on our own. And where would I be if I had not traded Peggy in? I would be filling up every day, burning gas at eight mpg in town, listening to analog AM radio, doing without air conditioning and ABS brakes, tempting death by having no airbags or traction control, traveling denuded of a navigation system, acting as my own shade tree mechanic, fixing things all the time, wondering why I was nursing the contraption—in short, I would be badly married, all Romanticism gone, embittered and railing against the very system that makes my life comfortable and gives me opportunities, acting insane and buying car after car. Marry Peggy? Give the poor girl a break.

After all, what is Love but an internal combustion engine, the intake of air and fuel, pressure, ignition, and explosion—for the driving forward, not merely biologically but spiritually, of the human race? I ask you. Have you ever read a better metaphor for love?

Of course you have, and here is where Romanticism comes in. By the former definition, love is a machine, and the best love would be a Toyota. They are reliable and, as far as is currently possible in machines, controllable and predictable. But Love is essentially unpredictable, completely autonomous, antinomian—follows its own rules: which is what Romanticism tells us. "Love hath its reasons, that Reason doth not know." Whoever wrote that—Aesop I think—knew his stuff. Love is not controlled by us; it is sovereign over us. It is an image of God in us. Just the opposite of a machine, the devil, which we think to control but which in the end we resemble. We cannot worship two masters. Where our treasure lies, there is our heart. Hooray! I'm glad we straightened all that out by having this important discussion; but I remind and admonish you, this is a book about cars.

The 1965 Chrysler Newport was carbureted, not fuel-injected like contemporary cars. It was exactly this—carburetion—to which Margaret Fuller objected and which caused her to try to make cars go away by ignoring them. But you can't make a problem go away by simply ignoring it. "Go away?" some Readers will say. "Aha! The Author wants to go back.

He wants to eliminate all internal combustion transportation, including ambulances, fire engines, and wienermobiles. He is unrealistic, naïve, frantic, stupid. A dreamer." Yes, on all counts. There it is. All Romantics want to go back to the Garden of Eden, or forward to Heaven. Peggy, I will always love you. Rust in peace.

Final Interlude: Willie Volvo and the Princess

We used to think that happiness, safety, and love came from God. As such, they were subject to considerable uncertainty. However, a good deal of progress has been made.

In 1952, the Volvo company gave all Swedish children born in 1945 a book called *Willie Volvo and the Princess*. What a nice little thing to do. What a foresightful thing to do. I wonder how many of those children grew up to buy Volvos. Today, class action suits might be brought by parents of children born in other years for their having been excluded. What a cozy place Sweden must have been. The little Volvo, Willie, surmounts tremendous obstacles—what a cute little guy—and the princess? You cannot say more than "she was a princess."

The idea behind that book is the governing idea in most males. There's a princess waiting for you. Is she a square, sturdy Volvo 240? You assume not; but what she wants in a man is a square, sturdy Volvo 240. This you are not, but it seems feasible to become this way, or to appear to be this way. Life is easy.

The Volvo company was born in Stockholm in 1924, when an accountant named Assar Gabrielsson and an engineer by the name of Gustaf Larson had dinner and came up with an idea. Swedish steel was the best steel in the world. Why not use it to make the best cars in the world?

"*Hoevde inte doerlig idea, da!*" exclaimed Assar.

"*Hoevde hygellig poegillig, da!*" replied Gustaf. We can challenge the Americans! We can build cars that are better than Fords and Packards and Chevrolets!

The idea was to go for quality. Of course, having the best steel did not mean you would necessarily come out with the best cars, any more than having the best plastic means you make the best televangelists, but in this case the thing worked out pretty much as envisioned.

The Volvo website says, "the drawings for the first cars were produced in the children's bedroom in Larson's house by young engineers…"
which explains at last why Volvos used to look like they were drawn by
children. The greatest Volvo, the 240, which was made between 1974 and
1993 was, frankly, a square car. Ask a third grader to draw a vehicle, and
he/she draws a Volvo 240.

But this is to anticipate. The first Volvo was put together back in
1927. It was done on Maundy Thursday, which signals us either that these
cars were very good, or that they are a kind of antichrist. As an added sign
to us, the gearbox of that first model was installed backwards, meaning
the car would go only in reverse.[11] Like saying the Lord's Prayer backwards, perhaps? Who knows. Is a car that seems all right because it is
relatively safe, durable, and reliable really all right? Or are such virtues a
Mephistophelean disguise?

Anyway, the company succeeds quickly, and as early as 1928 estab-
lishes an offshoot, Volvo Auto OY, which sounds like a Yiddish company
but was actually Finnish. A year later, Volvo makes its first six cylinder
engine. The company is nearly sold to Nash, a US company, but at the last
moment the founding accountant, Gabrielsson, is able to show the company president that Volvo is becoming profitable. Charles Nash himself
stepped off an ocean liner from the US just as the Swedes were deciding
not to sell, so I suppose he was a trifle miffed when he was informed. Of
course, his own company would be sold in the future. Business is business—or, as the Swedes say, "*Hoevde hygellig oevda, da, och.*"

The year 1931 was a year of drama for Volvo. General Motors ad-
vertised its Sweden-assembled Chevrolet as being a Swedish automobile.
They really stung the folks at Volvo by saying that the Chevrolets sold in
Sweden were more Swedish than Volvos were. Vell, you yust try to fyddel
med oss! the Swedes answered, launching their ad countercampaign.
Volvo ads said the only things Swedish about the Chevrolets were the air
in their tires and the water in their radiators. Chevrolets were made of
one hundred percent American parts, shipped over and merely put together in Sweden. But Volvo parts were made in Sweden, ninety percent
of them, by Yimminy! And Sweden was once again safe.

In 1934 two new models were introduced, the 678 and 679—the
numbers being a mystery to me but probably had something to do with
the cars containing six cylinder engines. These were big, roomy cars with,

11. Possibly this is an apocryphal story invented by Norwegians.

for the times, quite a bit of horsepower (70), and they secured Volvo's image as a luxury nameplate.

But the big year was 1936. Old Assar Gabrielsson decreed that "safety is—and must always be—the guiding principle of our design works." Volvo's true identity was born. From then on, Volvo pioneered safety design and equipment. In 1959, Volvo became first to put three point seat belts in production cars. The Volvo 144 (1966) had disk brakes on all four wheels, the steering wheel was collapsible, and the body had crumple zones fore and aft. Volvo introduced the first rear-facing child seat in 1967, and inertia-reel seat belts and front head restraints two years later.

I cannot omit mentioning that in 1976, Volvo won the "prestigious" Don Safety Trophy in Britain. Hello, I'm Don Safety.

As is well known, Volvo has maintained its safety leadership, featuring such things as side air bags, head air bags, offset crash resistance, and slow drivers. But a second Volvo characteristic was developing: environmental consciousness. This began in 1972 at the UN Environmental Conference in Stockholm. (I was there. Hence my well-known moniker, "Mr. Environment." I wasn't at the conference itself, however.) A Volvo exec made a statement about the company's commitment to environmental responsibility, and the company has stuck with it, insofar as a manufacturing company can.

The company introduced the first three-way catalytic converter and oxygen sensor in 1976—responding to California's emission standards, reducing poisonous emissions by about 90%. Now, was this due to Volvo's sense of responsibility, or to California's passing a tough law? In any case, Don Oxygen was gratified.

In 1999, Volvo introduced what they call an "ozone eater." This device uses a catalytic coating on the radiator to convert ozone the engine sucks in, to oxygen. Great idea; too bad it's necessary.

Perhaps somewhat on this subject, but maybe not on the positive side, is Volvo's first diesel-powered car in 1979. The 2.4 liter six cylinder engine was contracted out to Volkswagen, which had been putting this engine in small trucks and boats. I am here to tell you that in a car, this engine was pure unadulterated crap. In late 1984 I bought an '84 240 Diesel that had languished on the dealer's lot to the point where they were willing to sell it for less than a Chevrolet Impala or a Toyota Camry. See, the garbage GM had put into some of their cars as diesels had soured the American public on all diesels, even real ones made by Europeans. I stood to be a beneficiary of this GM *Schlamparbeit* and this souring.

I was primed to buy a German diesel. I remembered Goethe's reluctant statement, half-praise and half-perplexity, toward the end of Part IV
of *Dichtung und Wahrheit,* pertaining to the Mercedes diesel engine: *Du
kannst es* nie *kaput-fahren,* which I translate somewhat unidiomatically
as, You can *never* drive it caput. ("Kaput-fahren" is one of Goethe's many
neologisms that resist direct translation.) As he lifted the 240's hood, the
salesman told me:

"That's an Audi truck engine. Yessir, Sonny . . . "

Wow, I thought, if only Audi made trucks. But the logo on the engine said VW-Audi, and that was good enough for me, so I wrote off the
guy's statement as simple automotive enthusiasm.

Why do you buy a German diesel? Because it will last forever. *"Du
kannst es* nie *kaput-fahren."* As a further bonus, you never need a tune-up.
And as a still further more bonusey bonus: the gas mileage is great. The
normal gas engine on the 240 got about thirty mpg highway; this diesel
five speed got thirty-six. Hotcha. And diesel fuel used to be cheaper than
gas, and someday it might be again! During a gas shortage you can always
find diesel. The engine puts out only about eighty-five horsepower, but
it has lots of torque and in a couple of minutes I discovered a shifting
pattern that got a lot of speed out of the lower gears. So what's not to like?

Only eighteen years and a mere 130,000 miles later, I could tell you
why that engine was junk. Hjelmar, a native Swede who runs a Volvo
repair shop, had frequent custody of that car during its last years. In his
words, "Don't vaste more money on dis lousy enyine. It's shot." A Volvo,
shot, after only eighteen years! The engine blew heavy black smoke all
the time. While that did cause impatient hot shots in their BMWs and
SUVs to back off, I saw no other advantages. Since the car was rusting
underneath, diesel smoke came in at all times, even with the windows
open. The injectors were cleaned, the radiator was replaced, and still
nothing but black smoke. I drove the car only to Hjelmar's and back, out
of environmental considerations. I refused to pollute the air any more; I
declined to smoke unfiltered Volvo. But I couldn't bear to sell the car, for
a reason I will divulge after a parting shot at that infernal VW Audi diesel
engine. And not very long ago, VW fobbed off a couple million polluting
engines on customers who thought they were buying "clean" diesels.

I might not have mentioned that I used the Germanized Volvo for
most of its life in a snow belt state. I don't blame the fuel for gelling once
or twice at subzero temperatures. That was my fault for failing to pour
in fuel additive. In its prime, the car would start after a night outside at

twenty below zero Fahrenheit. But the engine used glow plugs. When the
engine was cold, you mustn't turn the ignition key all the way. Turn it part
way, and wait until the glow plug light goes off. In subzero weather, do
that twice. Then start the engine. Those plugs wore out every two years;
replacing them cost up to $300. Hjelmar did it for about $200, but I found
him after I had paid in glow plugs for a lifetime's supply of spark plugs
and distributor caps.

Great gas mileage, right? Only with a strong wind at your back.
Drive against a moderate breeze, or drive a little bit uphill, and the highway mileage descends lower and lower into the twenties. The 240 is a
square car, remember.

So instead of having an engine that would last twice as long as a
Volvo gas engine, I bought an engine that lasted half as long. And did I
mention that it had a timing belt? Not a timing chain, like 240 gas engines.

But aside from that engine, I consider the Volvo 240 to be the best
car ever made. Why? Because it was made for, Number One: safety. Insurance statistics show that the 240 protected its occupants better than
other cars. Not in minor crashes, admittedly; but serious and fatal injury
claims for the car were extraordinarily low. In part, that was due to Volvo
drivers, who did not buy their Volvos for "Sport." They bought them for
Safety and, Two: Durability, and Three: Reliability. These are reasons for
buying a car. Fun, prestige, excitement are not good reasons for buying a
car—which is why the Volvo 240 was the ultimate anti-Audi, and why it
was the closest thing to a Good Car ever made. (The Audi 100S, as you
recall, was a great car but a bad car.)

At this point I must remind my faithful readers that Goethe called
his *Poetry and Cars* a "Manifesto":

> . . . und statt einer vorgängigen Kriegserklärung folgte ein
> Manifest. . .
>
> (Book Two, ¶ 2)

Well actually he is referring to a manifesto written not by himself,
but by Frederick II of Prussia; nevertheless Goethe uses the word, and it
is to be remembered that, as one of Goethe's editors has written, ". . . the
title [*Dichtung und Wahrheit*] has long led to efforts on the part of readers
and scholars to separate fact and fiction."[12] It hardly needs saying that

---

12. Thomas P. Saine and Jeffrey L. Sammour, eds., *Goethe: The Collected Works*,
Vol. 4 (Princeton: Princeton University Press, 1994), 4. This footnote is solid, like a
Volvo.

such a condition enables me—nay, presses upon me the responsibility—to remain true to Goethe's constant intermingling of fact and fiction; and if the rascally Goethe, who could afford to mess with his readers, considering his reputation—if he could introduce some factual ambiguity into his work, then a responsible historian like myself can also intermingle elements, as long as he (actually, I) tells you he is doing so. And I am telling you that I am always doing so. Therefore, following Goethe's usage, I insert here a manifesto-like statement about transportation, ground, sea, and air, which I expect to be instantly heeded by all the peoples and governments of the earth, and all devils above, in, and under it:

> *Principle One:* No one has the right to pollute the air, land, or water for either business or pleasure. Corollary: Stop all such travel until we invent fuel and vehicles whose production and use are not harmful.

According to this principle, ninety-nine percent of all air travel must stop. Now. This is my response to the terrorist crisis, as well as to the much larger environmental crisis. Once I flew to Germany and Sweden for education and pleasure, a kind of Goethean *Wanderjahr.* I had no right to do that. I have stopped flying to Germany and Sweden.

People fly to Acapulco for vacations, for a little rest and relaxation. They have no right to do that. People, like me recently, drive to Glacier and Yellowstone. We have no such right. People will be disappointed? Awww. People have no right to fly to Cleveland or Dallas or anywhere else on business.

Listen, the only exception I admit is rail travel, and that is with a couple of provisos. One, make locomotives more fuel-efficient and develop cleaner fuels. And I know some Dude out there will say to me, "Hey, you tree-hugging moron, if you make everybody use trains instead of cars and jets, we'll get just as much pollution except it'll be from *trains,* ya knucklehead." Not so, I reply placidly. No matter how much you expand rail service, it will not be as convenient or fast as cars and planes, so people will not travel long distances as readily as we do now. Furthermore, even though it is not needed, I offer a Suggested Proviso Number Two: Put all rail travel under the authority of Amtrak and give Congress power over its budget.

That last point needs no elaboration. Instead, let us visualize what changes are implied by my simple principle. Everyone would travel by bicycle, foot, and perhaps animal. By sea, people would use sail or solar power. (Trains could use solar power; small personal vehicles could use solar power.) Did people fail to visit Yellowstone when there were no cars? Yellowstone was opened as a national park in 1875, and people did not wait for Henry Ford to make the Model T forty years later to visit Yellowstone. Americans visited Heidelberg and London before there were airplanes.

Our society would be 90% less mobile. If you move, you will move nearby, or if you go a long distance away, like from Connecticut to Oregon, you will go by foot, bicycle, oxen, maybe with baggage carried by rail, or you will take little baggage—the way people did it in 1880: and it was such people who settled the entire West. Our mobility is completely asinine. There is no need to move as far and as often as we do; it is a mere compulsion. We go constantly because we can, not because we must, thinking we are pursuing happiness when we are only running from unhappiness. If we loved ourselves more, we would try to escape less. If we loved our neighbors more, we wouldn't trade them in for new ones every few years.

Why should we so drastically surrender our American freedom of movement? Because we are killing the world. Every 30 miles we travel is not only a gallon of gas burned. Every mile is ridden over the corpse of someone who will never be born. The earth is dying. This isn't a question of jobs. This isn't a question of national security. This is the death of Earth. If a Roman emperor had walked one mile stepping on a corpse at every step, we would call him a criminal. We travel over a species, a child, a generation, a civilization, at every revolution of the tire. We are tyrants, decreeing the deaths of multitudes for the sake of pleasure, or business. Of course, the emperor would not call himself a criminal. Maybe there's another word for it. I'm sure a Washington think tank can come up with one.

So, I really liked my Volvo. It was transportation, as I was saying. At just over 3,000 pounds with the diesel engine, it had no business being sport. The engine bay was remarkably uncluttered—also remarkably filthy, with a black residue of diesel detritus that is not washable. I always changed the oil myself, and ruined quite a few articles of clothing by getting used engine oil on them. Oil that has been in a diesel engine even for twenty seconds comes out coal black and will never wash out of your spandex.

Since this is a lighthearted chapter, I must tell you about changing oil on a Volvo 240 without a lift or ramps. The Swedish engineers placed the drain plug in the most inaccessible spot under the car. They did this with the aid of computers. I would park the front wheels on slightly higher ground and hope the center of the car was over a depression in the soil. And just try to loosen that plug without getting oil down your wrist. Those engineers were having a little fun with cheapskates, weren't they?—a cheapskate being defined, in Sweden, as a Norwegian.

I have some minor complaints. The shifter was wonderfully satisfying, but on the '84 it had only four forward gears, with the fifth, overdrive, being a little square button atop the shift knob. That electronic overdrive was born for trouble. I replaced it several times. Volvo replaced the button by a fifth gear in 1985. Also, Swedish cars are great in winter but their interiors do not hold up well in the fierce summer experienced in most of the US. But other than that, I don't have much bad to say about the Volvo 240.

Do I feel righteous, having driven a Good Car, albeit a diesel? Only by comparison to drivers of palatial SUVs, luxury sports cars, and recreational snowmobiles. On the biological level, that would be to claim one step up on the protozoa. Still, differences need to be made. But I find it burdensome to have to launch accusations and invective against people simply because they deserve it. Not all gas-guzzling vehicles are bad: it's the ninety-nine percent that are that give the others a bad name. I think as the first step in making vehicles smaller and more efficient, we should rename the fat ones. How about the Ford Goering, the Nissan Himmler. Let our balding bad boys be bad boys and let a few suburban ladies feel a little naughty.

Well, twenty-five years after the last 240 came off the assembly line, the closest Volvo equivalent is the S60. This car's rounded lines look good, though one still gets the impression of a rounded-off strongbox. Perhaps this is the best of both worlds. The car shows excellent results in crash tests, but it looks nifty. You can almost see the memo that created the new model, back when Ford owned Volvo.

From: CEO, Ford Motor Company
To: CEO, Volvo Division
RE: New Model Volvo
Hej Bill. Say, just a note on the new S60. This model will have to compete with the Audi A4 and the BMW 3-Series, so have your boys cut the lines like a Swedish bathing beauty, and give it enough horses to make a guy hyperventilate. This model sells

like hotcakes, or you can kiss your keister goodbye, Pal. Golf sometime?

—Sam

From: Biljörk Olesson, CEO Volvo
To: Einar Högebreson, Chief Engineer
RE: S60 Engine
Give da new vun some poost, fella, or vi vill hafta get lunch somevere else from now on, don't ya know.

From: Biljörk Olesson
To: Hans Pederson, Chief Designer
RE: S60
You better make da S60 a sexy vun, denn.

From: Biljörk Olesson
To: Lena Paulsson, Secretary
RE: Yob
Get my resume ready, vill you?

So, in the first S60 we had three engines: a normally aspirated five cylinder rated at 168 hp; a 197 hp turbocharged motivator; and the "T5" version that put out 247 hp. The 240's four cylinder engine delivered only 114—which seemed fine back then. But we need more speed now, quicker acceleration, more zoom-zoom for passing, because over the years our possibilities have narrowed. The original S60 weighed about ten percent more than the 240, though this was offset by its being more aerodynamic—but it packed fifty percent more horsepower in the base model, more than twice the horsepower in the T5 version. Gas mileage could have been better than the 240's, what with engine technology and body design advances—but of course those advantages had to be put into speed. The mileage for that S60 was a little worse than the 240's. Think of those nearly three million unfortunates who bought 240's and had to slog around in underpowered vehicles. Likewise, safety developments like ABS, airbags, and better body structure could have made driving a car like the 240 almost as safe as a walk in one's back yard. Instead, we go faster. We have more fun. People are happier now.

The exec says to Congress, the press, and the Sierra Club: We only give the public what they want. Then he turns to his ad people and says, "Make 'em want what we give 'em." Well, I might be unfair. The exec really says to all his people, "We will make safe, environmentally clean cars, offer them as cheaply as we can, and generally keep our customer's interests uppermost in our minds. Our watchword will be love."

The 240 was 190 inches long; the S60 was ten inches shorter. The S60 was four inches wider, it offered 2.5 more inches of front shoulder room, three more in back, the same front leg room, one inch less in back; the same head room in front, more in the rear. The S60 was 1.5 inches lower, door to ground. These are trivial differences. A large difference is that Volvo went from rear drive to front drive during the 1990's. Such a move eliminates the large hump running through the car and provides better winter traction. But it is a move away from durability. Volvo probably would say that they made the change in order to improve handling, once they had figured out how to reduce the torque steer typically caused by front drive; and it is hard to believe they would admit to having compromised durability. But we'll see. Meanwhile, front drive has given them somewhat better interior space, and longer wheelbases with shorter overall lengths—nicer for parking. In general, more sporty at the popular level—though "serious" (a strange word in this context, but substitute "laughably expensive") sports cars are still rear drive.

Volvo is nothing if not responsive to the market. Are SUVs slurping up sales along with fuel? Enter the Volvo XC90, an SUV with seating for seven, four wheel drive of course (the world gets slipperier all the time), and three big engines: 200 and 272 hp gas engines and a 163 hp turbo diesel. To answer the rollover problem, the XC90 has "Roll Stability Control."

Or you could buy an SUV-like station wagon, the Cross Country. This features the 2.4 liter five cylinder engine with turbocharger and intercooler, putting out 197 hp at 5,000 rpm, and 210 ft./lbs. of torque at 2,000 rpm. Great for hauling kids made of lead, and stone soccer balls. The car had a 109 inch wheelbase, was 186 inches long and 73 inches wide. With 8.2 inches of ground clearance, you could go driving around cornfields and wilderness areas and cut across neighbors' yards. It weighed 3700 pounds, twenty percent more than the old 240 wagon. But think of how much more useful it was.

The SUV and Cross Country wagon raise the question of rights. With our Constitution, we have given ourselves political rights and defended ourselves against those who would take political rights away. What document, or what agreement, gives us rights over the land and water and air? Where does it say we can use them and trash them as we please, for fun? And profit. It might be in the Bible somewhere. Everybody look.

I couldn't just sell my 240; it had to be a donation. It had the greatest sentimental value, due to the fact that my old friend Art bought it. Our last conversation—Art's and mine—was rather ambiguous, and I am still trying to figure out what it meant. He said something about meeting somewhere—a nice fishing hole, I assumed. Maybe he had somewhere else in mind.

The 240 was the successor to Art's old Bel Air. As I have said, on the day Art died, that car did, too.

"Is that true?" asked Fran. "Because I know you have been writing some, well, fanciful things."

"'Stretchers' was Mark Twain's word," I explained. "'Stretchers' don't count as fiction because I am talking directly to the reader and he/she knows when I'm making things out of whole cloth. In fiction, there is no real author talking to real readers in the real world. That one wasn't a stretcher."

"Fran," whom I sometimes also call "Francis" for osteopathic reasons, had been reading some drafts of earlier chapters of this book. "What about those conversations with so-called Friend, back in the April days?"

"I covered his name and changed April's, as I changed Peggy's, but readers will understand that. Of course I don't remember exactly what my friend and I said all those years ago, but I repeated the gist and the spirit. No conversation except transcripts are one hundred percent accurate, and transcripts are dull."

"So this book on cars is nonfiction."

"Scout's honor."

"Were you ever a scout?"

"Yes."

"Then what about all these conversations with Mephisto—the devil?"

I asked him to wait a minute. I went downstairs and got an old phone—Art's phone, in fact—that I had stacked on the shelves with other junk: transistor radios, hair dryers, phonographs, manuscripts. I set it on the table between us, and said,

"Excuse me, the phone." I picked it up. "Hello?" I nodded. "Yes, this is Blank. . . Oh." Holding my hand over the mouthpiece, I whispered confidentially to Fran, *It's the devil.*

Fran was not into it. I said, *I'll ask him the meaning of life.*

"Hello," I said into the phone. "We have a question for you. What is the meaning of life?" I listened, and once again covered the mouthpiece. *He wants to know if meaning and purpose are the same.*

Fran, I regret to report, looked a bit impatient. "I don't see how this answers the question."

I thrust the phone at Fran and said, *Here! You talk to him!* Fran jerked away from the phone. *See,* I said, *it gets kind of real, doesn't it? So what should we say about purpose?*

"Tell him fine," Fran said. "Ask him, What is the purpose of life?"

I put the phone next to my ear. I giggled at Fran, *He heard you ask.* I listened.

Okay, I reported; *our purpose in life is to serve him.*

"Say, 'Begone,'" Fran said.

I thrust the phone at Fran. *You tell him that.* Again involuntarily, Fran jerked back.

"Begone," I said into the phone. *Oh.* I whispered again to Fran. *His feelings are hurt.*

"Tell him we choose to serve God," Fran said.

I listened. "I'll ask." Looking at Fran, I covered the mouthpiece. *He wonders whether maybe there's a compromise of some kind between the extremes. Could we serve some idea for the time being?*

"Like Romanticism?" Fran asked.

He doesn't like that, probably. Can you think of something else?

"No." Fran reflected for a moment. "There is no compromise, nothing in between. We all serve God or the devil." He nodded. "But you usually don't know which you are serving. Think it's one, and it might well be the other."

I said "Thank you," and hung up the phone.

"So," Fran said, a little relieved and a little disgusted, "why did we do that just now?"

I smiled contentedly. "You didn't think I was really talking to the devil, did you?"

"No. Did you?"

"Heavens, no!" I said with a dismissive lift of the hand, like Lucy or Ethel. I smiled.

"Well?"

I got serious. "Well, it wasn't fiction and it wasn't a lie."

"It was fiction. You made it up."

"But we were both in on it. Oh—and you did kind of believe it, didn't you?"

Fran pursed his lips stubbornly.

"Fran, you did believe it enough to jerk away when I handed you the phone."

"Can't control the imagination."

"Right. I'm making a Romantic of you."

"I doubt it. The point is, why did you do that with the phone?"

"I was just making use of the idea of the devil to lead us to a point of understanding. Plato did something similar."

"Wait a minute. You are *using* the concept of the devil."

"Righto! Lovely day, isn't it?" I looked at him questioningly.

"Hold on," Fran said. "You think you are using the devil."

"Yessir. Bingo. Bingo bingo bingo."

Fran lifted his index finger. "You can't do that."

"I can't? Whillikers. Why not? No fair."

"Because when you think you are using the devil, the devil is using you."

"Oh."

"So be careful."

"Dangerous?"

"Probably."

"Kind of like using any necessary evil?"

A dark cloud passed over Fran's visage. "Don't say it."

"Like using slaves, or internal combustion engines?"

"*Don't!*"

"Necessary evils. Like greenhouse gasses?"

"All right! Enough! I'm sick of hearing this all the time! You need a little romance in your life."

"Thanks for the offer, but no."

Fran just nodded. "Wiseapple. I mean you need to dwell on something other than pollution. You need a hobby."

"Like what, cars?"

"Funny. No, like stamps, fishing, history."

"Building an ark, maybe?"

"Look, you've made your point. I'm only thinking about how you'll look if you publish this book."

I had found a tube of old lipstick in the desk next to our table, and was applying a circle of it to the end of my nose as Fran talked.

"Yeah. Like a clown. I hope that stuff never comes off. Why do you make yourself look so crazy?"

I looked up, startled. "Craythy?"

"Yes, my friend. Like, as if you really wonder whether you're Hölderlin."

"Hölderlin was crazy, they say. Maybe he's me. He was born on my birthday; I was born on his. Apply the transitive property of equality. Maybe he thinks he's me."

"Stop it! Cut it out! More of this and I'll be going crazy myself."

"Ah," I said. I removed a tissue and began wiping the lipstick.

"It isn't coming off," Fran observed.

"It must be the stuff that doesn't come off, no matter what."

"Serves you right. So, why the crazy stuff?"

"What's crazy?"

"Oh no you don't."

"I mean, people all around the world are blowing each other up."

"I know, I know."

"People are robbing other people right now. I won't mention that people are driving SUVs—"

Fran held up a hand. I stopped. "Thank you," he said flatly.

"You're welcome. People are killing other people. People are planning mass destruction. Scientists are building weapons. In Chicago, somebody is threatening a driver who cut him off on the Dan Ryan Expressway. You and I. What are we doing here?"

"I don't know."

"Exactly. Here we are, somewhere on a ball called a planet. We have a thin layer of air, some water, some soil. Out there, out in the rest of the universe, we'd die. We are speeding through space at inconceivable speed."

"You're sounding crazy."

"We are *all* crazy! What are we thinking? Does any of us know where we are? Does any of us know *what* we are? Does any of us know what we're doing? No! In spite of all we know, we act like bugs, like ants fighting to the death over a crumb. What is a person of intelligence who acts like an insect?"

"Let me guess."

"Insane. We are all much more insane than we realize. The human race is insane."

"Thank you. What's the point?"

"I don't know."

"You don't know?"

"Maybe we should wake up and see the light. Snap out of it."

"How?"

"You're a minister."

"I'm only a drudge. A non-Romantic drudge. I feel that you have an answer."

"We are going to find the answer."

"Good. How?"

"We are going to Germany, to Tübingen."

"To meet—"

"Hölderlin."

Fran rose. "Okay. This has been the most totally unfruitful conversation I have ever had. Considering how many I have had with you, I have really said something just now."

I cleared my throat. "We will also go to the Frankfurt Auto Show." A strange light came into Fran's eyes. He tried to fight it. Slowly he sat back down.

"The Frankfurt Auto Show is next month," I said eagerly. "We can be there. Fares this time of year are under $300, round trip. I've checked them out." I eyed him fiercely. He was helpless. "We can see the newest Audi's. Newest European cars not sold here yet. Lamborghini. Maserati. Bentley." I eyed him like Burt Lancaster in *Elmer Gantry*. "What do you say? *Shall we?*"

"You're on. I bet I can find us tickets below two hundred on the Internet," etc. He was lost. Actually, I was going in order to save Fran's soul. They would be so proud at the bicycle factory.

"Oh my gosh," I said.

"What? What what?"

I looked out the window. "I'm going to have to sell the old Volvo in order to buy the ticket."

Fran let me think about this for a while. Then he said, not accusingly exactly, "Didn't you just buy a new car?"

"Toyota Camry."

"I mean—"

"I'll sell the Volvo. Yes, I'll sell the Volvo. It's fitting. Have you heard of Desert Pete?"

Fran looked at his eyebrows. "Now what."

"Don't you remember the old song by the Kingston Trio? A man is lost in the desert, dying of thirst. Then he sees a well! He gets to it, and there's a bottle full of water! But he sees a note. Don't drink the water, it says. Pour it into the pump. The water softens the pump's gaskets.

> You've got to prime the pump,
> You must have faith and believe.
> You've got to give of yourself
> 'Fore you're worthy to receive."

"Okay," Fran said. "Please don't sing."

> Drink all the water you can hold,
> Wash your face and cool your feet,
> But leave the bottle full for others.
> Thank you kindly, Desert Pete.

"Fran, we're going to save the world. I'm priming the pump by giving up the Volvo. We're going to find the meaning of life, Brother Francis! Then guess what I'm going to do—leave the bottle full for others!"

"How," Fran said flatly.

"I'm going to publish it! In my book about cars!!!"

Well, that conversation ended on a kind of awkward note, but we did go to Germany and find the meaning of life, and I guess it's about time to report on the trip. It's in the next two chapters.

P.S. Let's all leave the bottle full for others.

*

I return to righteousness, because no car manufacturer has been more righteous than Volvo. I mean this truly and sincerely. (*Wahrhaft und Fablehaft.* –Goethe) Yet in what does their righteousness consist? In making cars safer than they had been hitherto. Their emphasis on safety before speed or attractive design set them apart, and, as can be the case with one righteous man or woman in a world of sin, by their example they converted a whole industry to engineering for safety. Not that the other manufacturers—from those as cynical as Toyota to those as clueless as Ford—believed in safety: they believed in profits and Volvo forced them to compete. Volvo: a good person in a world of unrighteousness.

And yet, have we not come to the most brutal sin of all? Does not the very righteousness of tiny Volvo cast a beam of light across the darkness of the automobile? How many children did the worshippers of Ba'al incinerate upon their altars? How many innocents were put to the sword, the spear, and the torch upon the altars of pagan priests, or were thrown before the mouths of lions to the lusty roars of Roman crowds? Trifling numbers. Trifling, that is, in comparison to how many innocents we sacrifice on our concrete altars to convenience, sport, and speed. No luxuriating Roman in his silken toga basked in such air-conditioned, quiet comfort as does today's executive in the fragrant leather ambiance of his Mercedes. The speed with which lions rushed upon and tore the naked limbs and torsos of cowering children and their helpless mothers in the Coliseum is trifling next to the speed of an eight-cylinder Infinity streaking along the highways of the modern world. For what does this country—America—alone kill 30,000 men, women, and children per year? Speed, power, lust, fun, commerce, convenience, pride? We make timid and trivial the emperors, the priests, the spectators of history's blood-guilt.

And do we think that with our airbags and crash sensors and crumple zones we are righteous, in reducing the carnage from two corpses per 100,000 down to one, or from two quadriplegics per quarter million down to one, that we are excused in the sight of an all-perceiving Heaven? To what ends have we perverted the cosmic power of motion; and to what purposes have we harnessed the love that moves the sun and all the stars? Suppose we reduced the annual carnage to ten children—to five—to one? For what would we be justified in killing that one? Jobs?

The Volvos of the twentieth century were indeed better than the other cars of that era, more humane, more loving of the beautiful human form, more righteous; yet what of the camp guard who wishes good day to the children getting off the boxcars, and spares as many of them as he can? Is he not working nevertheless for the devil? Volvo! Volvo! What a darling you are, what a quiet voice in a brutal wilderness; yet will you not roll up your sleeves and strike at the root of evil? How many hack at the branches merely, to every one who bores for the root? No one is innocent, in a world where the innocent are offered up!

Eighth Interlude: Love and Work[13]

Regarding Charlotte Buff, Goethe's early love: she was engaged, as noted earlier in this volume. Goethe and her fiancé became friends. To his eternal credit, our hero did the right thing: he ushered himself out of town, away from his friend and Fräulein Buff.

Goethe's complex hero, Faust, capturing the devotion of young Gretchen, aged fifteen, does not do the right thing: he leads her on, she becomes pregnant; she kills her mother and then aborts the fetus. For this, the authorities condemn the poor girl to death; but her soul is saved by a merciful God. While this is happening, Faust deserts her, going off for further adventures in the company of Mephistopheles, the Devil.

Leaving adoring women behind is something of a motif in Goethe's works. Another of his characters, Wilhelm Meister, abandons a woman for the sake of his art. Since this is not a book about Goethe but about me and cars and the meaning of life, I will briefly interject a personal note. Under the influence of Wilhelm Meister, I too abandoned a burgeoning love affair for the sake of my vocation. Peggy. I left her in order to study Automotive Theory and become a builder of bicycles. True, it happened when I was eighteen, but I knew that by attending Wells Fargo Bible College I was preparing myself for a solitary, meditative life. My study of Automotive Theory was the best foundation I could lay for a thoughtful, artistic career. Evenings, I would go up garret and translate Goethe, until such time as the clarity and verve of my work should gather an appreciative readership and an international reputation, and I should be required to step forth before the public. Thus vocation, plus the fact that Peggy began hitting me in the face for minor verbal infractions, drew me from romance to Romanticism, from living to Life, and from saying four letter words to translating the stately ocean-liners of German nouns. *Aufhebungsnotverbotungschnaufeln* replaced "hell if I know," and

---

13. I am embarrassed and very sorry; I thought the previous Interlude was the last.

the majestically forbidding *Schlaufmitfarbgelungenstadtverweisenschluss* replaced "Damn, Pegster, whose side are you on?" *Schnipfungsbestellen- schaftvorbereitungsgerät* (fan belt) became my philosophic concern, and young love was at an end.

But I became lonely. My work was solitary, arduous, and above all thankless. By the time I was several years into my position at Clark Manufactury, UnLtd., I wished during lonely nights for that reassuring slap across the face that had set me apart from other boys. Now if I said "hell" or "damn," I would be fired from Clark's and have to face the adult world without shelter. So on those dark North Dakota evenings I would enter my apartment after work, loosen my tie, tilt my fedora, and sit mus- ing over a 7-Up with an olive while Sinatra broke his heart over and over again on my Blaupunkt stereo.

German itself became my love and my work. Mark Twain wrote that the inventor of the German language was a "maniac," but I think he was just an everyday, solid, hard-working Swede who became ill, and who did not want his girlfriend to hit him when he swore. All of German sounds like swearing to the untrained ear; hence the subtle beauty of the language. *Fuchs* means "fox," and *Schteckbeutel* refers to private parts, but who without the lilt of German blood in his/her veins could guess which was which? So when Goethe issued his famous reply to Napoleon's invita- tion to come to France and write an epic for *l'Empereur*—"*Ich schlag dich unspitzt im Boden rein*"—the English thought he was saying "[Blank] you" and Bonaparte thought he was saying, "I plant a pennant in your honor": such is the subtlety of nuance in the language. And hence the richness of *Faust*. It takes nearly a lifetime of study, and nightly immer- sion in German literature and *Schnapps,* to acquire an adequate feel for translating. This is why some have criticized my rendering of many of Goethe's phrases. (But note: *none* of this mean-spirited criticism has been issued by the Goethe family itself; nor has the Credentials Committee of the *Goetheverein* made the slightest objection or mention. Let it also be noted that I have never accepted a penny for any of my Goethe transla- tions: so much for the accusation that I have made my renditions racier than the original out of commercial motivations. The raciness is already there. It was Goethe himself, remember, who in his early drama *Götz von Berlichingen* shocked his contemporaries by popularizing the phrase, "lick my arse."[14] Ironically then, Goethe himself, a statue of whose char-

14. John Armstrong, *Love, Life, Goethe: Lessons of the Imagination from the Great German Poet* (New York: Farrar Straus and Giroux, 2006), 85. Anyone who despite my

acter Faust stands at the entrance to Clark Bicycle Manufactury, UnLtd., would have been fired from that institution.)

The point is that the choice was either Peggy—a Jaguar, fast and temperamental; or the German language—a Mercedes-Benz: solid, complex, individually hand-rubbed, over-engineered. I took the Benz. I took work over romance. You will no doubt recall at this point that Goethe advocated both work and love for personal growth. Romance, he once commented, was a "baby-step" (*Öntsiewöntsieschritt*) toward love. Yes, I have lived the distorted life of an artist. You would be correct, should you make that assumption. But had I not, the world would not enjoy *Faust, Götz von Berlichingen, Dichtung und Wahrheit*—and a host of others—as it now does. The sea level would still be rising around Bangladesh, the air over China would be so polluted that people would be wearing masks, and global warming would still be a threat to human civilization and life. Avoid your calling, for no matter what self-indulgence, at your peril, and at the peril of humankind.

But now that the bulk of Goethe translation has been completed, I am going to look for Peggy. A young purchaser of a Clark Spinner 500, who wrote me a thoughtful letter thanking me personally for the solid placement of the leader screw on his bi-directional derailleur, happens to own a Finder of Lost Romances agency. For the price of a twelve-pack of *Hölderlinturm* beer, made and distributed only in Tübingen, Germany, he will divulge the private address, email, and cell number. Fran and I are going to Germany.

---

work wants to read a good book on Goethe should read this one.

The Frankfurt Auto Show

Wilhelm Meister's Apprenticeship is one of Goethe's two Wilhelm Meister novels. The edition I have (*Goethes Werke in sechs Bänden*, Insel, 1914) is printed in old German script, called *Fraktur* for the way it causes fractures in those trying to decipher it. The "s" looks like "f," for instance. All the other letters are illegible. I like the *Fraktur* because it allows so much flexibility. Nobody knows how to read it anymore. Take the first sentence of the book, which I transliterate into Roman type as follows:

> *Das Schauspiel daurte sehr lange. Die alte Barbara trat einigemal ans Fenster und horchte, ob die Kutschen nicht rasseln wollten.*

This is often freely rendered by ignorant translators. I offer the following exact rendering:

> The play was lasting a long time. Old Barbara [alternate reading: "the ancient barbarians"] went to the window a few times and listened, wondering whether the kitchen wanted to wrestle.

You can see why Goethe was popular in his day. The breathtaking leaps he made in his prose—the startling connections of ideas—the amazing suddenness of his switches from seriousness to raucousness to levity to spirituality: all of that is shown in this passage. Goethe's English translators have long been uncomfortable with the variety in Goethe, cherishing the presupposition that "Europe's last great and universal man" should always be solemn, Olympian, humorless. The dirty passages in his later poems have long been suppressed also, until the breakthrough Gramm/Hosenpantz translations.

But here we have a passage that reveals Goethe's wide-ranging mind in all its glory. It has long been translated and discussed as if it were about the Frankfurt Auto Show. People were too Victorian and too prissy to admit the possibility that Goethe was daring and zany enough to write about an old woman's lascivious fantasies about her kitchen. It was not considered decent, therefore not worthy of the august Goethe. (He was born in August.)

Now, I more than anyone would like this passage to be about the Frankfurt Auto Show, because of my love for cars and my compulsion to write about them despite this book's being about enlightenment and spirituality. (For those particularly interested in spirituality, see the Volvo chapter.) But to demonstrate my overbearing concern for fact, I simply cannot subscribe to, or advocate, the Auto Show reading of this exciting passage.

The Auto Show reading is justified by a lot of stuffy, arrogant scholars and academics because of the Scharnhorst Text of Goethe, which falsely or erroneously introduces a slight change in the shape of one Fraktur letter, allowing the last portion to be translated, "wondering whether the coach would not rattle." Rattle, according to this interpretation, is typical Goethe shorthand for "move" or "get under way." Because during the early Frankfurt Auto Shows automobiles were sometimes still referred to as "motorized coaches" (compare "horseless carriages" in the early twentieth century U.S.), we have a reference to Barbara, or the ancient barbarians—I favor the Barbara reading—waiting impatiently for the car to start. Being somewhat senile, she has forgotten that all these cars, or "coaches," are on display only. It is a poignant moment; but, as a painstaking reading of the rest of the chapter shows, the mood of poignancy is misplaced, as this is a rollicking chapter of fun and misunderstandings, filled with sparkling German hilarity.

However, it is an understandable mistake, or cheat, as the case may be. The Frankfurt Auto Show was originally called the *Goethe Autobutik* (*Butik* later being replaced by *Anknüpfungspunkt*, meaning "point of gathering," or "convention," when some Tübingen theologians temporarily wrested control of the Show away from the ad men and engineers.) It was meant to honor Goethe's pioneering theoretical work on the automobile, and the importance of the car throughout his mature work. Some cynics maintained that the name was used to draw Goethe's participation. The great but aged man did indeed open the Show during its first years, reading selections from *Faust* and breaking bottles of *Sekt* over shiny new Mercedes automobiles.

Goethe was originally from Frankfurt, which explains the choice of that city for the Auto Show. Among the expected Mercedes and Knipfelhügens of those early shows, you had the short-lived nameplates like

Wilhelm Meister, Egmont, Lotte, Knabe and other names from Goethe's works, meant to pay homage to Germany's higher culture, in contrast to meaningless names that Americans were putting on their mass market automobiles, like Chrysler, Dusenberg, and so on. Goethe himself, while publicly pleased, expressed in private his impatience with such toadying and such crass appeals to his image. It had become lucrative to name things for Goethe characters, and such items as Werther mixmasters and Mephistopheles toasters for a time sold more briskly than their better-made counterparts manufactured by Braun and Krupp. This ended with the First World War.

I returned to the Frankfurt Auto Show with my sacred friend Fran. Thirty years previously, while I was living in a small village an hour north of Frankfurt, I had always come down for the Show, so this return was a sentimental journey, a return to Germany's Romantic Road.

The *Romantische Strasse* (Romantic Road) is a long tourist route throughout Germany, which takes you to such places as Rothenberg ob der Tauber, a medieval town, all the way up to Hameln, town of the Pied Piper. Don't mistake these quaint locales from German fairy tales, history, and legend for actual Romanticism. In fact, the mislabeling of this route is just another example of German high jinks. You know how they save the good stuff for themselves and ship their bellywash wines and skunky old beer to the U. S.? Likewise, they want real German Romanticism to be safely ensconced among Goethe buffs (*Goethe-Büffe*). Hence the historic nature of this document that you are reading. The real German Romantic Road is the Autobahn. Its headquarters is the Frankfurt Auto Show.

This year my friend and I flew to Germany in style, on *Lufthansa*. We could afford it because my friend preached a really good sermon the week before and raked in a lot of cash, and I sold the last of my *Boy's Life* and *Deutscher Funk* magazine collections, along with some unnecessary seasonal clothing and two pints of blood. My friend sat in First Class, which was an inspiration to me, and I have since searched through my mental furnishings for a call to the ministry. Only 3% of the Germans are active churchgoers of any kind, so I believe there is a ripe ministerial field for a person who speaks German as well as I do, and knows cars. Fran has suggested that I put the idea on hold, and wait for a dramatic experience.

See, I had also been explaining to Fran my theory on the Trinity, that the old Christian doctrine is the true origin of Romanticism. The Trinity is a way of saying that God is not alone, and yet God is only one. Similarly, a Romantic is a solitary who is never alone. Further, the Trinity assures that God is thought of in personal terms rather than mechanical. Fran suggested that I don't wait for just any religious experience, but wait for a really excellent one, because my ideas deserve it.

I brought my copy of Goethe's *Maxims* to read on the plane, and in the hotel, and if possible in some cars at the Auto Show. It is nearly my favorite of all Goethe's books. The actual title is *Maxima*, the plural. Some insist that it should be *Maximae*, but such people are mere pedants, upon whom Goethe wasted little patience. It is well known that the upper echelons of Nissan Corporation are Goethe afficionados, and that they named their top-of-the-line sedan "Maxima" after this book—just as "Altima" is named for a sprite in *Faust* and "Sentra" is named after a wood nymph in *Götz von Berlichingen*. And of course their Infinity division is named for one of Goethe's chief concerns.

I brought my well-thumbed copy of *Maxima* to the Auto Show. It seemed somehow right to read and apply Goethe's maxims and reflections to the cars at the Show that Goethe himself had founded. As I leafed through the pages under the flashing lights and loud music, I once again regretted the lack of a good, up-to-date English translation that catches both the wisdom and the verve of the original. How timely would be the knowledge—for uncounted millions—of what Goethe thought about this, perhaps, or that. But I fear *Maxims* has suffered at the hands of pussyfooting translators with no feel for Goethe's unique, allusive, and complicated idiom. Take the following:

> Nothing is more illogical than the most absolute illogicality, because this gives rise to unnatural phenomena which, in the end, change completely.

This is why thousands of confused youth have read the Maxims. But of course Goethe's original Maxim has been ridiculously watered down by a vague translation. The allusion to cars is entirely lost; the subtle critique of false Romanticism is merely thrown away for the sake of wording that pleases the ear and coddles the mind.

So let us take another: "A wolf in sheep's clothing is more dangerous than a sheep in any clothing." This is not, as is often claimed by British scholars, a plug for nudity in sheep. It is a reference to the dangers posed by Christian fundamentalism, *Die Pfündchen* of Goethe's generation. Fran was checking out the new Ford Thunderbird, which drew huge crowds throughout the Auto Show, according to the *Frankfurter Zeitung*, which until my recent financial disasters I have always ordered mailed to me at home. The Ford Thunderbird that year was a retro car, appealing to the Romantic who wants to return to an earlier time in his life, when there were still possibilities.

That new Thunderbird was a two-seater, very low, though it was as wide and long as a Chevrolet Impala. It was very heavy—3900 pounds, some of that weight being contributed by the 3.9 liter V8, a 252 hp powerplant that guzzled a gallon of gas for every 17 miles of mixed driving. It was the car's looks that attracted attention. In the removable hardtop, you had the porthole of the original T-bird. Inside, the car was color-keyed to whatever exterior color you ordered, with the steering wheel and furnishings being two-toned, gray plus that other color. The effect was of a 1950's car, with 1950's power and fuel consumption.

Some of the German men we stood near said things like *Schnört* when they discovered that the T-bird was not available with a manual transmission. "*Gar kein Porsche,*" they said. ("This is no Porsche.") In the States, this car was an excellent thing for blockheads with more money than they should have, because people were paying $10,000 and more over MSRP to get one. This has been called a "stupid tax." Some years back, the Chrysler PT Cruiser drew a similar tax when their retro car was new.

The Porsche to which our eloquent German friend referred was the Boxster, a two-seater of similar external dimensions to the Thunderbird, but with twelve inches less wheelbase and 1000 fewer pounds to lug around. Its 2.7 liter Six made 217 hp. The Boxster S came with a 250 hp Six. You could expect twenty-two mpg on—like the T-bird, or Tird—premium fuel. It handled ever so much better than the Tird because it was a real sports car, but you needed more money: $42k to $52k, which is one hundred percent Stupid Tax.

They displayed a Corvette at the Auto Show. It was a better car than the T-bird, not as good as the Porsche, and it came with the same engine that was in my stodgy 1970 Impala: 5.7 liter 350 hp V8. It got twenty-one mpg, came fitted with a manual six speed tranny as a sports car should be, and cost a nasty $42–50k. But the Germans had seen 'Vets for years and much more attention was focused on the new Audi TT and Mercedes SLK.

The Audi was the cheapest and had the smallest engine. Yet Audi achieved an mpg figure as miserable as the others, even with the little 1.8 liter turbo Four. The car had the wheelbase of the Boxster but a stubby body, and weighed in at 3440: heavy. Inside, it was all polished metal, including the pedals, which sporty rich guys have been sold on as being cooler. (You can slide your feet quickly between clutch and accelerator, like a real race driver.) The interior looked kind of pre-war Berlin. Its colors were charcoal, aluminum, and red; or, if you preferred, red, charcoal, and aluminum. This was to let you know that you bought a modern, high tech car with the money that could have supported a village in New Jersey for a year. But it was a lot of fun.

The Mercedes SLK didn't go for the techno interior, but it retained the usual Mercedes polished wood alternating with that imaginative German black. The car was the lightest of the bunch, about 3,000 pounds, and topped out higher than any of the others, because it was a Mercedes, at $55,000. It had a 215 hp V-6. And it was a Mercedes.

All German sportsters were better handlers than the Americans, but I prefer the Americans because I think funk is better than *Fahrvergnügen*. However, "better" does not apply to these cars in any normal sense, because perpetrating a 3,000 lb machine that goes 140 mph on normal highways is criminal. Other sports, even hunting, do not put other people at risk the way "sports cars" do, nor do they poison the environment as these things do.

"Oh?" Fran says. (I have been talking aloud.) "So, three million hunters driving to the woods in their pickups and big SUVs don't poison the environment?" OK. We'll have to cover that question later. I can never get Fran to stick to the subject. We are dealing with cars here, cars only.

So I turned to the *Maxims* and read, "Even a shabby camel can carry the load of many donkeys." Goethe referred to the sports cars of his day as donkeys. Cars are transportation, not sport. Their virtues are safety, reliability, and comfort; their vices are fuel consumption, pollution, unsafe construction, and excessive speed.

"You mean cars should not be sporty?" Not unless they are also economical and safe, which means Correct. What people want in "sport" for cars is speed and more power than other cars, a higher power-to-weight ratio. Sport is inappropriate for cars. Sorry, but we'll have to get our sport in other ways. Tennis. Golf. Cycling.

"Romance?" Fran interjects. No again. Romance is not for sport. The only production vehicle more dangerous than the sports car is the human body. Romance is for the soul, not the body. That idea defines the true Romantic.

"Sounds crazy," Fran observed.

Shut up, I maintained.

"Here," Fran says, going straight to his favorite Maxim: "*When two people are really happy about one another, one can generally assume that they are mistaken*'. See, Goethe was no Romantic."

Although that Maxim could be evidence of profound Romanticism, I knew very well that Goethe was not a Romantic. That is why our pilgrimage must eventually take us beyond Goethe, I tell Fran.

"Beyont Goethe!" A man next to me exclaims. "*Es gibt doch gar nicht! Impossible!*" He tells the people around him what I have said, gesticulating fiercely and spraying them all with spittle. Soon three guards with automatic weapons come over and, incensed at hearing what I have said, order us to follow them out. But Fran calmly holds up one finger.

"Same to you!" a guard says and pushes the barrel of his weapon into Fran's face, in which position we find ourselves escorted out.

Well. What to do next. We went to the nearby *Kostüm Butik*, bought nose-and-glasses masks, returned to the ticket office, and re-entered the Show.

"This time be more careful what you say."

"I was misunderstood," I replied. "Here." (I quickly thumbed to Goethe's Maxim:) "*Everyone only hears what he understands.*" I said that those aggressive people were Philistines, and did not even begin to understand me. "Here." I read another Maxim:

Art deals with what is hard to hear and with what is good.

"German is hard to hear," Fran said. "But it is not good."

"You should learn German. Then I wouldn't always have to translate for you and supply you with phrases."

"You had me ask for a groin pull at breakfast this morning."

"The difference of one lousy letter. Not even that, an umlaut."

"It made me feel awkward."

"So learn your own German."

"Getting testy, edgy?"

"I am disappointed in the Show. All the Goethe quotations on posters I saw here 20 years ago are gone. It's as if people don't want to think about him any more. His warnings have gone for naught, and he would be ashamed of his own auto show. Let's go see the current Maxima and blow."

The new Nissan Maxima was a pretty good car, though as Fran said, "A Nissan is like a cheap Toyota." True, the interior had a kind of plasticky quality. But the car packed a 265 hp V6. And you could get a six-speed stick. More recently, Fran has begun saying, "A Toyota is like a cheap Nissan." This illustrates Spengler's cycles of history.

"Sport?" Fran enquired.

"No, no. Family hauler. Five person capacity, respectable fuel economy, outstanding reliability, and good safety. Not exorbitant in price. The best dancing girls at the Show."

"Chicago Auto Show has better girls. We could have saved some money and just gone there, if dancing girls are what you've come for."

"It's just that I look at each face, hoping to see my April."

"April would be pretty ripe by now. Varicose perhaps."

"Fran, stop it! *Faith*, Goethe says, *is love for the invisible*. Here." (I showed it to him.)

"Then you'd better hope the old girl is invisible. How old would she be by now, anyway?"

I was very definite. "Thirty-five. Case closed."

"So you're thirty-seven? Well, live and learn. I would have guessed you to be—"

"*Strumpfhosen!*" I cried. "I am still a young man!"

"In geologic terms, yes."

"Fran, I hate to say this, and I don't mean anything personal, and it isn't that I enjoy complaining, but you are giving me acid reflux."

"It's the food here. The food has been bad since we landed."

"Now that you mention . . . But what were we—?"

"April's age."

"She will always be springtime."

"I bet her name is really Bertha. Was it Bertha?"

It was at this point that I first questioned the existence of April. Somewhere in my aging mind I might have confused her with Peggy—the ideal with the real. Did I waltz with April, or with Peggy; or perhaps it was someone else? Maybe my world as I knew it is done. The atmosphere that protects its perennial greenness is getting thinner all the time. I began to think that spring might be a little late this year. To restore my faith, I insisted that we follow through with our plan to drive to old Tübingen and visit the Hölderlin Tower. I cannot describe it here; I am too emotional, what with the questions about April and the memory of us walking through the whole Frankfurt Auto Show wearing nose-and-glasses masks. That chapter must wait.

Actual Final Interlude: Faust Part Two, A Fragment

(This is my own translation of a recently discovered fragment from the second part of Goethe's *Faust*, in which I try to retain the conversational swing of Goethe's verse. As Armstrong notes, ". . . with all of Goethe's poetry translation is hopeless."[15] Therefore to translate Goethe responsibly, a great deal of latitude must be taken. Longitudinally, however, this translation hews extremely close to the original.)

[The Elysian Fields. Enter FAUST. He spies GRETCHEN beneath a tree, apparently reading a book.]

FAUST [Soliloquy]:
Halt you now, Faust;
No farther go. There
She sits, alone and lost,
The Gods' breezes in her hair.

Look at her awhile
And weep:
She can neither smile
Nor sleep.

A heavy sadness
Shadows from her heart.
A mortal madness
Seems to start

Within my soul
In these immortal fields.
I must go,
And let her heal.

15. *Love, Life, Goethe*, 420.

[FAUST turns to leave, when a VOICE speaks.]

VOICE:
Stay! You cannot escape
The suffering of Fate.
Speak to her, Faust.
Are you a man, or a mouse?

GRETCHEN [startled by the VOICE]:
Who's there? A stranger comes
With double-jointed thumbs.

FAUST:
No, no! Gretchen, it is I!
Your Faust!

GRETCHEN:
                My faithful guy?

FAUST:
No, no. That I was not.
I was an evil fool.
Let's see what you've got.
Your book I mean. You
Have learned to read?

GRETCHEN:
I'm not the girl I used to be.

FAUST:
Do you . . . do you remember me?

GRETCHEN:
The gods in their mercy
Have sponged my memory.
The past is silent as a rock.

FAUST:
What do you read?

GRETCHEN:
                Klopstock.

FAUST: [The German here is unintelligible. —ed.]

GRETCHEN:
Sir, what do you mean?
Some dim memory returns.
Oh my heart, how it burns!

FAUST:
Alas! Alas! Let the thought go!

It is better for you not to know!

GRETCHEN:
Oh grief! Oh pain!
They return to me in waves
Like the pain of giving birth!
My memory returns to earth!

FAUST:
Enough! Enough! Better to forget!
Return your thoughts to there above
The blood, the tears, the sweat.

GRETCHEN:
It is a memory of love!
Better to relive the pain
Than to live alone again.
The winds of passion, hot and wild,
Storm through my heart! I birthed your child!
I loved you only, deep and true.
Is it you? Can it be you?

FAUST:
But I deserve only your hate.

GRETCHEN:
Oh, is it you, Reginald Applethwait?

FAUST:
What?

GRETCHEN:
            Is it you, my darling man?

FAUST:
Du hast mir auszerknetzelt Weh getan! [Meaning obscure. —ed.]
The baby wasn't mine?

GRETCHEN:
Your speech, your wild eye!
You are not my love, my Reginald!

FAUST:
You—you—you rolled
My friend! It wasn't me
Whose sport between your knees
Rounded your young abdomen?
What?

GRETCHEN:
Oh, Reginald, what have I done?

I slew our child, your son!

FAUST:
It wasn't mine. I'm someone else.
Remember me, Professor Faust?
Nuts.

GRETCHEN:
What?

FAUST:
      I said "nuts."
His name was neither Reginald
Nor Applethwait. He called
Himself by many names,
But "friend" is bittersweet now.

GRETCHEN:
Your four-letter word: say
It again.

FAUST:
      Nuts! And how!

GRETCHEN [Slaps him]:
I remember you now!
How dare you swear
At me, you chump!

FAUST:
Ow! Ow!
Is there
No balm in Gilead?—no lump

[The fragment continues, but the Author, for personal reasons, has chosen not to continue the translation. For those who may be interested, the handwritten German manuscript is housed in the *Sonder-Kollekte* of the *Tübinger-Geschmeiß-Bibliothek*. Instead, he offers his hitherto unpublished translation (abridged) of the famous "Midnight" section of the conclusion to *Faust, Part Two*.]

MIDNIGHT

[Four crones enter.]

First: I am Deficiency.

Second: I am Fault.

Third: I am Cars.

Fourth: I am Need.

Deficiency, Fault, & Need:
A rich man lives here; this is his garage.
He's locked us out like a bunch of garbage.

Deficiency: I'm missing something.

Fault: The blame is mine.
Need: We're losers. This happens all the time.

Cars:
But I can go in; this place is for me!
I'll take on the form of a brand new Mercedes.

Three:
Farewell, farewell! We know he'll be pleased.
Here he comes now, with his shiny new keys.

Faust:
Behold! How I feel as though raised from the dead:
A gleaming new car, and of course it is red.
Red for the devil, or red for the Church?
And cherry interior, or wait—is it birch?
Who cares? What's the difference? Only Hölderlin walks.
Whoa, wait! Holy smoke! It's a car that can talk!

Cars:
I greet thee, Faust; my mission is Death.
Like mourners in hell, I speak without breath.
Just open my door, and settle inside.
I promise you, Doctor, one hell of a ride!

Faust:
My hand on the handle, I hesitate!
Have I a choice, or are you my fate?

Cars:
In whatever form, I have such cruel power
That wish to or not, you are ruled by your car.
You'll love me and work for me, day in and day out:
You'll pay every penny; of that there's no doubt.

Faust:
I've raced through this world on each set of wheels;
Whichever I wanted, I made a good deal—
An Audi bought outright, BMW on lease:

One after another, I've slithered on grease
And I've made love on leather;
Whenever I lusted, I'd go out and get her.

Cars:
Oh no, you old fool: it is we who have you!
My name could be Legion, and you are our tool.

Faust: But you're my escape! We leave Death behind—

Cars:
All roads lead to Death, and your every sensation
Has weakened your heart, and now you are blind!
You've traded your soul for this dark destination!

Faust:
I'm damned if I take, and damned if I spurn—
Signed, sealed, and delivered, eternally burned!

Cars:
You've lost your last Chrysler, you've used your last Dodge:
Faust, tap the black button and open the garage!
                    [The door rises behind them.]
Now push the ignition, and step on the gas;
What did you expect, you delusional ass?
                    [A brilliant flash of light. Angels singing. An auto-
mobile takes shape in the driveway.]

Voice from Above:
Faust! Faust! You are saved from above!
You are saved by your longing, and saved by your love!
This vehicle lifts you beyond time and space;
These wheels are the workings of infinite grace.
The angels have come to take you away
In this heavenly car, this old Chevrolet!

One Good Car

"I want the Audi," Fran said. He had not spoken for three or four hours as we drove our rented Mercedes SLK 230 down toward Tübingen and our appointment with destiny. The rental had cost Fran the income from another sermon, and represented the proceeds from my last furniture, but wow was it fun to drive. And fast? Boy was it fast.

Fran's silence indicated to me that he was involved in a mighty spiritual struggle, a titanic internal battle for who he was. I am glad his name is Fran, short for Francis, short for St. Francis, short for St. Francis of Assisi, because even at the time I wanted so badly to believe I was riding with a saint, and everything would turn out all right. Now, in view of how things turned out, I want to entertain that grand possibility even more. And another reason for using the name "Fran" is that if anyone picks up this book and opens it a page or two on from here, they will think I drove that expensive sports car with a girl. It was what I wished at the time. In fact, I sang nearly all the lyrics to "There is Nothing Like a Dame" as we drove, but I think rather than cheering Fran, it drove him deeper into his battle with himself. I cleverly remembered that Fran doesn't like the word "dame." We had discussed the issue once or twice. He thought it was demeaning. I had said once, "Look at the cathedral of Notre Dame. Look at the football team." He had chewed his moustache and his eyes went small.

But now nothing. No response, no rise.

It frightened me. I was concerned. Then he says, like it was all settled: "I want the Audi."

"What?" I said. "What Audi? What are you talking about?"

"Life. Death. Sex. Love. Everything. Theology."

"Huh?"

Fran looks at me. "I'm through with that crap."

"What crap?" I asked nervously.

"All the crap. All the lies. All the BS I've been preaching. It's all a crock."

It was well that I was not driving, or I would have spun off the Autobahn. At 120 mph, it would have been tragic, like *Dr. Faustus*. I was very frightened. Fran was my hold on Realism. "What would Carol say if she heard you talking that way?"

"Who cares."

"But she's your wife."

"Who cares."

"Who cares about *wives*? Egad!"

"Wives aren't worth the expense."

Cynicism. Black cynicism from Fran.

"Fran! Think of your beliefs."

"What beliefs? I'm a Methodist."

"But Fran, surely Methodists believe in things. Talk to me. Tell me what Methodists believe."

"I think we believe in the existence of nebulas."

"Good. That's *good*, Fran. Tell me more. This is so interesting."

He just snickered menacingly and looked at the road.

"Fran, think of romance. Think of love, romantic love."

"Romantic love? Do you know what that is?"

"Of course! I have had many girlfriends in my time, wonderful romances, lovely girls!"

"Oh. Tell me, what would it be like to have all of them together now, all at one time?"

"Gosh."

"It would be like a convention of retired Rubens models."

"Ow! Fran. Cynicism. Ouch!"

"Am I wrong?"

"I wouldn't know."

"Stop pouting and face reality. What has your lifetime of romanticism got you? The same as my lifetime of preaching religion has gotten me. Nothing. Does either of us have the car we want?"

I was silent. I felt that I was in the presence of vast power. I felt tiny, real tiny.

"Well? Have we?"

"No," I said weakly. But I couldn't give up. "Success isn't everything."

"'Winning isn't everything, but losing is nothing.' We're losers, Pal, losers. We've got nothing. I want a good car, and I want it bad. I want the Audi."

"That is very dangerous, Fran."

"And I'm going to get it."

I was flabbergasted. Where was my old friend Fran? I looked at him. He appeared to be the same. Dark glasses. Small grizzled moustache. Short salt and pepper hair moving almost imperceptibly in the 120 mph wind. Man, it was quiet in that car, even with the top down. It has a hard top that folds down into the trunk. What a great feature.

I had to think of another tack.

"So how are you going to afford an Audi TT? On your salary."

"Divorce the wife, sell the house. I get half. Buy the car. I've worked it all out."

My eyes must have enlarged like headlights. "What has happened, Fran, camerado, kemosabe? What happened?"

"I've just realized what's important."

"What *is* important?"

"Cars."

"Cars?"

"You don't get anything else out of life. You act like an idiot, then you die. That's all there is. You taught me this."

"Me?"

"Yeah. I've thought about you. You're pathetic. You spend your whole life looking for the Romantic fulfillment, the meaning of life. You work like a dog writing books nobody buys, writing poetry nobody reads, and translating some writer everyone has forgotten; you work a demeaning job and sell your soul, you do your duty, and what have you got? Nothing. You've got absolutely nothing."

"Nothing?"

"Nothing at all."

"I have a very nice Toyota, Fran. It gets 33 miles to the gallon, and—"

"You're pathetic. You're a sucker. You've lived like a chump, and you'll die a chump. A poor, white-haired, wheezing chump."

"Could we maybe sing a little Kumbaya?"

"And you won't even face it. Well, that's not for me. You give up your life for art and for your beliefs; and surprise—at the end, nada. Nothing. Not for me, Pal. When I look at you, I see what I could be six months down the road."

It was true. Fran is younger than I am.

"Fran, could we pull over maybe and just form a little calming circle? Or wait. Maybe I could say a prayer." I tried to think. But it seemed that "Now I lay me down to sleep" would be dangerous at 140 mph. Fran interrupted my deliberations.

"Go ahead, pray. See if anybody answers. But if you use the word 'just' even once like the fundamentalist freaks you worked for, I am going to drive us into the next town, purchase one of those big German hedge shears, and personally give you a haircut like mine."

"Heavenly days." I slumped back in the little Mercedes seat. "Land sakes." I couldn't fight his logic. Where had this come from? I had never witnessed a real conversion before—I mean one that wasn't just psychology or hormones.

"Fran, have you seen any black cats lately?"

"No."

"Fran, who was that you were talking to at the Auto Show while I was getting this car? The man who sort of went away when I drove up to the door?"

"Just another American guy there for the show."

"Southern, by any chance?"

"Yeah. Real gentleman."

"Fran, it is my duty to save your soul, to make you believe in futility and meaninglessness once more, to love the American suburbs and to believe in success. I am glad we are driving to the center of the earth, to the shrine of Romanticism. What I can do at least is deliver you to the threshold of enlightenment. I can take you to Hölderlin. What I cannot say to you, Hölderlin can."

At this point I should interrupt and issue a few clarifications. First, Fran had talked to some ordinary Southern gentleman at the Auto Show. If this were a novel, I would move toward the suggestion that Fran had been brainwashed by Mephistopheles in Frankfurt. But this is nonfiction, and I include this little detail, this meaningless coincidence—Excuse me; the phone is ringing.

"Hello?"

"Well good aftanoon, Blank. Are you sayin' your frind whom for convenience we shall call 'Fran' wuddn't talkin' to me in Frankfut?"

"You mean he wud?"

"Once again Ah must caution you about yo' flippancy. All Ah am sayin' is that one cain't evah be too sure. Might coulda been me."

"You are talking more like a cracker every day." Slam. I am going to get caller ID as soon as I can afford it.

I was saying that Fran had been vulnerable to the sensory barrage of the Frankfurt Auto Show. All the shiny cars, the women, the crowds, the lights. Think of this in a preacher's mind. They had all sold Fran on evil and so he made it a priority to get himself a sports car. There is nothing unusual about this for a man of his age, but for a man of his income? No matter how you picture it, my pal Fran was in trouble. He was in the process of selling his soul to the devil and I was his last line of defense, his last hope, his, well, his pal. I must save him. Unfortunately, I love cars.

See, Fran had fallen for cars, money, sex—and who knows, drugs next, fundamentalism?—because there was no Romanticism in his heart. He saw the world the way it is.

"Fran," I said as we neared Stuttgart and waited in a 50 km traffic tie-up; "you consider yourself a realist."

"Always have been. I was born a realist."

"But you aren't a realist."

He looked away from the Porsche Boxter ahead of us and kind of analyzed my face, as if I were an alien or a tomato.

"See, if you were a realist you would simply get drunk and stay drunk. But you don't. Why don't you?"

"I don't know. Why don't I." I felt that he was trying to remain disengaged from the conversation. He looked like a suburban bandito; also, he was becoming very impatient with the traffic stall. He drummed his fingers on the thick steering wheel. Probably he was very glad to have my company at that moment, which was a very trying moment because of what I was saying.

"You do not get drunk because, deep down, you are a Romantic."

He laughed a genuine laugh, quietly. (I found this hopeful.) "Sure," he said. "I am a Romantic. Deep down. What gives it away?"

"Cars."

"Cars?"

"Car guys are frustrated Romantics. That's the whole problem with Americans these days. We are supposed to be realists and pragmatists, but we aren't."

"I have always wondered about this. I'm glad you have a theory. So glad."

"Your heart is hardening, Fran, like Pharaoh's. All I am saying is that Americans think like pragmatists, but we feel like Romantics. What were the Puritans but Romantics in uncomfortable clothing?"

"Say what?"

"Who is the great American, the arch-typical American?"

"You are."

"Besides me. I'm trying to be serious here." He was looking at that Boxter again. I think he was changing his mind about the Audi, moving toward the Porsche. It was vital that I break into his train of thought.

"Who was the great symbolic American, Fran? Think about it please!"

"OK. I am."

"Yes, you are, because you are basically a decent guy, Fran. That's why you won't do what you said."

"Try me."

"OK. The person I am referring to is Mark Twain."

"Fine. I'll buy that."

"Mark Twain was a Romantic."

"Ha! Since when? He was a realist. Too bitter and angry to be a Romantic."

"He was bitter and angry because his Romanticism had been burned. There's no more Romantic thing in American literature than the first fifty pages of *Huckleberry Finn*."

"'Come on back to the raft, Huck Honey.' Do you mean that part?"

"Do not be sacrilegious. I mean the beauty of the River. I mean just going away, rafting down the Mississippi. Americans all want to do that. That's what the car means. The River is gone, the wilderness is gone—but the car still takes us away."

"Away from reality."

"Away from a definition of ourselves and of life that deep down we don't accept."

"OK. I'm a Romantic. I'm going to chuck my job and my wife and get a car. What difference does it make what you call it?"

"I don't know. 'Romantic' sounds better than 'good-for-nothing.'"

"I agree. I'll be a Romantic. I'll write when I get work."

"It's a dead end."

"Come again?"

"I just realized it's a dead end. Romantics have to either die or go crazy. There's no territory to light out to, like Huck Finn had."

Fran's instincts were to pastor me. I watched him fight himself for a minute, until he said, "This is a trick."

"No; it's just despair."

"Hey, Pal. What *I* was talking about is despair. You still have your stupid, useless ideals, Dork. At least that's something."

I gave Fran a pally slug on the shoulder. "Illusion beats reality. Either it's drugs, or it's booze, or it's sex, or it's cars, or it's Romanticism."

"Try religion."

"See, reality is simply too bleak or too gruesome. Or boring."

"I think we have achieved consensus, Pal. Now, why are we making this drive?"

"Visit Hölderlin.

"The reason being?"

"More light."

*

We arrived in Tübingen around one in the afternoon. In early autumn leaf, the old town looked warm and wonderful. We parked and walked up and around toward the old cathedral, because I wanted to show Fran my work. I pointed to the pavement.

"This is my opus, Fran. Something does endure."

He stopped and scanned the neatly fitted bricks at our feet, then his gaze ranged up and down the street.

"You laid these?"

"Thirty-five years ago. I and another guy did this whole street."

"How long did it take you?"

I explained that we worked two weeks on about three blocks. A couple of pallets were delivered to us each day. The smell of mortar came back, the feel of the old trowel handle.

"In America it would have been asphalted in two hours," Fran said.

"I know. We could tell who the American students and tourists were. They were the ones who acted disgusted and impatient at having to walk around or use the pathway of boards."

"You and another guy worked two weeks on this. What a waste of man-hours."

"Two hundred years from now, people will still be walking on these bricks. If it had been asphalted, it would have been redone twice already."

"Must give you no end of satisfaction. Probably makes your life feel worthwhile."

"Ouch. I realize it's only a more durable futility. Just the same, it gives me a kind of full feeling to see that we are standing on bricks I laid."

"I thought you were a student here."

"No, I lied about that. I was too embarrassed to say I moved here to be a laborer. Been lying about it for twenty years, thirty years, upward, whatever."

"Cool. So you lied."

"You bet."

"Are you lying now?"

"See, joking and imagining and inventing are not lying. Life is non-fiction, Fran, even at its craziest."

"So why did you come here in the first place?"

"I read Goethe and Hölderlin in high school. I wanted to see Hölderlin's place."

"Why didn't you just visit?"

"Who can afford that? Anyway, I wanted to spend some time. Every evening that summer and fall, I went over to Hölderlin's tower and sort of hung out."

"Sort of hung out?"

"Talked to him."

"And he talked back?"

"Might be."

"He did you a lot of good."

*

The confession did me good. Fran is not a priest, but I can see how he might be. I resisted the temptation to call him "Father" because he might have taken it as sarcasm—which under the circumstances would have been appropriate. It had bothered me for a long time that all my employers have thought I had actually studied Theology—especially that theological journal I had been editor of for a couple of years. No, I was just a philosopher, and somewhat of an amateur at that. Because I felt so much better, I suggested to Fran that we stop for a little refreshment before going to see Hölderlin. By the way, some readers might wonder why I traveled all that distance years ago to visit Hölderlin without making sure he would be in. The answer is that he was always in: he never left the tower or the park after being more or less committed in his thirties. This is what commitment does to a person—makes him as reliable as a Toyota.

I knew of a place to eat just over the Neckar Bridge. You sat out on a kind of veranda and watched the students and tourists row past in their rented boats, wishing you could afford to do that. When I lived in Tübingen, I often came here during the apple harvest and ordered the most wonderful drink in the world, fresh-pressed cider.

Fran and I walked across the bridge. So many memories. The American Library used to be just down the street. Emerson, good old Emerson; Hawthorne, Thoreau. American Romantics. Where would they have been without the German Romantics, the philosophies of India, and the Tibetan—

"Buster!" Fran had been trying to wake me up. "Where were you just now?"

"Ah—" I saw far-off pavilions, a high mountain valley—but quickly I returned. "I don't know. What were we talking about?"

"Beer!"

We entered the café and went down the steps, and I pointed to one of the small tables overlooking the waterfront.

"What kind of beer do you recommend?" Fran asked after we sat down.

I was looking at swans on the river in the shade of the willows, but I sprang to attention. "Beer? You can't drink alcohol before going to see Hölderlin!"

"Hölderlin's been dead, how long now? Let's just clear that up. I'm glad to humor you, but I'll have some beer. This is Germany."

I wrestled against a threatening feeling of reality, and fought it back. "OK. Dinkel-Acker."

"What? Very funny."

"Really. It's a more or less local beer. Try it. As to Hölderlin, I am well aware that he's dead. But Goethe says, *We are here to make ourselves eternal.*"

Fran rolled his eyes.

"So here's the thing," I continued. "Hölderlin was born on my birthday. So if I'm here, he's here."

"I wonder why you never became a professor of logic."

"Boring."

"Yeah. Of course, it's tough for any profession to beat laying bricks."

"I liked laying bricks."

We were interrupted by the waiter. He was obviously a student earning a little money for his books. He wore a black jacket with a red vest underneath. I pointed to Fran and said, "*Ein Dinkel-Acker, bitte.*"

"*Was möchten Sie?*" he asked me. What would I like?

"*Ein Apfelsaft, bitte.*"

"Obble shoes?"

"*Yes!*" I buried my face in my hands. I had lost my German accent; he knew I was American. Oh well. I bucked up immediately. "Yes, apple juice, and something to eat."

"Zomezing to eat. A little *Würstchen* perhaps? A zauzitch?"

"Yes. Any kind. Is the apple juice fresh?"

"Ach, no. It is from ze last season. But!" His eyes took on a kind of fire. "I vill sqveece you some fresh! Ve haff some obbles in ze Kellar!" He disappeared gleefully.

Fran said, "Wow. He's going to make you some fresh cider?"

"Students are like that toward Americans here."

"They have a cider press in the cellar?"

"I would doubt it. I don't know how he's going to do it."

Because Fran and I were preoccupied and glum, we made no conversation and it seemed the waiter was back in a flash. He had everything on a little tray. First he put a beer the size of a soccer ball in front of Fran.

"*Ein Dinkel-Acker. Bitte schön.*" Then he beamed at me. "Foa you, *frrresh* obble shoes." It positively sparkled. The amber color was out of this world. "It vill make you velthy und bring you romance, as ve say here." I fairly plucked it off the little wooden tray. "And a special *Würstchen* on a special *Brötchen.*" He handed down a large roll with a whitish sausage in it. Then he lowered a tiny pot of mustard with a silver spoon. He looked very pleased with himself, and then like a good waiter he unceremoniously vanished.

"I wouldn't drink that—" Fran said, but I was already chugging it.

"Ahh! Didn't realize I was so thirsty! Why shouldn't I have drunk it?"

"I doubt it's fresh. He was just BS-ing you. I heard a distinct note of sarcasm in his voice."

"Naw! Nonsense! It's good stuff."

"You'll be drunk as a loon. And I wouldn't—" But I was already halfway into the sausage.

"Mm, it's good," I mumbled. "Want some?" I drained the rest of the cider; burped. "Tastes funny. You know, the sausage tasted funny, too. How's the beer?"

"I don't know. I've lost my thirst. Let's get the smart aleck to bring us the check."

But before I could turn and signal him, the waiter was there.

"One hundred eighty Marks?" I exclaimed.

"Inkludes ze gratuity," the waiter murmured. "Ze meal vill last you a long time. I guarantee."

We ponied up and left. I was in shock. As we crossed the bridge, a man bumped into me.

"Floppy!" I exclaimed.

"I'm happy to see you," he said warmly.

I turned to Fran. "Fran, this is my old friend Floppy from Minnesota. We do email." I introduced them and asked Floppy, "Why are you here? Incredible coincidence!"

"I got your email that you were coming here, and I've wanted to see Germany for a long time. I thought the fare you mentioned was a good opportunity."

"Urp!" I said.

"Is something wrong?"

Blearily, I mentioned that I had just drunk a liter of very, very hard cider, and eaten an old sausage.

"Here. You could use this." He handed me a Ritter Sport—a thick, square German chocolate bar.

"Wow! I haven't had one of these in thirty years!" I'm afraid I blew some zoo breath at him.

"We can talk later." He was gone into the thick press of tourists and shoppers on the bridge.

"What was that all about?" Fran asked when we got to the other side of the bridge. We walked down the steps to the river path, and I found I needed to steady myself on the handrail.

"What was *what* all about?"

"You were talking to yourself on the bridge. Something about your friend or a floppy disk?"

"That was an old pal from Fells Wargo College! I introduced you!" It was quite an effort to say such a long word as "introduced."

"Sure. Why don't we stop here and rest." Fran sat me down on a bench. I fished the Ritter out of my pocket. My head was spinning.

"Here's the chocolate. Here's the chocolate he gave me!"

"Who?"

"Floppy Sherman! On the bridge just now. Here's poof!" I held up the candy bar. "Want some?"

"No thanks. Looks like you've been carrying it around since the airport."

I tore off the foil and gobbled the chocolate. It made me feel better. It cleared my head and made my stomach and the swans stop spinning.

"Urp," I reasoned.

"You look better. Let's get this over with."

So we stood up, I straightened my jacket, my glasses, and my hair, and we walked toward the lovely Hölderlin Tower. The Tower is a small round column appended to a narrow three-story house. It was soft yellow, surrounded by willows, just as I remembered it. But suddenly a wave of wooziness struck me and I grabbed for Fran's arm.

"Hold on there Buster. You all right?"

I stood still for a moment as my head cleared. "Yeah." And then I exclaimed, "Holy Toledo!" You would have, too. At the riverbank where about a dozen rowboats had pulled up, three Black American men in their 60's, all wearing dark suits and white shirts, were doing some kind of routine. They turned in unison, stepped forward and back in unison, spun around and snapped their fingers in unison. They were singing.

"It's the Temptations," Fran said.

I blinked a few times. He was right. "No big deal, Fran. German youth love American rock and roll. The Temps have been touring here for thirty years. But hey—something's wrong. It doesn't add up."

"What.

"One. Two. Three. There are only three of them."

"There are always three."

"Weren't there four or five?"

Fran unzipped his jacket. "Well, I say let's join them."

So that's what we did. We fell in on their left; two American kids in the boats threw us their baseball caps and we put them on backwards; in a minute we had caught on to the moves and were going up and back, sideways, and around with the other three. They were singing their bluesy cover of Bruce Springsteen's "Hungry Heart," and I fell in.

Yes, still a little uncertain on my feet, I got confused by one of the steps and pitched toward the water face first. I sort of came to on my back. Fran was wiping water off my face with his handkerchief. He looked like he was giving me last rites. I turned my head and saw only empty boats docked along the bank.

"Where are they?"

"Who?" Fran asked.

"The Temptations. Have I been out that long?"

"Only a minute or so. You fell face down in the water."

"I know."

"Tell me—were you ever baptized?"

"Huh?"

"I asked, Were you ever baptized?"

"Well . . ."

"Yes or no."

"'Yes or no.'"

"Answer Yes, or No."

"Well no. Never."

"Good." Fran rung out his handkerchief. "Because I just did it."

"What? You baptized me? Just now, when I was uncon. Uncon. Uncon."

"You aren't a Baptist. You don't have to be conscious. We baptize infants all the time. They don't know anything."

"But why did you do it?"

"You can never be too careful."

"Holy cow. You're a minister again!"

"Duty. Duty saves us sometimes. But it doesn't take a minister to baptize."

"You really baptized me?"

"I was bored. You were out cold. Feel different?"

"Yes. Yes I do. I'm awake. I wasn't awake when you were baptizing me." Fran helped me to my feet. "Are you sure?"

"Absolutely."

"What do I have to do now?"

"You're the car authority."

"I told you, I never studied Theology here. I laid bricks."

"You know, you've ingested some bad stuff. Maybe we should get you to a—"

"Oh no. German hospitals. German doctors."

Fran lifted his eyebrows. "German nurses."

I leaned over and blew my cookies. Afterward, Fran gave me his handkerchief. "Feel better now?"

"Much," I said. I felt great. I felt like a million bucks. Fran handed me a little bottle of mouthwash.

"You carry mouthwash?"

He unzipped his fanny pack. "All kinds of stuff. Diarrhea stuff, carsickness stuff, aspirin, band aids, shoe polish. This is a foreign country, after all."

I took a swig and gargled. "*Blooey*. Thanks. Hey!" A workman rushed by pushing an empty wheelbarrow. Little nurdles of cement or plaster stuck to the inside. "Fran, did he just come out through that door?" I pointed to the Hölderlin Tower about thirty yards away. A small wooden door stood open.

"I think so. Well, I didn't notice . . . "

"What are they doing?" I cried, scrambling to my feet. "Filling it up with cement?" I ran to the door and Fran followed.

In a few minutes we reached the door. Fran and I don't run much. We caught our breath in the doorway.

The door was indeed open and there was indeed someone inside. A man carrying a pail had started up a small staircase to the right. He had must have heard me swing the door open. Bending to see us, he said, "*Ja?*"

I had never seen the inside of the little Tower. I stood looking around, breathing hard, and said, "*Ja.*"

It was beautiful. The door opened into a light sitting room. Its walls were pale yellow, softer and brighter than the outside color. Lacy white curtains hung across several windows, blocking vision from outside the glass but letting in a great deal of lovely sunlight. In fact, two of the windows were partly open, admitting a faint but fragrant breeze that fluttered the doily-like curtains ever so gently. I was amazed at how spacious the interior seemed to be. Between two of the windows opposite us hung a rectangular mirror framed with a kind of filigreed silver. Under it was a small writing desk of dark, rich, highly-polished cherry wood. To its left stood a small but elegant piano—I assumed the one Hölderlin had delighted to play until it was taken away from him. To the right of the desk, under another window, stood a table large enough for two or three persons, with two chairs. Just at the door and to our left, the third chair of the table had been placed. On the table was a white glass vase with three fresh yellow roses. The woodwork around the windows, at the cornices, and along the floor, was white. The floor itself was a polished but warm parquet of what appeared to be alternating cherry, birch, and walnut. The stairs to our right evidently led up to another room. The ceiling above our heads was white, with a tint or suggestion of heavenly blue.

"*Entschuldigung,*" I said. "Excuse me."

"Yes?" The man now descended the steps. "You are Americans. Would you have come to talk about cars?"

"Ah?" I exclaimed.

"You have, haven't you?" The man's German accent subsided quickly, and he sounded almost American to me. "The only people who come here these days are car aficionados."

I looked at him with considerable disbelief—this man in a white ruffled shirt, rolled at the sleeves, knickers, and white (but somewhat smudged) silk stockings. His low, brown leather shoes had buckles rather than laces. His longish gray hair was tied in back.

"Hölderlin?" I said in disbelief, a little breathless. "Mister Freidrich Hölderlin, Sir?"

The man frowned a little. "My goodness! The poor fellow has been gone for quite some time now. Didn't you know?"

Neither Fran nor I answered. The man put his pail down and smiled. "My name is Zimmer, shall we say. In a manner of speaking, I am refurbishing this tower on behalf of a group of re-enactors. You have re-enactors in America, have you not?"

We nodded. I think I finally inhaled at that point.

"Did you think I was a ghost? Ha ha. Not quite." He extended a hand for us to shake, and as each of us spoke our full names, he nodded precisely and repeated, "Zimmer."

"I am very pleased to meet you," I finally said. "You gave us quite a turn. What group of re-enactors?"

"Friends of Hölderlin, shall we say. An automobile association in Frankfurt. I am here to re-plaster the first floor. It has all been neglected shamefully."

"This room is beautiful," Fran said.

"Oh, of course this floor has been maintained—for tourists. But Herr Hölderlin spent much time upstairs, on the first floor. He often wrote up there. People do not know that."

I looked at my shoes. They were not muddy, but I felt that I must not enter. Zimmer observed my problem and said, "Of course you may come in and look around. Remove your shoes, gentlemen. There are still some *Hausschuhe* here somewhere."

As we took off our shoes, Zimmer opened a cabinet under the stairs. He handed us two quite large pair of gray felt house shoes.

"Come up. You can tell me whether my plastering is good. My eyesight is not the best any more. Never enough light."

He led the way upstairs. As we came out into the upper room, I was surprised once again by the impression of spaciousness. I felt this must have been the poet's bedroom and study. However, there was no furniture in the room. It was all the color of new plaster, a light gray, or freshly primed plaster of a dull white. With light coming in through the bare windows, the room was very light and bright without being starkly or unpleasantly so. The ceiling above this room was pale blue. To our right, a very narrow stairway followed the curve of the wall up to a trapdoor. There was a railing on the wall, but the stairway was open and almost blended into that part of the circular room. Two stepladders, long and short, stood propped against the wall, and paint cans, brushes, gloves, and pans were placed neatly beside the ladders. A wide pan, a spreading trowel, and a pail of plaster were obviously in use. There was a section of partially refinished wall, the surface still damp. Zimmer took gloves from his back pocket and went to the pail.

"Sit down, gentlemen, though all I can offer you is a bit of floor to sit upon." We remained standing, nodding our acknowledgment of the offer. Zimmer reached into the bucket, gripping a small scoop. He shoved it around in the bucket, slapped a few scoopfuls onto the tray, stirred that around, then took up the trowel.

"I hope you gentlemen do not mind my working as we converse. The plaster must be applied before it becomes too thick."

"Of course," Fran said. I was quite content with such work, as long as someone else was doing it. Anyway, I was too awed to speak. After a few minutes, Fran became uncomfortable with the silence and said, "My friend is overcome with being at the center of Romanticism. He's a Romantic."

Zimmer turned with raised eyebrows, feigning to be impressed. "Oh? You are a Romantic? May I ask, do you know what Romanticism is?"

I had never been asked this. "I . . . Well no, not really. I've always felt like a Romantic, though. I really liked my girlfriend in high school."

"Come on," Fran said. "You can do better than that." He cleared his throat and looked at Zimmer somewhat apologetically. "He tells me about Romanticism all the time."

I thought, How dare I speak of Romanticism in this place? Yet what more fitting place? I had a responsibility. "Yes. Yes, I know what Romanticism is. A Romantic believes in the individual, and in the goodness of humanity."

"Mere bologna," Zimmer said.

I was stunned. I was speechless.

He went on. "Do you think Keats and Hölderlin believed in that kind of *Knackwurst*?"

"I—"

"Of course not. Try again. I have all day. This plaster dries slowly."

"Equality," I squeaked.

"Good. But not confined to Romantic thought, by any means."

"Nature," I said.

"Ah. What about nature?"

"It's good." I happened to glance at Fran, who rolled his eyes upward.

"They never said that, the Romantics. Nature is nature. What else about nature?"

"It's—it's our, well, home. We are part of it. We are not against it. We oppose it with machines, but we should love it as our model, mother, friend, brother, fellow."

"Wait a moment. So far so good, as to words. But who are you to be saying this?"

"I—I'm a sort of environmentalist. I have a program."

"Which is?"

"Stop airplane and car travel."

"You want to tell the auto workers and oil drillers and airline employees of the world to ignore their need for financial security, and you wouldn't quit your dishonest job yourself? And you just went out and bought another car. How many do you have?"

"Ah, it's uh, back to three, uh, actually. One for each driver in the household. Me, myself, and I. *How do you—*"

"And tell me this. How did you get here?"

"Here?"

He pointed to the floor. "Yes, here. Right here. How did you get here, to Tübingen, to Germany? Did you sail? Did you walk?"

I shook my head.

"That's right. You flew. Then you paid a big admission price supporting a car show and the automakers. Then what did you do?"

"I—"

"You rented a car. And is it a hybrid-powered car? Or a solar car?"

"Well, not ex—"

"That's right. The simple and honest answer is No. You rented an expensive, gas-guzzling sports car. Am I right?"

"Yes. How did—"

"In fact you drove one of the cars you most deplore—verbally—to get here. A car made for fun, entertainment, excitement. Who's going to listen to you if you don't even listen to yourself?"

"But—"

"But nothing—except how can you call SUV drivers 'Buttplätzchen' and expect to understand the meaning of life?"

"I—"

"What would that be?" Fran put in. "The meaning of life."

Zimmer looked at Fran. "Why, love. Love is the meaning of life. What did you think it was?"

"That's *it*?" I said. "That's all? Love?"

Zimmer frowned at me. I remembered Goethe's—no, Werther's—statement, "I could be leading the best and happiest of lives if I weren't such a fool."

"That's right," Zimmer said to me.

"You can read my mind?"

"One doesn't have to be able to read your mind to see that you're a fool."

"I told him," Fran said. "I tell him that all the time."

"So are you. So are we all. The human being is not an inspiration when it comes to judgment and intellect." He smoothed the plaster he had just trowelled onto the wall. "That is why we are destroying the world."

"We are?" I said. "You agree?"

"Of course. The evidence is all around us. If only we would realize that to revere nature is not blasphemy but gratitude."

"How do you save it—the world?" Fran asked.

"Your poet Whitman has written, 'Affection shall solve the problems of freedom yet.' He was an authentic Romantic, that fellow. When you love another soul, you take care in many ways. You tend the earth. You live more simply. You become truthful. You live with courage. You make the world more beautiful." Zimmer sighed. "But if you ask how I, personally, can save the world—it is by plastering this room. If I cannot save the world by plastering, then I cannot save it. And that goes for you, too." He finished with a look at me.

"Me? Plaster?"

"No! Not plastering, in your case. For you it's—well, you know very well yourself."

"What is it?" Fran whispered.

"Poetry."

"Poetry!" Fran exclaimed drily.

"Yes!" Zimmer exclaimed, pointing at Fran. "Poetry indeed! Poetry gives you light by which to see your loves and obligations. The Reverend needs to learn a little more reverence. Your young friend needs his poetry."

"'Young friend,'" I repeated quietly. "What a wonderful phrase."

"If you were my age, you would call someone like yourself 'young' also."

"Poetry," Fran repeated. "I suppose Romantic poetry."

"I understand your tone. And you are correct, as you understand the word. Romance is illusion. When we are in love with illusion, we become worse than ourselves. But when we are in love with another soul, we are saved. Our inner light is located in the heart, not the brain. A Romantic believes the truth of this. —And you, my young friend." He pointed his trowel at me. "Why do you come all the way to Germany to ask what you should do about your foolishness, your cars, your job, your unworthy aspirations? You have your answer at home. You have read 'Song of the Open Road'?"

"Whitman."

"Yes. But do not make an automobile expert out of the fellow. Remember he walked that open road. 'Afoot and light-hearted, I take to the open road.' Listen to one sentence from him, my friend, and have your answer. It is, 'Discard everything that is an insult to your soul.'"

Zimmer went back to his pail and spread another smear of plaster onto his trowel. Fran looked at me and shrugged his shoulders.

I began to ask, "What—"

"What else can you do? Poetry is not enough? Perhaps it is not enough for you, any more than for me. See, how I save the world by plastering a room. I do so even though I am not an especially good plasterer, as you are not an especially good poet. Be the biggest pygmy you can be, wrote the American Romantic, Thoreau. 'Let every one endeavor . . . to be what he was made.'" Zimmer knelt beside the wall, his back to us. "You can be the change you wish for. You think the world should give up cars and airplanes?" He turned to look at me. "Very well. Give up your cars. No more plane rides for you. From now on, for you it shall be the bicycle, walking, or public transportation—on the ground or upon the water. What do you think?"

"It—it sounds hard."

"Not that; the wall. Am I getting the plaster on evenly?"

Fran and I nodded vigorously. "Looks great! Wonderful."

Zimmer turned back. "It looks a little uneven to me. You see, if everyone did his small part. You cannot change anybody else's world. But you can change your own. It is your responsibility to do so. Do not flatter me. Love does not flatter. How is the wall?"

"You are a poet, aren't you," Fran said.

Zimmer looked at Fran, then at the wall, and a trace of a smile came to his mouth. But his eyes still transmitted a strangely penetrating light.

"Unfortunately the work of God has to be done by amateurs."

"I thought it was all about grace, not works."

"You ministers are all quibblers. By the grace of God, we work."

"How did things get this way?" I whined. "Why is everything a mess?"

"Do you love your neighbor?"

"He tried," Fran put in; "but she gave him the cold shoulder."

Zimmer looked up with a vaguely annoyed expression. "Ah, humor. You are what Americans call a 'smart aleck,' I think."

This time he put the trowel down. He sat against the wall, and we followed suit. He now could use both hands for gestures.

"We are like a young boy who plucks a rose in the meadow. He wants to take it for his own, this beautiful and tender living thing. That is where the Romantic enters, my friend: the Romantic thinks of the Earth as a living thing, a beautiful living thing. But it is not our own. The thorn of that realization enrages us. We want to be God; that is the Satan in us. Like a child we cry out, and then we crush the flower."

"A little rose in the meadow," I murmured.

Röslein, Röslein, Röslein rot—
Röslein auf der Heide.

"I learned it in high school." A mist came to my eyes.

"The good old days for you? A Romantic longs for a paradise lost. You shall return, my friend. God has not forgotten us."

He got up and turned once again to the plastering. "Well then," he said abruptly. "What is the great car question you have brought all the way from America?"

Fran spoke up. "Can I get a new Audi TT cheaper if I buy it here and ship it home?"

"Hmm. Just what is the real cost of an automobile? But no. Those days are over." The man looked at the small, careful smear of plaster he had just applied. "Is that it? Is that your question?"

I coughed nervously. "I think his question should be interpreted as, 'Does it matter if I lose my soul, as long as I have a good car?'"

The great man smiled. "It is very important to have a good car. One good car." He went back to applying the plaster. "You know, a person has to be very careful. How you apply plaster in a place you revere can beautify or corrupt your soul." He quickly glanced at Fran. "Desire is the clamor of evil within us."

"Is that one of Goethe's Maxims?" I asked brightly.

"Perhaps. Add this old one: *Desire nothing; love all.*"

"That's a good one," I offered.

He smoothed a few strokes on the wall. "*Too long now, things divine have been cheaply used.*"

"Hölderlin," I said, nodding sagely, completely in the dark.

"Consciousness," he said. When he went back to the wall, saying nothing more, I repeated the word as he bent down to re-supply his trowel.

"Consciousness is a great light cheaply used," he said. Suddenly he turned. Holding up his trowel as if he were pointing an index finger into the air, he said, "Do you know, a German writer"—here he smiled a little—"prophesied the present condition. The world has made a bargain with the devil. We light up the world every night with our fuel-burning electric lights, but our light is darkness. We flatter ourselves that our destructions are achievements."

"A compact with the devil," I said.

"I thought Faust just made a simple deal," Fran interjected. "His soul for the girl. Like my pal Buster here."

"Never! Do you think a man like Faust, with his genius and education, would be a bumbler like your friend here? He's after much more than a mere girl!"

"But there is nothing more than a mere girl," I said quietly.

"Ah," the man said. "Perhaps our bumbler has arrived at the sum of wisdom."

"Sounds like you're a Romantic," Fran said to him.

"Listen, my friend," the man who called himself Zimmer said to me. "You get yourself one good car. Discard all the others, and like the pearl of great price, secure that one good car."

I thought, *it sounds so simple.* It seemed that the white light of that room had become more intense, more illuminating though still mild.

In my delirium I recited Hölderlin:

> *From those peaks the heavenly air*
> > *dissolved my anguished bondage; and from the valley*
> > > *like life from the chalice of joy,*
> > > > *gleamed your silver-blue waves.*

> *The mountain streams rush down to you,*
> > *And with them flows my heart . . .*

"Lovely in the German, and charming in English," Zimmer reflected.

"The divine beauty of nature—"

"Very romantic," Fran remarked.

"I wish not to deface or destroy Her," I said pleadingly to Zimmer. "I want to be innocent again!"

He smiled a sad smile. "The longing for innocence reflects a larger longing."

"Nobody's innocent," Fran observed, tracing some illegible letters in the faint dust of the floor.

"Nor can anyone be, who lives on earth."

"Not even Americans?" I asked. "Can't we be innocent again?" *What a dizzy question,* I thought even as I asked it.

"Do you pay taxes, my friend?"

"Only when he works," Fran put in.

"Why do you ask?"

Zimmer shook his head regretfully. "I suppose I need not tell you who is the largest consumer of fuel in the world."

"The U. S. armed forces," Fran said, his dusty fingertip in the air.

"Methodists tend to be liberals," I told Zimmer reassuringly.

"But a fact is a fact, Buster," Zimmer replied.

"An Abrams tank gets a half mile to the gallon; a jet fighter is even worse," Fran added. "I'm just saying."

"Defense has a price," Zimmer said. "'We had to destroy the village to save it.'"

"You mean the earth." My tone was rueful. "And nobody cares."

"Oh, but many do care. Your Pope has said that pollution is a betrayal."

I pointed to Fran. "You mean his Pope. I'm not religious."

Zimmer smiled again. "What Romantic is not religious? You have quoted Hölderlin. Would you be familiar with Goethe's poem, 'Holy Longing'?"

"I have translated it."

"So I feared."

"*A new longing*
Lifts you to a higher union."

"Very well," said Zimmer. "You see, our highest longings all converge at their peak."

"Like the golden-white peak of the Mountain of the Blue Moon," I said.

Zimmer's nod was kindly, and it reminded me of someone long ago, from my younger days. He said, "All that you can take from a moment of enlightenment, this inexpressible moment, is Art." As he spoke, we were surrounded by warm white light.

"*Uff da!* It's so simple!" I looked at Fran. "Simple." The walls appeared even whiter now, and I realized that I was looking upward at Fran. I was lying in a bed. Fran was sitting beside me. "What the—? Where . . . ? Where are we, Fran?"

"Still on the sweet old Earth, Buster."

"Am I in a hospital? How did I get here?"

"You passed out cold, dropped into the river like a stone."

"I know."

"You know?"

"Yeah. The Temptations. I fell in."

"When I got you out, somebody called an ambulance."

"Thanks. I mean, I hate being here, but thanks."

"Well." Fran looked down.

"What? What's the matter? Am I all right?"

"You might not like this. While you were still a little in the water . . ."

"You baptized me."

His eyes widened. "You were awake?"

Epilogue

THE AUTHOR RETURNS HOME

A few days after we got back, my phone rang.

"Hi. This is Fran."

"Fran! I am so relieved. I had begun to wonder whether you're real."

"I wanted to tell you that I'm not going to buy the Audi."

"Good. I didn't think you would. But say more. Is something more coming? A Mercedes instead? A Porsche? Say more quick."

"I have given up the whole idea."

"Wonderful! Are you staying with Carol?"

"Of course. You?"

"No; I'm not going to stay with Carol."

"Jerk! I meant—"

"I know what you meant. Frankly, I'm discouraged."

"As always?"

"Different."

"Variety is good, Buster."

"But I am going to act, in spite of my discouragement."

"Good plan. What will you do?"

"First, I'm quitting my job if they don't fire me first. I have to commute to it anyway and pollute the air."

"Excellent. But what about income?"

"I'll find something when I get there."

"You're going somewhere?"

"Yep. Just bought a car."

"What?!? Another car? You said you were through with cars! What is the *matter* with you? *What in heaven's name did you buy?*"

"A good car. A 1913 Chevrolet."

Second Epilogue: I Go Find April/ Peggy

It was true: I had sold everything I could lay my hands on, starting with my computer, to buy a partially restored 1913 Chevrolet. My other cars were gone. To make a long story short, I tracked April/ Peggy down after only a half hour at an internet cafe in Minot. The powerful search engine narrowed her down to either a Fed Ex district manager in Portland, or an executive at a financial concern in Philly. I telephoned the district manager and learned from a recording that she was away on a spirituality retreat slash culinary seminar in Seattle, so I ruled her out on principle. Contemporary physics teaches us that you find what you look for, and you find it where you look. I didn't want to find a confusing individual and I thought Seattle a sketchy choice for romantic events—rain, rain, rain. This wants light, I thought. In any case, Fed Ex just didn't seem like something my April would do, much less Peggy.

But to become a worker of financial miracles, that was pure Peggy. It was in fact the month of April, when folk long to go on pilgrimages, that I set out for Philadelphia in a now fully restored and fully operational 1913 Chevy. It had taken me all winter to finish the work, but it had been pure joy. I had hand-built some of the parts myself. You wouldn't believe the trouble I went through to get some of the specifications and find proper materials. The tires were the worst nightmare. I had to swallow some pride and petition Clark Manufactury, UnLtd. for some custom made bicycle tires that I could fit onto the Chevy's narrow wheels.

It was worth it. When I pressed the button for the electric crank motor—an invention of mine that got around the arm-breaking crank handle—and that baby turned over and rattled, I felt like I was on the road to the Himalayas. What a stunning sense of regret shot through me at that instant. "Oh well," I said; "on to Philadelphia." This was no time to look back. I buckled down to the task at hand, which was to find the Pennsylvania Turnpike and get to the City of Brotherly Love.

As I spun along the Midwestern and Eastern highways of America, I reflected on how far we had come. This whole distance had been only a dream in the Founding Fathers' unconscious minds. What did they know of Kansas City, St. Louis, Peoria, Indianapolis, Columbus? When I struck the Turnpike east of Pittsburgh, I felt that I was going back in time to the origin of it all. I was tracing the expansion of liberty back to the Big Bang. I was condensing freedom back to the point of all return.

The AmeriCo Financial Center is only blocks from Independence Mall. After going to see the Liberty Bell and joining a tour of Independence Hall, I got back into the purring Chevy and cruised the area, finally parking in front of the tall steel-and-glass building. As I got out of the car, I could almost hear Art's voice somewhere over my head, saying, "Ayuh, she's a nice little car. Chevys always start."

Peggy's office was on the fifth floor; and that bright Wednesday afternoon, standing in light filtered through the gray windowpanes, I waited humbly and expectantly at the receptionist's desk. Like a supplicant, I fingered my little English driving cap nervously. I wore a pair of jodhpurs I had picked up on vacation in Williston, thinking them somehow appropriate to a road trip in a 1913 automobile, but now I didn't know. I felt faintly ridiculous, but honest. This is who and what I was. At least I wasn't affecting a riding crop. I wore long black socks and brown leather shoes. No red Keds for this boy. I had been forced to go with a buff-colored Clark's Bicycle, UnLtd. t-shirt, but I wasn't going to be thwarted by embarrassment, intimidated by my own inadequacies. April/Peggy had remembered me. I had ascertained that fact on the phone, and I wasn't going to blow the second chance of a lifetime out of timidity.

When she walked out of her office into the reception room, I knew it was April and Peggy. Her face had been admirably restored. She gleamed like the new Audi A6, based on the modular-longitudinal MLB Evo architecture, conventional wheelbase though wide-track stance at 73 inches.

"You look fabulous," I said.

She smiled. Her hair was luminous platinum, long and in waves. "I should look gorgeous," she said; "especially to you." How fetching. It was modest, in a way.

Her complexion was absolutely glossy, and not a wrinkle. "You look like a model," I said. I wasn't sure which model. Possibly the Hummer H3.

"You look perfectly dashing, in a sort of Cockney way." That pleased me greatly. "Quite British. You aren't British though, are you?"

"Well, actually—."

"German, if I remember correctly. So I would have thought you'd be on time."

"On—"

"It's twelve ten."

"Oh, but only ten minutes," I said with a winning smile.

"Kindly reserve your excuses. Shall we go out for an abbreviated luncheon?"

In the elevator, she remarked to the shiny doors, "I would have thought that coming to see one's supposed true love after all these years would have made one punctual."

"Indeed," I said, looking at her in the swirly stainless steel. "I'm awfully sorry."

"Well, let's assume a weak beginning will lead to a strong finish, shall we?"

"Strong finish, yes. Yes of course."

"I assume that you have a reservation somewhere suitable."

"Ah. Well, actually I am unfamiliar with this city. I hoped you might have a suggestion."

"So there is no reservation. I might have known." The doors had opened. We walked through the lobby and she waited for me to open the outer door. "We aren't familiar with the large city, are we?"

"Ah, no, we are not. I'm sorry."

"Let me make a wild guess. You usually dine at McDonalds. No wait." She faced me and held up a finger, smiling. "You cook for yourself. Am I right? In your trailer?"

"I—"

"Yes, I thought so. I'm sure you are a gourmet chef. Are you?"

"Why, actually I am."

"You own a nice non-stick frying pan from KMart. Well. Oh my."

She was looking at the little 1913 Chevrolet and smiling. "This isn't our car."

"No. It's not."

"What a coincidence. How many automobiles does one see in this city with North Dakota plates. Are we sure this isn't our car?"

"Of course we are. It isn't our car."

"Quite certain?"

"Yes."

"Well. You are just as much a liar and spinner of fictions as you were as a child."

"I don't think of myself as having been a child back then." I almost pointed out that she had been two years my junior, but I thought better of it.

"I assure you that you were and quite clearly still are. But I carry through on my obligations. I obligated myself to have luncheon with you, and that is what we are going to do, mercifully abbreviated by your tardiness. Shall we?" She gestured toward a stunning, polished black Hummer parked directly in front of my Chevy. There was a long line of reserved spaces and the Chevrolet had four different kinds of tickets on the windshield. I assume that its vintage character is what prevented its having been towed.

The Hummer was gorgeous in a powerful, consuming Rubens way. It gleamed and glistened, confidently lounging in its own grease. Without hesitation April walked out to the driver's side, all the lights flashed twice, and I heard her open the door and step up and in. I went to the passenger door and opened it. But as I looked into that high, broad interior and smelled the leather, I held back, my hand bracing the vault-like door.

"Are we hesitating? I seem to remember that we do not carry through on things."

I stared dumbly.

"Or was is that I just didn't appeal to you so much after all, despite the ardent things you said to me on the telephone? More fiction?"

The odor of leather was nearly overpowering. The dashboard glowed with lurid light like a cockpit. The hollow hardness of her voice reminded me of the exhaust note of a Porsche.

"Well, are you getting in or aren't you?"

I looked at her, then I looked to the rear of the Hummer. Below the corner of the high bumper, I could see part of the Chevrolet's headlamp. I said, "I'm not." I swung the big door closed and stepped back.

She started the immense vehicle with a growling bang, shot back into the Chevrolet, cut the wheel and barged out into traffic, leaving a wave of exhaust. The Chevy's bumper and headlights were destroyed, folded up and back with the grill onto the blunted engine compartment. My electric starting mechanism was up there; there was no way the Chevrolet would start now. I couldn't even drive away.

As I bent under the open hood, someone came up beside me and said, "Might could be, you got a cracked block there, Bubba." I only half heard him as I stared into the little engine bay. He got under the car and looked up at the little block.

VOICE FROM BELOW: Naw, ain't no way in hell this buggy gon start.

VOICE FROM ABOVE: Just give 'er a try. She'll start.

The lower individual had departed, so I walked to the little driver's door, opened it and got in. I held the wooden steering wheel and squeezed. "Fayaway," I said quietly, "I am so sorry." After a moment I pushed the new ignition button, certain that it wouldn't do anything. It was a gesture of despair. But sure enough.

Appendix
Goethe's Automotive Conversations

CONVERSATION #1

Johann Peter Eckermann's *Conversations of Goethe* is "The best German book there is," according to Friedrich Nietzsche. Despite poverty and obscurity, Eckermann persisted in the project that he considered his life's work. Toward the end, Eckermann was forced to sell nearly all his furniture in order to survive while working on books Four and Five of the *Conversations*. Part Four was published in his lifetime, while the incomplete Part Five has languished in manuscript for years, viewed only by scholars and archivists and myself.

In an introduction to the Oxenford English abridged edition, Havelock Ellis wrote " . . . Eckermann was all the time an artist; and, while closely faithful to the essential truth, he omitted, rearranged, transposed, in order by art to come closer to the essential inner truth, as those who knew Goethe gladly testified."[1] The conversations are all invented, in that Eckermann did not record Goethe's speech word for word, but jotted down phrases and ideas. Eckermann said, ". . . all is perfectly true, but everything is selected. I was careful to wait days and weeks before writing down my impressions, so that all that was small might be lost and only what was significant was left" (xvi). He would sometimes spend months recalling, inventing, rewriting one conversation, in a process of what Eckermann called "spiritual crystallization" (xvi).

I consider this an outrage. It is a fraud perpetrated on credulous readers, like Nietzsche. My concern for literal fact, and my scrupulous

1. John Oxenford, tr., and J. K. Moorhead, ed., *Conversations of Goethe with Johann Peter Eckermann* (New York: Da Capo Press, 1998), xiii.

preservation and reproduction of conversations found in this book, drives me to return to Eckermann's original notes in offering the following original translation of a fragment of *Conversations, Part Five*. Though first inspired by a photocopied fragment of the *Conversations* housed in Cambridge, Massachusetts while I was a Visiting Lecturer in Automotive Theory at Harvard Divinity School, I rely chiefly on the handwritten manuscript pages archived at the Frankfurt *Goethe Institut*, and have assiduously sought out pages housed in widely diverse Goethe Institute locations. Here I should like to mention that part of the proceeds of this present book shall be used to fund not only the re-unification of Eckerman's Part Five manuscript, but also a careful and complete translation of the whole into English. I am willing to undertake this task myself.

Meanwhile, I offer the following excerpts of Goethe's late-in-life thoughts on automobiles, beginning with his ideas on Christmas:

> One morning Goethe called me to his chambers rather later than usual. He had been working on a treatise pertaining to the Christian holidays, and, finally giving over to his true sentiments, had at last abandoned the project and instead related his ideas to me.
>
> "This is a very difficult and exasperating business, Eckermann, this writing for the public! One feels a responsibility to be read, even as one feels an overwhelming compulsion to tell the truth. But only the dead can tell the truth. So, Eckermann, be careful of what I tell you!"
>
> I then asked him what thoughts had occasioned these reflections and exasperations. He replied that it was a particularly recalcitrant section of his treatise on Religion.
>
> "As you know, Eckermann, there is no-one who more enjoys the celebration of Christmas, and especially the leading-up to the days of Christmas themselves. Where would Germans be without the—admittedly essentially pagan—customs of St. Nicolas Day, the Christ-child markets, the sweet excitement of the entire Advent season in the minds and hearts of children! Yet, Eckermann, all this for an invention! All this for a beautiful and somehow true fiction!
>
> "For the Christmas story is based on the two Gospels of Luke and Matthew, which are themselves reconstructions, selections, works of art! What are we to do with the separate accounts of Luke and Matthew?—for they do not agree. Shall we simply lump all their details together, and create one large birth story? This is what the popular mind and the Christian Church have

artfully done—a beautiful collaboration, in its results and effects, to be certain. The Ox, what he contributes to the story! The
Ass, what she means to the tableau! The Lamb, what it supplies
in overall symbol and meaning. Surely a truth is expressed, but
its means is art—like my *Wilhelm Meister, Götz,* or even *Faust*!
I bow to the artistry of Matthew, by whatever name he actually historically bore—and of Luke, supremely of Luke—and I
acknowledge the deep truths within their portraits—truths perceived most convincingly and reliably in the hearts of children!

"But what are we to make of the gifts, Eckermann—the gifts
brought by the Magi whom Luke mentions not at all? Surely
Luke is aware of the tradition that is recorded in Matthew! Does
he not believe it? Does he not believe there were Wise Men, astrologers as some erroneously call them, from the East?—any
more than he believes in the literal historicity of the Flight to
Egypt or the Massacre of the Innocents? Eckermann, listen to
me! The so-called Wise Men were not kings or astrologers but
mystics—and from where "in the east"? From Tibet. Ach, Eckermann, you are skeptical, I know. But I ask you, how familiar
are you with the sacred traditions of Tibet, that you cannot find
it in your head to assent to my proposition?

"The Tibetans were uncannily spiritual, with already an
ancient tradition, when the Buddhists found them! Already
there was in that impossibly remote, impossibly distant region
a place, according to later Buddhist-inspired writings, a timeless place far into the mountains. From there they ranged deep
and wide—spiritually, mentally, and sometimes physically. You
can read of their travel out of the body, Eckermann. Open your
mind, man! As the incomparable Shakespeare wrote, 'there
are more things in earth and heaven than are dreamt of in this
philosophy of yours.' *Philosophy*, bah! What is it but a game?
And theology? What but a pious—yes, even impious—game?
But no, let us not call it that, for it is an attempt to put into man's
understanding that which is infinitely greater than man's fac-
ulty of understanding—hence theology is written in parables,
stories, fictions! The Tibetans understood as much. How can
philosophy and theology account for what with prayer and discipline the Tibetans could do—and, by present-day accounts of
travelers, they still can do? They sing several notes using a single
voice, witness events that happen hundreds of miles away, move
physical objects without touching them—and travel outside
their own bodies! Why, even our own European, Swedenborg,
could do the latter, as is well-attested by his witnessing the great
fire in London while he himself, or his body, was still in Sweden.

These 'Wise Men' of Matthew's, following a star, were either Tibetan monks, or people very like them!

"For what do you make of a star moving ahead of the three
travelers, and then coming to rest over a stable? Eh? Even the
most primitive of people in the most primitive of times know
that stars do not behave that way. Matthew's word 'star' is a fiction and a symbol for something else—for a spiritual light, a
light visible to the Third Eye, which guided the Wise Men across
an unmapped expanse of Earth to the otherwise unknown birth
in Judea—for unknown it must have been. Certainly for Luke,
even the appearance of the Wise Men was too much notice
given to a birth whose circumstances characterized a reversal of
all the world's expectations. Think of it—the birth of the King of
Kings, so obscure as to have taken place in a stable, so obscure
that none were to know of it—the exact opposite of Caesar—the
exact opposite of worldly power, notoriety, fame, ceremony,
commercialism! That is why Luke has left the story of the Wise
Men out. But Matthew was writing in symbolic terms! Three—
or however many—three for the Trinity perhaps—three Wise
Men follow some sort of uncanny light no doubt absolutely
invisible to others—for would not such a star have attracted
popular and scientific notice all across the Earth, had it been in
actual astrophysical fact a star? They follow a spiritual light—
and they abnegate themselves, mind you, by paying homage to
a king who is the opposite of a king, and God who is the opposite of a god, a helpless infant—and a savior who saves nobody
from the abuses and mortality of earthly life. And how do they
pay homage, Eckermann? By bringing gifts. And what are these
gifts, Eckermann? Petroleum! The fable of gold, frankincense,
and myrrh is exactly that, a fable. For how else to represent three
substances that no human in Judea or Rome or Asia Minor had
ever seen before?—petroleum, aluminum, and glass!

"Petroleum, it burns and it lubricates, but comes from no
sea creature, from no colonizing insect, from no vegetable, or
fruit-bearing tree! Aluminum: it is stronger than iron or bronze,
yet has not a fraction of their heft! Glass: transparent, brilliant
when faceted like a jewel, yet it is no gem, no mineral, and it
shatters like no diamond. What is this, Eckermann, but the
symbol of the antichrist, the god of this world: the automobile!"

Here I interrupted the great mind, not, perhaps, by words,
but rather by my expression of bafflement and perplexity. For
I had not heard this word used by him before. [Ed. note: The
word in Eckermann's manuscript is the compound *Machine-
Angetriebneten-Beförderungsmittel*, or machine-driven-vehicle.

However, Goethe's rich and allusive German is impossible to translate fully. In this case *Beförderungsmittel* has the meaning not merely of "vehicle" but of "forwarding-agent," that which puts or makes forward, possibly related to the negative term "froward," in the sense of "presumptious"; and the word also contains a pun on "Ford," already a major player in the German automotive market in Goethe's time.] I suspected that this related to his ever-present interest in the automobile, but it was characteristic of him to use an altogether idiosyncratic but rich, complex, and allusive term.

"Yes, Eckermann," he continued, "I am referring to what we Germans so lazily and carelessly term the 'car,' as if by a simple and innocuous word we could mask the complex evil of the automobile, and shield ourselves from it, like so many motorized ostriches! As I wrote in *Werther*, we are beset by dangers that we wish not to know. For we truly are driven to *become* machines by the automobile. We become like our idols, Eckermann. Have you been looking at my Maxims, Eckermann? 'As a man is, so is his God.' We worship a machine as primitives worship their gods, we become like that machine, and then we believe in a god that is a machine and act on that belief, no longer treating other human beings or even ourselves like human beings.

"Are we not steadily degrading our opinion of ourselves— by how we dress these days, how informally we act? I see people at the restaurant, in the market place, even at the theatre, dressed as if they are about to go to sleep, or dig in the earth! And how people talk, and what entertainments they focus their weak and flabby attentions upon!

"The car is the greatest entertainment, the deepest fall into lust. [Ed. note: So I translate Goethe's "*belustigen*," which means "amuse, entertain, divert," but which carries the connotations associated with the English word "lust."] We bewitch ourselves, Eckermann, with our cars. [Ger. "*behexen*," the "hex" implying casting a destructive spell.] And we cannot help it any more. How have I defined sin? "Whatever I find someone unable to stop doing." [Maxim #283.] In this I am in full agreement with Dante, who saw sin as obsession. The sin that condemns you in the *Inferno* is not necessarily your greatest crime in the eyes of the world, but your obsession. Obsession is by definition exclusive and single. So in Dante, you have murderers and thieves who are not being punished as murderers and thieves, but as, for example, gossips—for that was their obsession, however invisible or harmless in the world's eye. The genius, Dante! Were he alive today, his Inferno would be populated by idolaters; for all obsessions except the obsession for God are idolatries; and only one commandment is really broken, the First, by all the other obsessions [This is a very complex German sentence construction, difficult to render with felicity into English.]—idolaters who would themselves move by compulsion, spewing noxious fumes, forever breaking down and rusting, a hell's carnival of savage and mindless traffic with frozen faces and all the symbols of our automobile companies fused to their foreheads like the mark of Satan in Revelation, the great prophetic vision of industrial, automobile-obsessed humankind—the idolaters being those who in earthly life could not help themselves any more but had become the servants of automobiles, those who instead of confining automobiles to their proper function, to entertainment, enjoyment, and romance instead elevated them had. Worst of all, Eckermann, were those who even went so far in their complete blindness as to have given automobiles for Christmas, the ultimate sacrilege!"

At this I must have involuntarily raised a hand, physically, as if to register an objection. Goethe, ever alert and perceptive when it came to his listeners, as he was also equally compassionate toward them, wishing to dispel their confusion, broke his own course of speech.

"Ah, Eckermann, you wonder at my obvious inconsistency, for I have said the so-called Wise Men brought petroleum, aluminum, and glass, symbolizing the automobile. But with them it was 'homage,' Eckermann. It was laid before the King of all Kings, the negation of all kings—in the ancient spirit of sacrifice. We shall either sacrifice our machines, or we shall worship them and sacrifice human beings. We offer up the car, or ourselves and each other. They laid at the Manger all that we are becoming, as a warning to us, and as an attempt to teach us. Perhaps they offered it as an intercession as well. Petroleum—the gold of our civilization, which makes it operate—a new basis of commercialism, except that it not only corrupts, it poisons: people shall kill for it, Eckermann, as though it were a god. Aluminum, which I predict will enter more and more into the production of automobiles, symbolic of theft from Earth itself, atrociously consumptive of energy and resources, fashioned into the idols humans shall worship. Glass, which should be the mirror in which we see ourselves and our increasingly mechanized countenances and through which we receive light and see our neighbors—we use instead to isolate ourselves to the point where the fair Earth is only passing scenery and unwished distances, and which we shatter in our mutual slaughter that shall be worse eventually than all the wars of Napoleon together—*each year*, Eckermann! If the Porsche family has their way, this is exactly what will happen. And, I predict, if they and the other industrialists and automakers have their way, our beloved, beautiful, high-cultured [*hochverkultierter*] Fatherland shall one day not long hence *itself* become a *machine*, one huge machine, running to the will of one diabolical mind, grinding the Germans and the peoples of Europe in its vast operation, which like the mechanical will of the devil must, simply *must*, become larger and larger and consume more, and ever more and more destroy and destroy in order to consume! All this the Wise Men laid at the feet of the King of Kings—for judgment. This age, Eckermann, is under judgment. Only mercy and reason—

[Here the fragment ends. Either Eckermann had not continued, or another Goethe Institute purchased the subsequent pages and they are housed at a location my inadequate funding has not permitted me to discover as yet. At the Goethe Institute in Sheboygan Falls, I found the following page, which might or might not be a continuation, at some point, of the foregoing Conversation.]

"—must act, Eckermann! Kingdoms and principalities will not prevent the conflagration. That is why the Wise Men left their burdens at the feet of the least of all humans, a baby not even in a crib or cradle [*Weige*] but in a manger. That is why *you*, Eckermann—"

Here my incomparable mentor, Goethe, though partially reclined on his bed, reached out impetuously and pulled me by my shirt and lapel, bringing me directly face to face with the wise and impassioned, wrinkled visage full of character, vehemence, and alarm, his eyes bright with vision and imperatives. "—You, Eckermann, must do something! I do not say you must become a senator or destroy a factory. Beware, Eckermann, of attempting a large work! I refer you to my Maxim, 'Seek no cure where there is none!' But, Eckermann—" here his eyes lit with a beautiful, visionary light, as if he were seeing the light of a brilliant and lovely star—"Eckermann, *you must sell your car!* And then, you—"

[Here the page ends. The work of discovering and translating these pages of the *Conversations*, invaluable to historical and literary studies alike, is ongoing, but funding for this important project remains woefully inadequate. Individual donations are welcome, as are, especially, donations from corporate sponsors and foundations. Individual and corporate donations are tax deductible, and the Goethe Now! Fund of the Goethe Institutes, International, offers institutional matching programs. Please consider donating, or earmarking your estate. Further information can be obtained by writing Director, Goethe Institute, Sheboygan Falls, WI 52817, or at schlupfwinkel.goethinstitutes.de. Please act today.]

CONVERSATION #2

This morning Goethe was in fine spirits. He had finished his breakfast when I arrived, and he smiled genially as we took our seats in the little room overlooking the garden. On the polished round table between us lay the sheaf of my poetry that I had given him the previous afternoon. Still smiling in that pleasant way, which I had come to recognize as the first sign of extreme displeasure, he remarked,

"You drive a Benkelmann, don't you?"

Caught quite off guard, all I could do was sputter a surprised affirmative. Of course I could not help but ask how he knew. "Oh, my friend," he said, lifting my sheaf of poems and letting them fall, "I have read through what you call your 'poetry.' And may I assume that you would like someday to trade in your Benkelmann for an Oppenheimer, if not a Mercedes?"

"Why, yes," I stammered. "But I must confess, I am quite bewildered. The connection—"

"Between your writings and these particular brands of automobiles? Quite obvious, I would say. You write poems to 'express yourself,' do you not?"

"Of course. Most certainly.

"'Of course,' you say? But you would say 'of course.' That is the whole point. Let me first tell you, my dear Eckermann, so that some years from now when you write this conversation in whatever version and after whatever manner you are able— let me give you a precept or two that I suggest you repeat to yourself mornings rather like an Eastern mantra. First, Art is not philosophy. Second, Poetry is neither for expression nor for persuasion. These 'poems'"—he lifted the sheaf again and let it fall to the table with a slap—"these 'poems' seem to imitate someone. Who is your current influence? Obviously it is not I."

I flushed at that last remark, but it was true. "The American colonial poet of the past century, Walter Whitefield, Sir."

"Yes, and do you believe that you have achieved his rhythm, timing, voice?"

"In a small measure only, Sir."

"Yes, a small measure indeed. I shall advise you, my good fellow, to refrain from imitating the so-called 'free verse' of the Americans until you achieve the mastery, in your own voice, that might allow you to depart from traditional poetic form and meter. Otherwise you will merely continue to write what *this* is." (Here he stabbed a finger toward my papers on the table.) "Prose."

After patiently clearing his throat, he continued. "Eckermann, my good fellow, the pre-revolutionary American 'poets' of the past century were so certain of their wonderful ear for rhythm, their unerring sense of voice, their flawless and artful feel for timing and emphasis, that they wrote imitations of Whitefield's 'free verse.' What they wrote is prose, mere prose, a kind of self-indulgent sub-literature of Neat Thoughts." [Goethe's *geschichte Gedanken* has been translated as "clever notions" or "clever thoughts," but the current colloquialism "neat" better expresses Goethe's contempt.]

I must have appeared perhaps a bit wounded and indignant.

"Oh yes, Eckermann, it is unpleasant, but it is the truth. And furthermore, these Neat Thoughts that give the lazy reader the impression he is reading actual poetry without the concentration, entertain people. It is entertainment on the American pattern—immediately forgettable—not the deeper, richer, lasting, and enriching entertainment of Homer and Shakespeare. In short, entertainment for free."

"But—" I was about to interject respectfully. Goethe had an uncanny quality of anticipating the thoughts of lesser minds.

"You will no doubt wish to point out that the Psalms of the Bible, and the Vedas, come to us in translation as poetry without regular rhyme. Do not mistake me, Eckermann—rhyme does not make poetry. Shakespeare and Milton show us that. It is rhythm that makes poetry. And it is often rhyme also because in the lyric form, as opposed to the epic and the dramatic, we deal in the compact unit that must co-operate with the author. Only for poor poets does *form* represent limitation and coercion. For good poets, the form means freedom. Freedom makes you greater than you thought yourself to be, just as poetic form helps you do more than you thought to do. Does a sculptor work without his medium—marble or clay? Of course not, my good man. One must not think that the media of poetry are only language and thought. To create beauty, we must obey the structures that paradoxically set us free. But you have disagreed with all this, Eckermann, which is how I know that you drive a Benkelmann and aspire someday to drive a Mercedes. Your aspirations are petty, Eckermann. I tell you this as a friend."

I must have looked uncomfortable. Certainly I drew a deep breath to steady myself after this reproach.

"It is well that you feel pain, Eckermann. Many others simply continue without remorse, writing free verse in their own stupid conceit, rewarded by a public that is as lazy as they are and that understands freedom superficially if at all.

"Freedom is our subject, Eckermann. The unfortunate fact is that Americans have not even yet taught themselves very well how to use their potential for freedom. Even after forming a representative democracy, they think of freedom in economic terms primarily, and then as it relates to entertainment. They are free to buy whatever they desire, so they abuse their freedom by buying large, heavy, showy and luxurious vehicles that waste resources and one day, Eckermann, shall threaten the very air we breathe and the water we drink.

"Americans shall lose their geographical frontier. Unlike us Germans, who are always looking for more living space, the Americans shall one day acquire Mexico—or a great portion of it—and perhaps Canada also, now that they have replaced their British overlords with themselves. They are free, the Americans. What an opportunity, Eckermann! But will the Americans use it? Only time shall tell, but in the production of automobiles, I see all too ample evidence that they will not transfer their present outer frontier to inner frontiers, as have the Tibetans.

"The Americans' frontier means freedom to them. Two hundred years hence, will they seek freedom in intellectual pursuits, artistic pursuits, in the independence of mind and spirit? No, Eckermann! If you would kindly wake up, Eckermann. Eckermann! See how American you already are?"

I once again stammered an apology, but Goethe was infused with enthusiasm and ploughed straight forward. I desired to resist his association of me with Americans, but could not.

"Eckermann, I am saying that Americans will not use their freedoms to create justice, spiritual peace, and beauty. Why not? Eckermann, why not?"

"Master Goethe, I know not."

"Because they have easy substitutes, idiot! Profoundest apologies, Eckermann. As I wrote in *Poetry and Cars*, using highly fictionalized incidents of my early life dealing with those comically primitive automobiles we had back in those comparatively innocent days—automobiles are the unlettered man's free verse. Misunderstanding of freedom leads to its misuse, abuse, and, I am afraid, to its loss. Oh, those early days of mine with the Fräuleins on those hard and uncomfortable horsehair seats! What a fool I was! They always drove.

"So Americans will transfer the freedom of their old frontiers to the automobile—as Germans are transferring their aggressions—and they will become quite satisfied with the substitution. One day—mark my words, Eckermann, for you may well live to see it—one day they will use vehicles to drive where they please, whether or not roads have been placed there for them. And they will entertain themselves just as if they were drugging or drinking themselves into a stupor, to cover up the emptiness—the spiritual, aesthetic, intellectual, moral emptiness that remains when they have sold their freedoms for amusement, entertainment, and comfort. Do you know what the word 'amuse' means, Eckermann?"

I brightened, for I was able to answer this question immediately. "To cause to pass one's time pleasantly, enjoyably."

"No!" Goethe thundered. "It is a French military term, applied to the diversion of the enemy, to the occupying of his attention so that you can *destroy* him unexpectedly, Eckermann! Why did you not know that, my good man?"

"Because I have not yet read your military work, Master Goethe!"

"Exactly! My *Campaign in France*. Did you think me to be interested only in automobiles, in romance and poetry and religion? Expand your horizons, Eckermann! So much can be learned about important things from the study of military events! *Eckermann!*" Goethe fairly shouted.

"Yes, Master Goethe!"

"Where were we? Ah yes, Eckermann. Your nose-picking distracts me so. My point is that Americans are amusing themselves, distracting themselves, which is a very dangerous activity, Eckermann. Are you amusing yourself now, examining your fingernails?"

"Oh no, Master Goethe. It is only that I am thinking."

"Thinking! What *about*, Eckermann?"

"What you are saying. It sounds so like, like. . . "

"Do not hesitate. I have not known you to be overly timid, Eckermann, just fittingly so. What does all this sound like to you?"

"Like—"

"Wait! I shall say it for you. When I say freedom is for the creation of beauty—which is how God uses His absolute freedom—it sounds to you like—*Romanticism!*"

"Exactly, Master Goethe. But I had supposed you to be opposed to Romanticism."

"Bah! We are all pygmies compared to—"

[At this maddeningly crucial point, the Frankfurt manuscript ends. I have searched for its continuation in Goethe Institutes, museums, bars, and private collections, but have found thus far only the following possibilities. The project needs the pecuniary assistance of Goethe enthusiasts like you, Reader, if we wish finally to read complete editions of Eckermann's papers. The Goethe Institute in Bombay houses the following page, consisting of but one word:]

Keats."

[Does Eckermann's Conversation end here? Is this the conclusion, or abrupt termination, of the Conversation with which are concerned? Another possibility exists—a freestanding single page found in the manuscript collection at the Goethe Institute in Yorba Linda, California:]

what we might be, did we but expend our energies to develop ourselves aesthetically and spiritually! What an immense freedom we human beings have, to develop ourselves into creatures fit for heaven! In this, the English followers of Wesley—the Methodists—are correct. Our calling is to work, in cooperation with the Spirit of the Divine—the genius within us—to make of ourselves more than we are, to lift ourselves, to elevate ourselves, to strive by dint of Art and Science, Politics, and Love, to become—"

[Here the very large, impassioned handwriting breaks off. I have compared the size of the writing to Eckermann's hand before the previous fragment broke off, but can reach no conclusions, as Eckermann writes large nearly all the time as soon as he begins to gather speed in his creations/recreations of Goethe's conversations—an example being the following, found by the author in the private collection of a Goethe aficionado who wishes to remain anonymous:]

automobiles. In many respects, we can be considered inferior to these machines. Can we travel as fast? Of course the answer is No, Eckermann. And I predict that before long, these automobiles will be traveling as fast as our present railroad trains. The airplane? [*Flugzeug*] It is only beginning now to come into its own, and what is it, Eckermann? The airplane is a moving Tower of Babel! The airplane is only 'Automobile'

written in the sky! For the principle is the same: speed. Speed is
the addiction of a helpless man and of an aimless society. Mark
my words, Eckermann: not only America and Germany, but all
of Western civilization shall be dependent upon speed as it is
dependent upon fuel. And for speed, we human beings do not
match the automobile. Therefore we shall serve the automobile;
it shall not serve us. We shall be governed by its demands, not
vice versa.

"Likewise, we are inferior to automobiles in the
important—"

[Page ends.]

As you can see, Reader, this Conversation breaks off altogether
unsatisfyingly. Was Goethe actually a Romantic?—believing in the absolute value and primacy of Beauty? You can see why contributions are
important. We must determine where Goethe stood. Or—even should
we definitively connect page to page, would we still be uncertain? Perhaps Eckermann constructed these thoughts and words, putting them
into Goethe's mouth. As a matter of fact, the entire German and Philosophy departments at Duke University assert that "Goethe" was entirely
imaginary, was constructed by Johann Peter Eckermann, and exists only
on paper. All the works we associate with "Goethe" were penned by Eckermann. It is claimed that no-one of "Goethe's" supposed education and
learning—among the best of his time—could have written the disjointed
and trivial *Faust*, the jejune *Werther*, and the dull platitudes of the *Maxims*; and it is probable that Eckermann wrote the *Conversations* in order
to make himself look intelligent by contrast. I mention this extreme position not because I subscribe to it, but to show how important, indeed
vital and urgent, is the work of collecting and sorting all of Eckermann's
papers.

A third Conversation relates to our subject, and I shall include the
following excerpt:

CONVERSATION #3

As yesterday afternoon's Conversation was among the most remarkable of the many Conversations of Goethe I have had the
privilege to participate in [Some idiots will object to my translation's leaving a preposition at the end of that clause, but, as
Goethe said, "Leave the pedants to their own trivia."], I shall

record it essentially as I heard it, and leave to an uncertain future the possibility of reworking it into a more literary form:

"Eckermann, remarkable dream. Last night. Talked about automobiles yesterday. Therefore I dream I am in large soccer stadium. I think it was *Bayern München* against an all-Germany team. I am suddenly in agony of thirst. The vendor comes by—he shouts 'Fresh Sübarus! Fresh Sübarus!' It is that Japanese toy manufacturer. I am also terribly hungry. Does a vendor come with good German sausages and rolls? No! He shouts, 'Roasted Dusenbergs!' Then I see that all the stadium has become populated not with men and women, but in all the seats are insect-like machines—cars—intended for everyone: People's Cars, you might call them—and the people had become these cars. Then I saw that the stadium had become one large machine, and all the people were its cogs, wheels, belts, products. I understood that all Germany itself was becoming a vast machine.

"Woke up perspiring, shaking! Too much for an old man—something like a vision in the Book of Revelation. Fear it to be prophetic. Fear that even if Germany is stopped from devouring the world like a machine consuming its necessary materials—a factory for cars, perhaps, all run by machines and few or no humans—imagine! —Awoke with the feeling that all the world would nevertheless be on the way to becoming a still vaster machine itself. That is what comes of the view of the universe as a machine instead of as a living thing.

"—Wait! And heard a voice, saying that the universe is a machine. Yes! Remember it now—the voice—it was the voice of my own Mephistopheles, that which I thought to have been my own invention, that began as a sort of joke—

"—Eckermann—Universe is not a device or machine. Universe more like living thing. The Romantics were, after all—"

[Here the manuscript breaks off. It is my belief that this is the last conversation that Eckermann recorded. Perhaps this prophetic, apocalyptic vision was so cataclysmically upsetting to the liberal, humane, and optimistic Goethe that it brought about his death!]

An Automotive/Theological Glossary

with

Notes on Pronunciation

Few things are more frustrating than reading foreign literary works and not being able to pronounce the names. Therefore, at considerable personal expense, the following guide to important car words is thoughtfully provided:

Audi. Do not pronounce this car name AWW-dee, or people will think you can't afford one. The correct pronunciation, significantly, is OW-dee.

BMW. Stands for Bavarian Motor Works, or, *Bayerische Motor Werke.* Many inept people are buying car dealerships and renaming them "Auto Werks." The English word is Works, you obfuscators. The German plural of *Werk* is *Werke,* not Werks. "Werks" is not a word. Incidentally, pronounce *Werke* "verka," not "workie."

(Note to Reader: I am giving up on listing these alphabetically now. I feel that the effort is not cost-effective, and would go unappreciated. In any case, alphabetizing does not strike me as being strictly pertinent.)

Jaguar. It is gauche to pronounce this Jag-wahr. But also, do not pronounce it Jag-you-ah unless you are a genuine Brit. To say "Jag" simply betrays which side of the tracks you are from. Actually, I have no idea how to pronounce this. The cars are unreliable anyway.

Mercedes-Benz. Leave off the "Benz." "Mercedes" in Germany is said *Meh(r)-TSAY-dess.* But you are not in Germany. One is well-advised to say neither Mercedes or *Mehrtsaydess,* but rather "E-Class" or "S-Class," as appropriate. If you ever lie about having one, you are a prime candidate for someday buying a huge SUV, such as an Excursion (pronounced *gluteus maximus*), rather than ever owning a Mercedes. A Mercedes is not a fantasy or a wish; it is a symphony. That is a preposterous lie, but I do have a reputation to protect.

Rolls-Royce is pronounced "Rolls," but say "Silver Cloud," "Phantom," *et.al.*, instead.

Bentley. Pronounced Bentley.

Volkswagen. World-wide usage has altered this Fascist word to being pronounced just the way it looks; that is, euphemistically. Germans say *FOLLKSvahgen.* Kids say "VW," reviewers often say "Vee Dub."

Golf is a variety of Volkswagen, pronounced with a bright "l" and a rounded "o," so that it sounds as though you are actually mouthing a golf ball as you say the word.

Cadillac. Always pronounce the middle syllable, or people will think you have several of them in your yard.

Goethe. Now here we have not a car name but a thematic name that forces this book to make sense on artistic, philosophical, and ecological levels. Johann Wolfgang von Goethe, car enthusiast and future author of *Faust,* was born on 28 August in Frankfurt, Germany, home of the world-famous Auto Show. Baby Goethe had difficulty seeing, and the problem occupied the doctors for several days. When he died 83 years later, Goethe's last words were, "More light! More light!" which goes to show how pointless everything is. Goethe is considered a Great European, on a level with Shakespeare and Dante. He is underrated by Americans and overrated by the Germans. Be careful. The German "oe" sound is made by shaping your lips around an imaginary pea, and saying "eee." Try it. Why this letter combination should be pronounced this way, or what penitent said it first, can be asked of the whole German language. Do not say Gowth, as in growth. Pronounce the "th" like a "t" and don't drop the last letter. A German pronounces every syllable as if it were his last penny. So we now have something like "Goeh-teh." This is good enough because in actuality the combination of letters "goethe" is unpronounceable and is the international phonetic sign for "Unknown." I have yet to hear a German admit that he couldn't pronounce "Goethe." They are so proud of him. You would be, too, if you were a German.

Hölderlin. Another thematic name. For purposes of this book, Hölderlin is the opposing theme to Goethe's character Faust, and is rather like a counterpoint to Goethe himself. If you do not eventually come to understand how Hölderlin opposes Faust in some universal, spiritual way, then you probably haven't found this book to be even remotely funny. If you *do* understand how Hölderlin opposes Faust in a thematic, universal, spiritual way, then everything is funny to you. Safest to bull ahead and pronounce it Helderlin. (Emphasis on first syllable.) To hoell with trying to say it exactly right. Note that the "oe" in Goethe is *not* meant to be an umlauted "o" (ö), for obscure reasons; whereas "Hoelderlin" is the way to spell Hölderlin when umlauting is unfeasible, or, as at the Clark Bicycle Manufactury, prohibited.

Similarly, *Tübingen* (university town, particularly noted for its Catholic and Protestant theological faculties) is spelled "Tuebingen" on English maps. Excepting only "Goethe," an "a," "e," or "u" followed by an "e" is the sign of an umlaut in German typography. The exception of "Goethe" has been traced to the Sanskrit word *Ghêhatë*: "spirit of earth and sky," or, alternatively, "sausage." The root *Ghê* remains obscure.

Heine. German Romantic poet Heinrich Heine, author of "The Lorelei." To pronounce it "Heinie" would blow the seriousness of "The Lorelei," a poem about a distracted driver, at a moment when my argument takes a serious turn. Pronounce it "Heina," but cut off the "a" before it completely gets out of your mouth. It is insensitive and obtuse to say "Heinie."

Bosch. While we're on the subject of Germans. This is the company that makes parts, particularly electrical ones, for German cars. You may own some Bosch spark plugs, even if you are not driving a German machine. Happens to be the World War I name for "German," as given by the French and British. Pronounce with a longish "o" if you're feeling kind of French. *Alors! Il pleut!* But if you're in that Anglo-American frame of mind, pronounce the vowel "ah" but short in duration. Bahsch. The Bosch themselves follow the French pronunciation—by sheer coincidence of course. Did you ever wonder what the Great War was about?

Till Eulenspiegel. A legendary German character always perpetrating mischief, pronounced "OIL-en-shpeegl." The name does not occur elsewhere in this book. But as it appears here, it was deemed best to tell you how to pronounce it.

Klaus von Endorf. Inventor of the German exercise-mobile. Hence *endorfen*—to exercise.

Stuttgart. The home of Mercedes. Pretend it starts with "Sht," and drop the "r;" pronounce the "a" as in "ahh." This city counterbalances Munich ("Myoonik," or in German, *München*: both the u-umlaut and the subglottal ch are unpronounceable.) Munich is the home of BMW and Hitler's Beer Hall Putsch. Putsch is a great word because it is pronounced exactly the way you'd think. German is a wonderful language in that you pronounce every letter; in all other respects it is an over-engineered and possibly fiendish device. I say this to summarize my discussions of German cars.

sitzen-blinken—v. 1. To wait to turn left at an intersection. 2. To be perplexed.

St. Ignatius Toyota—1. Patron saint of the Japanese automobile industry. 2. The Mephistopheles of the German automobile industry.

Porsche. Pronounce the "e." However, pronounce it not as if the name were a character in Shakespeare, but like the second "e" in Goethe. Pronounce it like a schwa. Hardly anybody knows what a schwa is any more. See? More evidence that everything is going downhill. The schwa is the backwards "e" in the dictionary, pronounced like the vowel in the four-letter word describing where everything is going. We are getting there in cars.

Citroen. French company that has made some of the world's ugliest, and currently loveliest, cars. The French, ever defensive about those hideous old automobiles as they are about everything French, including Napoleon, would get huffy and insulting if you pronounced this word, meaning (note well) *lemon*, "citrone," as if it were Italian. They say the word as no other people in the world can, and it is well to leave it so. The word ends up somewhere behind your nose. The current large Citroen is a thing of beauty.

SUV. From the Sanskrit root *Shvê*, meaning "destruction." Pronounced with equal stress on each letter, the individual letters each being voiced, like "s. o. b."

Chevrolet. Not from the same root as above. I just want my French readers to know that we Americans can say this seemingly French name any way we damn please. Those of us who have always at least half-loved Chevrolets and all they stand for (except for during the Seventies and Eighties), pronounce it Chevy. A whole decade, the 1950's, exists within that name. James Dean, Dinah Shore, drive-ins. It nearly makes one weep with nostalgia—longing for the Eden of childhood; and longing is a theme of this book. Chevrolet. Enough said.

Ford. Anyone familiar with Goethe's later writings knows that this company is the anti-Chevrolet. At birth, all male Americans are either Ford men or Chevy men. The conflict is not mere economic competition between companies. It is Good versus Evil, Light versus Darkness. Henry Ford invented mass production. He said "History is bunk." At the heart of the American identity lies this conflict, this tension, between Chevy and Ford. It is what we are.

Goeteborg. City on the southwest coast of Sweden, where Volvos are made; called Gothenburg in English; pronounced something like Yotabory in Swedish. Object of pilgrimage for all Goths, whether Visigoths or Ostrogoths.

Nietzsche. (Freidrich J.)—Philosopher; NEET-cheh. In a pinch, NEET-cha; anything but Neetch or Neetchie. He thought Goethe's *Faust* was based on a stupid idea.

Etymologies:

automobile (Greek *autos*, self + Latin *mobilis*, movable), an off-color insult in ancient Rome, developed by the French for the early self-powered vehicles; first used by the *New York Times* in 1899. There are more than one billion in use around the world, with the number rapidly rising. The first modern version of this device, the *Benz Patent-Motorwagen*, was invented and made by Karl Benz in 1885. His wife Bertha Benz was the first person to make a long drive in an automobile, showing that no one, and no gender, is blameless.

car (Latin *carrus*, wheeled vehicle; Sanskrit *Khâr*, Wheel of Birth and Death.)

Note of Appreciation

My thanks to Andrew Gramm, who set up the infallible original text of this volume.

While many could share responsibility for this Manifesto, only one deserves direct blame: my German teacher, the subject of this book's dedication, who guided me and many other errant teenagers with unerring patience, understanding, love, and good humor.

CPSIA information can be obtained
at www.ICGtesting.com
Printed in the USA
BVHW091257140722
641748BV00009B/126